Praise ☑ P9-DES-520

"A leading man as wicked as he is irresistible... Heart-wrenching, redemptive, and stirringly passionate. A series opener to be read and savored."

—*RT Book Reviews*, 4.5 Stars

"Exquisitely imagined... Darkly atmospheric and delectably sexy, *Kiss of Steel* is an extraordinary debut."

—*Booklist* Starred Review

"Dark, intense, and sexy... A stunning new series."

—*Library Journal*

Praise for *Heart of Iron*

Maggie Award Winner, Best Paranormal/Fantasy

"Deliciously atmospheric, completely enthralling...a sexy literary merger of Bram Stoker, Jules Verne, and Jane Austen."

—*Booklist*

"McMaster's second book dazzles and seduces. She crafts complicated, damaged, and driven characters whose unlikely passion is unforgettably powerful. Will leave readers breathless."

—*RT Book Reviews*
Top Pick of the Month, 4.5 Stars

Praise for *My Lady Quicksilver*

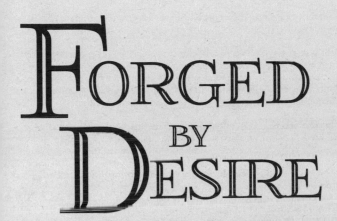

FORGED BY DESIRE

BEC MCMASTER

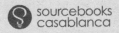

sourcebooks
casablanca

Published by Sourcebooks Casablanca, an imprint of Sourcebooks, Inc.
P.O. Box 4410, Naperville, Illinois 60567–4410
(630) 961-3900
Fax: (630) 961-2168
www.sourcebooks.com

Printed and bound in Canada
WC 10 9 8 7 6 5 4 3 2 1

This one is for Kara. My baby sis forever.

One

HE DREAMED OF RED SILK...

In his dream, Garrett Reed straightened the white bow tie he wore, glanced once at the crowd of elegantly dressed aristocrats, and then turned and opened the hackney door.

"About damned time."

His gaze slid over the woman within, taking in the acres of tight red silk and the froth of lace framing high, creamy breasts. Perry cursed under her breath as she tried to gather up her skirts and the brass-plated fan she used as a weapon. "You could offer me your hand."

As he should have. Garrett was still trying to gather his wits. He'd never before equated Perry with dresses; indeed, he'd never have thought that she could actually pull off this subterfuge. The entire time he'd known her, she'd worn the tight black leathers of the Guild of the Nighthawks, hunting murderers and thieves across the rooftops of London with him. At first glance most people mistook her for a lad, and Garrett himself rarely thought of her as a woman. At least until tonight.

It was his own damned fault. He was the one who'd

told her he didn't think she could do it. A dare—fool the aristocratic Echelon into thinking she was one of their own.

Belatedly he offered her his arm. Perry stepped down, her gloved hand resting lightly on his forearm and her eyes raking the crowd for any signs of their targets. As he should have been doing. Garrett was still moving a step behind, unable to concentrate on more than one thing. And that one thing smelled like French vanilla perfume.

"Can you see Lynch? Or Rosalind?" Perry asked.

Garrett slid his hand over the small of her back. He couldn't stop looking at her, as if a part of him still couldn't believe that this elegant, beautiful woman beside him was the same partner he'd worked with for the last nine years.

As if sensing his gaze, she glanced up at him, a slow smile creeping over her lips. "I've never seen you struck dumb before."

"I'm not without words," he countered, guiding her toward the marble stairs that led to the opera house.

"You've barely managed a conversation since we embarked in the carriage. I do hope I haven't stolen all your wits."

Garrett leaned close enough to murmur in her ear. "If you keep going, you could steal something else as well."

Those eyes were watchful, as if she wasn't quite used to flirtation, especially not from him. "If I wanted your heart," she whispered, "I'd cut it out of your chest with my knife."

"I prefer something subtler."

Perry's painted red lips curved up in a genuine smile, though her eyes still searched the crowd. "Concentrate."

"I am." He glanced again at the faint swelling of her breasts—breasts he'd never noticed before. A tight fist of need clenched in his gut.

"On the reason we're here."

Garrett plucked the opera tickets from the inner pocket of his coat as they approached the main doors. This was the true test. Neither of them was of the Echelon, the aristocratic blue bloods that ruled London. If they were turned away here, the Nighthawk Guild's Master, Sir Jasper Lynch, and his secretary, Rosalind, would be alone inside.

With dozens of humanists who were plotting another terrorist attack on the Echelon. They wouldn't discriminate between the blue blood lords they despised and a blue blood rogue like Lynch.

This wasn't the first time the humanists had struck. But the attacks so far had been small, merely tests. Several lords had been driven into a blood frenzy by small mysterious devices the terrorists called Doeppler Orbs. If they set enough of these orbs into action in a theater full of blue bloods, it would be a bloodbath.

Perry's hand tightened on his sleeve as he handed the tickets over to the liveried servant. The man scrutinized the pair of them through a monocle, then nodded and let them through.

Shadows flickered through Garrett's vision, the darkness in him bubbling up. It was far too easy to summon these days, and much more difficult to dispel.

Garrett forced a smile to his lips and swept a pair of champagne glasses from the tray of a passing servant drone. The automaton rolled away through the crowd with a faint teakettle hiss, the sound itching along Garrett's skin. He forced himself to continue, to ignore it. It hadn't always been this way. His craving virus levels had been sitting at a reasonably healthy thirty-two percent for the past three years.

But a week ago, a blue blood lord in the grip of a blood frenzy had tried to rip Garrett's heart out of his chest and very nearly succeeded. It was one of the few ways to truly kill a blue blood, and in the effort to heal itself, his body had relaxed the fight against the virus. Garrett's virus level had more than doubled, leaving him struggling to fight a hunger he hadn't had a chance to acclimatize to.

He was barely managing to rein himself in these days. He couldn't let anyone see how close to the edge he was. Especially not Perry.

The noise swelled to a dull roar. Brightly colored silk filled the room, and feathered headdresses bobbed like a menagerie of birds. Garrett grimaced as he directed Perry to a small, out-of-the-way place beside a marble column. He usually liked these events, but since the attack, the presence of too many people only seemed to crowd in on him.

"There's Rosa." Perry tilted her head toward the stairs as she sipped her champagne.

Indeed, when he looked, he saw the coppery curls of Rosalind's coif beneath the candelabra's light. A dark shadow almost obliterated her as a man swept her out of the way of the crowd. Lynch.

Garrett turned his back on them. Lynch was a recognizable figure. If any of the humanists saw him here, they'd know what he was about. However, Garrett and Perry were unknowns and needed to keep it that way.

"Keep an eye on them," he instructed quietly, pressing close enough to Perry that her skirts brushed against his polished shoes. "But don't stare. And act like you've seen all of this a thousand times before. You're my thrall, remember?" The thought sent a flash of darkness through his vision. The idea of Perry as his personal blood slave was heady.

For a moment he almost envied the blue blood lords parading their thralls—young ladies who exchanged their blood rights in exchange for protection, gifts, and an honorable thrall contract—through the room. Garrett's gaze drifted to Perry's throat and the fierce, flickering beat of her pulse.

Idly fanning herself, Perry glanced around the room with a slightly bored expression. "I do know what I'm doing."

"So do I."

"Yes, but playing a cad is already within your repertoire." The fan stirred cool air over his lips as he reached out and leaned his hand against the column behind her. Perry's expression lashed pure heat through him. "That was never in any doubt."

"If I doubt you, it's only because you've never played the lady before."

"Perhaps you simply never noticed."

He looked down. There was a slightly challenging note beneath the words.

"You do play the role well." His eyes narrowed. It was an unspoken rule that when a blue blood showed up on the guild's doorstep, nobody ever asked about their past.

Most blue bloods were created during the blood rites, a rite of passage offered to certain privileged sons among the aristocracy and strictly controlled. Accidents occurred, however, when the merest scratch could transmit to others the virus that made the blue bloods what they were. Those accidents were declared rogues, forced to join either the Nighthawks or the Coldrush Guards that guarded the Echelon. Kept alive only for their usefulness.

He'd never asked about Perry's past, though he'd often wondered. Women were strictly forbidden the blood rites for fear their gentle natures would succumb to hysteria at the fierce hunger of the craving. He wasn't certain if any of the men who'd decreed such a law had actually met Perry, or the only other female blue blood, the Duchess of Casavian.

"Indeed, you play the part almost too well," he continued, to see how Perry would react.

The fan fluttered, stirring the black curls of her wig and the lace trim of her dress. It drew his attention to the faint pulse in her bare throat, to the fine tracery of blue veins beneath her creamy skin. Hunger burned within him. Again his vision flickered to black-and-white tones. The world became a little distant, as if something was drawing him away from it.

"I wasn't born in breeches, Garrett."

She'd said something. He yanked his gaze up, trying to focus. "I hope not. I'd have thought you'd have been naked." It was what he would have said a month ago. An idle flirtation that didn't require much thinking to mouth. Reaching out, he caught the top of the fan, feeling the razor-sharp edge against the pads of his fingers. It was irritating him, making the hairs on the back of his neck rise.

She rapped his knuckles with it. "Behave."

"Just playing a role, my love."

"So am I. *La femme fatale.*" She sliced the fan in the air just in front of his nose, forcing him to take a step back. With a slow, wicked smile, Perry strolled out from under his arm, catching up her skirts with one hand as she deposited the empty champagne glass on a drone's tray. He followed her lead as she stalked away.

Dangerous woman.

"That way," Perry said, pointing along the corridor with her fan. "Rosa and Lynch are heading for the stairs. Which means we need to disappear until the crowd has thinned."

Then it was their task to search the foyer and backstage for either the humanists or the Doeppler Orbs.

"I am your humble servant," he replied, following in the wake of her swishing bustle.

"Servant, perhaps," she murmured under her breath. "Humble? Never."

The bell rang, signaling that the patrons ought to be seated. Suddenly Garrett and Perry were fighting against the tide of the crowd. A young lord's shoulder hit Garrett's, throwing him off balance, and he bared his teeth in a silent snarl. He could smell blood in the air, his gut clenching. It was probably in the champagne.

Bloody hell. He needed to get this over with and get out of here.

"Perhaps you'd care to use the powder room?" His hand slid to the small of Perry's back, helping her keep her balance against skirts that had to be somewhat unfamiliar. Fingers flexing against the supple muscle along her spine, he let out the breath he'd been holding. Touching her felt like holding on to an anchor. In the darkness that was slowly becoming his world, Perry was a reliable, solid light that slowly drew him back to safer shores.

"We're alone." Garrett pushed ahead of her and pressed his fingertips to the door to the powder room, listening for a moment. *Nothing.*

He shoved the door open and stalked inside, shrugging out of his evening coat. A white silk waistcoat strained over his chest, gleaming back at him from the floor-length mirrors. A pair of white leather holsters rode over his shoulders, with two small pistols that would each fit in the palm of his hand. There was a knife in his boot, but the main weapon was his body.

Behind him, Perry locked the door. She lifted her heel onto a champagne-colored divan, then slowly dragged a fistful of her skirts up, revealing her flesh-colored stockings. He caught a glimpse of her gray eyes, watching him in the reflection. Watching his reaction.

She might not have owned an abundance of curves, but she had legs as long and lean as a dancer's. "Perry," Garrett warned. This was no longer fun. She was pushing him toward the edge, and he was far too close to it as it was.

Her gloved hands slowed, dragging her skirt a fraction higher until her garter ribbons were revealed. This time Perry watched him openly, her gaze locking on his in the reflection as she slowly dragged her pistol from the holster strapped to her thigh.

Garrett tugged at the gleaming white silk of his bow tie. "Bloody hell. That's enough, Perry. You win. You look entirely fetching in a gown. And partially out of it."

"I'm nowhere near finished, Garrett."

This was a side to Perry that he'd never seen, never even dreamed existed. As a Nighthawk, she'd been forced to expel the myth that her gender made her vulnerable in any way. She generally preferred her own company and rarely jested, let alone flirted. It was as if putting on the dress had relaxed her inhibitions, and his dare had only served to throw down the gauntlet between them.

The predator inside him noted that they were all alone, locked inside by her own devices. It stirred restlessly.

She snapped open the barrel of the pistol and checked the ammunition. When she looked up, the heeled slippers brought her face almost to his. His cock hardened, each muscle in his abdomen tightening as if for a blow. *Don't.*

Their eyes met. "Do you remember when you laughed at me and said I wouldn't know one end of a dress from the other?"

"So this is revenge?" His lashes lowered. "Don't play games you can't afford to lose. I'll only offer my surrender this once." He gave in. Let his eyes bleed to black for her. To show her just how close the line was for him.

Perry sucked in a sharp breath but she didn't back away. And that was the mistake they both made.

His hand slid up her cheek, the silk of his gloves cupping her face in his. He knew what her blood tasted like. She'd cut her wrist for him when he lay gasping on the floor a week ago, with his heart ripped half out of his chest. Perry's blood had healed him, but the desire for it had never quite gone away.

And this time he wasn't injured.

Perry caught her breath and wrenched away from him. Her eyes glittered darkly in the mirror as they met his. "You're right. I accept your surrender."

Garrett stepped closer, sliding his hands over her shoulders. "I'm no longer offering it," he murmured and pressed his lips against the smooth silk of her neck.

"This isn't… We shouldn't—"

He could feel her trembling. God, he wanted her. One hand slid around her waist, drawing her back into his arms. Perry's hand caught his, holding it against her abdomen as if uncertain whether to draw it away or tug it closer, but the softening of her stance betrayed her. She melted back against him with a low moan. "Garrett…"

The thought skittered away, drowning in a flood of darkness as the hunger washed over him. His lips trailed against her nape, the edge of his teeth riding over that flawless white skin. The hunger in him burned hot, until he could barely see or hear anything that didn't have to do with her.

All he wanted was her. All he needed… And, damn her, he was going to take it.

Hand fisting in the pearls at her throat, Garrett yanked her head to the side. He couldn't remember triggering the concealed knife in his sleeve, but the hilt of it was warm in his hand. Their eyes met in the mirror, and his irises were black flame. *Shouldn't do this. Control yourself.* Then the moment was gone and he slashed the small blade across her throat.

Warm blood splashed against his mouth as Perry gasped. He lapped at it, suckling hard. *Not enough. Never enough.*

Soft cries cut the air as her body jerked in release. Then she was melting against him, her weight falling into his arms and her blood wetting his lips.

He caught a glimpse of those amazing gray eyes, wide and alarmed, but couldn't stop himself from drinking more, feeling her weaken, hearing her heart shudder in her chest, her breath catch in her lungs. Blackness swept through his vision, turning the world dark. Prey. His prey. And she was all his. He'd drink her dry, steal the last shuddering breaths of ecstasy from her body as he—

"*Garrett, stop!*" she whispered, and he realized she'd been saying it for a while now. "Please, stop…"

The dream shattered.

❧

Garrett sucked in a huge breath and bolted upright, breathing hard. His fingers clenched in the blankets as they fell into his naked lap.

The world was dark and silent, the steel shutters drawn across his window to keep the sunlight out so he could sleep. Yet everything in the room was clearly visible, his blue-blood senses so superior he could make out each piece of furniture and article of clothing. Holding his head in his hands, he rocked back and forth, trying to fight the raging desire that burned through him.

Perry. At the opera.

The dream struck him every time he closed his eyes, though events had not played out that way in life. Perry had stopped him before he took her blood, slamming him back against the wall with her own eyes bleeding to black and their breath mingling. They were so close to kissing that if the screams hadn't started echoing down the hallways outside, he didn't know what would have happened.

"Bloody hell." Swallowing hard, he brought his shaking hands down from his face. The dream always ended that way. The hunger overwhelming him until all he cared for was her blood. Sometimes he woke before the end. Those were the better nightmares.

Sometimes he had to witness the whole damned thing.

A month since that incident at the opera, and he couldn't forget it. He'd never thought of Perry as a woman, as a *beautiful* woman, until that night. Now the thought haunted him.

His hands were still shaking. Garrett sucked in a steady breath and lowered them. Movement fractured off the small mirror attached to the vanity. Himself, still in shades of gray instead of color, his eyes as black as the demon inside him. The hunger.

Shoving the blankets aside, Garrett made his way to the vanity and stared at himself in the mirror, taking slow, steady breaths until he could see the blackness washing out of his eyes. *Come on.* The muscle in his jaw tightened. He could control this. He *would*.

But it was growing harder and harder each day. No

matter how much blood he drank, the hunger kept growing until it was a gnawing pit within him, eating away at bits of his soul until he was afraid one day he wouldn't wake up from the dream. One day, the dream would be real.

"Damn it," he muttered, grinding the heels of his palms against his eyes. Anything to force it down.

The intensity was ebbing slowly, his heart returning to its normal rhythm. Garrett slowly lowered his hands, staring at the blue of his eyes in the mirror. Almost normal. Only a shadow existed, a warning that the demon of his hunger haunted him still.

Pouring water into his shaving jug, he splashed it across his face. The heavy brass spectrometer in the corner caught his eye. There was no point avoiding it. Ignoring the truth didn't make it go away.

Taking up his razor, he slashed a small cut across his finger and squeezed it to make blood well. It oozed slowly through the cut, the dark bluish-red that gave blue bloods their name. Slowly the drop quivered on the tip of his finger, then fell into the glass vial at the end of the spectrometer. Garrett squeezed another two drops out, but the cut was almost healed. With a grimace, he turned the dials on the spectrometer to start the acidic reaction.

The device spat out a small roll of paper with several numbers printed on it. He ignored the first three and went straight to the craving virus percentage.

Sixty-eight.

Garrett stared at the piece of paper for a long time, then scrunched it up in his fist. The numbers were still burned across his retinas. They'd increased since his last reading, which had been yesterday morning.

Suddenly it wasn't enough to clench the paper in his fist. He tore it into fine shreds, discarding them among the ashes in his cold hearth. He had a duty to report this. Any blue blood that reached CV levels of nearly seventy percent was staring the Fade in the eye. It was something every blue blood feared, the final, unstoppable progression of the disease.

Soon his skin would start paling, the color bleaching out of his hair and eyes as he evolved—or devolved—into something inhuman, something utterly vampiric. A blood-thirsty monster incapable of rational thought, driven only by its hungers. The albinism probably would have started already if his levels had climbed slowly, but the swiftness of his increase had saved him from that at least. He had time to hide this.

A rash of vampires a century ago had made it compulsory to deliver reports of high craving levels to the authorities. Nearing seventy percent was cause for increased surveillance. Any higher and they'd consider executing him.

Panic burned through his chest. He couldn't let anyone know. He had to find a way to deal with this. He wasn't ready, hadn't done everything he wanted to… Garrett turned and scraped the spectrometer off the bench as incoherent fear roared through him. Kept going. Smashed the mirror, the shaving bowl, ripped the linens from the bed.

None of it made him feel better. None of it made the truth go away. He froze in the middle of the room, quivering as the rage left him. The carnage was catastrophic. The type of thing the authorities would expect to find if they discovered how high his CV levels were.

Water spilled across the floor, mingling with the small patch of blood from the spectrometer. Instantly the puddle diluted, but all he could see was blood. Could smell it, feel the need for it bubbling up within him.

And suddenly Perry flashed into his mind, an image from his dream, smiling up at him from behind her fan as she flirted with him. Blood welled from her throat and the smile died as she clapped a hand to her throat, blood pouring through her white satin gloves and running down her arm and décolletage.

Garrett collapsed to his knees on the floor, sinking his head into his hands again.

If he didn't report this, then the consequences could be catastrophic.

For he knew who his first victim would be.

Two

"NEW DUKE FOR THE COUNCIL! EXILED LORD RETURNS from Scotland! The Moncrieff is back!"

The woman who called herself Perry jerked to a halt in the middle of the footpath as the young paperboy's voice carried over the crowd. A feeling of old terror momentarily froze her in place. The Moncrieff. Her breath caught, a familiar sensation of light-headedness assailing her, bringing with it a surge of panic she hadn't felt in years.

No. She'd buried those feelings years ago. Fought to find a measure of control over the hysteria. She wasn't the same girl who'd run in fright then. She was ten years older. Stronger. No longer powerless.

"Perry?" Her companion realized she'd stopped and turned to glance at her with his entirely too perceptive blue eyes. Dressed in the crisp black leathers that heralded a Nighthawk, Caleb Byrnes was seemingly unaware of the eyes that followed him. Women were watching him and wondering if he'd look that good without his body armor. "Are you all right?"

"I'm fine." Perry forced herself to start moving again, almost mechanically.

If the story was true and the Moncrieff had been named one of the dukes who ruled the Council, then their paths would likely never cross. He would be part of the aristocratic Echelon, with its own glittering, blood-driven world, well out of her spheres.

They wouldn't meet. They wouldn't. And if they did, would he even recognize a girl the world thought dead?

She shivered. She wasn't fooling anyone, least of all herself. The Moncrieff wouldn't have forgotten her. Could you forget a woman whose disappearance named you a suspect in her murder and earned you exile for ten years?

Perry had to know more. "Stay there."

London was foggy this time of morning, with most of the crowd of pedestrians comprised of men in suits and top hats as they scurried toward their places of employment. A little boy tugged at the leash of a mechanical dog and it staggered after him, its boiler pack evidently running short of water, judging from its awkward gait. His mother grabbed his hand, her bustle swishing as she led them both toward a steam carriage.

An omnibus blared past, silencing the cry of the paperboy, and Perry stilled, trying to track him. Shutting out every other noise until she could find him.

There. Ducking across the street behind a coal-laden dray, she slid between a pair of hackneys and onto the opposite footpath.

"Sorry, lad," a man muttered as they brushed

shoulders, then he glanced back sharply at her face as if realizing his mistake.

It wouldn't be the first time she'd been mistaken for a boy. Perry wore her dyed hair clipped short at the nape. The stark black leathers of her uniform clung to her long legs, and she wore her corset tight enough to smother any hint of betraying curves. Not that she'd been blessed with an abundance of them in the first place.

Better if the world saw her as a man. A man had certain freedoms a woman did not, and in this world, where women were denied the blood rites that turned them into blue bloods, it would be safer for others to think her a lad.

Besides, no one would recognize her like this.

The paperboy scanned the street with his cap pulled low over his eyes and fingerless gloves clutching the paper tightly. He saw her and interpreted her intensity for interest immediately. "Here, sir. A shilling to hear the news."

Perry tossed him the coin, then snatched the paper up. She'd barely finished shaking it out before Byrnes was at her side.

"You do realize it's almost seven in the morning? And we have a summons to attend to? His high-and-mighty lordship won't take kindly to either of us being late."

"Don't speak of Garrett in such a way." She scanned the page, ignoring the grainy photograph of the duke until last. *The Moncrieff's exile over… Reinstated by the prince consort as one of the seven dukes that rule London… Replacing the House of Lannister after their treachery…* And there. Perry's breath caught, her heart giving a painful twist in her chest. *The Earl of Langdon was unavailable for comment following the news. The disappearance of his daughter has never been explained, and he still resides in seclusion at his estate.*

Finally her gaze dropped to the photograph.

There he was. He'd barely changed from the day she'd fled from him, staring imperiously out from the image as if looking straight at her. Moncrieff, with his sandy blond hair swept back from his brow, stylish sideburns, and those piercing blue eyes, gray in print, but she could imagine the sight of them as they swept over her.

The paper crumpled in her fist.

Byrnes's eyes narrowed as he watched her. "Someone walk over your grave?"

"I was curious to see who they would replace the Duke of Lannister with on the Council." This appointment would give the Moncrieff a great deal of power.

Byrnes took the paper, shaking out the folds with a soft, ruffling noise. The newsprint stained his bare fingers. "Duke of Moncrieff." His eyes scanned the lines of text. "I wonder what he was exiled for."

"He was suspected of murdering his thrall, Miss Octavia Morrow." Amazing how cool and dry her voice sounded. "They never found the body, however, so he was only exiled."

"Why accuse him of murder then? The girl might have run."

"And broken her thrall contract? The punishment for which is sometimes execution?" Perry glanced away. "It would have to be strong inducement indeed for her to consider running away."

"Hmm." Byrnes folded the paper under his arm. "I can't see why you're so interested. One duke is much the same as another. Murderer or not."

"I should tell Lynch that you hold such thoughts." The previous Master of the Nighthawks had recently been elevated to the dukedom of Bleight after challenging his uncle—the previous duke—to a duel.

"Lynch being the only exception."

Byrnes wouldn't have been her first choice to work with. But her partner, Garrett, was currently serving as Master of the Nighthawks after Lynch's promotion, and for some insane notion, he had set Byrnes upon her.

After years of working solely with Garrett, knowing how he moved and thought and anticipating his directions, trying to work with a man who wanted no help from her was a lesson in frustration. She'd long been used to the Nighthawks ignoring her skills because she was a female. Byrnes's only saving grace was that she didn't think her gender had anything to do with his perceptions.

"Come. We're late—and you know who shall bear the blame for that."

Perry fell in behind him as he strode toward the guild headquarters, his long legs eating up the distance. She barely noticed the people around her, her hands tucked into the pockets of her long leather coat and her gaze on the cobbles in front of her.

The only thing she noticed was the paperboy's distant cry echoing in her ears. "*The Moncrieff is back! Read all about it!*"

No reason to suspect their paths would ever cross.
But a shiver ran down her spine all the same.

～

"So kind of you to join us."

Perry shut the door, her gaze raking over the inside
of Lynch's study. Or Garrett's now, rather. She had to
stop expecting to see her old master here at the guild.
He often visited, but he'd made it clear that he had a
life outside the guild now.

The room was almost precisely the same as it
had been under Lynch's reign. The enormous desk
dwelled beneath the windows, curtains drawn back
to allow light to enter, and dozens of books lined
the mahogany shelving. The whole place looked and
smelled like *male*. If she took a breath she could almost
capture Lynch's presence. Not his scent of course, for
blue bloods had no scent, but the familiar accompa-
nying odor of leather and ink, his cheroots, and the
enticing, mouthwatering scent of the blud-wein he'd
liked to drink.

Two men sat on the sofa before the cold fireplace.
Perry nodded at Fitz, who nervously toyed with the
frayed sleeve of his tweed coat. He hadn't aged a
day in the time that she'd been there. Perry herself
had stopped aging at roughly twenty, her skin still as
smooth and creamy as a youth's.

Fitz's left eyebrow was growing back in after a
laboratory accident, his blue eyes wide behind his
glasses. A slender man with shoulders narrower than
hers, he'd found his place in the bowels of the building, turning that significant intellect toward matters

of a mechanical or alchemical nature. The man was a genius. His inventions had eased the difficulty of investigations dramatically.

At his side, Doyle was his polar opposite. The only human member of the guild, he ran the place like Garrett's quartermaster, his grizzled bark stripping the hide off a number of the raw recruits. Once, long ago, a blue blood novice had made the mistake of challenging Doyle, considering himself above a mere human. They still whispered about it down in the novice halls.

"Apologies," Byrnes said with a slightly mocking drawl, tossing his coat over the back of an armchair and easing his large frame into it. "Perry wanted to stop and survey the society pages."

That brought her attention to the last person in the study. Not that she'd been unaware of him since she'd entered. No, she'd felt his gaze on her the instant the door opened.

Looking up beneath her lashes, she caught a glimpse of Garrett's blue eyes on her and nodded. Hot blue eyes with a question in them.

"The fault was mine," she admitted, slipping her own coat from her shoulders.

There were three seats remaining. One crushed between Doyle and Fitz, or the entire sofa facing them, where Garrett would no doubt take up residence. Cursing Byrnes under her breath for moving faster than her, Perry crossed the room and tentatively slid her own coat over the back of the sofa.

As soon as she sat, Garrett pushed away from the fireplace behind her. She felt his presence stirring the air as he brushed past. Perry stiffened. So much had changed in the past month and it was entirely her fault.

For years her devilishly handsome partner had looked at her as just another Nighthawk, while she'd been plagued by foolish, girlish ideas. Something she'd never acted on, of course, or betrayed even the slightest hint of, but she couldn't seem to banish the feelings.

She thought she could control them. And then last month two things had changed her entire world. Garrett had been seriously wounded by a rabid blue blood lord to the point where she'd almost thought she would lose him. Only her blood had saved his life and she'd sat by his bed for days, a horrible, sickening feeling inside her.

Then barely a week later, once he was healed, the incident at the opera had occurred.

She could never think of it without referring to it as the "incident." Stupid, reckless pride. That was the cause of her current predicament.

"Don't play games you can't afford to lose. I'll only offer my surrender this once."

Advice she wished she'd listened to.

Garrett settled onto the sofa beside her, his arms stretching out along the back of it and jolting her out of the memory. Ever since that night, she'd hardly seen him. Not only had he partnered her with Byrnes, but he was frequently "busy" attending to guild matters. It could have been coincidence. Perhaps.

"Find anything interesting in the newspaper?" he asked.

"Nothing worth repeating."

"Then is it possible at all for us to have this meeting?" Frustration edged his words. He tugged his pocket watch out of his leather coat. "You're fifteen minutes late. I'd expect it of Byrnes…"

Byrnes arched a brow but said nothing. The two men had been at each other's throats for the past month. It didn't help matters that the ruling Council of Dukes hadn't officially confirmed Garrett's advancement as Master of the Nighthawks. The Council had allowed Lynch to establish the guild under their control forty years ago, and Byrnes was taking full advantage of their indecision in this matter.

"We're here now," she replied.

"Excellent." Garrett scanned the room. "I have here a writ from the Council. They have agreed to examine my claim as Master of the Nighthawks. If no one has any objections, of course?"

Though he didn't quite look at Byrnes, Perry did. The other man shrugged as if he didn't care, but his arctic eyes gleamed. He and Garrett had been with the Nighthawks for a similar length of time, and both had worked within the inner rank of Lynch's Hand—the five who had been his most trusted lieutenants.

Lynch had created the Nighthawks forty years ago, and in all that time there'd never been a thought given to succession. Lynch had always seemed invulnerable—until he'd met Rosa, the devilish revolutionary who'd stolen his heart and set his feet on a new path.

"No objections?"

Silence greeted the room.

"Moving on, then." Garrett briskly placed the letter beside him. "Matters of importance include

Lady Walters's missing diamonds, a murder in Bethnal Green, and some sort of rumors about fighting in the Pits…" His voice droned on and Perry found herself only half listening, which was unusual.

She'd known this new life she'd found wouldn't last as soon as she'd read that the Moncrieff had been exiled for ten years. This year made only nine, which meant the prince consort had recalled him for some reason—and not only recalled him, but offered him a seat on the Council of Dukes who ruled the city.

Such a position was an honor. What the devil had Moncrieff done for the prince consort to reward him as such? And what was she going to do?

Everyone thought Octavia was dead, murdered by the Moncrieff's own hand and buried in an unmarked grave somewhere. She'd made sure of that—the blood that had washed his bedroom left little doubt that someone had died there.

The only person who might suspect she was alive would be the Moncrieff himself.

Shock was starting to wear off. She'd hoped their paths wouldn't cross, but she knew him too well. Now that he was back in London he'd be looking for her, trying to read a trail that was nearly ten years old. With luck, he'd never find her, but if he did…

"We also have a supposed sighting of a ghost, down at Brickbank where they're rebuilding the draining factories."

That jerked her out of her reverie.

Perry looked up and realized that Garrett was watching her. "*What?*" Was he jesting with her? Trying to see if she'd been paying attention?

"A ghost?" Byrnes asked in disbelief. "Sounds like someone's been at the gin again."

"A ghost sighting and two bodies," Garrett repeated, "at the draining factory this morning."

The enormous factories near Brickbank were where the blood gathered in the blood taxes was stored, purified, and bottled for the Echelon's private use.

"Perry," Garrett continued, "I want you on this, along with myself."

He hadn't worked with her in more than a month. If she hadn't been trying so hard to avoid him, she'd almost suspect he'd been avoiding her too. Which was ridiculous. What had happened at the opera—the almost kiss—was likely nothing to Garrett. Flirting with women was the same as breathing for him.

"As you wish." She let out a slow breath. This was her job. It didn't mean anything and she could do this, pretend that there was nothing between them but friendship. She'd been doing it for years.

"Excellent." Garrett straightened, looking around. "Nothing else?"

Byrnes glanced at her, then at Garrett. When she arched a brow at him, Byrnes gave her a tight little smile that could have meant something or nothing at all. "Nothing that would interest anyone else." He stood and stretched like a cat. "Though I will be sorry to lose my partner."

Perry shot him a withering glare.

"You're not," Garrett announced, leaning back against the sofa and staring Byrnes down. "You're exchanging partners. I'm sending you out with ~vice."

The stretch faltered. "I work better alone. You know that."

"You're one of the best trackers the Nighthawks have," Garrett replied, just as quickly. "I want some of the better novices to be paired with you at times, so they may learn."

"They'll slow me down."

"Then hurry them up."

Garrett pushed to his feet, clasping his hands behind his back and turning away from Byrnes, effectively ignoring him. Doyle and Fitz sat quietly on the opposite sofa, watching the byplay with entirely different expressions. Fitz looked like he'd rather be anywhere but here, and Doyle seemed to be mentally placing bets.

Doyle scratched his chin and, with a slight grunt, climbed to his feet, working out the kink in his hip. "You boys want to play cock o' the yard, you ought to get yourselves down to the trainin' room and work it out. The guild don't need us fightin' among ourselves with all this upheaval." He paused in front of Byrnes on his way out. "My money's on Red, just so you know."

Byrnes gave one of those slow shrugs he was famous for. He stood and clapped Doyle on the back. "Don't get too cozy with it, then."

With a rough laugh, Doyle escorted him out of the room. Fitz slunk after them with an almost apologetic look at Garrett. One of the reasons he lived in the dungeons and played with clockwork weaponry was because he abhorred violence.

Perry found her feet, eyeing the door.

"Perry."

Damn it. She froze and glanced at Garrett reluctantly. "I was going to get ready. I'll meet you downstairs and get the boilers going on the steam coach."

Garrett turned to face her, his hands still clasped behind himself and his eyes spearing through her. Authority suited him. "You'd tell me if you were troubled about something, wouldn't you?"

What? Heat crept up her neck and into her cheeks. "Of course. Why would you say such a thing?"

"You seem distracted. Being distracted can get you killed, and I won't have that."

The flush burned hotter. Perry dug her short nails into her palms, trying to force her body to stay still. To not look guilty. "I'm fine. I shall meet you by the carriage and we can go examine the draining factory."

Garrett nodded. He wasn't satisfied, not nearly, she thought, but at least he didn't push her.

Letting out the breath she'd been holding, she managed to escape from the room.

A month ago, she *might* have confided in him.

Three

THE FIRST DRAINING FACTORY LOOMED OUT OF THE FOG like an ancient steel ruin. Fire had done what the years hadn't yet achieved, rusting steel and destroying everything else until the main factory looked like a shell of its former self. Blackened steel spars ended halfway in the air, where the heat from the fires had sheared off the beams, and the brickwork of the enormous furnaces was pitted and choked with coal.

Five of the factories had been gutted in an attack several months ago by the humanist movement—those members of the human population who were dissatisfied with their lack of rights. That left only a single factory in use by the edge of the Thames, its smokestack belching thick, black smoke into the air.

Work on the factories had resumed almost as soon as the fires went out. The sudden shortage of blood left the Echelon bleating for more, and in response, the prince consort had decreed that rebuilding the factories was the first priority in restoring this section of London. Never mind the blackened and charred houses that had been caught in the blaze. The occupants there were only human, and working class at that.

Garrett closed the black lacquered door to the steam carriage as he stepped down. Perry had swept her driving goggles up on top of her head, the glossy black strands of her hair tumbling in disarray. Cursing under her breath, she pulled the lever that shut off the oxygen valve to the boilers and waited for the steam carriage to hiss itself into a whispered death. Little half-moons of soot stained her cheeks, a sight that almost brought a smile to his face.

She didn't look at him. She hadn't in over a month, not directly. As though looking at him meant she too would have to confront what had happened at the opera. The turning point in both their lives.

A sudden reckless frustration swept through him. "Here," he said, stepping forward and offering her his arm to help her down.

"You've never helped me down before," Perry said with a sudden scowl. "I know you're struggling to reconcile the fact that I'm actually female, but that doesn't suddenly make me useless. Just because I wore a dress, it doesn't change anything."

Swinging her legs off the driver's seat, she slid down into the spare few inches between his body and the carriage. For a moment Garrett was tempted to step back, give her space.

Instead he stilled.

Perry realized that too late, freezing in place as she brushed her gloves off against her tight leather breeches. Slowly she lifted her head, gaslight catching the gleaming gray of her eyes. There was an inch between them at most. A single tantalizing inch that he was too aware of.

"It's difficult to *stop* picturing you in that dress," he replied, forcing his voice to stay soft. He could almost feel the heat of the hunger swimming through his eyes, threatening to drop him over the edge. "Considering how much of you it flaunted."

"You can't help yourself, can you? I never should have worn the dratted thing."

Reaching up, his gloved fingers swept at the sooty rings her goggles had left on her cheeks. The motion soothed some part of him. Maybe this was what he needed. Something to ground him. "I said that you could never pass as a female, and you wanted to throw my words back in my face. You succeeded. Admirably."

Twirling at the bottom of the stairs, the red skirts sweeping around her and the thick, luscious curls of her wig trailing over her shoulder as she shot him such a direct look he could hardly breathe all of a sudden. "Well?" she'd challenged.

That moment. The moment it all changed. Like some enormous hand reached out and closed its fingers around his heart and lungs, squeezing, forcing the breath out of him.

Garrett didn't know how to react now. Perry had recovered flawlessly, resuming her aloof, taciturn persona as though nothing remotely unusual had occurred that night. Gone were the practiced flirtation, the smiles that lit her from within…but he couldn't forget them. How did you forget something like that? Pretend it had never happened? Pretend that his eye wasn't drawn to her now in a way that was distinctly masculine and not at all friend-like?

The problem was that he now knew a sensual woman existed beneath her logical, focused exterior. If she were any other woman, he would have pursued her relentlessly until he had what he wanted. But this was Perry. Someone he admired, respected, someone he'd give his life for. To cross that line meant their entire friendship—which was evolving, admittedly— would change. And then? He didn't have a bloody clue what that would mean. But he knew it meant more than sex, more than friendship. Perry deserved nothing less—he just wasn't certain he could give her what she wanted.

His hand dropped as he searched her gaze. His skin felt hot; no mean feat considering how cool his blood ran now that he was a blue blood. But the hunger in him had settled, comforted by her nearness. He didn't know quite what to think about that. It wanted her, craved her, yet it gentled at the touch of her skin. She made it easier to breathe again.

Perhaps he'd been wrong to avoid her so much for the last month. Or perhaps not. He didn't understand any of this.

"You enjoyed making me act like a fool," Garrett murmured. "Don't even try to deny it. And now you have to deal with the consequences."

Her eyes suddenly gleamed. "You're right. I did enjoy making a fool of you. The problem is that I only intended for you to act a fool for one night. Not this whole bleeding month."

Sliding past him, leaving behind the ghostly fragrance she washed her clothes in, Perry strode toward the factory.

Garrett followed her toward the gaslights burning at the front of the factory and the people gathered there. He didn't even understand why he'd pursued this—pushing at her, trying to elicit some sort of recognition, some sign that things had changed between them. Hell, he didn't even know why he wanted to acknowledge that things had changed.

"You're a fool," he muttered to himself under his breath. What the hell did he want from her?

Far better if he kept his distance, forced their relationship back to the familiar grounds of friendship. His hands shook as he slid them into his pockets. Better for both of them.

Still, he knew he couldn't avoid her forever. A part of him yearned for someone he could trust at his side. Fitz was the only one who knew his blood levels were high, and Garrett couldn't confide in him. Fitz was the man to speak to if one wanted to know how to calibrate a brass spectrometer or repair a boiler pack, but when it came to dealing with personal demons, Garrett might as well be speaking another language.

And he was starting to feel lonely. He was surrounded by Nighthawks all of the time and yet forever aloof. Lynch was the only one who might have understood how that felt, but Lynch was gone now, dealing with the pressures of the dukedom and enjoying his new wife's company. Besides…after what Garrett had done to Rosalind, Lynch barely spoke to him.

Not only had he lost Perry, but the only other man he'd counted as a true friend. And both times were his fault.

One of the men in front of the factory doors turned

and half blinded Garrett with his lantern. His workman's shirt was stained with coal and grease, and the pants he wore had seen better days. One glance at his pale face and the strain that tightened his mouth, and Garrett knew he'd been the one to find the bodies.

The man saw him, his shoulders sagging with relief. "Me lord Nighthawk. Thank the heavens."

"I wouldn't be thanking the heavens just yet," Garrett murmured under his breath with a glance at the horseless carriage alighting behind his own.

The man followed his gaze and paled. The gilt-covered carriage, with its inlay of mother-of-pearl, signaled its occupant more clearly than a fanfare could.

"Looks like we're about to receive a visit from a duke," Garrett said. He could just make out the hawk emblem carved in gold on the side paneling, with a ruby for an eye. "Or a duke's heir. Barrons, by the look of it."

The heir to the Duke of Caine stepped down from the carriage, his dark eyes raking the scene. Tossing his gloves and top hat to his footmen, the young blue blood started toward Garrett with a deliberateness of purpose.

They'd met before, as Barrons's role on the Council of Dukes was that of liaison between the Council and the Nighthawks, and he had even been counted one of Lynch's few friends. Garrett's dealings with him, however, had been as second-in-command of the Nighthawks. Now he walked a fine dagger's edge. He was acting guild master, but not yet officially recognized.

As if he didn't have enough on his mind.

"Barrons," Garrett murmured, with a slight nod of the head that wasn't as deep as usual. He had his own position to establish.

Faint humor stirred in the other man's predatory gaze. "Master Reed," Barrons replied. His bare knuckles tightened over the silver-edged handle of his sword-cane as he glanced up at the enormous building behind them. "I hear we have reports of ghosts and two bodies."

"News travels swiftly." Garrett had barely received the report himself.

Dark eyes flickered to his. Unreadable. "The Duke of Malloryn and I are responsible for the rebuilding of the draining factories. We can't afford to have anything go wrong with the one draining factory still in working order." Gesturing to Garrett to fall into place beside him, he continued, "The foreman sent a clockwork raven to Caine House as soon as he heard the news."

I wonder if that was before or after he sent one to the Nighthawks? Garrett's lips thinned. He liked Barrons, but the absoluteness of power that the Council wielded didn't sit well. And they frequently meddled in affairs that belonged firmly in the Nighthawks' jurisdiction.

"I'm afraid I've only just arrived at the scene myself," Garrett replied. "If you give my men an hour or two to examine the factory, I'll have a report directed to you."

"You needn't bother," Barrons replied, with that faintly mocking smile on his lips again. "I know how this works. Consider me a silent bystander. I won't get in your way, and I won't tamper with your evidence. I'm only here to observe."

To observe what, though? The mystery? Or my effective-ness as commander?

"As you wish," he replied, for he couldn't very well insist otherwise. Ignoring Barrons, he glanced past him to the foreman who was following dutifully at their heels. "Mr. Mallory, yes?" Garrett gestured for the man to step up to his side.

"Aye, sir," the fellow replied, doffing his cap nervously.

"Tell me, what time did you find the bodies?"

"'Twere half five, sir. I come in early, as I wanted to get the fires burning hot before the workers arrived. We been working night and day since the burning of the factories, but we have the night off on a Sunday." A nervous glance at Barrons told Garrett all he needed to know about the man's religious convictions.

When the Church in Rome had excommunicated them as demons, the Echelon had burned most of the churches and cathedrals and forbidden the masses from worshipping in public. Most of the working class, however, held private gatherings in secret places to worship. The more the Echelon tried to weed faith out, the more it dug its roots deep in the population.

Humans might be forced to yield to the blood taxes and their place in the social hierarchy, but they'd be damned if they'd give up their religion. Such a thing, however, was dangerous to speak about in front of a blue blood lord. Only a year ago, the prince consort had ordered ten men flayed for attending such a gathering.

"I'll pretend I didn't hear that," Barrons murmured. As if sensing the foreman's nervousness, he nodded toward the door. "Do you mind if I observe your men's examinations of the bodies?"

Effectively giving Garrett time to question the foreman alone. "Go ahead."

The moment he was gone, color began to return to Mallory's cheeks as though he were unaware that he still stood beside a blue blood. "Do you think he'll report me?"

"I think," Garrett said, "that Barrons is rather more liberal than one would presume. He needs to get these factories rebuilt as soon as possible and keep this one running smoothly. Informing on you defeats his purpose."

The foreman breathed a sigh of relief, his fingers twitching as if to make the sign of the cross. "Aye. He's better than some o' them others."

"I agree." Garrett smiled. "Do you mind if I record our conversation?"

"With what?"

Garrett retrieved the small, brass recording device from his pocket. "We call it ECHO." Echometry communications…something starting with *H* and observations. No matter how many times Fitz told him, he never could remember it all.

Once the information was recorded, Garrett could play it back over a phonograph in the comfort of his study. Fitz was working on making something smaller that could repeat the information instantly.

Mallory peered at it. "Why, I ain't never seen the like. Records me voice, aye?"

"Clearly enough to fool your wife." They shared a smile.

"Aye, well, go ahead and question me, sir. I'd like to hear me voice, I would."

Gesturing him through into the factory, Garrett clipped the ECHO to his lapel. "Monday, twenty-first of November. This is Acting Guild Master Garrett Reed, recording a conversation with Mr. Mallory, foreman of Factory Five. So, Mr. Mallory, last night the factory was closed and you arrived at half five this morning to stoke the boilers. Can you explain to me how you found the bodies?"

"Aye." Mallory leaned close, speaking slowly and loudly, as if to a deaf man. "I come in through the side door and turned the lights on back there. Didn't need to light the whole factory, see? Just down here where the furnaces stand."

"You may speak normally," Garrett instructed. "The ECHO has an accurate recording radius of twenty feet."

"Aye, sir." Mallory shuffled in embarrassment, then pressed on. "Through here, sir. You'll see the row of furnaces there? They're what we use to purify the blood."

The enormous row of furnaces radiated waves of heat in the chilly morning. Gaslight gleamed on the heavy black iron, though almost everything else fell into pools of darkness. The Nighthawks were instructed to leave any scene as it had been found, at least until initial observations had been recorded.

"So you lit the furnaces? How long did that take?" He could see the wheelbarrow tracks and taste the coal dust in the air. Coal bins were full to overflowing and a shovel still sat in one of the wheelbarrows.

"Aye, lit them up. Then I went upstairs to boil a spot o' tea at half six, so I must have been down 'ere an hour." Mallory gestured to a grimy clock face on the wall. "Been a factory man all me life, sir. It's habit to keep time."

No doubt Mallory did the same thing every Monday morning at precisely the same time.

Garrett followed him up the stairs to the factory. Morning light gleamed through the dusty windows, casting a grayish pall over the enormous room, and it was frigidly cold up here. Somewhere in the eaves a pigeon fluttered and cooed, frantically searching for a way out. Huge steel cables hung from the ceiling, suspending the walkways that overlooked the main room and led to the offices upstairs.

A dark figure caught his attention: Perry. Dressed in her tight black leathers, she almost blended into the shadows that swallowed up the walkways above. The only thing that caught his eye was the pale oval of her face, almost as familiar to him as his own. She paused here and there as if examining the area. Scenting the air, he knew. Perry could track a man to the London borough where he lived, purely by the scent trail he left.

"All the factories shared the mess hall outside," Mallory explained. "But there were a gas stove and kettle in Mr. Sykes's office. He's the overseer."

Garrett tore his gaze away from her. *Focus.* "But he's not here?"

"Ah, well. Ain't his practice to be here till midday or thereabouts. I sent word to his house, but ain't heard back yet."

"Sleeping off a soused head?"

Mallory looked relieved. "Something like that, I'd expect."

Garrett questioned Mallory thoroughly until they finally found themselves maneuvering from the enormous row of machines toward the bodies.

This was where Garrett differed from Lynch. He liked to take a man's measure, to hear the story from witnesses before he sought out the bodies. Lynch, however, took his evidence in scientific facts and autopsies. Lynch could guess what type of man had the means of doing something like this, but he lacked the ability to converse with people easily. Garrett knew people inside and out. He could put them at ease with a few well-placed words, and he listened. People liked to talk about themselves, given an attentive audience.

Both methods worked and Garrett stuck with what he knew. He wasn't Lynch. He could never *be* Lynch. And the Nighthawks and the Council would just have to get used to that.

By the time they came upon the bodies, Mallory had relaxed enough to forget his words were being recorded as he spilled details of the ghost he'd seen. *"Way up on them ramparts, where your Nighthawk's standing. 'Twere a woman, sir. I could see right through her, and she gleamed fair pale…"*

Mallory stopped in his tracks as soon as he saw the pair of bodies, and this time he couldn't stop himself from making the sign of the cross.

Two of the Nighthawks, Faber and Scoresby, had secured the area and Scoresby was setting up the mechanical shutter camera with Barrons looking on in curiosity. Dr. Gibson would be arriving soon to make his own analysis and take the bodies away for autopsy.

No help for it. Garrett looked at the bodies. Pale

and naked, their fingers tangling, almost as if reaching for each other. One was a brunette, her dark curls covering her features. The other had long, blond hair with ringlets framing her heart-shaped face.

"Poor wee lasses," Mallory muttered, working his cap in his hands. "Can't think what they were doing here at night."

Garrett knelt down and, using a stylus, lifted one of the girl's stiffening arms. Dark stitches in her skin showed where deep cuts had been made to her chest. Almost as though something had been removed inside, then the skin replaced. But little blood spatter around her. He felt her throat, but the skin was quite cold and cadaveric rigidity had begun to set in. Dr. Gibson would no doubt discover more.

"Found anything?" Perry asked, appearing on quiet feet. He could never work out how she did that, as her boots had small heels on them.

"This one was already dead," Garrett murmured. "Look at the bruising on the bottom of her arm—and body. She's been moved from where she died, but the death occurred sometime last night, I'd say. Gibson will have a more accurate idea of time."

He circled toward the other girl, stepping carefully. "This one, however, was killed here." Blood splashed from the gaping chasm in her chest, the ribs splintered and the flesh around the wound mangled. "I think the heart has been removed from both of them, but this was done quickly and far less efficiently than the other girl. He was hurried here. Not as precise."

A glance showed arterial blood spattered across the nearest machines and drying on the timber floorboards.

Garrett's nostrils flared at the sight of blood, and his gaze shot toward the stairs that led down to the furnaces. He had to focus. "You heard nothing when you came in?" he asked Mallory.

"Nothing, sir."

And he would have heard precisely that with the furnaces roaring. Garrett frowned. "I believe you startled the murderer and he killed the second girl here, while you were below. The first young lady was already dead and perhaps he was moving her." Did the second girl struggle? Was that why he killed her? Had she tried to scream for help when she heard Mallory moving about?

"How?" Perry murmured. "Carry one body over his shoulder and the other young woman in his other arm?"

"That argues for either brute strength or help. No sign of the heart?" Garrett directed the question at Scoresby, who was taking photographs of the scene.

"No, sir."

"How did he move the first body here and murder the other girl? She would have been struggling, I'd assume?" Barrons asked.

"Don't ever assume. What are your thoughts?" Garrett knelt down, directing the question to Perry. "Think there were two of them?"

"Possibly." Perry circled the girls, her lean form drawing his gaze. He waited patiently while she knelt and examined the blond, looking at her hands and fingers, then her face. She quickly performed the same examination on the brunette.

When she looked up at him, her gray eyes were solemn. *Troubled.*

"You recognize one of them?" he asked.

"No. But I do recognize the sort. Look here," she said, lifting the blond's hand. A ruby ring decorated the girl's middle finger, though red marks showed where someone had tried to remove it.

"She came from money, then," he mused.

"Not just money, Garrett." Perry turned the girl's palm toward him. "No calluses, no signs of wear… Her skin is pale and flawless. Like she spends most of her time wearing gloves and has never performed a day's work in her life. This"—she pointed to the ring—"is not just a common ruby. See the silverwork? The way the carved roses curl around the ruby and hold it in place?"

He leaned closer, aware of leather straining as the other men did too.

Perry's thumbnail flicked one of the silver thorns and it popped out, a bead of clear liquid seeping from the end of it.

Barrons sucked in a sharp breath and Perry looked up. "You've seen them," she said, and it was no question.

"It's a fashion among the debutantes of the Echelon these days," Barrons admitted, scratching at his jaw. "I don't recognize either of the girls, though, which is not unusual. I rarely mingle for societal purposes these days."

"It's not just a fashion," Perry corrected. "It's a weapon. A poison ring. The liquid inside is hemlock, designed to paralyze a blue blood long enough for the girl to get away if he attacks her."

Garrett reached for the girl's hand and examined the ring. Hemlock and its effects on a blue blood had only been discovered recently, and the information was still circulating throughout London in humanist pamphlets.

He'd heard rumors recently that some of the younger lords of the Echelon had begun to play dangerous games, taking what they wanted from the sheltered young ladies for the night and casting them aside without a thought. Once blooded, a young girl's entire reputation could be ruined and she would be seen as anyone's for the taking. A blood whore.

The rings must have come into fashion shortly after word of hemlock's effects reached the Echelon, as a girl's only means of protection against such a scenario.

The other girl's fingers were bare but there was a mark on her right hand that attested to the presence of some sort of jewelry in recent times. Something she wore frequently enough that it had left its mark on her.

"Look at their hair," Perry said. "It's thick and glossy with health and long enough to be looped up in fashionable styles. If a young working girl had hair like this, she'd have sold it. Their nails"—she held up the blond's hand—"are perfectly manicured."

All signs he probably wouldn't have looked for. Perry's skills ran in the other direction from his.

"Plump girls," Garrett began to notice. "Neither of them knew hardship."

"If word of this gets out..." Barrons trailed off grimly.

"We'll find out who they are," Perry replied, her voice hardening as she folded the girl's hands over the ragged hole in her chest. "And then we'll find the killer."

The firmness of her tone surprised him. Garrett examined her face, but it was expressionless as usual. Perry always kept her emotions locked firmly under key, but she couldn't hide them from him. What was it about this situation that bothered her?

Wiping her hands on her breeches, she stood up and let out a breath.

"Scoresby, make sure you photograph this entire area in detail," Garrett said. "Faber, I want the whole factory searched for anything out of the ordinary, including anything that might have created this 'ghost.'" Although he had his doubts about precisely what Mallory had seen. A man stumbling across two bodies in the dark was often confused. "When Dr. Gibson arrives, help him to load the girls into the medical van." He looked at Perry. "Ready to question some of the jewelers?"

Barrons was still staring at the bodies. "I believe I can spare you some time with that inquiry."

"You know where the rings come from, my lord?" Perry asked.

"My ward, Lena Todd—now Lena Carver—is responsible for distributing them among the debutantes. It was her idea, you see." Barrons's head lowered in thought. "She might know if any of the debutantes have gone missing."

"Lena Carver." Garrett frowned. "The new verwulfen ambassador's wife?"

"Aye," Barrons replied.

"Bloody hell," Perry muttered under her breath.

Bloody hell, indeed.

∾❦∾

By the time they exited the factory, several other Nighthawks had arrived, along with Dr. Gibson. Garrett gave them directions, then commandeered one of the novices to drive the carriage.

Perry reluctantly handed over her driving goggles and glared at Garrett as he held the door open for her.

"I always hold the door open," he pointed out.

Perry glanced up at him from beneath her thick, dark lashes as she climbed inside. "And do you always stare at my backside when I climb in?"

Garrett choked back a laugh and followed her inside. "Guilty as charged, I'm afraid." Slamming the door shut, he felt the familiar throbbing hum as the boilers started. At least now their conversation wouldn't be overheard.

When she didn't reply, he looked up. Faint rosy circles colored her cheeks, despite the infinitely cool look she gave him.

"Good God. Are you blushing?"

"You would have to say more than that to make *me* blush. I've heard all manner of vulgar commentary from you over the years, enough to grant me some immunity."

The steam carriage started forward. Perry glanced out the window, the gray light of a frosty November morning washing over her features. The unsettling urge to push at her hit him again.

"Don't pretend you're in any way innocent," he replied. "Do you remember what you were whispering in my ear at the opera?"

Her glare practically incinerated him. "I've tried to forget the entire incident."

"Did you succeed?" His voice roughened.

This time she looked away, turning her face to the window and granting him her profile. She was a long time in replying. "Quite."

Liar. "Perhaps I should remind you."

"Perhaps we should concentrate on the task at hand?"

A thousand responses leaped to mind, but Garrett said nothing. Simply watched her, reading the clues that he hadn't noticed until now. How wound up she was. Tight as clockwork.

Not about him, he was certain. Or she'd have been like this since the opera. No, this was new.

"This case bothers you," he said.

"No more than usual."

"You're always on edge after something like this," he noted. "But you don't get quiet. You get angry and you don't relax until we can get in the training room and you can punch the bag a few times. Or me."

"Do you want me to fight with you?"

"I'd like you to tell me what's bothering you," he replied, though he could have taken up the gauntlet.

Perry's gaze dropped to her hands. "It's nothing."

"Is it about the case?"

"I… It's… I never like seeing young girls like that. They were what? Sixteen? Seventeen? They've barely lived."

"A lot of them are." He stared out the window as they passed through the streets. Here in the heart of the city, the cobblestones gleamed and elegant passersby laughed beneath their bonnets and top hats. A far cry from the streets outside the city walls that kept out the rabble, the kind of people that he'd once come from. "It's the children," he admitted quietly. "They're the ones that bother me the most. Them and the whores."

"Whores?"

Garrett shrugged. "They don't have anyone to protect them. Circumstances force them to do what they must, and most of them die cold, lonely deaths. Do you know why that bothers me so much?" he asked. "It's because I see my mother. I see her body." A flash of it swept through his vision. Mary Reed, lying naked and broken in an alley after her night's shift. Robbed of everything—her clothes, her meager coin purse, her dignity.

He'd been all of nine and left to fend for himself. Oh yes, he knew how those children and whores died. It was one of the reasons he'd chosen to step away from the gutters and better himself, one of the reasons he'd joined the Nighthawks when it became apparent he had the craving virus. He hadn't been able to protect his mother, but there were always others.

He forced the memories away. "Do you see yourself in those young girls?"

She shook her head abruptly. But the stillness was there in her shoulders.

"Or is it something else?" He watched the way she took a quick breath and looked away again. "It is. Something else is bothering you."

"Garrett, leave it alone."

Like hell. But he'd long since learned that if he kept questioning her, she'd obstinately dig her claws in and say nothing more. Perry was possibly the only person he couldn't eventually wear down.

"As you wish," he replied softly.

Stillness fell between them, broken only by the steady hiss of the steam engine. Garrett stretched his arms out along the back of the seat and watched her stare out the window stubbornly, pretending that she didn't feel his gaze.

The silky, black strands of her hair, cut longer in front and shorter at the nape, fell over her forehead. A boyish, careless cut, but one that drew his gaze to the smoothness of her throat and the long line of her nape. He'd pressed a kiss there at the opera. Felt the kick of her pulse against his tongue as he fought the urge to bite her, to mark her as his. It was the first time his demons had ever come close to overruling him.

"Do you think the verwulfen ambassador will be home?" he asked, mainly to break the thick silence in the carriage. He hated the way silence seemed to settle over them now. As though both of them were far too aware of what had changed, yet neither wished to mention it. Sometimes he felt like he was truly losing her. If the opera had never happened, he could have confided in her about his CV levels and found some sense of solace, at least.

Now he could not. Because she was the greatest torment he faced, and how the devil could a man admit that to a woman? To a friend? Every moment she was with him, he couldn't stop thinking about her—the sound of the soft, little moans she would make as he pinned her beneath him, the taste of her skin, and the wetness of her blood splashing over his lips... He shifted and forced his thoughts to other things. To two poor girls with their hearts cut out of their chests.

"I hope not," Perry murmured.

Garrett shared her sentiments. Verwulfen were another species indeed. Dangerous, ridiculously strong, and impervious to pain when in the grip of *berserker-gang*, the strange fury that drove them while they were in a rage. The Echelon had ruled them too volatile to live freely ever since they'd exterminated the Scottish verwulfen clans at Culloden, locking them in cages and considering them slaves. Dozens of them had been thrown into the Manchester Pits to fight to the death for the joy of the crowd, or even the rough Pits in the East End of London, but times were changing. Several months ago, a treaty had been forged between the Scandinavian verwulfen clans and the Echelon, with a law decreeing all verwulfen in the Isles free of their shackles.

The man responsible for that was Will Carver. Once second-in-command of a dangerous rookery gang. And now Garrett and Perry had to question Carver's wife.

Garrett knew how well that interview would proceed.

❧

Luck wasn't with them. The ambassador was home.

The ancient butler ushered Garrett and Perry into a study where a pretty young woman sat behind a desk, patiently showing a hulking brute a letter. The man's coat was strewn carelessly over the back of a chair, and his shirtsleeves were rolled up to his elbows. Despite the cut of the clothing, he seemed ill at ease in it. As if he still wasn't used to finery.

At Garrett and Perry's entrance, the pair looked up,

their almost identical bronze-colored eyes locking on the two Nighthawks. While a smile dawned on Mrs. Carver's lips, her husband merely examined them with a dark glare.

"Good morning, Mr. Carver." Garrett bowed his head. "Mrs. Carver."

"Is it a good mornin', then?" Carver replied, straightening to his full, almost intimidating height. "Nighthawks in me study don't usually herald good news."

"Not good news, no," Garrett replied. "I would like to have a word with your wife, if I might."

"I don't think so," Carver growled.

"Will." Mrs. Carver shot him a demure look from beneath her lashes. Though Carver's lips thinned, he stepped back and folded his arms across his chest, letting her have her way.

"What may I do for you?" she asked, leaning back in the chair and eyeing the pair of them. Her dark hair was gathered into a neat chignon, yet delicate brown ringlets framed her pretty heart-shaped face. She was the sort of woman that might have drawn Garrett's eye a while ago. Perhaps a month or more ago.

Perry stepped forward. "A pair of bodies was found at one of the draining factories this morning—"

"What are you tryin' to say?" Carver snapped.

"One of the girls wore the same ring your wife does," Perry replied. "We're trying to ascertain the girl's identity. Nothing else. Barrons sent us here to inquire about the ring."

Garrett let her lead. Perhaps Carver would find it less antagonizing to deal with a woman. And it gave him time to study the pair of them.

Mrs. Carver looked genuinely distressed at the news. She touched the ring on her right hand, her brow furrowing. "That's terrible news. But I don't know if I can help you. There are dozens of these in circulation. They—" She broke off.

"We know their purpose," Garrett added, "and it is none of our concern. We merely wish to identify the bodies. The other girl looks to have had a similar ring on her finger, but the ring was removed."

Perry swiftly reeled off the details of the girls' appearances, impressing even Garrett. When it came to conversation, he could recall almost every word spoken, but Perry's skills of observation were unparalleled. It was one of the reasons they worked so well together.

Mrs. Carver slowly shook her head. "I'm sorry. That could describe almost two dozen debutantes."

"Would it be possible for you to view the bodies?" Perry asked. "To help identify them?"

Carver shifted but his wife laid a hand on his wrist, stilling him instantly. "I can try. I find it difficult to deal with such things now that my senses are so enhanced. The smell—" She grimaced. "I shall try."

Garrett's estimation of Mrs. Carver rose. She might look like a bit of muslin, but she had a core of inner steel, it seemed. "I shall send word ahead to headquarters. Would you care to take our carriage?"

"Now?" Mrs. Carver asked, her pretty, almond-shaped eyes widening.

"No time like the present," Garrett replied smoothly. If they were correct in the assumption that the two victims were of the Echelon, they needed to track this killer before word hit the news sheets.

Or worse, the Echelon gossip mill.

❦

Perry watched as Dr. Gibson gently peeled the sheet away from the face of the first body. The girls had been brought back to the cold, sterile room in headquarters that Dr. Gibson used for his autopsies. Thankfully, the doctor hadn't yet started.

Gaslight painted a distinct, icy-blue glow across the dead girl's face. Garrett moved into view, escorting Mrs. Carver and her hulking husband.

Carver looked bothered by the smell, standing over his wife and scrubbing at his nose. His broad shoulders strained at his coat, and his long, tawny hair brushed against his lapels. He was not the type of man who would normally catch the eye of a young debutante—as Mrs. Carver had once been—but every married woman or widow in the district would recognize the underlying virility and touch of carnality that rested uneasily beneath his skin. Even Perry did. Verwulfen were dangerous men, and Carver more so than most.

However, he was particularly careful with his wife, his hand sliding over the small of her back. Almost gentle. As if he took some comfort in the touch too.

Mrs. Carver tugged off her gloves, then glanced at the girl. Instantly the color bleached from her face. "Oh."

"You recognize her?" Garrett asked intently, his blue eyes even brighter in the gaslight.

Shadows sculpted the high arch of his cheekbones and brows. A devilishly handsome man, and intimidated by nothing. Comfortable in his own skin to the point that eyes automatically turned when he entered a room. This was what Lynch had seen in him when he reluctantly named him as his successor. This was what Perry saw. There had been other options for guild master, but Garrett was the best of them.

Perry folded her arms across her chest and leaned against the wall. She felt comfortable in the shadows, letting Garrett handle the matter. And she too found the cold, chemical scent of death unnerving.

"It's Miss Amelia Keller," Mrs. Carver said. Her expression softened and she reached out, as if to touch the girl. Carver might be all brute, but his wife suffered the finer emotions. "She was on the cusp of making a thrall contract with the Earl of Brumley."

"Was there a reason she sought you out for the poison ring?" Garrett asked.

"The same reason they all do. It's becoming quite the sport for blue blood lords to ambush young ladies the moment they step outside a ballroom or when their chaperone's back is turned."

"So nobody wished her harm? Specifically?"

"Not that I'm aware of. However, I knew her only peripherally." She exchanged a glance with Carver.

"Verwulfen have been given the pardon now," he muttered, "but not all o' them pasty-faced vultures like dealin' with us."

Mrs. Carver had fallen far from her former rank within the Echelon by not only marrying a verwulfen, but becoming one.

"They come to me when they're desperate," Mrs. Carver added.

"What about her fiancé, the Earl of Brumley?" Perry asked.

"He doted on her. He was nearly twice her age, and I believe he considered himself quite fortunate to have landed her," Mrs. Carver replied.

Garrett nodded at Dr. Gibson, who whipped the sheet back over the girl's form. "And the other," he murmured, moving around the steel examination table.

This time Mrs. Carver was prepared. Her nostrils flared minutely when Gibson lowered the sheet. "She smells like...some sort of chemical. Something like ether and perhaps laudanum. Fresh blood too."

"You can distinguish that?" Perry asked, for she herself could barely make out the individual chemicals.

"My sister, Honoria, has scientific tendencies," Mrs. Carver replied, screwing up her nose. "After visits with her, I'm more than aware of what certain chemicals smell like."

"And the girl?" Garrett pressed.

Mrs. Carver examined her for a long time. "Miss Fortescue, I believe, though I could be mistaken. I've seen her but once, and from a distance. She did not come to me for the ring. She must have received it through an associate of mine."

Garrett thanked her for her help and quietly escorted the Carvers to the door. When they were gone, Perry could no longer stand it. She dragged the sheet up over Miss Fortescue's face and let out a sigh.

"This one's going to be a right pickle," Dr. Gibson

muttered, wiping his hands on a cloth. The ex-army surgeon was fastidious.

"Daughters of the Echelon," Perry agreed. "They'll be screaming for heads to roll." She circled the table. The sheet clung to each girl, a dimple revealing where the chest cavity had been spread. For a moment her gorge rose, and she swallowed. Her own nightmares were ten years old. This couldn't be happening again. What were the odds?

But he's back in town, an insidious little voice whispered. *And if the Moncrieff is back…*

A vision flashed into her mind of the monster who'd once strapped her to a steel examination table like this and…done things to her. Horrible things that were best not thought of again. A clammy coldness circled her brow, and her nostrils pinched together. *I killed Hague. I know I did.*

The whirling arc of the sword as she cleaved Hague's face in two, blood spraying across the Duke of Moncrieff's bedroom… When she ran, he'd been screaming—or trying to anyway, through what was left of his face—but what man could live through such a thing?

"Your initial observations of the bodies—what were your findings?" she asked.

"It's a mystery, to be sure. I would suspect Miss Keller died almost ten hours ago. However, the coldness of the factory might mean time of death was actually earlier. The removal of her heart was done more precisely than even I could attempt. Evidently he had time to perform the procedure—and that's what this was. A procedure.

"I don't know what he hoped to achieve, but he's performed the process many times before. There is some organic substance on her skin that I can't quite identify, and the aorta and pulmonary artery leading from where her heart once lay are…in a state of post-mortem healing. I cannot even describe it."

Healing. A sense of cold lashed down Perry's spine. "Have you tested her for any sign of the craving virus?"

Gibson looked up from the sheet-covered body, his bushy brows beetling over his eyes. "It's not standard procedure on females."

"But her body is healing," Perry argued, flexing and unflexing her fingers. "And I'm proof enough that accidents occur." She wanted to be out of here now. As far away from the bodies as she could get. As far away from… Was it time to run again? She'd thought she'd found some sense of safety here. The guild had become her home in a way that the Echelon had never been.

And leaving Garrett… Her breath caught, indecision sweeping through her. Stay? Or run before the Moncrieff found her?

"I'll test them for signs of the craving virus. Whoever our killer is, he's had a lot of experience with a scalpel. He's also very strong."

"We're looking for someone from a medical trade then."

"A surgeon, a barber, a butcher… Someone who uses a blade in their day-to-day life." Gibson sighed. "The other strange thing is that there are no defensive wounds whatsoever on Miss Keller, no signs of struggle or hints of skin beneath her fingernails. As if she simply lay there while he performed the deed."

"Chloroform or ether?" Perry asked. "Mrs. Carver could smell ether, after all. Perhaps she didn't fight because she was unconscious or dead from inhalation."

"Maybe. Miss Fortescue was another matter." He used a stylus to lift back her bloodied lip. There was some foreign substance caught in her teeth. "She bit him. Hard enough to tear skin. She was struggling when this happened, and I would presume that he had his hand over her mouth."

"Mallory startled him in the process of moving her." Perry was starting to draw conclusions.

Gibson nodded. "Perhaps. From the wounds on her chest, the removal of *her* heart was done in a hurry. And I'm fairly certain I can make out a stab wound, though I'll know more once I've completed the autopsy." Moving away from the bodies, he cleaned his hands. "God only knows why he took the time to remove her heart, if he thought Mallory might find him."

Perhaps because he couldn't bear to leave it behind. She'd encountered a man like that once.

That was her cue to leave. Perry muttered her good-byes and closed the door behind her with a soft *snick*. She stayed there for a moment, forehead pressed against the cold, iron-bound door, as memory assaulted her. A cold, sterile laboratory, outfitted with dozens of shelves featuring glass jars full of strange amorphous shapes… Her vision clearing as she blinked her way back into consciousness… Light reflecting back off steel implements… The jars… Something about the jars…

About the shapes in them.

A human heart. And other organs. Hague's little trophies.

Hague had been only a human, a scientist who worked for the Moncrieff. There was no way he could have survived what she'd done to him the night she'd fled.

Was there?

I cut half his face off. His jaw was dangling by a single scrap of tendon... The thought made her stomach revolt, but she forced herself to push through it. She'd seen Hague go down, bleeding all over the Moncrieff's fine silk sheets. She could remember *that* from the morass of nightmarish images that were all that remained of that night. Stricken with the first stages of the craving virus, she'd barely been lucid as she fought her way free of the laboratory and staggered out into the streets.

But she'd never seen Hague actually die. For the first time, doubt assailed her. He was the type of man who would have stayed long enough to remove a girl's heart. He'd have *needed* to. It was an abnormality in him that she'd never encountered before. And though he'd been human, the Moncrieff was not. If the duke had returned home from his club in time, he might have been able to save his precious doctor by using his blood to infect him with the craving. He'd always boasted to her of his high CV levels. Such a thing could heal almost everything, and Hague had been a genius, irreplaceable.

They'd blamed the Moncrieff for her disappearance, so he must have returned soon enough after her escape. All they'd found was blood splashed across his bedroom. No sign of Hague's body, but she'd assumed the duke covered it up. Couldn't have anyone seeing what was going on in the cellars, after all. Which was probably why he'd set the house on fire.

"Don't ever go down those stairs. That floor is off-limits," the duke had told her when she'd first come to his house.

"But why?" Perry had asked, always curious and insatiably so at seventeen.

"Perhaps I have the bodies of my former consorts hidden down there," the duke had replied with a slight smile, as he referenced the old tale.

At least there was one thing she could say about him. He'd never actually lied to her.

Slowly Perry pressed her fingers against her chest. There was no scar there, thanks to the craving virus, but she could almost feel where the blade had cut in, slicing through her flesh while she screamed and strained against her manacles. Cold trickled down her spine like a trail of marching spiders.

"Just be still, mijn lief… This won't hurt for very long…"
Unlike the duke, Hague *had* lied.

Four

INFORMING SOMEONE THAT THEIR DAUGHTER'S BODY had been found was never a pleasant task.

The moment the butler opened the door, Garrett knew it was going to be one of those meetings. He and Perry were ushered into Lord Keller's front parlor, while the butler went to fetch his master. Perry traced her fingers over a fragile glass vase. Garrett had the uncomfortable feeling that she was no longer with him; there was a sense of distance about her.

"Are you all right?" She'd been quiet on the ride over, distracted again. Those small silences might have fallen one too many times in the last month, but they'd been silences full of things left unsaid and swift little glances that each of them stole when they thought the other wasn't looking. Silences that seemed thick and lush and full of what had happened at the opera.

This was different.

"I can't help thinking that this is where they'll display her," Perry whispered, trailing her fingers over a lace doily on the back of an embroidered armchair. "It's already like a crypt."

A stuffed parrot stared glassily back at him from its perch on some ornamental table display. Garrett silently agreed. The parlor was still, waiting. Full of polished furniture that would never see use until someone passed away and needed to be displayed. Even the ormolu clock on the mantel had frozen. No doubt someone had simply forgotten to wind it, but the silence held a deafening feel.

The staccato of shoes echoed on the marble tiles in the entrance, and then Lord Keller appeared, the silver wings of his hair powdered and swept back from his forehead. His skin bore traces of rice powder and his lips had been slightly rouged, which gave him the appearance of something that had returned from the dead. One of the more old-fashioned members of the Echelon then, still wearing his Georgian pumps and silk stockings. Some of the older blue bloods did that, lingering in their pasts.

Keller's gaze raked over them. "Nighthawks in my home." His lips thinned and pressed together, as if to contain something. "You've found her then."

So Miss Amelia had been missing? Why hadn't anyone sent word to him?

"My lord, I'm so terribly sorry," Garrett said. "We discovered two bodies this morning at the draining factory, and Amelia has been identified by a contemporary. We would like you to confirm this identification."

Keller sank into the nearest armchair as if someone had cut his strings. He bobbed his head, pressing his fist to his mouth, unable even to speak.

As usual, Perry looked uncomfortable at the sight of such a display. The butler hovered in the door, and

Garrett gestured for him to find something alcoholic. He knelt and took Lord Keller's hand.

The man squeezed his fingers almost painfully, swallowing again and again. The silent display of grief lashed at Garrett. This was the part of the job he hated the most, but he did it, because he knew he was better at it than the others.

"Here," he said, offering a bloodied glass of whiskey when the butler returned.

Keller forced it to his lips, coughing some of it down.

"Is his consort here?" Garrett murmured to the butler.

"She passed away three years ago," the man replied.

"Children?"

"Miss Amelia was the only child. He does have a brother, though, in Kensington."

"Send word." Garrett turned back to the grieving lord. "My lord, you mentioned that Miss Amelia was missing. Might I ask the circumstances?"

The session droned on as Keller sputtered his way through several glasses of whiskey and blood. Miss Amelia, it seemed, had returned from a ball early the previous morning, made her way to her room, and was missing by the time the afternoon sun started to set. Keller had immediately set his people to searching for her, fearing the worst. Assassinations or kidnappings were not uncommon among the Echelon. They were practically expected, in order to further one's family name or House. And Lord Keller couldn't fathom his shy daughter sneaking out of her own volition.

"Her relationship with the Earl of Brumley was cordial?" Garrett asked.

Keller looked up. "Brumley? Of course. Brumley would never have lifted a hand against her."

They'd have to confirm that—and Brumley's whereabouts. Perry began shifting restlessly. Garrett glanced at her and she tipped her chin up.

He nodded. *Go.*

Perry excused herself to search the debutante's room, while Garrett began making a list of those who might be enemies of Lord Keller and his House.

&c&

"Well?" Garrett demanded, strolling along the footpath in Mayfair with his hands in the pockets of his leather great cloak and a bowler hat perched cockily on his head.

He could have been any one of the blue blood nobility on the streets here. Others barely gave him a glance as they hurried about their business. Perry was a different tale. Eyes caught hers and skittered away, then back with a slight widening as they recognized her gender and the body armor she wore.

How ironic that in the world of the Echelon, a man like Garrett, born to streets far to the east of here, fit in, while she, who had been born onto silk sheets, did not. He was a damned chameleon, mingling with every level of society as if he belonged, an ability she'd never owned. Indeed, she'd never felt as though she belonged anywhere—not the Echelon of her youth or even strictly the guild. She was always slightly aware that she was a woman in a man's traditional role. Easier sometimes to fade into the background and pretend that she wasn't there.

"The window's on the second story," she murmured, glancing up at the gleaming white brickwork of the Keller mansion. A black iron fence guarded the house, with thick, lush roses twining around each bar of the fence. The alley that ran along the side of the house was cobbled and wide enough to fit a dray. "There's no way a sheltered debutante like Miss Keller climbed out."

Garrett strode down the alley and looked up. "I could climb that."

"I never doubted your skill at entering any sort of bedroom."

He flashed her a grin. Her heart kicked in her chest like a mule.

"Where there is a will…" Garrett reached up and gripped the downpipe, lifting himself onto his toes. Above him, iron squealed as a screw threatened to pull loose. "However, not using this."

"Most blue bloods could climb the wall. There's no sign of entrance in the room, however. No marks on the sill or scratches on the lock. No dirt on the floor. No sign she slept there, either," Perry replied, following Garrett as he turned back toward the street and the steam carriage. "The bed was freshly made and the sheets smelled laundered. I asked the maid, who admitted they were changed yesterday."

"So she vanished sometime after she came in?"

"Or perhaps she said her good nights, kissed her doting father on the cheek, and slipped out the back while nobody was looking."

Garrett walked backward in front of her, his hands in his pockets. "He claims there was no one else courting her. The thrall contract was all but signed."

"Brumley's old enough to be her father. If she had a younger beau, then he would be a secret." Some of the games that young blue bloods and potential thralls played were carried out in secret, after all. She could well remember the little clockwork butterflies Moncrieff had commissioned to lure her into darkened spaces. A little code, just between the two of them during the initial stages of their courtship, when she'd been young and captivated by him.

One would flutter onto her shoulder, and then he'd call it back to him with the beacon and she'd follow, slipping from the ballroom with her heart pounding madly in her ears... The thought made her toe catch on an upraised cobble. Garrett caught her arm as she tripped, and Perry grabbed a fistful of his coat, the nearness of his mouth swallowing up her vision as she staggered against his chest.

There was an awkward moment as his eyes widened and they tried to disentangle themselves.

The moment stretched out, Garrett's expression strangely unreadable. Then he shook himself and graced her with one of those charming, insincere smiles he had in abundance. "Well, I'm used to women throwing themselves at me, but this—"

"Don't flatter yourself," Perry replied, stepping away from him and straightening her long leather coat. The feel of his hard body lingered, igniting her own. Strike her blind, but she was no innocent. Sometimes she wished she was, just so she wouldn't know what she was missing out on. "I'm a woman of rather discerning taste. Whereas you have none."

"Taste? Or discernment?"

"Both could be applicable." Could he see the flush of red in her cheeks? Perry strode ahead. "Come. We still have to visit the Fortescues. They'll be slighted by anything less than the guild master himself. Let some of the men do the groundwork."

"I'll send Larkin and Hayes to question whether Miss Keller had a secret beau, one she didn't want her father to know about." His brow furrowed. "I hate it when you're right."

"One of us has to be the voice of reason."

"What would I do without you, Perry?"

Idle words. But they froze her on the inside. "Let's hope we never have to find out." This time she darted ahead and held the coach door open for him, forcing a teasing smile to her lips. "Shall we, sir?"

"Only if you don't call me 'sir' again."

❦

The visit to the Fortescues was no less draining. Garrett straightened his coat as he hurried down the portico, Perry at his heels.

"Well, that went well," Perry murmured.

Garrett reached out and jerked the door open. "After you."

A long, slow look from those dark gray eyes. A ridiculous little game, but it eased the tension in his shoulders. He needed her for this. To help him forget the horrible way Lady Fortescue had started crying, those watery green eyes staring at him in silent condemnation, as if he hadn't done enough to save her daughter.

He'd never been able to divorce himself from the burden of the job the way Lynch and some of the others managed, but today had been worse than usual, with every little fidgeting move Lady Fortescue made rustling her bombazine skirts in a way that prickled beneath his skin. It didn't help that a part of him saw only prey when he looked at the poor widow.

"Three days Miss Fortescue's been missing," Garrett said, frustration leaching out of him, "and no one saw fit to mention it to us."

Perry glanced at him as she sat. "Not unusual if her mother thought she'd run off with some man. I get the feeling Miss Fortescue was somewhat fast, judging by the list of potential beaus we have."

"Lady Fortescue asked for Lynch."

"Because Lynch is all they know," Perry replied. "This transition period was unexpected, and you're an unknown. That will change."

"Mmm." He stared out the window.

The next stop was the Earl of Brumley's manor. It was a modest abode, by Echelon standards, on the outskirts of Kensington.

"Ten pounds says Brumley's involved," Garrett murmured under his breath as he knocked.

"On what do you base that theory?"

"He's older, she's younger. No doubt she attracts the eyes of other young blue bloods... Besides, years of experience in cases like these often prove the husband figure guilty."

A frown worked over her brow. "I'll take your bet," she replied. "From what I recall of Brumley, I don't think he had the capacity to do this."

The moment they were ushered into the earl's presence, Garrett realized he'd been mistaken. Brumley was seated behind his desk, wings of silver lining his hair. The minute they entered, he pushed away from the desk and then maneuvered his wheeled contraption out from behind it.

The craving virus could heal almost everything, but not amputation of the lower leg, it seemed. In the working classes, mechanical limbs were often grafted in place of an amputation, but this was the Echelon. Such a thing was considered to make one less than human, part machine and therefore with fewer rights. Brumley had evidently disdained such a mechanism.

"Lost it in the Crimea," Brumley said stiffly, noting the direction of Garrett's gaze. "How may I help you?"

The man's abrupt manner spoke of years in the military, which was unusual. No doubt Brumley had been a younger son or cousin. Not expected to become earl.

The moment Garrett explained what they were there for, the earl's entire mien changed.

"I...see," he murmured, a distant, hurt expression crossing his face. Whatever he'd felt for Miss Keller, there had been affection and respect. The earl was no fool, however. His gaze sharpened. "Who?"

"We're uncertain as of yet—"

"Hence your appearance here," Brumley said. He turned and rolled to the decanter in the corner to pour himself a blud-wein. "As you can see, the chances of me being involved are limited. At the least, I'd need servants to carry me, and I could barely travel to the factory itself without a fully staffed carriage."

"Do you know who might have wished her harm? Or how she could have turned up at the factory?" Garrett asked.

"Amelia was…not the sort to make enemies." For a moment Brumley's countenance softened. "She was kind. Perhaps too kind. She spent most of her time involved with her charities or visiting with me. Balls never interested her. No, I cannot even fathom how she came to be in that area."

"Did she know Miss Fortescue?" Perry asked.

"Everybody knew Miss Fortescue," Brumley replied dryly. "But Amelia had little to do with her. I cannot form a connection there either, beyond a vague association."

After fifteen minutes, they'd gleaned what they could from the earl. He saw them to the door of his study, then paused. "You'll tell me? If you find who did this? I should like to know."

And in that instant, Garrett saw not a man in a wheeled chair, but a man who could and would take revenge. A hard man with years of killing behind him. Someone who might not have risen to the position of earl through happenstance.

"As soon as they are taken into custody," he replied.

Brumley would have to be satisfied with that.

The afternoon was clouding over as they left the building. "So Miss Keller's a saint and Miss Fortescue is a sinner," Perry murmured. "And there's little connection between them."

"That he knew of," Garrett replied. "Why those two girls? And why the factory? How does that play into this?"

"Time to go back to the factories then," she said. "We need to find that connection."

Five

THE ROCKING OF THE CARRIAGE LULLED HIM INTO A brief sleep during the journey back to the East End. By the time the carriage disgorged them into the bustling streets near the factories, workmen swarmed the streets, heading home—or to the nearest pub—for the rest of the day. He and Perry worked their way through the costermongers and barrow boys, questioning them about anything they might have seen that morning, before meeting back by the corner of Craven Street and Old Bailey. It was cold work, and though he didn't feel it as strongly as a human, he tried to breathe some warmth back into his cupped hands.

"No luck?" Perry asked him.

"Someone mentioned a creature prowling these streets that he called 'Steel Jaw.' He reeked of gin though, so I'm not inclined to believe him."

"Steel Jaw?"

"Someone along the vein of Spring-Heeled Jack." Garrett shrugged. There were dozens of so-called mythic creatures and devilish murderers prowling the stews.

"Ha'penny for your luck, guv!"

Garrett stopped in his tracks, his attention focusing on a brash young lad sitting on the stoop of a disused shop. The moment their eyes met, the boy jerked his chin with a wink. "Why, a rum cove like you, bet you're sharper 'n a shiv." He gestured to the box crate set up in front of him with three chipped cups on it. Swiping one cup out of the way, he revealed a bottle cap and then tossed it in the air. "Think you can guess which cup she's under?"

A second later the bottle cap was gone and the cups were in motion, dancing under the boy's nimble fingers.

Garrett knelt down, leather straining over his knees. "This one?" he asked with a slightly questioning lilt, tapping the middle cup.

The lad snatched it out of the way, revealing the bottle cap. "Aw, strike me blind, guv. They says you gotta watch you Nighthawks. Here, again. A flatch, sir?"

"You've got deep pockets," Garrett drawled, reaching inside his coat for his change purse. He flipped a brightly polished ha'penny onto the top of the crate. "What's your name, lad?"

"Tolliver."

"Off you go then, Tolliver. Let's see how good you are."

The cups started their madcap dance. Perry stepped closer, leaning over Garrett's shoulder to watch. For a moment he almost forgot what he was doing, feeling her breath on the back of his neck.

"Which one, sir?"

"Hmm." He reached out, hand hovering over one

of the cups. Then the other. The lad's eyes brightened
but his expression stayed the same. He might have
been all of eight.

"This one," Garrett said, picking the cup on the right.

The bottle cap gleamed underneath it. The lad
begrudged him the chink, and Garrett tapped the crate
to say, "*Again.*"

"You do know thimble-rigging's illegal?" Perry
murmured under her breath. "Why are you encourag-
ing him?"

Because he knew what it was like to have no other
way to earn coin. The prince consort's brutal crush
on the streets dated back to Garrett's time as a lad,
when the prince had been nothing more than an
advisor to the king, before he'd overthrown him and
married the young princess. Humans became little
more than cattle then, the blood taxes doubling, and
even honest men forced to supplement their trade
with dishonest work.

Or children.

Garrett tapped the crate. The cups moved faster this
time, the boy determined. Any man watching would
barely be able to tell which cup was which. Garrett
won another coin. And another, disappearing them
into his coin purse. The boy's brows drew together,
the world vanishing around them as he moved ever
quicker. "And now?" Tolliver challenged.

"I think…I think it's right…here," Garrett said,
flicking the bottle cap out of the crease between his
thumb and palm and tossing it on the crate.

The boy gaped as the bottle cap danced a
jig. Then he snatched up the cup he thought it

was under. Empty. The other two yielded the same results. "Blimey, 'ow'd you…" The thimble-rigger's voice trailed off, his eyes narrowing. "You bloomin' cheat! You think I'm gulpy? You owe me five ha'pennies."

Garrett fetched them out with a smile, holding out his hand. The boy cupped his palms underneath and the ha'pennies poured forth, along with a couple of shillings, and even a pound note or two. They vanished just as swiftly.

"Good show," Garrett said. The boy gaped up at him, a hole in his ragged coat.

"'Ere, 'ow'd you do that?"

"You got used to me tapping the crate," Garrett replied, feeling generous. "You didn't even see me swipe it."

"Aye, but you ain't s'posed to—"

"Nick it?" Garret asked, with a faintly amused grin. "That's because you didn't expect it."

A smile split that smudged face. "Thought you was a Night'awk, not a broadsman."

"Weren't always," Garrett countered, tipping his head toward the north. "Grew up in Bethnal Green. Dipped my share of pockets. This your stretch?"

"Aye. Lease it good an' proper off Billy the Pyke."

A self-appointed landlord, no doubt. "Lot goin' on with them drainin' factories. Were you round abouts when they went up?"

The boy launched into an excited diatribe about the night the humanists burned down the draining factories, complete with expansive hand gestures. "…Like the fires o' 'ell, all blazin'! Why, you could see nigh on nothin' for miles, there were so much soot and coal in the air."

"Bet you see a great deal, hmm?"

"Everythin' on this stretch. Keep me nose out for Old Tom Piper."

"And them murders. More excitement by the look of it."

"Bloody nobs," the lad agreed. "They says them girls were of the Great 'Ouses, if'n you can believe."

"Aye, I can. You see anythin' this mornin'?"

The lad shook his head. "Only the usual. Old Man Mallory up and about, Mr. Sykes, and the milkman passin'—"

"Mr. Sykes?" Garrett frowned. "The overseer?"

"Stopped in at half two. 'Ad a lush dove with him, both of 'em swayin' like they was three sheets. No doubt she charged double. He's no flash gent."

"He took a whore back to the factory with him?" Garrett's voice sharpened. The logbook had indicated that Sykes had signed off at six the previous evening and not returned.

"'Appens regular-like. Got an 'earty appetite, 'e does."

"Did you see them come out?" Perry asked.

Tolliver shook his head. "It were cold enough to freeze me old Nebuchadnezzar, so I were 'uddled right back under the stoop. Mighta missed it."

"What did she look like?" Garrett asked.

"A whore. Rouged up and wearin' a heavy cloak." Tolliver shrugged. "It were *cold*."

There was nothing else to be had. Garrett slipped the urchin his coin and told him where to find him if he remembered anything else.

"I bet Sykes didn't enter that in the logbook," Garrett murmured, leading Perry toward the factory. "Ten quid the 'whore' was Miss Keller."

The feel of a set of eyes on him turned his head.

"What?" he asked, enjoying the look in Perry's eyes.

"What was all that?"

"The people here don't always trust Nighthawks. To them, we're naught more than the Echelon's fist. Now he knows I was one of his once. Besides, he needs the coin more than I do." No doubt the poor little blighter slept on that stoop at night, something Garrett had firsthand knowledge of himself.

The draining factories loomed ahead, abandoned shells with workmen hustling over them like beetles on a carcass. Indeed, each bare spar looked like broken ribs, sheared off at the midpoint.

"I knew you grew up somewhere in the East End, but Bethnal?"

"Why not?" he challenged.

She tugged on his coat. "With all your cologne, fancy waistcoats, and polished boots, who would ever expect it?"

"People see what you present to them. I learned that early enough. I was sixteen when I found the Nighthawks," he replied. "My grandmother was a weaver with a bit of book learning—enough to teach me some words. I used to mimic her finer speech as a lad, and when her and me mam died, I became one of the swell mob.

"When you're born on the streets, you soon realize the only way out is up. And the only way to stay up is get rid of any trace of where you were born."

Like his speech. He often silently repeated the things blue blood lords or merchants said, trying them out for himself. It was rare that he slipped up these days, usually only when he was angry.

"That was almost frightening, the way you started dropping your *g*'s. You sounded fit to join one of the slum gangs."

"Aye, well, when I was first infected, I actually considered it. The Devil of Whitechapel and his gang are the only ones who dare defy the Echelon. He's got a certain swagger a street lad tends to admire." And Garrett had been full of anger then—at the man who'd cut his mother's throat and stolen her purse; at the Echelon; and most especially at the prince consort, whose crushing taxes had forced his mother into disreputable work.

"What happened?"

"I tried to pick Lynch's pocket instead," Garrett admitted with a wince at the half-remembered thrashing he'd received. "He made an impression. So I followed him home and sat outside the guild for a week. Lynch finally took me in. Anything to stop me from freezing to death on his stoop." The smile on his face slipped slowly.

Perry saw it. "I've never asked," she said hurriedly. "How were you infected?"

"Three months before I dipped Lynch's pocket, I may have had a slight altercation with a set of young blue blood lads. Practically dripping lace, they were, which in my neck of town was worth a fortune. I ended up with three fat coin purses, a handkerchief or two, a pair of broken ribs, a slash across my face, a black eye, and a split lip."

"And the craving virus, I presume."

"A somewhat unwanted side effect. Obviously one of them was bleeding—and so was I."

"You seem to have acquired somewhat of a nasty habit in your youth," she said dryly.

"I'm completely reformed." He slid a hand over the small of her back as he helped her around a semi-frozen puddle. Even through the smooth leather of her coat and corset he could feel the muscles working along her spine. What would it be like to run his hands all over her body? She wasn't soft like most women—except in those places deemed desirable by a man—and the thought intrigued him. Strong, sleek limbs, meant to wrap around a man's hips…

"You wouldn't know what 'reformed' means." Perry shot him a smoky look that burned right through him.

Garrett's fingers danced over her waist, a smile lighting his lips. He liked her like this, warm and teasing. For a moment he managed to slip beneath the careful guard she held in place and to see within. And she was letting him touch her, which was a secret delight he'd never thought he'd own. How had he not been aware of this side of her?

Perhaps because she didn't want me to see…

"True," he said, holding up her coin purse.

Perry's hand shot to her hip. "How did you…?"

He tossed her the coin purse, and she snatched it out of the air. "I was a fingersmith, a good one too. Only man as ever caught me was Lynch."

A trio of objects slipped from his sleeve, and he juggled them in front of her. Perry's jaw dropped lower as she snatched a small gold lump out of midair. "That's

my ring!" She grabbed again. "And my pocket watch."
The moment she saw the last object he held in his hands,
the color washed out of her cheeks. "Give that back!"

He caught a glimpse of a small round coin with a
falcon's head stamped on it, like one of the sigils the
Echelon used. Fist closing around it, he held his arm
high. "What's wrong? Something personal?"

She grabbed his arm and spun him directly into the
wall of an alleyway, yanking his elbow up behind his
back. A knee dug into the back of his, rendering him
incapable of moving. Not that he wanted to. Perry's
entire body pressed against his, her breath in his ear.
"Give it back."

She dug his fingers open but the object was gone.
Snatching at his other hand, she opened it too and
snarled in frustration. "Where did you put it?"

One last sleight of hand as she'd manhandled him.
"You're a Nighthawk," he replied, swallowing tightly
as he lowered his arm and pressed his fingertips against
the rough brick. "Why don't you find it?"

I dare you.

The silence practically blistered his ears. Then one
of her thighs wedged between his and spread his legs.
The shock of it stirred hot fingers of need through
him, and Garrett turned his face to the side as she ran
her slender fingers up his flanks. They darted into his
pockets, coming away empty. Rough hands, jerking
against his hips. Up his sides.

"You're enjoying this," she growled, her hands
growing reckless with frustration.

"Of course I am. A man'd pay more than five quid
to get a touch up like this elsewhere."

He sensed the moment she realized what she was doing. One palm curled over his hip lightly, the pressure almost negligent. The sudden pounding of her heartbeat echoed in his ears. Tension vibrated through him and she felt it, he knew. How could she not? Every muscle in his body was locked steel, tight with desire.

Damn you. Do it.

The pressure of her hand against his hip increased, a languid touch that almost became a stroke.

As if something had been decided.

Garrett almost lost his breath, his brain slowing to a crawl as everything inside him went molten. There was a tremor in his fingers, echoing through his whole body.

"You'll owe me more than five quid then," Perry replied in a voice that had turned to liquid smoke.

The rational part of him was arguing against this. But he'd finally found her again—finally found the *her* that was beneath that damned facade she kept erected against the world. And she was sex and sin and all manner of beguilement.

The shock of her hand sliding over his buttocks made Garrett's hips jerk. He was hard in an instant, the ache in his balls so tight it almost hurt as he ground them against the harsh brickwork.

Each touch was torturous. A slow, leisurely glide down the inside of his thighs that made him tense.

"*Perry*," he ground out as her strong fingers caressed his calves and circled his boots. *How bloody eloquent.* All of his charm and wits seemed to have fled. Perhaps south, with the rest of his intellect. He ground his teeth together as she began the return journey.

"Not hidden here," she murmured, stroking his outer thighs.

"Obviously." Somehow he bit out the word.

Her hands curled over his arse, sliding over the tight leather and then delving between the backs of his thighs with a touch that rocked him to the core. He made a small sound in his throat, more of an exhale than a word. *Hell.* She knew what she was doing. Turning him inside out. How could a man think? Heat blinded him, darkness shadowed his vision. It should have been a warning, should have told him something, but he didn't care. All he cared about were those devious hands and where they were going.

"You may be able to steal my bits and pieces, but I love it when I steal your words," Perry whispered, her breath curling over his ear as she pressed against him. Her arms curled around his body, her lethal touch sliding up the hard planes of his abdomen and over his chest. Thorough as sin, stealing over and under his skin. Every touch echoing through his raging erection as if he could feel the whisper-soft stroke of her fingers there.

Heat raced through him. Someone, somewhere had struck a match and set it to a line of gunpowder. The shock of it, that this was *Perry*, nearly undid him.

He should have stopped her. This was taking things too far. But the part of him that was purely male caught his tongue. Why stop her? Just how far would she go? The words broke on his lips. *Stop. Tell her to stop.* But those hands were still doing wicked things to him, stirring the darkness within him, the hunger…

The alley was thick with silence. Only the sound of their

harsh breaths. A silence of their own making, cocooning around them like velvet gloves. Intimate. Dangerous.

"Not here," she whispered, hands sliding up under his arms. "Not there... Spread your hands against the brick."

He hesitated and suddenly the long tip of her sword cane slid between his legs, a lingering threat. The way they'd both been taught to act when apprehending criminals.

"Spread them," Perry insisted, her breath hot against the back of his neck.

Garrett slowly pressed both hands against the brickwork. A hot shiver ran through him. Darkness uncurling like a serpent in his gut, sliding through his veins like poison. This was the last chance to stop her. He could feel it. But everything in him wanted to see where she'd take this.

He'd never felt this way before. Usually he preferred to be in charge, but there was something tempting about the way she took control. A game of command between them. Garrett slowly straightened his arms. Every inch of her pressed against him, hips flush against hips. Perry's breath caught and he could smell the sweet vanilla oil she sometimes wore.

With her pressed this close, all he could do was tremble as her palms caressed his shoulders. "I always took you for an innocent," he murmured.

"Of what crime?" The shock of her hand sliding over his hip.

"Are you?" he insisted.

A minute pause in her wicked search. "A lady never reveals her secrets."

"You never reveal anything." He wondered if she heard the touch of irritation there.

A soft, wicked laugh, her breath wet against his ear. "If you knew my secrets, Garrett, you wouldn't be so curious, would you? As soon as a woman's mysteries are revealed, you're hying off on the next challenge."

Garrett glanced over his shoulder, his lips an inch from hers. "You're talking about other women? Now?"

"What would you like to talk about?" Her finger traced teasing little circles around the waistcoat over his nipple. Slowly tiptoeing down.

Every muscle in his abdomen clenched. If there'd been a thought in his head, it was gone, lost in the feel of her hands. *Hell.* There wasn't much of him left to search. She couldn't be an innocent; she knew only too well how a man's body reacted and how to do the most damage to him. The thought fired his blood.

"What would you like me to reveal?"

Soft, tantalizing words.

And the surge of answering thoughts was a tangle in his head. "Everything."

Where had that come from? Every choking emotion from the last month rushed over him. The aching, self-imposed loneliness... The fear, the lack of sleep, and the wish, deep down inside, that he had someone to talk to about it. Someone to tell him that it was going to be all right. *Her.*

He wanted to know her. To learn her secrets, to discover everything she kept hidden within her. She'd said he liked a mystery. Well, she was the greatest mystery he'd ever come across. Everything he'd thought he knew about her had been smashed by this change between them. He liked it only too much.

And he knew she could feel it in the sudden

shudder racking his body, in the way her eyes met his, gray against blue, and then swiftly lowered, sooty black lashes hovering over her cheeks. For a moment, the smile slid off her lips, the laughter dying. *This. Yes, this.* Hovering between them. Unsaid, unspoken, burning in the air every time they were together.

Even as her hands slid lower, *lower*...tangling in his steel-plated waistcoat and the softness of his shirt. Fingertips darting under the edge of his belt. Suddenly it was skin on skin and Garrett realized he'd stopped breathing. No doubt a while ago.

Perry's hand stilled. A tease. Utterly torturous. But the look in her eyes was terribly serious. She was shutting down before him, as if that single uttered word had been a key twisted in a lock. *Everything.*

"No. You're not going to stop there." He caught her hand as it withdrew, holding it trapped against the smooth skin above his waistband.

"Garrett." That was the Perry he knew. Expression melting smoothly off her face, her voice hard and tight.

He'd pushed too far and now she was pushing back, erecting those damned walls she'd never let him past. How he hated those bloody walls.

Garrett turned, her hand tugging at his. He held her by the wrist, forcing her to meet his gaze. Eyes a man could drown in. They weren't smiling now.

"And just like that, she disappears," he murmured. He could think now. Breathe. Barely.

A flicker of uncertainty in her eyes. "*She?*"

"The woman inside you."

"You're speaking in riddles." Another tug at her hand. This time she got free. "I am the woman I am."

"Are you? Or is it simply more convenient to pretend to be devoid of any feminine wants and pleasures?"

Perry's gaze dropped, as if to look elsewhere, but somehow it never made it past his lips. Instantly he stiffened.

"You want me." His voice was rough. "I'm not a damned fool. Sometimes, when you forget yourself, you let it show. And you can't blame me for wanting to know more, for wanting——"

"More?" she suggested, taking a step away from him. "Everything?"

His hand dropped to his side.

"I'm not doing this," she said. "You're right, sometimes I do forget myself. And you're a handsome man, Garrett." Here her cheeks colored and she faltered. "You know that. I know that. Every woman from here to Hampshire knows it——"

"That's not fair, bringing my past into——"

"But it's true," Perry countered. "I shouldn't have done this. I'm sorry." Then she turned and stalked up the alley, her shoulders squared.

"Where are you going?"

"I'm going to do my damned job!" she threw over her shoulder. "Which is not lingering in alleys with my superior or…or discussing inappropriate relations. I intend to go question the people on the streets, those who might have seen or heard something. As we should be doing now!"

Throwing the job in his face. As if she damned well hadn't been the one to start this mess. Heat burned up his throat. "Superior?" he asked. "As though we haven't been friends for years?"

He went after her, matching her stride for angry

stride. Perry shot him a dark glare, but her cheeks were pale. "You *are* my superior now. And this is highly unprofessional."

"Also, incredibly convenient."

Perry stopped. "What do you mean by that?"

"I mean"—Garrett leaned close, cupping her cheek with one hand and tracing the edge of her lips—"that you'd rather throw my rank in my face than discuss what happened."

A long, dangerous silence. "Because nothing did happen, Garrett."

He threw his hands up in defeat as she hurried away from him. "You stubborn—"

"What?"

"Nothing," he called after her, shoving his hands into his pockets. "Because nothing happened."

One last dirty look, and then she was gone, vanishing into the pedestrian mass on the street.

"Nothing," Garrett muttered.

Which was why he felt like she'd punched him hard in the solar plexus, why he felt like he couldn't quite catch his breath. Or feared he never would again.

"Bloody hell." He took the coin from a hidden pocket in his sleeve and looked at it, at that haughty falcon's head embossed on the silver. Nothing there, either. Nothing to say why she'd been so keen to get it back.

With a silent snarl he flipped it in the air and pocketed it again. She damned well wasn't getting it back, not now.

Not unless she paid the price he wanted.

Six

She was a fool who just couldn't stop playing with fire.

And now she'd gone and opened Pandora's box, and clearly Garrett was curious about *this*—whatever this was—too.

But just curious? Perry felt a small thrill at the idea that he desired her, yet she knew it wouldn't be enough. Garrett liked *women*. And she was never feminine enough for men. No matter how hard she tried to hold herself back and pretend to be just an accomplished young lady, she could never quite manage it.

She'd seen that look of disappointment in too many eyes to expect more here. And once the challenge was gone, Garrett's interest would fade. Someone else would catch his eye, and then their friendship—the one thing that had held her together all these years—would be destroyed.

That was the one disappointment she didn't think she could ever stomach.

For the next hour, they worked the streets surrounding the factory. Questioning people. Everyone

knew about the murders it seemed, but the facts
were skewed. A ghost who'd torn apart three girls.
A factory man who'd finally grown weary of his blue
blood masters and murdered two of their own. The
theories came thick and fast. Steel Jaw, one vagrant
whispered. A terror who'd begun stalking the East
End months past.

"Ridiculous," Perry murmured, but this was the
second time she'd heard that name.

Hague had been adept with biomechanics, after
all. Most of his core work revolved around creating
truly functional steel inner organs, unlike the crude
chest pumps or iron bellows that sometimes worked as
lungs. It would hardly be a stretch of the imagination
for him to create a new jaw for himself.

If he lived...

Growing far too easy to believe that now. Slowly
her gaze lifted, locking on the silent brick chimneys
of the draining factory at the end of the street. Like a
hulking stone-and-steel behemoth, lying in wait.

Perry couldn't tell Garrett her theories, not without
letting him know how she knew, and then he would
want to dredge it all up. The ghost of Octavia Morrow
prowled restlessly within her. *You always knew she'd
never stay dead. Not entirely.*

If she told anyone, it would be Garrett. But...her
fists clenched and unclenched. If she told him, then
he would be involved. Or rather, he would *involve*
himself. She knew him only too well. Then there'd
be a target practically painted on his chest. Perry was
never going to let that happen.

And she had no proof. If it was Hague, how

had he gotten to the two girls? Why the factory? Connections... She needed to find connections. Not just dwell on the past and the fact that Hague had once cut the heart out of a girl in Moncrieff's cellar. Once. He'd taken other organs from the other girls. It wasn't his modus operandi.

He was dead.

Garrett rubbed at his temples, strain showing in the fine lines around his eyes. "I think we've gotten all we can. Time to head back. Get some sleep perhaps."

Perry only half heard what he said. She was still staring at the factory. She needed to find this mysterious Steel Jaw. Find out if he and Hague were one and the same.

The thought made her feel violently ill.

"Of course," she murmured, wondering just how she was going to manage this.

෬ඏ

Garrett awoke with a shout.

Sucking in air, he stared at his hands, at the fading image of blood coating them. *A dream. Hell, just a dream.* He let out a shaky breath and sank his head into his hands with a quiver. Not *just* a dream. They never were; they felt so real. A craving for blood and sex, his cock sinking into Perry's warm flesh even as blood dripped from the gash in her throat.

"*Fuck*," he whispered, dragging himself out of the bed on shaky limbs. Yesterday, what had happened in the alley had been a mistake. It only haunted his dreams more, made him crave her more intensely. More than anything, he wanted to be able to pursue what had happened between them, but he didn't dare.

You selfish bastard. Wanting to seduce her, even now, knowing what was happening to him. He had to stop this…this…whatever it was between them.

By the time he'd recovered well enough to check his blood levels, the faint morning sunlight was beginning to seep through the steel slats that covered the window. His CV levels held at sixty-eight percent. Every day he waited for the brass spectrometer to spit out his reading, wondering if today would be the day they finally hit seventy.

Not today. Garrett splashed himself clean, then dressed swiftly and made his way downstairs, even though few others would be up and about. Night was a blue blood's haunt, though the job often forced him to keep odd hours.

The moment he entered the dining room, he knew she was there. Those smoky gray eyes met his, dark shadows circling them. Perry looked as well-rested as he did, hunched over a mug of blood-laced tea with her feet tucked up on the chair.

"Did you get any sleep?" she murmured.

"An hour or two. Maybe." Garrett gave her a nod, tearing his gaze away from her and toward the sideboard. He helped himself to a flagon of blood. The instant he put his lips to it, the world shifted, his vision darkening.

Bloody hell. He drained his glass. Then another. Only then did the sharp, gut-clenching ache recede enough for color to come rushing back into the world.

"Where do we start?" Perry asked, pushing the newspaper aside.

Business as usual, then.

Garrett leaned his hip against the sideboard. He didn't quite trust himself to sit beside her. "I'm waiting for Gibson's final autopsy reports. Larkin and Hayes should be back this morning, hopefully with some information about our debutantes—their regular movements, who saw them last, that sort of thing."

It was different from the way he usually managed an investigation, this delegation of tasks rather than running the footwork himself. He didn't know if he liked the waiting or not. He'd spent half the night trying to compile data into something that resembled a theory and still had nothing. "Anything occur to you last night? You look like you've barely slept, either. Something keeping you awake?"

"Bad dreams," Perry murmured, rubbing at her chest absently.

Here in the guild she often stripped out of her coat, leaving only the billowing black sleeves of her silk undershirt and the hard leather of her armored corset. Leather straps and gleaming silver buckles crisscrossed the corset, hiding a virtual arsenal. Hiding too the faint hint of curves that he knew existed there.

Somehow not being able to see her breasts made him want to strip her naked even more than a gaping display of flesh would have. Perry was a mystery; he wanted to uncover her, wanted to discover every little secret she owned, like an archaeologist unearthing a hidden treasure.

"Anything you wish to discuss?"

One dark brow arched. Of course Perry didn't want to discuss it; she never discussed anything personal with him. His jaw tightened. He was beginning to realize just how one-sided this relationship was.

Then she sighed, her gaze dropping to the bleached timbers of the table as she stared through it. "The girls... Finding them like that. I just kept seeing them. All night."

"We all have our moments." His had been a particularly nasty fire down in Abbott's Lane. He hadn't been able to get the stink of the dead prostitutes out of his nose for weeks. "Do you want a sabbatical?"

"Of course not. I'd rather find the bastard who did this."

Garrett nodded, his gaze dropping to the paper. "Let me guess...it's the talk of the town?"

"Surprisingly not," Perry replied, giving the paper a nudge toward him. The tension was leaving her shoulders, as if she thought she was safe now. Talking work, rather than anything personal. "The prince consort's upcoming exhibition has stolen the front page."

Garrett crossed to the table and shook the paper out. "You sound almost put out."

"Frankly, I'm not. Doyle's already chased three journalists from the door. You're going to have to give them an interview shortly, or they'll begin making up all manner of nonsense. And then we'll have both the front page and a murderer named something ridiculous like the 'Phantom of Factory Five.'"

His lips thinned. That was one part of the job he wouldn't relish. "Do you honestly believe the rubbish about ghosts?"

"No. But in my experience, newspapers rarely concern themselves with facts."

That stole a smile from him. Most people couldn't tell when she was jesting. Not an inch of her expression or tone ever changed. Only through years of familiarity had he aligned himself with her dry sense of humor.

"Exhibition," he murmured, scanning the front page and a grainy photograph of a pair of handsomely dressed foreigners stepping down from the rail of what looked like a dirigible. Garrett looked closer. England had sunk its resources into the seas, building steam liners and the enormous iron warships they called Dreadnoughts, but many foreign countries preferred air travel to the sea. From the military cut of the men's dark uniforms and the heavy fur hats they wore, he suspected they were from one of the more northerly European countries. "I'm surprised we weren't given the contract for security."

The prince consort had vowed to stun the nations with a display of fine British technology and all the wonders the Empire could offer at his exhibition. Garrett had loosely followed the news in the papers, but he'd lost track recently. "Opening this weekend," he murmured. "Exclusive to the Echelon and their invited guests for the first week, then open to the public for a shilling entrance fee after that."

"What's caught your attention?" Perry could follow his mind as easily as if she held a map.

One could only wish the opposite was true. In that, she was distinctly female.

"'The Russian ambassador,'" he read, "'the Scandinavian Embassy, several Bavarian and Saxon dukes…' There are a lot of foreigners in the city at the moment." He frowned, something tickling his mind. "What am I forgetting?"

"With an event like this, there'll be all manner of welcoming balls and social niceties planned," Perry added promptly. "Both Miss Fortescue and Miss Keller could have come into contact with our foreign visitors."

"No. That's not it." Garrett closed his eyes, racking his brain. Where the devil had he seen something about foreign nobility? His eyes shot open. "The factory logbook. A week ago. A party of noblemen was escorted through. Some bloody names I couldn't pronounce without mangling them fiercely."

"It should be in the evidence locker by now. Scoresby collected it."

"Excellent." He folded up the paper and discarded it on the table as Perry uncurled herself from the chair.

The storage facility was located in an adjoining building. The yard between was almost empty at this time of day, with only a stable drone spluttering over the cobbles, its circular brooms sweeping away the debris. The automaton moved with swift efficiency, courtesy of Fitz and his mechanical meddling.

Pushing into the library, Garrett nodded to the warden and strode to the locked clockwork doors that opened into Storage. Dozens of interlocking gears covered the heavy brass door. The only way to open it was to correctly turn two or three gears, so that the whole thing would turn. Turn the wrong one, though, and it would lock tight.

"One would presume the draining factory party was comprised of Russians or the Bavarians or Saxons." Perry followed him inside. "The Scandinavian verwulfen clans would have little interest in learning how to collect and store blood."

"I'll send Hayes and Larkin out to check the docking records at the airfields to see who arrived and when."

"I thought you liked Sykes for the murders." She closed the door behind them.

"I do. But I'm going to keep all the possibilities open."

Storage was a set of rooms with cold iron lockers in rows. A good thing they kept new evidence compiled in the lockers nearest the doors. Tugging out his identity card—a square brass card with ridges and indentations in it—he slid it home into the slot on the nearest locker. Metal teeth crunched through the matching holes in his card, and then the locker opened.

The logbook was heavier than he remembered. Garrett flipped through the pages, with Perry peering over his shoulder, her body nestled close to his. The moment he caught her faint vanilla scent, his body went still.

Sometimes he could forget her or the cursed heat of the craving within him. And then she would do something to draw his attention back to her, even something as innocuous as standing beside him.

He breathed her scent in, tasting the vanilla oil on his tongue. Sweet. Where did she wear it? A touch to her wrists and the side of her throat?

Garrett swallowed hard. He tried to blink away the flashes of dark shadow that threatened to consume him. "Count Mikhail Golorukov, Countess Yekaterina Orlova, Prince Pyotr Demitzkoy, and Duchess Elizabeta Kalovna."

"They're definitely Russian," she murmured in a small voice that drew his attention.

Something about her expression warned him that she'd noticed his withdrawal. Hopefully not the reason for it. "How do you know such a thing? I couldn't tell a Bavarian designation from a Russian one. I can barely pronounce either."

A little shrug that could have meant nothing at all. "I read the papers."

"Well." He snapped the logbook shut. "At least we have some names to ask questions about—a connection between the Echelon and the factory. I'll send Larkin to inquire quietly into Golorukov and Demitzkoy."

"I wouldn't presume that the killer is a man."

"Not that I doubt you—or any other woman—could kill someone, but statistically the chances are higher, you must admit." He started toward the door.

"In normal circumstances I might agree with you. But we're dealing with the Russian court. Both men and women are allowed to be infected with the craving there, and each is equally as dangerous as the other. They make the Echelon look like a bunch of lambs. Or so I've heard."

Garrett held the door open for her. "Fine. Then we shall quietly investigate all of them. And their retainers. And anyone else they happened to bring. Satisfied?"

"I'm simply trying to be thorough."

The memory of her hands skating over his abdomen the day before shot through his mind. Garrett took a deep breath. Thoroughness was her forte. "Well, we certainly can't accuse you of being slapdash. What next?"

"It's Tuesday," she said.

"Followed closely by Wednesday, yes."

Perry glanced over her shoulder, the weak light from the library's sconces dappling her face with shadows. "Lynch shall be arriving shortly for our appointment if you've no current need for me."

The door jerked out of his hand, the gears springing out and rotating into a variety of higgledy-piggledy positions. "How could I forget?" Garrett murmured. Lynch and Perry sparred every Tuesday morning at ten o'clock. "If you'll excuse me, I believe I'll chase Dr. Gibson down over those autopsy results."

Seven

THE FEEL OF THE HILT IN HER HAND WAS A WELCOME respite. Perry slid the weapon—an elegant rapier, in a style similar to that preferred at court—from its rack and let its weight balance on her fingers. She stared down the long sliver of its blade, wrapped her fingers firmly around the hilt, then stepped back.

Perfectly balanced.

The room had been an orangery before the building became home to the guild headquarters. Lynch had ruthlessly stripped out all of the plants and transformed the room into a boxing saloon of sorts. Heavy matting protected some of the floor, and boxing bags swung from the iron rafters. The ceiling and most of the eastern wall were made of glass, through which one could see the denseness of London stretching into the distance.

It was empty of Nighthawks now, for Lynch despised being a form of entertainment. Every Tuesday morning he booked the room for the pair of them, and others knew better than to enter.

The only witnesses were Rosalind, who Lynch

could never say no to, and Charles Finch, the enormous bruiser who presided over the room as the weapons master. Rosalind crossed the floor in a swish of dark green taffeta skirts and peered out through the glass windows, her leather gloved fingertips pressing lightly against the glass panes. Rain patterned the glass, distorting the view of the city.

As usual, Lynch's head turned to track Rosalind. He did that often. As if just the sight of his wife was a pleasure in itself. A small, wriggling worm of jealousy bit at Perry, but she'd long since accepted that no man would ever hold her in such regard. And though she might have dreamed of it, whenever Garrett looked at her lately, it was with a sense of wariness, as if he was trying to puzzle something out about her.

Yesterday had changed nothing. For one blissful moment, there'd been a hint of *something* between them, a dangerously seductive glimmer of something more than friendship. He'd given her *that* smile, the predatory one he reserved for ladies he was pursuing, and then all of a sudden he'd reverted to the friendly distance he'd been holding her at for most of the last month.

"Shall we begin, Your Grace?" Tension coiled within her, just begging to be unleashed in one way or the other. "Or would you prefer us to leave you alone with Rosa so you may stare at her ever so prettily?"

Lynch shot her a long, slow look. "If you call me 'Your Grace' again, I've a mind to take you over my knee."

"You're showing your age," she retorted. "You sound like my grandfather."

"Father perhaps," Lynch grunted, selecting his own blade. "I'm old enough."

"I've noticed you're slowing," she replied. "I'm sure Master Finch has some liniment somewhere for your aching joints."

Lynch's gray eyes flashed fire and he shared a rare smile with her. It softened the hawkish features of his face, and she knew that few ever won that smile. The former Master of the Nighthawks had forged a family, a force, out of those the Echelon decreed rogues, and he'd done it by making himself into a finely honed weapon. Cold steel tempered only by his wife's fire and the few careful friendships he'd established among his fellows—Doyle, Byrnes, herself, and even Garrett, once upon a time. "Careful, Perry. Or I shall be forced to prove just how slow I can be."

His rapier slashed toward her with stunning speed. Perry parried with a shriek of steel, leaping back out of the way.

Lynch circled her. He no longer wore the leathers of a Nighthawk, but he'd not disdained black. Stripping out of his coat, he tossed it aside and rolled his broad shoulders. There was not a single sign of weakness in his flesh. He was pure muscle, built to take his enemies down.

He'd need it, now that he served on the Council of Dukes that ruled the city.

The pair of them settled into a slow dance of feinting. Perry's muscles loosened, her feet seeming to float beneath her of their own accord. This was the time when she felt most alive. No time for troubling thoughts.

"For goodness' sake, stop playing with each other,"

Rosalind called. "We have an appointment with Sir Gideon Scott for a luncheon with the Humans First Party."

"As you wish, darling." As he swept in front of his wife, he shot Perry a grimace Rosa couldn't see. He'd accepted the dukedom for the power to keep the deadly prince consort at bay, but politics tended to make Lynch's eyes stutter shut.

The next second, his blade was slashing toward her. Perry parried, her wrists light and fluid, almost like an artist wielding his brush. That was what Garrett had never understood, and why he had little talent with a sword. He preferred to slash and hack with wide, ringing strokes that never landed because Perry was simply too quick for him, darting beneath his guard to tap him on the chest, the arm, the wrist, just to prove that she could.

Lynch, however... He'd also been born to the Echelon and had learned to duel at his father's knee. Every dispute in the Echelon was settled with a blade, and it was the only way to promote oneself in the world. Kill the head of your House in a duel, and you inherited their position of power.

Steel rang on steel, and Perry shot Lynch a swift grin as the edge of her rapier slashed through his sleeve. No time to congratulate herself; he thrust toward her, using his greater height and reach as an advantage. Perry had to arch back to avoid being skewered.

The blades began to dance quicker and quicker, the ringing sound echoing in the rafters. No time for thought, only action, her arm moving before her eyes even saw the telltale hint of movement in her adversary's body.

Lynch swept low, his boot hooking behind hers.

"Bloody—" Perry went down with a snarl, hitting the floor and rolling up over her shoulder so that she was on her feet again. She barely had her footing when he was upon her again, beating down hard on the sword in her hand. Her wrist jarred but she held on grimly, trying to scurry back across the floor to gain some room to straighten.

There was none. Lynch was ruthless, sweeping the tip of her rapier out of the way so that the blade was flung aside and pressing his own up under her chin.

Perry froze.

"Old dogs know many tricks," he said, breathing hard. "You duel with all the politeness of one of the Echelon. Don't forget you're a Nighthawk. Fight like one."

Perry let out the breath she'd been holding as he stepped back. Her rapier lay on the ground several feet away. She glared at it.

"You'll regret such advice when she kicks you in the unmentionables," Rosalind teased, coming forward with his coat.

Perry rolled to her feet, bending to fetch her discarded steel. "I could never do such a thing to you, Rosa. I promise I'll aim for something less debilitating."

"How considerate." They shared a smile, though Perry still felt a little shy around the other woman. They'd known each other only a month, and yet it was nice to be friends with another woman for a change.

"Your concern for my consort is touching," Lynch drawled. "Don't think I'm going to drop my guard, though."

"I wouldn't expect it." Perry shared a grin with him. If Lynch was foolish enough to think she wouldn't use every advantage, then he deserved what he got and he knew it. "Can I ask you something?"

Lynch paused in the act of handing Finch the rapier. "Of course."

"You've heard about the murders at the draining factory?"

"Yes."

"A party of Russians was taken through there a week ago."

"Yes, I know," he said. "I was there, with several others of the Council. A grand display of our greatest technology."

Of course he would have been. "Did any of them seem particularly interested in the facility?"

"Not even remotely," he drawled. "Countess Orlova could barely stop yawning. They didn't understand why we would want to store our blood, rather than drink it fresh from the vein. It's…a different culture and they're not bound by the same afflictions we are."

"You mean, by humans who refuse to be cattle?" Rosa asked with a deadly sweet smile.

"Precisely. If they want blood, then they take it. No matter the consequences. They own many serfs and, regrettably, have little concern for the sanctity of human life." He paused. "You think they had something to do with the murders?"

"It's a theory, among others. We're trying to ascertain the link between the draining factory and two debutantes."

"Certainly unusual." Lynch frowned.

"Come on," Rosa clucked, holding up his coat. "We'll be late. And you're getting that look in your eye."

"Are you going to say good morning to the men before you leave?" Perry asked.

Lynch paused in the act of sliding his arms into his coat. Rosalind slid it over his shoulders, her expression neutral as she patted it into place.

"I don't think that would be wise," he replied. "I am no longer their master. They have another now. He needs to establish himself as the man in charge."

"A deed that would be slightly easier if you'd speak to him," Perry dared to say. "The men know you've not spoken a word to him in the last month. It makes it difficult for Garrett to establish his command, considering some think he's usurped you. There are rumors—"

"Then he needs to learn how to deal with them," Lynch shot back.

Rosalind straightened his lapels, shooting Perry a glance. "Perhaps if you greeted him in public as—"

"Enough." Lynch caught Rosa's wrists and glared down at her. "I asked him to do one thing for me. One thing. I trusted him."

"And if he had obeyed, you'd be dead," Rosa shot back. She tugged her hands free and smoothed a lock of her dark red hair into place. "Garrett broke his word and told me you intended to sacrifice yourself for me. If he hadn't, the Echelon would have executed you. It worked. We tricked them into thinking that I wasn't the revolutionary they were searching for. You lived and so did I."

The prince consort had demanded the head of

the revolutionary who led the humanist movement in London—or he'd take Lynch's in return. When Lynch realized that his pretty little secretary was the revolutionary "Mercury," he'd been unable to deliver her. Only by going against his word and telling Rosalind what Lynch had intended had Garrett been able to pull the wool over the prince consort's eyes and save Lynch.

Lynch, however, was only too aware of how lucky they'd been. Rosalind could have died instead.

"He traded your life for mine, and he did it know ing the consequences," Lynch said to Rosalind, giving Perry a tight nod. "I understand your loyalty to him. I appreciate it. But I am not in the frame of mind to forgive him for what he did." A slight pause. "I don't think I ever shall be."

"That's not fair," Perry snapped. "I was aware of what Garrett planned regarding Rosalind. I helped him. Yet you've not given me the cut."

"I never asked you to keep my secrets. You did as I would expect, given the closeness of your relationship with Garrett." Taking up his top hat, Lynch clasped hands with Finch and then strode toward the door. "Until next week."

The door shut behind him abruptly. Rosa let out a faint huff of breath. "Well. That was a spectacular failure."

"I shouldn't have pushed."

"Perhaps my husband needs to be pushed every now and then. I wish he could resolve this feeling of being betrayed. He misses the men."

"And they miss him," Perry replied, sliding her

rapier back into the rack with slightly more force than needed. Why had she said such a thing to him?

Perhaps because you're worried that you might not be here for long, a little voice whispered, *and you don't want to leave Garrett alone.*

"How is Garrett managing?" Rosalind asked.

"The one thing he is very good at is managing men. It's Byrnes I'm worried about." Perry glanced toward Finch. She knew he was unlikely to loosen his tongue, but some things should never be said in company.

Rosa slipped her arm through Perry's and walked her toward the far end of the orangery. It wouldn't matter. Finch had a blue blood's exceptional hearing.

As if noticing their intent, the grizzled weapons master called, "Might leave you two alone and fetch myself some tea."

As the door closed behind him, Rosa smiled. "A perceptive man."

"A rarity," Perry admitted dryly.

Rosa examined her. "And how are you doing? Truly?"

Nobody ever asked her how she was. Perry looked at Rosalind in surprise. "I'm fine," she said guardedly.

"Surrounded by all these men… I doubt you have anyone to speak to of…certain matters."

"Actually, Garrett and I often…" She stopped. He hadn't been her confidante in over a month. So many things in her life seemed to exist in the past tense now.

Rosa patted her hand. She had never been an affectionate woman, but it helped that neither of them truly belonged to a conventional female role. Rosalind had been raised to despise blue bloods and the prince consort. Lynch had changed all of her perceptions. Now rather than destroying them, she was trying to browbeat them into restoring human rights through Parliament.

"Things change," Rosa said wisely. "It is often difficult for men and women to have a true friendship without certain complications coming between them."

Heat warmed Perry's cheeks. "I don't want our relationship to change." She just wanted to take back that night at the opera, to have her friend back. Uncomplicated. Safe. Feeling as though she could breathe again when he was in the same room.

"Don't you?" This time the look Rosa shot her was uncomfortably perceptive. "I was there, remember I saw your face when you walked out in that dress and Garrett realized you had breasts. You wanted him to know."

"I was a fool."

"Better a fool than a coward."

Perry pressed her hand against the glass, her skin soaking in the coldness. She'd never spoken of this to anyone else, and it felt uncomfortable to be doing so now. "Rosa. Please don't."

"Do you know, you and I are very similar in some ways. I don't like to be vulnerable. That is why I fought so long against Lynch, against what I felt for him. It's a horrible feeling to be at the mercy of one's emotions, especially when you have spent so long forcing yourself not to feel them."

"That's not how I—"

"Isn't it?" Rosa glanced over her shoulder. "Do you know the one thing that changed my mind? The moment I realized that I could lose him—truly lose him. Nothing else mattered anymore."

"Garrett doesn't feel the same way that I do," Perry blurted out, then cursed herself. Now where had that come from? She curled her fingers into a fist and turned back to the sword rack. "Forget I said that."

Silence followed her as she crossed the room, broken only by the faint patter of rain against the glass behind her. Perry dragged the rapier free and examined the blade, running it between her fingers to feel for the faintest flaw. She took up a rag and the pot of oil that Finch lovingly caressed the weapons with.

The swish of taffeta skirts followed her. "I think that you have worked very hard over the years to keep him from thinking of you as a woman or real-izing that your own emotions hold such sway. And now he has realized at least one of those truths, and you are frightened."

Frightened? Perry pressed her lips together to stifle her retort. She was trying not to ruin their friendship. Fear had naught to do with it. "This is most unbecoming, Your Grace."

"If you call me 'Your Grace' again, I shall box your ears. I thought we were friends. Indeed, I'd hoped."

"I should like to see you *try* to box my ears," Perry muttered under her breath, sliding the oiled rag along the blade. She held it up, examining the gleam of fine steel, and then set it aside.

"Don't tempt me," Rosalind said dryly. "Do you want to know what I think of the situation?"

"Not particularly."

Rosalind shot her a humored look. "I think that if

you went knocking on Master Reed's door one night, this whole matter might be sorted before dawn."

Heat swam through Perry, a flush of both embarrassment and need. In her dreams she was brave enough, but not now. "If Garrett feels anything for me, then why hasn't he acted upon it? He's made it quite clear that he's avoiding me. I've seen more of you this past month than him." She didn't mention what had happened in the alley yesterday. Garrett had made it quite clear that if she hadn't come to her senses, he had no intention of stopping.

But that was sex. Of course he wouldn't turn such an opportunity down.

"There must be some reason he's been avoiding you. Come now. You're a Nighthawk, Perry. Why don't you figure it out, hmm?"

✍

"Any ill effects?" Dr. Gibson pressed his stethoscope against Garrett's bare chest and then tapped his ribs in several spots while Garrett breathed in and out.

"Nothing," he replied, staring at the white walls of the small surgery. He hated being here. He'd been trapped here for days last month while his body recovered from the crippling injury it had taken. The vulnerability had shaken him.

"Mmm." Dr. Gibson tapped along Garrett's back with two stiff fingers. "Your chest sounds fine. No sign of that wheeze that was bothering you at the start."

"I'm a blue blood—which means everything should be perfectly healed. Are we done?"

"Even a blue blood rarely recovers from a thrust

through the heart. If Falcone had gotten his fingers through the heart muscle, you'd be dead. You may put your shirt back on. We're finished with this part of the examination."

Garrett stood and picked up his shirt from the back of a nearby chair. "You mean there's more?"

"I need to take your CV levels," Gibson replied, staring down at his notes as he swiftly made a few marks.

Garrett froze with one arm through his sleeve. "Is that necessary? I monitor them myself."

Gibson scratched out another word. "As this is your final examination, I would like to be able to complete your file." He gestured distractedly at the corner. "The spectrometer is there, if you would?"

Garrett's heart started pounding in his chest. He slid the shirt up his arm and eased his other shoulder within it. If Gibson saw his CV levels, he'd be required by law to report them. The doctor was a man he considered a friend, but the truth was inescapable.

"How is the autopsy coming along?" he asked mechanically, tugging the soft black undershirt closed over his chest. He had to think of a way out of this...

"I'll have my reports in by the end of the day." Gibson looked up, momentarily distracted. He squinted through his half-moon spectacles. "A terrible shame, truly. Those poor young girls."

"Anything of importance you've discovered?"

"Only that our killer is a master with a scalpel. The hearts were removed while both girls were still alive. Miss Fortescue was sedated throughout the procedure—with chloroform, I suspect—and her breastbone was removed to get at the heart, then replaced and wired together." Dr. Gibson frowned. "It was most peculiar. The ends of the aorta and superior vena cava were in some state of healing, almost as if the murderer were performing some sort of... I don't even know what to call it. The closest thing I've ever seen is when they replace a man's lungs with bio-mech chest pumps, but everybody knows that you can't replace a man's heart and keep him alive. It's impossible."

Garrett started working on the buttons of his shirt, glancing at the spectrometer. "Any sign of the craving?"

"In Miss Fortescue, yes. The breastbone was starting to fuse back into the ribs and her CV levels were sitting in the low teens. Miss Keller was only missing for a day, so it's too early to tell."

"Is there—"

A sharp rap at the door preceded its opening. Lynch strode through, then faltered when he saw Garrett. Anyone else might not have noticed the hesitation, but Garrett knew him only too well. Grabbing the black leather coat that completed his uniform, he gave a clipped nod. "Your Grace."

Lynch ignored him. "A word, Gibson?"

"We'll finish this later," Garrett murmured, more relieved to see his former master than Lynch would ever expect.

They locked gazes and Lynch tipped his head in the faintest of nods, his lips pressed together thinly.

The hurt of it was like an icy stab to the chest. Garrett strode past with his coat in hand and shut the door behind him. Only then did he let out the breath he'd been holding. The hallway stretched out on both sides, empty and looming.

Once he'd been a trusted comrade. Now there was
nothing. Not even a greeting. As if Garrett was some
stranger. It ate at him, though he'd known how Lynch
might react when Garrett had revealed the truth to
Rosalind and begged her to sacrifice herself for Lynch.

Garrett crushed his fist closed, turning blindly down
the left hallway. *You earned his scorn*, he told himself,
trying to ignore the rising tide of darkness within him.
It didn't do a damn thing to halt the regret he felt.

With late afternoon light streaming through the
windows, the corridors were empty. Most Nighthawks
would be asleep, waiting for the moon to rise. That
was when the city was at its most active and also the
time that suited them best. The bright light of day
could be harsh on a blue blood's eyes and fair skin.

Almost four hundred Nighthawks filled the guild
at times, though there were several other groups of
them billeted across the city. Garrett found himself
striding the halls unthinkingly, not knowing where
he was going. Somewhere away from Lynch's scorn.
Somewhere he didn't have to be quite so alone…

෴

A knock at her door jerked her out of the stillness of
meditation.

Peace slipped from her body like water rushing
over her skin. Only Garrett knocked like that. Perry
cursed under her breath. After the conversation with
Rosa she'd been on edge enough for the hunger to
rise in her. Her usual blood-laced tea had barely sup-
pressed the urge, so she'd resorted to the meditation
techniques Lynch had taught her.

For a woman to have such hungers was socially unacceptable. Perry had to be in control of herself at all times, especially when she was on a case and needed her head clear. Stealing a moment like this was a necessity. With all the feelings he aroused in her, Garrett would only shatter any gains she'd made.

"Come in," she called, uncrossing her legs and stretching.

Her hard-won peace fragmented the instant Garrett strode inside her quarters. The short chestnut strands of his hair were rumpled, as though he'd raked a hand through them—or just risen from bed—and his blue eyes were hot with turmoil. It rode over the broad line of his shoulders, and each step he took radiated a predatory menace.

Her own needs spiked, driven by the hunger reflected in his body. For a moment the world was crafted of shadows, then she took a deep breath and let it spill from her. "What's wrong?"

The expression washed from his face. She could see him visibly rein himself in, forcing the hunger back. It lingered in the tension of his jaw, but a smile touched his mouth—a meaningless, hard-edged smile. "Nothing is wrong."

Lynch. For a moment her heart ached for two stubborn men who both refused to apologize.

He prowled her small room but saw none of it, she guessed. Perry rested her hands on her knees and watched him, waiting for him to speak. This wasn't the first time she'd received an inappropriate visit to her bedchambers.

Garrett plucked a half-open book from the small armchair in the corner and glanced at the title. "A gothic?"

Perry uncurled herself swiftly and reached for it, but he held it high, flicking it open to where it had rested. "'And then he tasted the breath of her, each lingering caress…'"

"Give it back," she growled.

Turning his back, he went on reading. Perry wrapped an arm around his shoulders and threw herself forward, trying to reach it.

"'For I love thee, Diana—'" His voice choked off as she wiggled against him, her fingertips bare inches from the book. "Christ, Perry, are you trying to strangle me?"

"Tempted to."

The next moment, he flipped her over his shoulder onto the armchair. Her legs dangled over the back of it and she rolled, righting herself. Garrett backed away, his blue eyes dancing as he held the book up again.

The words washed over her, horribly romantic words she'd been enjoying the night before to take her mind off the day's horrors. From his tongue, however… They shivered over her skin—tender, mocking words she'd always wished he'd say to her.

She shouldn't begrudge him the moment. Playful times like this always took his mind off his troubles.

But it ached, just a little. Why did she have to hurt just so that he felt better?

"That's enough," she said quietly.

Garrett kept reading. "'And the duke whispered in her ear, words that echoed along her spine—'"

This time Garrett was ready for her. When she leaped at him, he swept her up over his shoulder. The world upended. All she could see was the long, lean

length of his back, the curve of his muscled arse, and—
with a quick glance under his arm—the dratted book.

"Garrett!"

The room spun. Perry landed flat on her back on
her bed with a breathless gasp. Something red flickered
into view. The book. Garrett held it with negligent
fingers and a watchful gleam in his eyes.

Perry snatched at it—and missed. Rolling onto her
hands and knees she tried again. "Give it back!" The
words came out a little choked, a little desperate.

He watched her. Then held the book out.

Perry eyed it. As soon as she realized he wasn't
going to withhold it, she snatched it from him and
buried it beneath her pillow

Garrett collapsed back on his elbows on the mattress, taking up most of her bed as if he belonged
there. A dangerous thought. Dragging her knees up
to her chest—not to avoid taking up space, she told
herself—Perry leaned against her pillows and stared
back at him.

"Why are you so afraid to be a woman?" he
asked finally.

She ignored him. "You shouldn't be here. You're
going to start rumors."

"I enjoy being with you," he said carefully. "I don't
have to pretend with you. It's…peaceful."

Pretend? She looked at him sharply.

Garrett stared at the ceiling, his arms crossed
beneath his head. He gave a soft sigh and she saw
that the smile had faded again. This was why he was
here—to talk to her.

"Do you know what Lynch once told me? He said

I should be an actor on the stage. I've always known how to mimic people, even as a lad. Then when I became a thief for the swell mob, I had to learn to strip everything of my past from my speech and appearance. To be something I wasn't. I still do it. Only now, I'm Garrett Reed, Master of the Guild of Nighthawks." A harsh, breathless laugh. "Confident, in control, a man who knows how to react in every situation."

His confidence was one of the very things she found attractive—that, and his seeming ease in his own skin. He was everything she wasn't. Or was he? A frown touched her brow. She'd never seen him show even the slightest sign of conflict, but it was there now, in the distant gaze he leveled at the ceiling and the line of tension around his mouth.

"You don't feel you are those things?"

He turned those dangerous blue eyes toward her and she saw the truth in them. "I feel like I'm trying to juggle a half-dozen balls, and I don't know where they're going to land. Byrnes, Lynch, you... the guild... That, most of all. Am I doing right by it? By the men? I keep making mistakes, and everybody keeps reminding me that I'm not Lynch—"

"Lynch made mistakes," she cut in.

"Really?" A mocking arch of the brow. "Because I can't seem to think of any."

"Rarely. But you have to remember that he was in charge of the guild for forty years. He had more than enough time to perfect his leadership and learn from what he'd done wrong."

"Then you *do* think I'm making mistakes?" Garrett countered.

"Some, yes." His eyes flashed hot blue, but she held up a hand to stall him. "Byrnes, for example."

"He's the one who—"

"You do realize he doesn't truly want to lead the guild?" she cut in. "He knows he's not equipped to deal with it, nor does he particularly wish to."

Garrett's mouth opened and shut. "He's made it quite clear he disagreed with the choice Lynch put before the Council."

"Of course he did. He feels overlooked. And you reacted as if you saw a rival, when you should have been working together to sort this matter out. You give him the same work and cases you'd offer to any of the trackers, rather than using him as a trusted member of your Hand, so he resents it."

Garrett's teeth ground together. "He *isn't* trusted."

"That's arrogance speaking, not the man I know you could be. Not a *leader*."

A long moment of silence. "And how do you propose I reconcile this matter?"

"Give him the same work you give to any of us. Involve him in your decisions. Ask his opinion—he's good at what he does, Garrett. You can't ask for his respect if you can't give him the same."

"So this situation is my fault?"

"No. But you're the man in charge. He's not. You're Master of the Nighthawks now, which means you need to be the one to act decisively in this matter, rather than giving in to the actions you'd prefer to take."

Garrett rubbed at the bridge of his nose and sighed.

"You know I speak the truth."

"I hate it when you're right," he corrected.

Perry smiled her most secretive smile.

"And Lynch?"

It was eating away at him. Perry nibbled her lip. "He'll come around."

"You don't know that."

"Yes, I do. He's being stubborn and foolish. Much like someone else I know at times… But he's not a fool."

Garrett rolled onto his side. "When did you get to be so wise?"

"I'm always wise," she quipped back.

Lazing on his side, he reached out and stroked her bare foot. Perry froze. The room suddenly seemed far too small.

It would be wise to pull away, but as his gaze held hers, Perry found she couldn't move. Something about the moment seemed to draw her in. A longing she couldn't quite disguise.

He saw it. His thumb paused beneath the arch of her foot, a long, considering moment. Black heat suffused his eyes. Full of dangerous promises.

Perry couldn't breathe.

"Garrett?" She could feel it igniting in her too, the richness of the hunger seeping through her veins. Her vision darkened and she reached out to stroke his jaw—

Garrett turned his face away sharply and drew back with a shaky breath. "I'm sending you out with Byrnes to examine the factory again. The preliminary reports are back from the autopsy. Dr. Gibson believes the second murder occurred on-site or very close to the factory. The first girl was killed elsewhere, as suspected, and moved."

Byrnes? Perry's hand lowered. "Why?"

"That's what we need to know." He rolled to his feet, straightening his clothes.

"Not the murders. Why Byrnes? You know he and I—"

"I need a murder weapon," he replied, speaking over the top of her. "I need you to find either the knife or scalpel that removed Miss Fortescue's heart, or someone who saw something. And it's about time I dealt with the press. Is there anything else?" The look he gave her might as well have been offered to a stranger. The blackness had faded from his irises.

Yes. You're a nodcock. Her jaw locked and she glared back.

Garrett arched a brow, correctly interpreting the look. "Then I'll see you later this afternoon."

As he left the room, she refrained from mentioning that Byrnes wasn't the only one he wasn't handling very well.

She just didn't understand why.

Eight

BYRNES AND PERRY CAUGHT THE TRAIN TO THE NEWLY renamed Wapping station, which lingered in the remnants of the Thames Tunnel. The previous tunnel had been a marvel of modern engineering, burrowing beneath the river and providing pedestrian access to Rotherhithe on the southern bank. In recent years the East London Railway Company had transformed the tunnel to carry trains, and people were taking full advantage of that fact.

Perry disembarked at the platform, striding into the crowd. The guild's steam coach was reserved solely for the use of the guild master, so most Nighthawks had to find alternative means of transport. Garrett had offered the use of the steam coach until she'd reminded him very pointedly of that fact. A foolish victory, and one she regretted as they swam against the crowd.

"This is ridiculous," Byrnes muttered, leading her through the streets toward the draining factory. "The men have already been over the factory with a fine-tooth comb. What does Garrett think we're going to find?"

"Something sharp." A murder weapon, no less.

"Perhaps if we find it, I'd best take it in hand," Byrnes said. "Considering your current mood."

Perry stopped in her tracks. "My mood?"

"You have that look in your eye." Byrnes caught her arm and steered her forward. "The one that says you'd like something sharp and pointy, all the better to stick it down his throat."

"Unfortunately, your grasp of anatomy is almost as woeful as your concept of charm. I wasn't contemplating his throat at all."

Byrnes laughed.

The nearest storefront had no fewer than five cages in the window, with squawking parrots, a lark, and a nightingale captured within. In these streets, one could buy almost anything. Particularly the exotic. On Sundays the street was an open-air market, with raucous birds and monkeys for sale at every cart, fighting for space with barrows and stands, with cheapjacks selling whatever they could lay their hands on. Refreshment stalls offered apple fritters cooked while you waited. Perry had on occasion tried one, though she could only stomach a couple of mouthfuls before her cursed body rebelled against food.

Today the streets were manageable. The wreckage of the draining factories loomed ahead, with a full squadron of metaljacket guards keeping people at bay. Weak afternoon sunlight gleamed on the polished steel of the guards' breastplates, and the polished glass of their eye slits revealed a hint of pale blue gaslight within. It looked almost eerily as if the automatons were staring back at her. Workmen scurried behind them, with scaffolding surmounting the buildings and steam-driven cranes shuffling into place with a faint hiss. Earthshakers—the armadillo-plated automatons the Echelon owned—were being used to clear the wreckage from the burned-out factories.

Factory Five loomed at the end, with soot stains showing where the fire had almost spread. It was strangely silent down here, gravel crunching beneath her boots as she and Byrnes strode toward the factory.

"So what was all that about?" Byrnes asked.

"All what?" Perry pushed her brass identity card into the keyhole. The doors to the draining factory had been keyed to the senior identity cards of all the Nighthawks while the investigation was in place.

"Reed seems a little on edge of late," Byrnes replied, following her. "You wouldn't happen to know the cause?"

"No."

"How curious." He eased the door shut with a slow squeal of the hinges. "If someone perceptive—say, someone trained to investigate people—were paying attention, it might actually seem that the strain began that night we investigated the opera."

"Don't tempt me to find something sharp and pointy." A hand rested over the knife at her hip. "I'm most certainly not in the mood for your so-called humor."

His laugh was rough and low. "So you and Reed are both on edge. The plot thickens."

In the almost unearthly silence, the factory seemed watchful. Dull gray light streamed through the dusty windows high above, and the air was frigidly cold this close to winter. Perry took careful steps, eyeing the enormous glass vats that had once been used to store blood. The brass filtration devices beneath them lay silent now, the overhead cranes and rows of conveyor belts preternaturally still. The Echelon would be screaming for fresh blood and for this case to be solved. It wouldn't be long before the Nighthawks' opportunity to examine the factory vanished and the Council of Dukes demanded that the workers return to their labors.

After all, what were the lives of two young girls compared to the Echelon's needs?

She followed Byrnes, gaze locking directly on the spot where they'd found the bodies. His words finally got the better of her. "What do you mean he's been much changed since the opera?"

"You haven't noticed?"

"No." Her cheeks grew hotter. "Yes. I don't know—"

Crouching low, Byrnes examined the bloodstain on the floor. It had long since leached into the timber floorboards. "I think that you finally played your hand."

Perry could barely breathe through the sudden scorching embarrassment that bit into her. If Byrnes had guessed the truth of her feelings, then she would never live it down. "My hand? What the devil do you mean?"

Byrnes held up a hand. His brows drew together. "Frankly I don't give a damn, although it's proving to be rather entertaining." Cocking his head, he lowered it toward the floor. "The entire factory is meant to be off-limits until we clear it, yes?"

Ignoring her embarrassment, Perry nodded. "Yes."

"Then why is a furnace rumbling?"

Perry knelt down, listening intently. Beneath the floorboards, she could just make out the whispering sound of some machine. Beneath her fingers, the floorboards vibrated, just slightly. As she watched, dust skittered across the floor.

Her heart leaped into her throat. "There's something beneath the main factory."

"A boiler or furnace somewhere." Byrnes flashed her a grin. "One that's not on the schematics."

Behind him, she caught a glimpse of something moving. Her mind fought to recognize it, then Perry leaped forward, hitting Byrnes hard in the shoulder. They catapulted backward just as a winch screamed through the air where his head had been.

Perry rolled to her feet, looking up. The winch was suspended from an overhead crane. It reached the end of its swing and began the return journey, sweeping back toward the walkway that it had come from. The flap of a coat vanished around the edge of the offices overhead, footsteps echoing on the tin walkway.

"Someone's there!" she yelled, holding her arm up and pointing her wrist toward the railing. The pistol strapped there jolted forward into her palm, the magazine whirring as the mechanism readied itself. "Stop! Or I'll shoot!"

The ring around her thumb tightened as she curled it toward her palm. Almost enough tension to pull the trigger. The footsteps receded and Perry swore, darting around the swinging winch as she tried to get a better vantage.

"Strike me blind," Byrnes cursed, rolling to his feet. "I'll go up after him. Cover the other set of steps. He has to come down somehow."

Perry ran toward the filtration devices at the back of the factory, her boots echoing the fleeing footsteps. It was darker back here, the enormous glass beakers distorting the shadows. She slowed, one hand dropping to the knife at her hip and her other wrist leading, with the wrist pistol pointing up into the darkness. The footsteps had slowed too. She couldn't see through the thin tin sheeting, though.

"Byrnes?" she called.

In the distance she heard him hammering up the stairs toward the walkway. "Got him covered."

Above her a shadow rippled along the wall. Perry ducked to the side, moving silently. The shadow took a step, almost as if he was aware of her. *What the hell is he doing?*

Moving slowly, as if…as if he was luring her forward…

Perry froze, gently placing her foot down. The moment she did, a grinding noise sounded in the walls and she felt the floor give way beneath her.

"Byrnes!" she screamed as she vanished into the darkness below.

Nine

GARRETT SPENT MOST OF THE AFTERNOON GOING through the paperwork on the Keller-Fortescue case in his study—or Lynch's study. It still bore the echo of the former Master of the Nighthawks, from the heavy, leather-bound tomes that lined the bookshelves to the case files he still hadn't managed to put away and the ebony-framed map of the Empire that hung over the fireplace.

Scraping at the stubble on his chin, Garrett tried to clear his mind. The press had been dealt with and Hayes had made a brief report earlier. Miss Keller's only link to the East End was a charity she dealt with—a lending library for impoverished children. Miss Fortescue had never set foot in the place. Not a single person had seen them disappear from their homes.

As for the Russians, they'd arrived in England three days before the tour through the factory. He had a list of events they'd attended and was trying to match them against functions either of the girls had been to.

Garrett rubbed at his temples. He was reaching the point where the facts were becoming a useless jumble of information. God, he was tired. Every time he shut his eyes he could almost feel the dreams sucking him under.

Concentrate.

Miss Keller had died in the early hours of Monday morning, which at least gave him a timeline. Now he just needed to question the Russian party to discover where they'd been at the time of the murder.

The tick of the clock was a slow beat that only highlighted the silence. Garrett could stand it no more. He lowered his hand from his eyes and glared at the stacked bookshelves. If he couldn't damn well sleep or think, then it seemed past time to rid himself of at least one ghost.

Hours later, a swift rap at the door drew his attention. Books were stacked in piles by the door, along with all of Lynch's collection of necessities—lamps, maps, and even his inkwell. The room was bare.

"Come in," he called, dumping another pile of books by the door.

Doyle's eyebrow arched when he saw the mess. "We've got maids for this sort o' thing."

"Excellent. Have them box the books and all of the duke's personal belongings, and send them his way. I want the case files returned to the filing room and all these shelves swept clear of dust."

Doyle's gaze slowly took in the bare furnishings. "There's been a call of distress come in via telegraph from the garrison on Hart Street." He held out the small rolled sheaf that the message was printed on.

Hart Street. A ring of cold circled the back of Garrett's neck. The garrison was close to the draining

factories. Tearing the piece of parchment open, he
scraped his thumb over the small black ink letters.

*Urgent attention: Guild Master. Nighthawk missing at
draining factory five. Request immediate assistance.*

"*No,*" he whispered under his breath, knowing
instantly who the missive had come from. Perry would
have used longer sentences—and names. "No, no,
no." He snatched his coat off the back of a chair and
swung it over his shoulders, his gut tight with dread.

"Sir?" Doyle called. "Do you want the carriage?"

"I'll go on foot." It would be quicker over the
rooftops. He was moving, throwing the words over
his shoulder. "Send a regiment of Nighthawks to the
factory, and tell them they have twenty minutes to get
there or I'll have their heads."

⚬⚬⚬

Sensation returned slowly, pain spearing through the
back of her skull. Perry blinked and carefully lifted
her head. Her vision swam, and when she pressed her
fingertips to the back of her scalp, they came away
sticky. Blood.

Where the devil was she? A gaslight flickered,
highlighting a long, narrow room. An enormous steel
examination table dominated the room, the gaslight
gleaming on its edges. The moment she saw it, she
rolled to her hands and knees, cold dread spiraling
through her. Her stomach lurched at the movement,
but Perry fought to stay upright.

*The man—the killer, she suspected—running overhead.
The floor giving way. Hitting hard on the stone floor.* Perry
swallowed the fist of nausea lodged in her throat as

memory sank its greedy claws through her throbbing head. Nothing moved in the shadows, but she could almost sense someone watching her.

The thought was enough to send her scrambling for her knife. Her hands shook as she held it in front of her and staggered to her feet, leaning heavily against the smooth glass panel of the wall.

Until something moved behind the glass.

Perry jerked away, stumbling over her feet and staggering into the examination table. *Blast it.* Her heart pounded. "Byrnes!" she screamed as she stared in horror.

Glazed blue eyes blinked hazily at her through the bluish cast of the liquid behind the glass. A brass mask, much like those the poorer Londoners wore to help with the black lung, locked over the girl's face, with a tube leading out from it.

Perry took a step back as those eyes met hers and she sucked back another scream. *Still alive.* Her gaze lowered. To the woman's naked breasts and the long thin scar down the center of her chest. In the flickering light, it almost seemed she could see a shadow lodged like a fist in the stranger's chest.

Something skittered in the darkness. A rat, perhaps. As Perry's vision cleared, she realized there were half a dozen of the strange aquariums lining the room. Figures hung suspended in the clear blue water, their hair streaming around them like mermaids. Hanging there. Floating. Four of them in all, with two empty glass cases at the end.

Her breath came, short and sharp, her lungs clamping in her chest as if someone had knotted her corset far too tight. *No.* No, she wasn't back there. She'd escaped Hague and what he'd planned to do with her. This wasn't like her nightmares. She was free and she was strong. She could fight now, the way she hadn't been able to do back then.

It didn't matter a damn to her body. Her feet refused to move, nothing but a strangled sound choking out of her throat. In that moment she was just a young girl again, frightened and alone and useless. No air in her lungs. Nothing.

Stop it. She curled her fingernails into her palms, forcing them to cut into her skin. *Breathe. Just breathe. You're a damned Nighthawk now.*

Something shifted in the shadows behind her.

Perry screamed.

∽

Garrett slammed through the factory doors, breathing hard. The cold, gray light hit him, as well as the stale scent of the factory. He raked the scene with a glance, taking in the three men at the back of the factory. Byrnes looked up, no expression on his face. The other two Nighthawks kept hammering on the floor. Stomping on the floorboards as if to break through them.

There was no sign of her.

Darkness descended. He was halfway across the factory before he realized, his gaze locked on Byrnes's throat. Fingers curled into his palms, itching to strike out.

"Where the hell is she? Perry?" Looking around. "*Perry!*"

"The floor opened up beneath her. There's some kind of hydraulic system in it. By the time I got back down here, she was gone. I left for just a few minutes to get help. I—"

The next thing Garrett knew, he had his fists curled in the front of Byrnes's leather uniform, throwing him back into the glass beakers they stored the blood in. The sound shattered the silence, glass spewing across the floor as Byrnes grunted and rolled, coming to his feet with a dangerous grace.

"Feel better?" Byrnes spat blood, his eyes narrowing to cold blue chips of ice.

"*Where were you?*" Garrett roared. "Where were you when she was taken?"

"Chasing the man who tried to kill me!"

Garrett took a step forward.

Byrnes fell back into a defensive stance, his fists curled in front of him. "You only get one free hit."

"That's all I'll damned well need."

"Sir? Sir!"

Both of them looked aside, breathing hard.

The pair of Nighthawks from the garrison on Hart Street were watching. Garrett took a rasping breath, trying to hold on to himself. All he needed was word circulating through the guild about the division between him and Byrnes. And this wasn't about Byrnes. This was about Perry. He had to find her.

"Thomas." Garrett put a name to the face. "Can you hear her?" He crossed the room in long strides, examining the floor. "Can we get this open?"

"It's a trapdoor of sorts," Byrnes said, dusting glass shards out of his sleeve. "The floorboards are reinforced with steel. We're not going to get through it in a hurry."

"Then find the damned contraption that will open it." Garrett slipped a small tracking device from his pocket and wound it. It gave a steady blip as he released the clockwork mechanism, picking up the matching signal from the tracing device he'd planted on her years ago. "She's here somewhere." Damned thing wasn't more specific than that.

Byrnes looked up at the walkways above them. "He was up there. He must have pressed some mechanism."

"Keep working on the floor," Garrett snapped. "Get hammers, the crane... Anything. Just get it bloody open." He met Byrnes's eyes. It was easier to hold on to the anger and the darkness within him if he had another focus. Right now that focus was on finding Perry. "We need to locate the mechanism he used."

Twenty minutes later they were no closer to finding it. Garrett swore, kicking at the railing on the upper walkways. *Christ, if she's already...* No. He swallowed hard. She was alive. She had to be. He'd know somehow if she wasn't...

"We'll find her." Byrnes looked up from where he knelt near the fuse box. "She's clever enough to find her way out."

Garrett simply stared at him, devoid of...anything. *If I lose her...* It choked him, rising up in his throat like a fist, and he turned away, sucking in air. He'd been pushing her away for the last month, so worried about the progression of his disease that he'd never given a thought to how he'd feel if he lost her.

The truth hit him like the sledgehammers the men were using to tear up the floorboards downstairs. Perry was the only thing holding him together. The only one he trusted, truly trusted... He couldn't lose her. She was his everything.

Shouts echoed from below. Garrett and Byrnes strode to the railing, leaning over it with mirrored intensity.

"Getting through the floor now, sir!" young Thomas Wiley called. "Won't be long!"

Garrett thundered toward the stairs. At the top of them, Byrnes caught his arm. "Wait."

The urge to shove him aside rose up but Garrett held it down. Byrnes's head was cocked. Listening. Suddenly Byrnes turned, aiming a boot for the center of the foreman's door. It splintered away from the frame, and he shoved at it with his shoulder. "I can hear something."

Faint, echoing thumps coming from within.

As though someone was...inside the walls.

Garrett slammed his shoulder against the remnants of the door and staggered into the small room, Byrnes stumbling with him.

"Perry?" he yelled.

The sound of knocking vanished. Then resumed again frantically, coming from behind a bookshelf.

Garrett hammered on the walls. "Are you there? Perry, is that you?"

"Get me *out!*"

It was her voice, but he'd never heard her sound like that. Garrett started tearing books off the shelves, wrestling with the bookcase itself. It didn't move.

"Here," Byrnes said, yanking on the gaslight on the

wall. "I've seen these before. The bookcase is a door of sorts."

Slowly it opened, revealing a gaping black maw. Frigid air rushed over his face and there was Perry, curled up into a ball, her hands bruised and bloodied. His heart stopped beating in his chest for half a minute. He swore it did.

She looked up and he had no words for the expression on her face. Huge, barely lucid gray eyes that widened as they saw him, her hands coming up defensively. As though she didn't know who he was.

"Perry?" He reached for her, dragging her out of the small cavity. She staggered forward on jerky feet, tumbling into his arms. A warm, trembling weight. Shaking from head to toe. Not a single sound came from her. "Perry. It's me." He gently curled his arms around her, shaking a little himself. "I've got you. I'm here. You're safe."

Guilt smothered him, thick and choking. It was a wonder he could breathe. Garrett's arms tightened around her. "Damn it." He stroked her hair, fingers raking through the short silky strands. Clinging tighter. It was his own damned fault, sending her with Byrnes. Not watching over her the way he was supposed to. And for what? Because he knew he could barely control himself around her.

Looking up, his eyes met Byrnes's. Fury blazed inside him. *You were supposed to keep her fucking safe.* That was the deal they'd both agreed upon when he'd first sent them out together.

Byrnes gave a tight nod. Accepting the fact they'd discuss this later. "I'll let them know we've got her."

He might not have given a damn, except for the faint softening in his eyes as he looked at her. Then he was gone.

Darkness prowled the edges of Garrett's vision, but for once he wasn't drowning in bloodlust. He just wanted to hold her. To never let her go. *His*.

His eyes shot wide at the thought, his body stiffening. As if she sensed the change in his body, Perry's fingers dug in tighter, locking herself around him. The tension melted out of him again and he pressed his lips to her hair. "I'm not going anywhere, sweetheart." A little fiercely. "I promise."

Of all the times to be having this revelation... He felt dumbstruck. All these years he'd wondered if there was something deficient in him. Wondering why he could like women, but never seemed to feel anything more, and here it was, sneaking up on him when he'd least expected it.

Friendship was a blurred line, but the truth remained Perry was the reason he'd never found anyone. He cared for her. Deeply, irrevocably. The idea of not having her in his life left a gaping hole somewhere in the region of his chest.

Not going to happen.

Garrett glanced behind himself, then reached out and hooked a chair with his boot, dragging it closer. He slumped into it, dragging her into his lap and pressing her head against his chest. "Shush... I've got you," he whispered, rocking her gently. "Just breathe, love. Deep, slow breaths. You're safe. I'm never letting you out of my sight again."

The burning truth of that statement almost crushed

his chest. He pressed another frantic kiss to her forehead, then took her hand and slid it through the opening of his coat, directly over the steady thump of his heart. "There you are. Just listen to my heart. Listen to it beat. All for you, love. All of it for you."

Long, slow minutes followed. The men stayed away, which he grudgingly had to thank Byrnes for. There were enough rumors in the guild without bringing Perry into the heart of them. She'd always abhorred gossip, particularly about herself. If anyone saw them like this, there'd be no denying that they weren't just partners.

Not anymore.

Even if he didn't know what that precisely left them at.

Garrett's lips trailed across her cheek, listening to the soft sound of her breathing. She'd calmed down now, but she hadn't moved. Just lying there, listening to his heart. Her palm splayed wide over his bare chest. Somehow she'd wriggled her fingers between the gaps in his shirt. He'd been in such a hurry that he hadn't bothered with his armored waistcoat or even the leather body armor he usually wore when out on patrol. The feel of that small hand splayed over his bare chest rocked him to the core.

The minutes ticked by. He wasn't usually given to silence, but she was. She would speak when she needed to and not before.

"I'm a coward," she whispered. Those gray eyes looked up at him. So lost.

"That's ridiculous. You're the least likely coward I've ever met."

Perry shook her head and tried to brush the hair off her hot face. "I was so frightened. I haven't had one of my hysterical fits for…for years." Her lip trembled, gaze growing distant.

Garrett took her face in his hands, turning it up to him. "You were hardly hysterical. No more than I was." His voice roughened. "I wanted to tear those bloody floorboards up with my bare hands."

The feel of her skin under his hands was silky soft. He couldn't stop himself from stroking his thumb against the high curve of her cheekbone. Perry glanced down, as if surprised to find herself on his lap. Or his hands on her face.

"I'm sorry. I didn't realize—"

"Damn it, don't be sorry." Garrett brushed the damp strands of hair off her forehead and leaned back, hands cupping her cheeks. Those gray eyes were red-rimmed but clear of tears. Beautiful. It was as if he was seeing her for the first time all over again. *Seeing* her, truly seeing her. He stroked his thumbs over her cheeks. Then again. A little more forcefully.

He didn't know how he was going to make himself let her go. Moving slowly, he slid his arms around her and dragged her in close again. "And I don't think I'm quite ready to let you stand." He stroked her hair, nuzzling his face into it. "*I* need this. Just give me a moment."

The stiffness in her body melted out of her, bit by bit. Each time he stroked his hand through her hair she softened just a little more. And damn him for a fool, but he liked it.

He could also smell blood. There was a sticky spot

at the back of her skull. Garrett's fingers paused over it. "Are you hurt?"

"No. A little light-headed. And nauseous. My knees don't feel quite up to taking my weight, either."

It struck him then that the darkness in him hadn't risen at the scent of her blood. He was aware of it, of course, but the furious hunger rested inside him. It sat like a heavy weight in his chest. Softened. Lulled. Her hand stroked small circles over the muscle of his pectoral.

Garrett puzzled over that. He'd been so frightened he'd hurt her. But this... It felt right. She felt like she belonged exactly where both he and the hunger wanted her.

Damn, but he wished he had someone to speak of this with. Someone like Lynch, who'd had years to deal with controlling the craving virus. Someone who could give him some bloody advice.

The sound of boots ringing on the metal stairs intruded and Perry tensed. When she scrambled off his lap, he let her. Perry took several steps away from him, her face still paler than he'd ever seen it.

It was Byrnes. Of course. His gaze skated over Perry, then back to Garrett. "You need to come and see this."

"Is it important?" Garrett asked, shooting her another look. Still far too quiet. Trembling a little, he thought, but holding on to it.

Byrnes nodded grimly. "It's important."

Ten

"DO YOU WANT TO STAY UP HERE?"

Garrett's face slowly came into focus in front of her. Behind him, the Nighthawks had torn half the floor up with hammers and pry bars. The darkness below yawned like an enormous mouth, ready to swallow her up. The instant she thought it, heat washed out of her face, leaving her lips numb again. Deep in her belly, the fear stretched out its claws and let her know it was still there, ready to drag her under again.

Yes. She didn't want to go anywhere near that... that place. Not again. The thought set her heart racing, a tremble of cold rippling down her spine.

"You don't have to." Garrett saw it in her face.

Years ago, she'd fled from something like this, and it had cost her in nightmares that left her curled into a ball in her sheets, desperately trying to hold the sobs inside. Trying to get her lungs to open so that she could breathe again. Time had eased the frequency of her hysterical attacks, until today. She could stay up here, nice and safe, or she could force herself back into that nightmare. Stare it in the face and spit in its eye.

She didn't want to. But if she didn't do it now, she knew she'd wake screaming tonight.

Best to face it while she had people around her. Perhaps take a good look at what lurked beneath the factory and chase away some of the shadows. It was just a room. Just another room, full of ghostly girls trapped behind the thin facade of glass. All she had to do was keep telling herself that.

Somehow her head jerked in a nod. "I'm coming down."

Garrett squeezed her fingers. She hadn't even noticed he was holding her hand. "I'll go first," he said, stepping away and gesturing for a lantern.

"No. I'll go," Byrnes said. "Make sure it's safe. You're the guild master now." For once his words held no acid. The way his gaze sidled toward her made her realize that some part of him felt the bite of guilt.

Byrnes dropped into the darkness. Garrett followed, shooting her one last grim look before the shadows swallowed him up.

Perry paused at the edge. "Garrett?"

A light bobbed in the darkness: one of the phosphorescent glimmer balls they sometimes used. "Here. Someone help her down. I'll catch her."

If it was anywhere else, she'd have simply stepped off the edge and landed in front of him, just to prove that she didn't need his help. But she still felt fragile. Thomas held out his hand and Perry took it, letting him lower her over the edge. As her body vanished into the darkness, her lungs sucked in a deep breath. Then another. A little faster. She looked up as Thomas gave her hand a squeeze.

"We're right here, miss."

Hands slid up her legs. "I've got her," Garrett called. As Thomas's hand opened, she dropped into his arms.

Foolish to feel so frightened. And to let them see it too. She'd worked for years to uphold her reputation and make it clear she could do this job. It was harder for her. She'd had to prove her worth and value so many times in the last decade, and now young Thomas saw her as just another frightened woman.

"Bloody hell," Byrnes whispered, lifting the glimmer high as he examined the glass cases. Light rippled through the unearthly blue liquid inside, and the girl he was staring at reached for him. Byrnes scrambled back, his face paling as he tripped and landed in a sprawl. "She's alive. She's bloody still alive!"

"Thomas," Garrett called in a choked voice. "I need you and Atherton. Hayes, send word to the guild. We'll need Dr. Gibson here now. And the medic van."

It broke something inside her, staring at that poor girl. Something huge and fierce and choking rose over her, and then Perry was reaching for the pry bar that Byrnes had brought down with him as a weapon.

"Perry...?"

She swung it, driving it straight into the glass. Water spewed out, the girl's eyes widening inside the case as she fell forward and then Garrett was there, catching the girl as she slumped. Perry smashed the remaining glass out of the way as Garrett gently lifted the wet girl into his arms.

"Perry, stop. We need to do this carefully." He was

looking at her. Trying to get her to focus on him. "Put the bar down."

Perry lowered it. Not down on the ground. Her heart was thumping so hard in her chest that she felt like she was going to be ill. The skin on one of her bruised knuckles split as her fingers locked around the cold iron. "I can't." Choked words. "I can't put it down."

"That's fine. Hold it then, if you're frightened. Just don't smash any more of the glass. Byrnes? Your coat?"

Byrnes crawled to his feet, swinging the long leather coat off his shoulders. He held it out and Garrett transferred the girl into his arms. Byrnes closed the coat around her with an oddly gentle movement as Garrett reached for the mask that was strapped around her face. The clips sprang open beneath his touch and the mask eased away from her skin, the white imprint of it gleaming against her cheeks.

"You're safe," Garrett murmured. "He can't hurt you. Not again. I promise."

"No—" The girl's face crumpled, her fingers grabbing onto Garrett's coat as she sobbed. "Please... *Please*..."

Perry staggered away, unable to watch. It only reminded her of her own helplessness. She could hear Garrett's voice, though. Gentle words. Doing what he did best. "Byrnes will look after you. You're safe—"

Safe.

Picking up the lantern, Perry crossed the room, her boots crunching on glass. Behind her she heard Atherton and Thomas land in the darkness, where

Garrett swiftly gave them orders. She couldn't look at the glass cases or the women inside. Instead she stared at the steel examination table at the end of the room.

A surgery. Her hip hit a small rolling cart covered in gleaming implements. Just the sight of them made the heat drain from her face. A single light hung over the table, its bulb darkened. But she could imagine it bright and glaring. Imagine the gleam of it on steel, reflecting back off the scalpel—

—the straps cutting into her as she wriggled and jerked. Locked over her chest and arms, hips and thighs. Trapping her, no matter how much she fought—

"Perry?"

She jerked her hand away from the table. "Yes?"

Garrett stepped around it, his blue eyes burning through her. "Are you all right?"

"I'm fine." Better than those poor girls anyway. Wrapping her arms around herself, she shivered. Time to prove she was made of firmer pluck than this. To prove it to herself, if nothing else. "What do you want me to do?"

He looked at her, searching for any sign that she was going to suffer another bout of hysteria. Perry's cheeks burned. How she hated those episodes. The breathing was the worst, because she thought she'd never draw another breath again. It had taken years to learn how to survive them. Years of meditation with Lynch, and surprisingly, the martial art he'd insisted she learn had helped.

"I'm fine," she repeated, her voice just a little louder. "I want to help."

Garrett gave a clipped nod. "We're going to get

the other three out. I'll need you to help me." He
shot one last questioning look at the table, his expression darkening. "Then we need to work out how to
locate this bastard and find out what the hell he was
doing here."

✑

Water gushed over her, thick and salty. Perry caught
the last girl in her arms as she slumped forward out
of the tank, her wet stringy hair clinging to Perry's
face. Fingers raked over her, clutching at her arms.
Fighting her.

"I've got you," she whispered, staring into those
pale green eyes. "You're safe now."

For a moment she felt a sense of kinship. This one
was the fighter. But unlike Perry, she'd been unable
to escape. That could have been her. Locked up like
that. Or devil knows what else Hague had intended
to do with her. If not for the single buckle that had
torn from the straps holding her down, giving her
just enough space to free her arm, something like this
could have happened to her.

Byrnes helped her unclip the mask from over the
girl's mouth and nose. The suction gave a little pop
as they pried it loose, the stale taste of air leaching
from it with a hiss. That explained the metal canisters
clipped to the walls beside each tank. Aether. The
breath of life.

Perry dragged her coat off and draped it around the
girl's shoulders, her wet shirt clinging to her skin.

"Who are you?" the young woman sobbed.

"My name is Miss Lowell." Hopefully the sight of

another female would help to calm the woman. "I'm a Nighthawk. This is Byrnes, one of my companions."

The woman's eyes darted. "The...others? I know there were others. I could see them. See what he did to them."

One of the girls hadn't been breathing when they removed her from the case and another was in a perilous condition, the scar down her chest red and inflamed. The other Nighthawks had removed both of them to the medic coach where Dr. Gibson was fussing.

Perry gave a little shake of her head. "One is still breathing—her name is Alice. The others... Whatever he did to them, their bodies were fighting it."

Byrnes shot Perry a warning glance. But if that were her, she would want to know "What's your name, miss?" he asked.

"Ava." Haunted eyes glanced at the examination table, then darted away. "Ava McLaren."

There was a faint Scottish burr to her voice. Perry stilled. "How long have you been here?"

"Where are we?" A hesitation as Ava swallowed. "The last I knew, I was in Edinburgh. It was May."

Edinburgh. Perry squeezed her hand, holding on just a little too tightly. Edinburgh was close to the Moncrieff's family home—and place of exile. "It's November. And you're in London. We were investigating a pair of murders in the factory when we found you."

November, Ava mouthed. Any remaining color drained out of her cheeks, and she swayed in Perry's arms. It brought Perry's split knuckles closer to her face, and suddenly the woman stiffened, eyes locking on the torn and bleeding skin, her irises darkening.

A blue blood. Perry's gaze jerked to Byrnes.

He slid his arms around Ava, tugging her tight against his chest as he stood. "I've got her," he murmured. "You should see if you can stop the bleeding."

What were the odds of the woman having the craving virus? A woman who'd been held captive by a man who liked to cut out girl's hearts? It wasn't the same circumstances as Hague—just similar enough to make something tighten in her chest.

For a moment she was frozen, then Perry leaped after them, yanking at Byrnes's arm. "What did he do to you, Miss McLaren?" The words were harsh, but her heart was hammering in her ears. "Did he inject you with anything? Then cut you with a scalpel?"

"Perry," Byrnes snapped, turning his shoulder as if to keep her away from the girl. "Bloody hell, give her time to catch her breath."

Then they were gone and she had no answers other than those her mind could supply—and those she could imagine only too well.

Hague.

It had to be Hague. Didn't it?

❧

"I never…I never knew, I swear. They been 'ere, all along, ain't they?" Mr. Mallory stood by the door to the factory, twisting his cap in his hands as he watched them put the bodies of the first two girls in the medic van.

Garrett clapped a hand on his shoulder. "We need to ask you a few questions about your missing overseer, Mr. Sykes."

"Anythin' you need," Mallory replied, tears wetting

his eyes as he watched Dr. Gibson slam the door shut on the medic coach.

"Has anybody seen him?" Garrett asked. "None of my Nighthawks can locate him. There's been no answer at his address."

"You think he did this?"

"We're not certain," Garrett replied. "He is, however, a person of interest."

"No, I ain't seen him. Don't speak much, outside of work. He don't seem to speak much to anyone, actually. Just locks himself up in that little room up there, goin' over the books. Comes out every once in a while and just watches. Not like most overseers I've worked with. People don't— they don't like to cross him."

"Has he made any threats against anyone?" Garrett's instincts sharpened.

"No, quiet manner he has. Don't ever raise his voice. Just…watches. It gives a man the right shivers, it does."

"How long has he been here?"

"Near on six months as I can recollect. I wouldn't know the precise date."

Garrett asked several other questions but it was clear Mallory was shaken. Not even the ECHO could catch his interest this time around.

Outside it was mayhem. People strained along the fences, howling for details. He could see one or two familiar faces—the press with their bulbous cameras. Lurking about for him, no doubt. Well, they'd have to wait. He had more pressing matters to deal with. Gibson had pronounced the second girl dead and suspected an infection in her blood, considering the recent surgery. Alice had been subdued with a dose of laudanum and the doctor was seeing to her now.

Footsteps echoed him and he found Perry at his heels. Her lips were blue with the cold and she shivered, her arms wrapped around herself. Garrett glanced around for one of the blankets they'd dragged from the medic coach. "What are you doing? You're freezing." He draped it around her shoulders. "Get up on the seat beside Gibson and back to the guild. I don't want to see you again until you've had a warm bath and changed your clothes."

"I'm fine."

"Perry…" he growled.

"You're wet too."

His own shirt clung to his chest. "I'll return as soon as I get the men sorted out." More Nighthawks had arrived from the guild to go over the laboratory and transport everything back to headquarters where it could be examined at leisure.

"Get Gibson to test them for the craving," she said. "The last one we rescued—Ava—she's a blue blood."

"Truly?"

"I saw it in her eyes, Garrett. She wanted my blood."

It was only then that he remembered her bloodied hands. The moment he tried to look at them, Perry snatched her wrist out of reach. It stirred his anger but he swallowed it down, forcing himself to leave her be. Later. When both of them had time. Then he was going to sit with her and damn well make certain she was barely bruised.

"Perhaps you'd best sit with her," he instructed.

"She'll be frightened and unsure of what's going on. You've experienced it—"

A flash of something—fright—lit through her eyes. There and gone again. "I'll try to speak to her. She won't let go of Byrnes at the moment."

Both of them looked over to where the other man handed Ava up into the front of the medic coach. Once on the seat, the other man began rubbing at her hands to warm her up.

"Perhaps he's not a lost cause, after all," Garrett noted with some surprise.

"You only see him as a rival. I'll hardly claim him to be garrulous, but he looked after me, Garrett, when you sent us out together. He doesn't cluck over me like a mother hen the way you do, but he made certain he was always in the line of fire first."

Garrett sighed and rubbed a hand through the back of his wet hair. "Go. Bathe. That's an order. Tell Doyle he's to make certain you're warm and dry."

"I'm not telling him any such thing," she replied tartly, backing toward the coach. "I can look after myself, you know."

A smile teased his lips. Doyle would take one look at her and she'd be in the steam baths below the guild, with warmed blood being delivered in a flagon, and a warm dressing robe and slippers. Perry might not know it, but looking after her had become somewhat of a conspiracy among the men.

"Go then, my lady peregrine. I'll see you later, after this mess is sorted out."

Eleven

"YOU SENT A MESSAGE TO HIM, DIDN'T YOU?" PERRY growled, not bothering to knock.

Garrett paused in dragging on a clean, white shirt to glance at her as she entered his bedchambers. The color suited him. They were so often in black, but white highlighted the bright blue of his eyes and his gleaming chestnut hair. He swiftly did the buttons up over his broad chest, then started on the cuffs. "Sent a message to who?"

"Doyle."

A smile touched his lips. He was struggling with the buttons at his cuffs. "I take it you are clean and dry."

"And fed, watered, and scolded," she added, crossing to his side. "Here. Allow me." Her bandaged hands caught his wrist, tugging the button through the material. The hard flex of his forearm bunched beneath her grip. "My hands are healed already, courtesy of the craving, but he insisted on slathering on some foul-smelling concoction."

"Doyle doesn't have any daughters. So be gracious."

"You're not my father, either," she reminded him.

"Not even remotely. And don't try to categorize me as a brother or cousin."

A heavy silence fell between them. Full of a liquid awareness. Perry let go of his other sleeve, her cheeks flushed with heat. "I see you've been redecorating."

He followed her out into the remnants of what had once been Lynch's study. The bookshelves were swept clean and the desk, which had always overflowed with paperwork, was spotless. Someone had brought in a pair of red leather-studded sofas and a Turkish rug. They rested before the enormous hearth, with the faded square in the wallpaper above it indicating where a map had once hung.

Garrett tugged open a desk drawer and removed a dark green bottle and a pair of wineglasses. He shrugged, kicking the drawer shut. "It seemed time. I was growing weary of all the books. They're not mine."

There was more to it than that. Perry eyed his nonchalant expression and then the bottle. "Blud-wein?" In her state, it would go straight to her head.

A rare delicacy for a rogue blue blood. The sort of thing the Echelon drank, but supplies would be short now, what with the closure of the draining factories.

Garrett shot her one of his more devastating smiles. "One of the few things I kept from Lynch's stock. He owes me a decent drop."

She felt tired, glassy. Every so often she caught herself staring and knew she was ready for sleep. The shock of the day had torn through her like a knife. A long day, trying to settle Ava and Alice. Still it was nice to know some things hadn't changed. She and Garrett often relaxed together like this after a horrendous shift on the streets. And she needed it right now. Almost as much as she'd needed his arms around her at the factory.

Slumping into the corner of one sofa like a marionette with its strings cut, Perry tucked her feet up in front of her and wrapped her arms around them. Best not to think of that. After the horror of the day, Garrett had been there, the way she knew he would be. But it didn't change this awkwardness between them. And it seemed her past was starting to catch up to her.

She had no proof, nothing to go on but the little voice in her head that wouldn't leave her alone. *You know it's Hague. He's back. And his methods have evolved.*

But how could she point Garrett in the right direction without revealing all of her own tangled secrets? And if she did, would he somehow trace Hague back to Moncrieff? That was the last thing she wanted. The Moncrieff wouldn't hesitate to cut Garrett down. Indeed, if the duke had any inkling of her feelings for Garrett, he'd relish the opportunity.

Garrett set the bottle and glasses down on the carpet. Grabbing a lap rug, he draped it around her shoulders and tugged it tight around her, his hands hovering on the edges of the rug as if he didn't want to let go. "How are you feeling?"

"Tired." *Exhausted.* "What's wrong?"

His mouth tightened. "You were the one who was trapped down there. I should be asking you that."

"Yes, but you're acting strangely. I'm not." Perry tipped her chin up, refusing to let him see how much today had shaken her. Garrett knew she was capable, but she couldn't afford to have another moment like that one today. The men would expect it of her, and she'd fought too long and hard for her reputation over the years to lose it now.

Garrett laughed, more of an exhale really. "You like to make things difficult, don't you?"

She wasn't used to this. Not at all. Perry tugged the rug tighter around her. "I don't know what you mean—"

"We need to speak about today."

"I told you—I'm fine."

"I'm not." Tension ran in stiff lines through his body. He rubbed one hand over the other. "I was frightened."

The words stole her breath. "You? You're never frightened."

"I know that we lose Nighthawks on occasion. It's one of the hazards of the job. It's expected. But…not you." Those stormy eyes met hers. Locked on her tight. "I thought, for a moment, that I'd lost you."

Her breath caught. These were uncertain waters. Garrett was always cool and in control. Tonight was different. Something darkened his eyes, a sense of revelation. And whatever he saw, he didn't like it. "But you didn't," she replied, trying to make sense of it all.

"I thought I did. I've had the thought before—that time three years ago when I lost you in the tunnels beneath the theater—but not like this. And I can't—" His voice roughened. "I can't lose you. Things are… becoming a little complicated for me."

Well. She sat in stunned silence. How many times had she longed to hear those words over the years? Her heart clenched in her chest. *No.* She couldn't deal with this, not at this moment. He didn't mean it. He couldn't.

For a second, she thought she was going to suffer another attack.

"I shouldn't have pushed you to go with Byrnes," he admitted. "I should have been there for you, should have—"

"The floor swallowed me up," she said quickly, digging her nails into her palms. It helped take her focus off her breathing. "You being there wouldn't have made any difference."

"Yes, but…"

"You're feeling guilty," she said. "I don't blame you for what happened, and this isn't Byrnes's fault, either. If it's any consolation, I believe he's probably going to find it difficult to get any rest tonight, if only because he'll be worried you might try to strangle him in his sleep." She forced her voice to remain cool and calm. Inside she was trembling. "Now, could you pour me some blud-wein? I must admit that I am particularly craving a glass right now."

Garrett stared at her. "Your sheer practicality is almost cold-blooded at times. You know that?"

Perry sank back into the sofa. She wasn't cold-blooded, not at all. Today would haunt her, but not now when she was safe, clean, and dry. She'd learned a long time ago to appreciate these moments in life and not dwell on the others. She couldn't. Or she'd be a gibbering mess. "We saved two girls. We also have a strong lead on the Keller-Fortescue case. I'm so tired right now that I just want to…not think about it."

"It's so easy for you not to think about it, isn't it?"

"It's something I've learned over the years. From an excellent teacher, mind you."

Garrett shot her a rueful look. "That's different."

"Why?"

"Because usually…" He gestured helplessly. "It's just different." Going to his knees on the rug, he popped the cork on the wine bottle and poured her a glass. She was suddenly ravenous, her vision flashing through myriad shades of dark.

The fireplace crackled and he cleared his throat. "Drink up. Here's to merrier thoughts. Like revenge."

His glass clinked against hers, then he pressed it to his lips, his irises going black with hunger. A little flush of answering need swept through her and she drank greedily, trying to assuage it. Not that blood would ever slake *this* thirst.

"Revenge?" Perry asked, lowering her empty glass.

"Do you remember how you drove me insane following the Falcone attack? Not letting me out of bed, fluffing my pillows, fetching me blood and wine and anything else I needed."

"I don't know how you suffered through it."

He smiled, purely diabolical. "I suffered your smothering ministrations because I knew that you cared. Just as I do."

Perry sat up straighter. "You are *not* confining me to bed rest." Not with a madman out there who might—or might not—be Hague. She needed to be on this case. She *had* to know if her nightmares were coming true. "Don't you dare."

"This case is getting dangerous—"

"That's not unusual."

"Yes, but—"

"Garrett!" she snapped. "If you take me off this case I shall…I shall make you regret it."

"I shiver at your inventiveness."

"You should," she growled, snatching the bottle of blud-wein from him. "I can be hellishly inventive when I set my mind to it." It wasn't enough. She could see it in his eyes. Her voice softened. "You asked me once why this case bothered me. It's personal this time, Garrett. I can't just sit back and watch. I won't."

The instant she said "personal," his gaze shot to hers. "Why?"

A mistake. He'd never let up now. "Because I know what it's like to be powerless like that."

"Perry." He reached for her.

"Don't." She brushed his hand aside and poured herself another glass of blud-wein. "I don't want to talk about it." She held the bottle out to him. "I didn't choose to become a blue blood. And the man who did this to me… He wanted me to be able to heal from what he intended to do…for the hurt he intended to cause. I was less than a woman to him."

The sleepy lassitude of the blud-wein was working its magic, stealing through her veins and smoldering deep in her stomach. Letting her reveal something that she'd never spoken of to anyone before.

Garrett's face hardened. "He hurt you."

Soft, dangerous words. Perry looked up, surprised by the blackness sweeping through his irises. He'd drained one glass. He shouldn't be craving another so strongly.

"It was a long time ago."

Garrett's face was so expressionless that he might as well have been carved of stone. But stone didn't radiate fury and menace like that. Stone didn't look like it wanted to kill something. Badly.

"Garrett?"

"Is he dead?"

The harshness of his whisper bothered her. "Y-yes." Or at least she'd thought so. She wasn't so certain anymore.

"D did he…? What did he do to you?"

She thought she understood. Garrett rarely spoke of his mother, but Perry knew that the poor woman had been molested before her throat had been cut. He'd spoken of it once when he was drunk. "Not that," Perry hastened to assure him "The man he wasn't interested in me as a woman. Only in pain, in… He liked to cut." Bile rose in her throat. "Please don't ask me any more."

Hastily she drained her second glass. She needed it. Warmth spread through her, a slow seeping drug that swept away some of the nausea speaking of Hague resurrected.

Garrett slid his hand through hers, lacing their fingers together. "I wish that I could have been there."

"You *were* there for me," she replied. "You were there when I needed you. When I couldn't bear the thought of another man even touching me, let alone living among dozens of them. You taught me to trust again, when so many men had let me down."

His fingers squeezed hers. "I still wish I'd been there…when it happened."

"Then don't stop me now. If you want to help

me, don't take me off this case. I want to catch this bastard." Particularly if it was Hague. "Before he hurts some other young girl."

"Fine. You'll work the case. With me."

She'd be lucky if she was allowed out without three armored guards after this. Still she gave him a shy smile and slipped her hand from his, reaching for the blud-wein. "Thank you. Let's go over what we know. I don't think I could sleep just yet."

For the next hour, they talked about the case. Garrett created a map on the carpet, using the wine bottle as the draining factory and small copper pennies to indicate areas of interest. One copper penny for the man who'd mentioned Steel Jaw, another for Tolliver, another for Sykes.

"I almost forgot," Garrett said. "I've solved one mystery, at least."

Perry leaned her head back against the sofa arm sleepily. "Oh?"

With another of those devastating grins, he ducked behind the desk and returned with a small brass box with what looked like reams of transparent ribbons attached to the top—the same type of ribbon that was used in the ECHO to record sound. "I have found our ghost," he said, setting the device on the table and turning it on. "It was in the laboratory."

Vision flickered over the nearest wall, pale and muted from the competing light from the fire. But it was enough for her to see a woman dressed in white turning toward the projecting device, her eyes and mouth opening wide in a scream.

"What on earth...?"

"It's not perfect, but in the near dark, it would be enough to scare away anyone who stumbled across the killer's laboratory." Garrett flicked the switch off. "Humans are a superstitious lot."

"A bloody ghost." Perry shook her head. "What next?" Taking another sip of blud-wein, she relaxed again. "So, who do you think is behind all of this?"

"Sykes," Garrett murmured. "We still need to locate him and question him. There's been no sign of him since Monday. Almost as if he's vanished."

"Not unusual, once he knew we were looking for him," she reminded him. "Sometimes people run."

"Only those with something to hide."

Perry sipped her wine. "I'd like to look through his home, if I could. See if the scent trail matches anything I picked up in the laboratory at the factory."

"Tomorrow," he agreed with a frown. "We both need sleep or we're going to start making mistakes. Sykes had to have created that laboratory. It had to be someone who had access and could come and go at will."

"Garrett, there are dozens of tunnels beneath that section of London. It could be anyone."

"Yes, but there's also a constant ebb and flow of workers above. Someone must have seen something unusual—unless...unless it wasn't unusual for them." People rarely noticed others coming and going if it was a regular occurrence.

"But how would Sykes have met Miss Fortescue or Miss Keller?" Perry argued. "We'll need to question the factory workers."

"The men have started, but it will take days."

"Then get more men on it. You don't need to do all of this by yourself anymore."

Another slow smile. "I'm still getting used to this position, I suppose." He shifted a handful of shillings toward the factory. "Those can be Nighthawks. Hayes is good at questioning people. He can be in charge." He frowned. "Why is he taking daughters of the Echelon? That's the part I can't figure out. They're not prostitutes or women whose disappearance wouldn't be remarked upon."

"They have to have come into his sphere somehow, and maybe...maybe he sees them and wants them for his collection." She thought of Hague. "Some men—or monsters—are like that. They fixate on women they've seen." *Her.* Perry swallowed. The duke had told her after Hague first found her trying to free girls from his laboratory that she was safe. That he had a deal with Hague. Hague would do the duke's work, and the duke would look the other way when it came to some of Hague's...peccadilloes. That was the word he'd used. In return, Moncrieff's thralls were not to be touched.

Only she hadn't been safe. For days after the aborted escape attempt, Hague had watched her every time she moved around the Moncrieff's mansion, desperately writing to her father to break the thrall contract. The moment the duke was gone for the evening, Hague had drugged her and she'd woken up—

Perry forced the memory back into its locked box in her mind.

"What else?" Garrett mused, not noticing her discomfort.

"Someone needs to question Ava and Alice."

Silence fell. Perry drained her glass, letting the warmth of the blud-wein soften the tension in her muscles. *I'm not going to think of that. Not tonight.*

"We'll let them rest," Garrett replied. "Alice won't let anyone near her except Doyle, and Miss McLaren is still…unsettled. I'm not going to force that on either of them. Not yet."

"You could let Byrnes question Miss McLaren," Perry suggested. "She seemed to trust him."

"We'll see."

Perry curled up along the sofa. She was feeling deliciously relaxed now. "This is a most excellent wine."

"Perhaps you can send the duke your regards," Garrett replied dryly, draining the last of his glass and placing it aside. Leaning forward onto his hands and knees, he swept up the pennies and shillings.

The view was most excellent too, Perry thought, staring at his arse. Leather did all kinds of wonderful things for the male anatomy. A hot flush pooled low in her belly, igniting all sorts of wicked ideas in her head. Or perhaps that was the amount of blud-wein she'd consumed. It left her flushed and relaxed and contemplating things she probably shouldn't.

Slowly she closed her eyes, soaking in the warmth from the fireplace. Garrett cursed under his breath as he gathered up the rest of the pennies, the monotony of it lulling her even further. She felt utterly safe here, knowing that he watched over her.

"Perry…"

A presence loomed. She reached out to stop it, but then warm arms slid beneath her and the scent of Garrett's familiar cologne filled her head. "Never could hold your wine, Perry. Come on, I've got you."

Strong arms. She thought about insisting that he put her down, but she was tired, the world was hazy, and if she were honest with herself, she quite liked being here. Her fingers curled in the collar of his shirt, her head nestling on his shoulder. The world spun as he straightened and Perry let it, nuzzling in closer.

The next thing she knew, she was in the soft, gentle dark and Garrett was easing her onto her bed. Hands tugged at her boots, and one heated palm curled around her calf.

"What're you doing?" She yawned.

"Lie still." A breathless laugh filled the warm darkness of her room as Garrett tossed her boots aside, then knelt on the bed. "How the bloody hell does this thing work?"

Her corset. Deft fingers played over it, working with smooth efficiency to unclip each silver buckle. Then the tight laces at the front that held it all together. She lifted her arms up as he dragged it over her head, the thin cotton undershirt she wore clinging to her breasts. Looking down, she started on a button, but the damned thing was so small she could barely get her fingers around it and—

The next thing she knew she was flat on her back and Garrett swiftly undid her buttons. "Tell me you're wearing something beneath this," he murmured.

"My chemise."

"Good." He whipped the black shirt over her head. Then froze. "That is barely a chemise. That—*Christ*, that's a scrap of lace."

"Had to cut it off at the bottom," she murmured. The cool night air shivered over her skin. Idly she traced his knee, which rested on the bed.

He removed it. Quickly. "I would never have guessed. You. In lace."

"I like lace. Sometimes." She was still a woman, with her own needs and desires. No matter how much she had to pretend they didn't exist.

"Only where others can't see it," he muttered, starting on the buttons at her waist. "Blast it, how's a man to forget that?"

"You didn't have to undress me."

"It seemed a good idea at the time."

Her breeches slid down over her hips and she lifted her bottom off the bed to help him. The room spun. "Goodness," she murmured. His face swam into focus, thick lashes framing his dark eyes. "You're so pretty, Garrett."

"Now I know you're foxed." His voice was low and firm. "Stop squirming." One hand held firm against her thigh as he tugged the leather leggings down over her calves. Perry giggled, his fingers tickling her.

Even in the near darkness, she could see that he was smiling. Her heart gave a gentle tug in her chest and she reached out, touching his lips. Garrett tossed her breeches behind him and looked up.

The expression on his face did all sorts of damage to her insides—an equal mix of confusion and bemusement, with a touch of frustration. "What am I going to do with you?" he asked softly.

Why don't you kiss me?

Hands tugged at the sheet, pinning it down over her body firmly, and the bed dipped as he sat on the edge of it.

She thought for a moment that lips touched hers. Reaching up, her fingers grazed the stubble on his jaw, then Garrett caught her hand and tucked it beneath her pillow.

"I'll kiss you one day, Perry, but I'd prefer to do it when you weren't half-asleep and on the ran-tan."

"Not drunk," she murmured.

"Not at all." He smiled again and she blinked sleepily.

Had he said those words? Or were they only her imagination? Perry tried to open her eyes, but his tall form was moving away from her and she was so tired and... She curled into the pillow and let the darkness wash over her.

∾

"Good morning."

Garrett gave her a slightly smug smile as she filled her cup with tea and laced it with blood. He held his own cup in his hands, his elbows resting on the dining table, looking handsome and more refreshed than she'd seen him in days. *Bastard.*

Perry slid into the chair opposite him and glared. The morning light, which usually hurt her eyes only a little, was unnaturally bright. "I feel awful."

"You didn't have to drink almost the full bottle of blud-wein yourself."

"You didn't have to undress me, either."

A smile curled over those devilish lips. "No, I

probably didn't. But let's be honest… I was rather curious about what you're hiding under those harsh leathers, considering the way you flaunted yourself at the opera."

"Satisfied now?"

A long, slow, heated look. "Not at all, actually."

Perry took refuge in her tea, not quite certain how to answer that. It had been easy to flirt with him at the opera and the other day in the alley, but something… something had changed. There was an edge of seriousness beneath the lighthearted tone he used. A certain look in his eye. Testing her perhaps.

"Not going to ask me?"

"Ask you what?" Her eyes narrowed.

"If I peeked." Garrett's eyes twinkled over the top of his cup.

"I know you didn't peek," she replied, feeling all flushed and bothered. *Damn him.* "You're too much of a gentleman."

"Sometimes I'm not." His voice turned soft, drugging. "Sometimes I'm not a gentleman at all. You just haven't met that side of me yet."

And didn't that present quite an enticing image. Perry stared at him. Waking up in only her chemise and drawers hadn't bothered her until she'd seen her leggings hanging forlornly over a chair and began to remember last night. She could remember bits and pieces, here and there. The soft almost-ghostly kiss that she could have sworn she'd imagined. *Had* she imagined that? Her gaze focused on Garrett's devilishly sensual mouth. Fate couldn't be that cruel.

"You didn't peek," she repeated. "I know you too well."

Their eyes met. Garrett's smile widened.

Despite herself, Perry's heart started to race in her chest. She'd never expected him to level *that* look at her. She'd seen it enough times—aimed at other ladies—to know what it meant. The thought left her unsettled. For years she'd known exactly where she stood with him, even as it chafed at her. But now everything between them was unsettled. She didn't know what he was thinking, and the small reckless part of her that had flaunted herself in front of him at the opera and in the alley wasn't feeling quite so brave this morning.

"Besides," Perry added, "that would be cheating."

"Were we playing some sort of game? I wasn't aware there were rules."

Were they? She didn't quite know what this was. But one thing was certain. She'd lose. The stakes were far too high for her, while they meant little, if anything, to him. Perry didn't realize she'd been smiling at him until it died, melting away as if it had never been.

Garrett noticed. He always did.

"You're right," he said, his voice turning crisp. "I didn't peek. The lacy undergarments completely distracted me. I would never have presumed you to be the sort."

"Lacy undergarments?" someone asked. "To what do we owe the pleasure of this conversation?"

Byrnes settled at the dining table beside her, one brow quirking.

Immediately Garrett's lips tightened. Perry slid a hand over his, staying him. "We discussed this last night."

"My punishment?" Byrnes drawled, sliding an arm

along the back of her chair. Despite his careless words, he watched Garrett carefully. "You know I never meant to see her hurt."

"I wouldn't mean to kill you, either..." Garrett growled, shoving to his feet. He rested both hands on the table and leaned over it. "No, actually, that's a lie."

"You're being unreasonable," Perry told him flatly.

"Only where you're concerned, my dear." Byrnes gave her an enigmatic smile, kicking one foot up on another chair and spreading his arm across the back of hers. It was a nonchalant gesture, but the muscles in his arm bunched as Garrett's eyes darkened.

What the hell did that mean?

She shot Garrett a look, but he was staring at Byrnes with that unreadable expression on his face, the one that unnerved her. Byrnes stared back, a challenging little quirk to one brow.

She felt like kicking Byrnes's chair out from underneath him and then shoving the table into Garrett's thighs. Anything to break their locked stares. Around the room, some of the novices had begun to notice.

"You're drawing attention," she said quietly.

Both of them looked around. Garrett flexed his fingers into a fist, then released it, giving her a nod. Acknowledging that he'd been acting like a fool, at least.

"So where is the case at?" Byrnes asked.

Perry hastily filled Byrnes in on the events they'd discussed the previous night—anything to break the tension.

"Perry and I are going to have a chat with Fitz about what we discovered at the laboratory, then we'll investigate Sykes. Nobody's seen the foreman since Monday, which seems unusual." Garrett's voice softened. "How is Ava?"

"She woke up screaming several times. So I stayed with her." Byrnes met Garrett's eyes with a challenge, as if daring him to castigate him for it. "But she's recovering as well as one can, I suppose, considering what she went through."

"Do you think her nerves have recovered enough to be questioned?"

"She's stronger than she seems," Byrnes admitted grudgingly. "I'll try, but I won't push her."

"I don't expect you to." Garrett gave a clipped nod. "I also want you to pursue some information for me. I want to know if any of the Echelon have ties to the draining factory. Political, economical…anything of interest."

"I'm working alone?"

"For now. Before you get somebody else killed."

For once Byrnes seemed less than pleased with the announcement. Perry drained her tea and slammed the mug down, hastily climbing to her feet. "Come," she said, grabbing Garrett's arm and dragging him away from the table. "We're wasting time."

The moment the door shut behind them, Perry sighed. "You should stop baiting him."

"*Me?*"

Perry strode away from him, throwing her hands up. "Let's go see what Fitz has for us. He, at least, is a rational male."

The striking ring of a hammer echoed through the lower floor as they made their way to Fitz's dungeon. Garrett rapped on the door and held it open for her. The hammering never stopped as Perry stepped through, her eyes instantly watering from the smoke.

"Devil take it." Garrett coughed. "Fitz!"

The guild's engineer looked up, his eyes magnified by an enormous pair of brass goggles. Tufts of hair stuck up over the top of the goggles, making him look as though he'd been in the midst of an experiment gone awry.

"Rational, hmm?" Garrett murmured close to her ear as he pushed past her.

Fitz tossed the hammer aside and dragged his goggles up on top of his head. He blinked, as if only just noticing the thick haze in the room, then turned and swore. Smoke billowed from the chimney. Fitz pulled the lever to open the flue.

"Sorry, sir," he called, slightly louder than he needed to. "Didn't hear you knock."

Which was why nobody bothered anymore.

"What have you got for me?" Garrett asked, prowling among the workbenches littered with a scattering of items. Crates full of the mysterious pieces they'd taken from the laboratory.

"This," Fitz said, slapping Garrett's hand absently as he reached for one of the crates. "Don't touch." Gently he slid his hands under something and lifted it almost reverently. "Look at it! She's a beauty. I've never seen the like... I couldn't even begin to imagine how to create such a thing."

The smooth, polished brass lump in his hands began to take form. Bile rose in her throat. "It's a clockwork heart," Perry said.

"Gibson removed it from the chest of the first

unidentified victim during the autopsy." Gently
easing it onto a stand, Fitz reached for his forceps.
"Mechanical limbs are usually crude, unless they're
formed by the blacksmiths the Echelon control. But
I've seen their work—even their iron lungs—and I
can honestly say that I've never seen anything like
this. Watch." He gently slid the forceps under one of
the beaten brass sheets. The rivets had already been
removed and it opened, revealing a chamber of sorts.

"Whoever he is, he has the genius of da Vinci.
This is almost a perfect replica of a human heart, only
slightly enlarged. There are clockwork pieces inside—
here…" He tapped at the top of the specimen. "And
here." The bottom. "But from what I can see, I think
the entire thing works on pressure. As soon as one
chamber fills with fluid, the clockwork at the bottom
releases the mechanism blocking each valve, and the
blood pours through into the next chamber. It's…the
most amazing device I've ever seen."

It was vile. Pulsing with evil. Perry shut her eyes
and shuddered. "Put it away. I've seen enough."

Shooting her a surprised glance, Fitz complied,
nestling the heart back in the straw-filled crate.

"The same device resides in both Miss McLaren
and Alice, doesn't it?" Garrett asked.

Fitz nodded. "Gibson examined them. They both
seem quite well, considering their ordeal. He's going
to do some tests on the effectiveness of the device;
how much blood it can pump; whether its limits
impede either girl's rigorous movements—"

"No," Garrett said, the firmness of his voice echoing
a little. "They are women, Fitz. Not an experiment.

And they have just been rescued from a hellish ordeal. You are not to question either of them without my authority, and neither is Dr. Gibson. I won't have them performing some sort of macabre tests for your own curiosity."

In that moment, she loved him just a little more fiercely.

Looking chastened, Fitz gave a stiff nod of the head. "As you wish. I shall restrict my experiments to what I have here." He gave the mechanical heart another covetous glance. "Whoever he is, he has access to the craving virus. The one thing I am certain of is that all four girls were blue bloods. No human could survive this. And if you see here"—Fitz pointed to the aortic valve —"the heart was joined to the body with the process the Echelon's blacksmiths call fusion. Using the healing components of a blue blood's saliva, he managed to fuse the metal with the body."

Perry exchanged a glance with Garrett. "Our killer is far more educated than we imagined." Like Hague had been. It troubled her. "Could he be one of the Echelon's blacksmiths?" Such men were rare, devoting their lives to their bio-mech work. They were also strictly controlled, often accepting patronage with one of the Great Houses.

"The Academy of the Greater Sciences would have names of all of their previous students. I've not heard of a master smith who hasn't earned his degree in their hallowed halls," Fitz said.

"I'll send Byrnes to search the register," Garrett said. "What else do you make of our killer?"

"He's a scientist," Fitz said. "He doesn't see himself

as a killer, nor does he see the girls as human. They're experiments to him."

Both she and Garrett exchanged a glance. Garrett's lip curled. "Yes, I think you're correct."

"He has access to money," Perry added. "Setting up such a laboratory would have cost him a fortune."

She could see Garrett thinking. He frowned. "He has financial backing—either an inheritance of his own or patronage. Someone out there knows what he's doing, but why would they allow such a man to live freely?"

"Genius," Fitz murmured. "Whoever he is, he can create something no one else can."

"And if he leaves a trail of bodies behind him, who should care?" Garrett scowled. "I despise men like that, though it does sound an awful lot like a blue blood of the Echelon backing him. Who else wouldn't give a damn about the life of a human girl?"

"There's something else, sir. I've examined the laboratory itself, several times. Do you recall that space in the corner?" Fitz asked.

"With the drag marks on the floor?"

Fitz nodded. "There was something there, something that was removed. I found copper pipes in the walls nearby and managed to trace them back to the blood storage vats in the factory above. Whatever he was creating in that corner, he needed blood for it. There are marks on the ceiling too, like scorch marks. Whatever it was, it was quite large. He must have dismantled it to remove it."

"Blood," Perry murmured. "That sounds ominous."

"That corner was out of the line of sight from

where Ava and Alice were kept," Garrett mused. "They wouldn't have seen anything, either."

"What could he have been building?" The possibilities were infinite.

"A device of sorts, something powered by blood?" Garrett looked toward Fitz.

Fitz shrugged. "I doubt it. Steam power, I'd imagine, judging from the soot marks on the walls. However, it certainly used a great deal of blood—for some unknown purpose—if the sizes of the pipes are anything to go by."

Garrett swore under his breath. "Keep searching. I want to know everything I can about his laboratory and what manner of man he is. As for us…" He looked at her. "Time to go see if our mysterious, missing foreman is a diabolical genius."

"Sykes's house? You do take me to all the best places."

Twelve

SYKES HADN'T BEEN HOME IN DAYS.

The cold, almost-metallic scent of emptiness filled the small flat he rented. Perry dragged her fingertips over the dining table. All she could smell were the remnants of Garrett's cologne. He'd declined to put it on that morning out of deference for her senses, but it lingered in his skin enough for her to be haunted by it.

"Anything?" He leaned against the doorjamb, arms crossed over his chest.

"Nothing." Almost as if… "Nothing human anyway." Human scent imprinted everything they touched, most especially their homes. Only blue bloods gave off no scent. The bed was made, the sheets folded with an almost military precision. What wasn't she seeing? "What do you think?"

"I don't think he lives here."

"What?" As soon as she said it, she began to see the signs. If Sykes lived here, he didn't spend a great deal of time at home.

"Mallory said he likes to drink."

If Sykes was gin-stricken, then he didn't fit the

mold. The place was too clean. "So you think this is just a facade?" Perry asked, crossing to the door.

"Nobody seems to know much about him, except that he rarely comes in early." Garrett scratched at his jaw. "It's all adding up. Fifty quid it's Sykes."

"Fifty quid it's Steel Jaw," she countered, a nervous little shiver sliding over her skin. What were the odds that after she'd cut half of Hague's face off, now there were rumors of a man with a steel jaw prowling the East End, just as two girls were murdered—and the events weren't related? She could ask Garrett; he was a sporting man. If she could explain how she knew about the doctor.

Or perhaps Sykes, Hague, and Steel Jaw were the same person? But how would he disguise his deformation? Synthetic skin? It was never quite the same as real skin, but it helped disguise mechanical enhancements if one could afford the exorbitant price.

Then she remembered something. "Sykes has a beard, doesn't he?"

"As thick as the hair on his head allegedly."

Her heart started pounding. "Do we have any old cases like this?" Garrett had access to more case files than she did, and she rarely bothered to go through them. "Cutting out a girl's heart is a rather distinctive murder pattern."

She held her breath, hoping that Hague had been indiscreet in the past. Moncrieff had evidently covered Hague's tracks in the fire, but perhaps there were others. Men like that never stopped. They had to start somewhere, and perhaps Garrett would recall word of it. She needed to let him in on the Hague angle somehow. By herself, she was clever enough to pick out facts and put them together, but working with Garrett always produced better results.

"Nothing, as I can recall. And the experimental aspects are definitely unusual." He sighed. "Well, no sign of Sykes but we might as well search the place while we're here. Do you wish to take the washroom?"

"My pleasure," she drawled. "I shall leave you the bedchamber."

Several minutes later, she made her first discovery in a jar on the vanity. The jar was filled with inch-long hairs of a russet brown. "What the devil?"

Garrett poked his head through the door. "What is it?"

She held up the jar. "Someone collects his hair clippings."

"No toenails?"

"That's disgusting." Still, she opened the jar and unrolled the small leather kit that Fitz had given her onto the vanity. Tucked in each slot was a small glass tube with a rubber seal. Using thin pliers, she popped several hairs into a tube and capped it for Fitz to examine at the lab. Just in case.

The hair troubled her. If it was Hague's, then it was a good deal lighter than it had been. The man had thick, almost-black hair that he combed precisely into place. A little niggle of doubt washed through her.

"Anything?" Perry tucked the kit behind her belt. Garrett had given her a detailed description of Sykes from the witnesses—thick brown beard, gruff voice, tall and stocky with the sort of shoulders that belonged on a dockworker. It didn't sound like Hague at all, but he might have disguised himself. The hair proved otherwise, unless he'd taken it from someone else. One of his victims? Why would he keep it here? She leaned forward, her coat riding up over her hips as she took one last look behind the mirror.

"Nothing you'd wish to see." His voice sounded slightly distracted.

There was a flicker of movement in the mirror and Perry looked up, catching his eyes directly on her bottom. "You're right," she drawled, and those devilish blue eyes lifted to meet hers in the reflection. The damned man smiled.

Slowly her heart began to beat a little faster. *Treacherous thing*. It wasn't the first time she'd caught him admiring certain female characteristics. Still a part of her felt flushed and heated that this time it was her. As a young girl she'd been hopelessly tall and slender, and until she'd finally grown into her body, she'd been prone to clumsiness. Men hadn't looked at her then, not like this. The only one who'd ever seen something attractive in her had been a monster.

Dressing as a man had its advantages, but sometimes she wished she could acknowledge her female desires. Sometimes she wished that a man would look at her like that, and now Garrett was and she didn't completely trust it...

"Stop thinking so much about it," he said, lifting one hand to grip the door frame. An eminently masculine pose that flexed the muscle in those strong arms. That smile grew, stretching in an entirely satisfied way across his face. "You've colored up."

"I'm not thinking about it."

"No?" Far too satisfied with himself. "You look pretty when you blush."

Soft, dangerous words.

"And I'm not pretty when I'm not blushing?"

"You're pretty when you smile. That shy little smile I can win from you if I work hard. You don't smile enough, do you realize that?"

She didn't smile enough?

Garrett's arm lowered. "And you're pretty when you get that stubborn look on your face, which means I have no chance of winning the argument. I still try. Because I enjoy teasing you. Or when you're focused on beating me in the ring when we're sparring. And you're dangerously alluring when you're soft and relaxed and drinking blud-wein... In fact, I think I like you best like that."

His gaze lost its focus and she knew he was picturing it. Holding her in his arms. Slowly dragging her leather leggings down her long, slender legs... "You let me see *her* then. The woman I got a glimpse of at the opera. The woman who ran her hands all over me in that alley. The woman who smiles and teases and looks at me as if she's stripping me naked." He took a step toward her.

Perry took a step back. This wasn't what she'd expected. "*Her?*" she replied nervously. "You make it sound as if I'm two different people." Her back hit the wall.

"You are." Garrett stopped. Looked at her. "I know she's in there somewhere. You just like to hide her, to keep her locked away so that no one sees her. I don't know why. I know you don't like letting me—or anyone—know your secrets, but I wish you'd let me in." His fist tightened. "It's growing increasingly frustrating. I never pushed because I thought you would tell me in your own time. But you have no intention of revealing anything, do you?"

Because one secret would lead to another, and Perry didn't know how to tell him who she was. She wanted to, she suddenly realized, with a fierceness that almost ached. Garrett was the only one who might understand.

And she knew immediately what he'd do if he found out what the duke and Hague had done to her.

"There's nothing interesting about me," she replied quietly. For his own damned sake.

"I'd beg to differ."

That brought heat into her cheeks. "What are you doing?"

Garrett arched a brow.

"This flirtation," she said. "You never paid one ounce of attention to me before, and now you're flirting. And…you kissed me last night."

"Did I?" Noncommittal, damn him. "That wasn't a kiss, Perry."

Perry made as if to shove past him, but he was blocking the washroom door. Filling it with his body. Sometimes she didn't notice just how tall he was. "Move."

"Why should I?"

"I have a dozen reasons. Most of them involving rather painful nerves and certain pressure points."

Slowly he gave way, crossing his arms over his broad chest. Bare inches separated his hard body from the other side of the door frame. She could fit through. If she squeezed.

Damn him, why was he pushing at her like this? She was so angry she wanted to kick him. Did he think this was a jest?

Suddenly he leaned close, the heated spice of his cologne overwhelming her. The largeness of his body caged her in, trapping her against the doorjamb. If she turned her face, her lips would brush his jaw. *Do it.* Her treacherous heart leaped into her throat.

"I have one thing to say in my defense about the kiss…" Garret whispered, sending shivers across her skin. "You asked me to." Then he was gone, pushing past her and sauntering back into the main room. "The next time you ask, I'm not going to be a gentleman, Perry."

She collapsed back against the doorjamb as he vanished. *Bloody hell.* This was getting out of hand. Idle flirtation was one matter, but he didn't sound idle at all. Not anymore. No, he sounded as if he had no doubt that she'd ask him to kiss her again.

Stomach dropping through the pit of her abdomen, Perry pushed away from the door frame. Time to pull herself together. She could barely think with the nightmare of Hague and this mysterious killer looming at the edges of her life, and now Garrett was confusing her.

"This needs to stop," she blurted.

Garrett froze, a slightly incredulous expression lighting his face. "What?" His brows drew together. "Why?"

She skirted around him. "We both know this is a game. It's…it's been amusing, but…you're my friend, Garrett."

"Which didn't stop you at the opera. You weren't thinking about friendship then, Perry. Now things have changed—"

"I don't want them to."

His brows shot up. "You don't want—" Garrett gave a shaky laugh. "I cannot believe this. You"—his jaw tightened—"you have that look on your face."

"The one that says this isn't an argument you can win?"

Nothing.

She watched a dozen emotions roll across his face like clouds covering the sun. Thinking. Always dangerous. Garrett rarely fought with her. He outpaced her. One moment she would think the argument over, and the next she'd realize that he'd flanked her and was coming back at her from another direction.

"Whatever you're plotting, don't," she advised. "I can't think about this— about what's going on between us right now. I do know it probably isn't a good idea."

"Too messy," he agreed, with a telling gleam in his eye.

"Yes."

"And you would have to take a risk."

There was no answer to that. He wasn't arguing, but she couldn't see where his slippery mind was going with this...

The anger melted out of him. Definitely not a good sign. "Fine. Let's play this your way. No more touching. No teasing. Back to the way things were, which means—" He reached out, his fingers pausing just before they brushed the hair off her face. His eyes were smoldering. Daring her. The touch sent shivers racing along her skin. "Definitely no more kisses."

She swallowed. "You said you didn't kiss me."

"I lied." The hand dropped and Garrett stepped back, his expression closing over. "For what it's worth, I was willing to take the chance." With a clipped nod, he turned and strode out into the streets.

Perry stared after him. *I was willing to take the chance…* The thought of it ached more than she'd thought it would.

She'd earned that. And she knew it in her heart too. But Garrett didn't understand. If she didn't stop this now, he'd destroy her. She'd never be able to be what he wanted, and she didn't think she'd be able to withstand seeing the disappointment in his eyes when he realized that.

No more kisses…

Damn him.

❧

Hours later, Garrett stepped out of the White Hart with Perry at his heels. They'd spent the intervening hours questioning local businesses about the mysterious Mr. Sykes. This close to the factories, soot clung to the white walls of the pub they'd exited, making it seem as though it too was choking on the taste of coal. The moment he stepped outside the pub, the smell of piss and rotting fish hit him in the face like a shovel, and Garrett tried to stop breathing.

Perry's delicate little nose wrinkled and she tucked her hand up in front of her face, no doubt breathing in the scent of the Bourbon vanilla that she dabbed at her wrists. He'd bought it for her years ago when she complained about the filthy places he dragged her to. "For a man known to have a certain proclivity for drink, Sykes rarely imbibes much at all," she said.

Just one pint of ale every Friday night, the man behind the bar had murmured. Ten o'clock regular.

"So either Mallory is lying about him being a drunk—"

"Or Sykes allows him to believe it," she replied, a small frown furrowing her brow. "Why?"

"He needs an excuse to explain his absence at work. Mallory said in his first statement that Sykes never arrives before ten."

"So what's he doing until ten?"

A flash of the darkened laboratory swept to mind. "He's in the laboratory. I'll bet a quid on it." The more he thought about it, the more it made sense. "The factory shuts down at night—or at least it used to until the recent factory burnings put them on double shifts. The equipment we saw down there requires boilers. Noise and smoke. So he goes in the morning to see to the girls and do…whatever he's doing, because the work in the factory shields him from discovery. Nobody would hear him or notice a little extra smoke. Explains why he's there late too. Or maybe he doesn't leave. I'm fairly certain he rarely stays at his home."

Another little frown, her eyes a million miles away. "I like the theory, but I don't believe we should discard others." A little hesitation. "I want to go through some old case files when we get back to the guild. See if anything like this has happened before."

"I've never known you to be so eager to review old

files." Perry preferred to leave the paperwork to either him or the clerks.

She didn't reply. She was still staring at nothing as she strode at his side with her hands in her pockets. This wasn't the first time he'd thought that Perry was troubled. But if he asked her, he knew he'd not get an answer. Best thing to do was wait her out, much as he hated it.

Garrett glanced down, avoiding a wooden crate and the small boy curled up beside it. He absently flicked some chink toward the lad, who plucked the shilling out of the air in surprise. Nothing else he could damned well do to help the children littering the streets. For a moment his expression darkened and he shot a look toward the gleaming Ivory Tower that soared over London, home to the blue bloods and, most important, the prince consort and his puppet queen.

The crowd parted around them, men and women alike shooting them blank-faced stares. Nighthawks weren't as hated as the blue bloods of the Echelon, but they were still the law. For the humans that lived in this borough, they were little better than the pox. Recent riots had fueled the tension, and martial law had only recently been lifted. The prince consort might have crushed the spirit of the people for the moment, but Garrett had the vague sensation of thunder brewing in the distance.

He'd always felt safe before, but for some reason the hairs along the back of his neck were standing on end. This was more than the rumble of discontent among the human classes.

He knew that feeling.

The type of feeling he'd always had when he worked the streets as a lad. As if someone was watching them.

Placing a hand in the small of Perry's back, he directed her around a barrow boy.

"I thought you weren't going to touch me."

"I think we've got eyes on our tail," he replied. "Pretend you see something in the window that you're interested in."

The street was narrow, edged by several pubs and shops. With the afternoon light fading, the streetlamps were few and far between and wouldn't be lit by the lamplighter until later. Perry arched a dubious brow, then turned, dutifully pointing something out to him.

"A butcher," she murmured. A full pig carcass hung in the window and the butcher glanced up at their interest, his hands swiftly wrapping a piece of meat in waxed paper. "And they call us barbaric with our thirst for blood."

"See anything?"

A quick glance. "Dozens of people. It's late afternoon, Garrett. Are you certain you're not simply—"

"Five quid we're being followed," he countered.

She rarely took his bets. He always won. Perry's lips thinned. "Fine. Let's draw them out, whoever they are."

As she turned to separate, he caught her arm above the elbow, a fierce flash of heat spiraling through him. "No."

Perry twisted, throwing him off with a dark glare. "Don't," she warned.

"Perry." He caught up to her, the street vanishing

into a chiaroscuro landscape. The idea of watching her walk away from him into potential danger was more than he could bear, particularly following the incident at the factory. "I'm not going to let you—"

A distressed sound echoed in her throat. Garrett looked down in surprise.

"Don't hold me back," she whispered. "I know what happened at the factory. I know how poorly I reacted. I promise I won't do it again. I'll hold myself together. I can *do* this."

She was thinking he didn't believe her capable? "I don't give a damn about that." One look at her showed she didn't believe him. *Bloody hell.* "Fine. Separate. Let's play a little cat and mouse. You draw him. I'll double back and see if I can get a line on him."

At least if he sent her ahead through the streets, she'd be a little safer and he could keep an eye on her. Garrett slipped the small aural communicator from his pocket and clipped the brass clockwork piece in his ear, insisting she do the same with hers.

They separated, making a great show of her being interested in something farther down the street. Garrett shook his head, shoved his hands in his pockets, and stalked up one of the alleys, snapping his fingers to catch the attention of several sprawling youths as though to question them.

He gave her two minutes, feeling the tick of every second. Then he shimmied up one of the old rusted ladders attached to the building beside him until he stood on the rooftop, with its excellent vantage point.

She was gone.

Not something that should concern him, as she

could move quickly when she wished, but the knot of dread in his stomach wouldn't relax. Garrett traced over the rooftops. Laborers were beginning the long trudge home and the streets bustled with activity, hawkers crying out their wares.

"Lovely bit o' mutton!"

"Some flowers for your lass? Buy her favors! Pretty daisies! Or perhaps some violets?"

And there… The lean figure striding up the center of Abagnale Street. No sign of anyone paying her undue attention. Except…a tall man with his bowler hat pulled low over his eyes, Garrett couldn't see the front of him, but the man stopped as she did, pretending to examine the nearest barrow, and then continued on as soon as Perry started walking again.

What were the chances that the man following her sported an almost Prussian beard?

"Got him," Garrett murmured, knowing that she'd hear him through the aural communicator. "Thirty paces behind you. I think it's Sykes."

Even through the earpiece he could hear her intake of breath. "I'll play lure then."

Lure. His pace quickened, knowing she'd try to tempt the stranger out of the crowd. Which meant somewhere isolated.

The next corner she took, she strolled left.

"Perry, I can't see you," he snapped. "Get back on the main street."

"Is he following?"

Garrett risked a look. "Yes, damn it. Don't make any more turns. I'm coming." He began to run, skating over the roof tiles and leaping between houses. He was breathless by the time he reached the street she'd turned down, though not from exertion.

No sign of her. "Where are you?"

"Third alley," she murmured quietly. Which meant she didn't want others to hear her.

Sound crashed through the device in his ear. Garrett winced and clapped a hand over the brass piece. "Perry?"

No answer. Just another jarring sound. An almost feminine grunt, as if she'd been hit. "Got him!"

Garrett ran.

Hitting the edge of the roof, he leaped out into the air, landing with a thud in the alley below. Perry was grappling with the man. She hit him in the throat with an open chop of the hand, and the moment he staggered backward, she spun and kicked him in the face. The man stumbled.

That's right, you bastard. No easy prey here.

The moment the stranger saw Garrett, he took off, fists pumping at his sides as he pounded down the narrow reaches. Pitted brickwork lined the alley, full of shadows.

"Got him!" Perry darted after him.

"No!" Damn her! Garrett went after her.

It wasn't enough. The stranger ran directly at the brick wall at the end of the alley, then hit the ground in a slide, feet first. There was a small, timber door in the wall, probably an entrance into a cellar somewhere. The stranger hit it and vanished into the darkness as it splintered.

Perry sped up.

"Don't you dare!"

She hit the ground in a slide, her coattails splashing through a puddle of icy mud. Garrett lunged forward, snatching her by the arms as her legs and hips disappeared inside the small opening.

He yanked her back, jerking her legs out of the way. A second later a large meat hook bit into the dirt from within. Garrett caught a glimpse of a pair of dark, rabid eyes and then the man was gone.

"What the hell is wrong with you?" he roared. "We don't know what's down there!"

Perry scrambled to her feet, brushing off her coat. Her face had paled. "An onion cellar, by the smell of it."

Immediately he knew he'd taken the wrong tone with her, but she was going to be the death of him. "You didn't know that. And you could have ended up gutted."

"I'd heal," she snapped. "And he's getting away."

She shoved open the door of the building, revealing a small home with a pair of startled women looking up from the hearth. One of them pointed toward the window at the back, her hand clapped to her chest. "He...he went through there."

Out into the other alley. Garrett staggered to a halt in the empty confines, cursing under his breath. "Can you smell him?"

"Nothing but bloody onions." Perry exchanged a wary glance with him. "He has no personal scent."

A blue blood, then. Although from the speed he'd moved at, that was already certain.

"His clothes?" Garrett asked, for she could often track a man to within ten inches of his home.

"Laundered recently. Damn it. This whole area

smells like tar. I can't get anything else!" She kicked a crate, sending a cat flying from its midst, which startled the pair of them. "It had to be Sykes. He must have seen us at his home."

Bending over, Garrett caught his breath. Now that he had a moment, anger started to burn. "You nearly got yourself hurt. What the hell were you thinking?"

That put her back up. "I was thinking that this could be the bastard who cut those poor girls' hearts out!" There was a strange quiver in her voice. "I need to find him, and this was the best chance we had."

"Find him! Not get yourself killed! You're a blue blood, damn it, but you're not invincible!"

"Would you have stopped Byrnes?" she snapped. "I'm just as good as he is!"

"You don't have to prove that to me."

"Maybe I'm not proving it to you! Maybe it's for me?" There was a flash of wild eyes. Frightened eyes. Swiftly masked. "Forget I said such a thing."

Like hell. He grabbed her arm. "What's this all about? You've more than proved your worth over the years." Sudden understanding made his grip tighten. "This is about the factory, isn't it?"

Perry struggled. "It's…not just the factory."

"Yes, it is," he said. "You think you have something to prove to yourself." She looked up. The depth of emotion in her eyes almost drowned him but Garrett steeled himself. "You're off the case."

"*What?*"

"If you're not thinking clearly, then you're a danger to yourself." He dragged his arm out of the way as she reached for him. "No. I mean it, Perry."

Her jaw dropped open. "You son of a bitch. Don't you dare."

"Desk duty. For three days. Until you can prove to me that you can keep a calm head."

"You can shove that—"

"Don't make it a week," he warned.

"If you're doing this because of what's happening between us—"

"I'm doing this because you were reckless," he snapped back.

Perry's mouth worked, her eyes flashing mutinously. Pressing her lips together over some rather choice words, he imagined. "As you wish, sir." Biting the words out. "And now we've lost him. He'll be miles away or gone to ground."

Better that than to risk her life. His nostrils flared. He could, in part, understand her frustration. "Time to return to the guild and discover if Byrnes has had any more luck with Ava. And you could definitely do with a bath." He glanced down at her muddy boots and leggings. "If Doyle doesn't dunk you in the water trough outside before he lets you on his precious carpets."

He didn't say anything else. He wasn't sure if he trusted himself not to make the situation worse.

And he wasn't completely certain if she wasn't correct in his reasons for doing this.

❧

It was a long trip back, using trains and omnibuses the way they used to before he'd been promoted. Perry rubbed at her eyes as Garrett opened the front door to the guild. What a long, confusing day, capped off by that horrendous chase. She could smell the rot of the streets clinging to her boots and clothes and, worse, to her skin. All for nothing. The bastard had gotten away, and now Garrett was going to put her behind a desk for the next three days. He'd keep her there the whole time too, just to prove his point.

Had she been reckless? Perry stepped under his arm, deliberately ignoring him as he held the door for her. The moment she'd seen the stranger following her, a white light seemed to go off in her head. If she'd stopped and thought about it, she'd have talked herself out of giving chase into the cellar, but not because of the risk.

Because she was frightened.

There. She'd admitted it to herself.

Doubt gnawed at her from within. All she could see was that laboratory again. Screaming, pounding at the walls, lost in the dark... Unable to breathe. Her vision narrowing down to a tiny pinhole and numbness tingling in her lips.

No matter how strong she'd made herself, how many ways she knew how to kill a man, the moment her past reared its ugly head, she became nothing more than a quivering mess.

"There you are!" Doyle barreled through the foyer, his face flushed and angry. "I've 'ad lads out searchin' for you for 'ours. You oughtn't be traipsin' the streets like you used to."

Perry was brushed aside as the old man clucked and cooed over Garrett. She shook off her maudlin thoughts. Time for that later. She had to focus again. Prove to Garrett that she wasn't a risk to herself.

"You've a visitor." Doyle slipped Garrett's coat off his shoulders.

Perry flung off her muddy gloves and raked her hair out of her eyes. She needed a cheroot and a glassful of blood with a heavy dash of whiskey in it. Then those case files.

But first... She met Garrett's eyes. "I owe you an apology."

Surprise lit his features. Followed by wariness. He crossed his arms over his chest. "I'm listening."

"You were right. I should have thought about it first. It was reckless." Her cheeks burned. "And it did have something to do with what happened at the factory."

"Apology accepted." Garrett took the small tumbler of blood that Doyle passed him. "We'll discuss it later in more detail. You're still on desk duty for three days, however."

Doyle looked her up and down, eyeing the small trail of mud she was leaving on the rugs. Trying to pretend he wasn't as curious as hell about that little encounter. He gossiped like an old woman.

"Thank you for accepting my apology, sir."

"Don't know 'ow she always gets covered in muck, and 'ere's you with the polish still on your boots," Doyle muttered as Perry stalked past him. "By the way, I put 'Is Grace upstairs in your study. Sent the best of Lynch's blud-wein stock up too."

"His Grace?" Garrett murmured.

Perry was only half listening. But she paused at the base of the stairs as Doyle continued setting Garrett to rights, brushing off his coat and straightening his collar.

"Didn't you get me message? I thought one of the lads must've caught up to you. Let you know the duke was 'ere," Doyle said.

Duke. She had this horrible sensation of lightness, as if she wasn't in her body anymore. Perry's foot moved mechanically, started up the first stair, but her head was turning, locking on Doyle, on the way his lips moved, even though she felt like she couldn't hear the words anymore. There was a strange buzzing in her ears.

"The Duke of—?"

"Moncrieff," a smooth voice announced from above.

Thirteen

EVERYTHING IN PERRY WENT STILL, HER LUNGS LOCK-
ing tight as though there was a clamp around them.
His voice swept through her, taking her back ten years
into the past. Smooth, cultured. The kind of voice that
slid over the skin like velvet in certain situations, or
could cut like a knife in others.

A man stepped out of the shadows on the floor
above, pressing both ringed hands on the railing as
he surveyed the room below. The slightest of smiles
touched his mouth as his gaze locked on Garrett.

Had he not seen her? Did he not recognize her?
Perry made a small, choked sound in her throat, but
none of the men noticed.

"My apologies," Moncrieff continued. "I heard you
speaking and thought to introduce myself." He started
walking along the railing toward the stairs. Still not
looking at her.

Perry's gaze shot toward the door in the room.
She couldn't run. Not if he wasn't hunting her. And
not without alerting Garrett or Doyle to the fact that
something was seriously wrong.

She could see how that would play out. If Garrett caught one hint that she was terrified of this man, he'd set himself between them.

No. She had to be strong. For his sake.

"Alastair Crawford, Duke of Moncrieff," he announced, taking the first step down. "Recently returned from Scotland."

Perry pressed her back against the wallpaper, trying to push herself through the wall. She didn't know what to do. In all the scenarios she'd imagined, she'd never pictured this. Never pictured other people being involved. Her heart was thundering in her ears, her body trembling as if to flee, but there was nowhere to go. Moncrieff wasn't stupid. He'd have the building watched, guards in place—

Garrett started toward them, giving her a deceptively lazy look. He'd picked up on her tension, at least. "Your Grace, a pleasant surprise." He paused at the foot of the stairs, placing his body between her and the duke. "Garrett Reed, Acting Guild Master of the Nighthawks. What may I do for you?"

"A word, if I might?"

The Moncrieff's entire focus was on Garrett. And that made the coldness shiver deep inside her. If he wanted to cut at her, that was the best way to do it.

Garrett shot her a questioning look.

Somehow she forced a smile to her lips. *No. Nothing is wrong.*

The moment his back was turned, she let out the breath she'd been holding. *Everything is wrong. I have to leave.*

Her heart fisted in her chest. For years she'd worked

out precisely what she'd do if the Moncrieff ever found her, but she'd never considered just how much it would hurt to run. To leave behind everything that she knew. Everyone that she cared for.

Perry stared at Garrett's broad back as he strode up the stairs, her heart breaking in that moment. She'd miss him so desperately. He was the one who'd made her stay here, made her feel safe and wanted. Slowly he'd helped her learn to trust again, to relax around other blue bloods. All of the quiet, teasing conversations they'd had flickered through her mind. All of the moments she'd wished she'd been brave enough to turn her face and press her lips to his. That moment today, when she could have admitted to him how she wanted to take that risk too.

Gone.

She looked up. Realized that another pair of eyes was watching her. Drawing their own conclusions, no doubt. Perry swallowed against the fist in her throat, forcing all of the expression off her face as the Moncrieff glanced back at Garrett.

And smiled.

Her first instinct was to run or hide. But he'd seen her. Looked right at her. He had to know it was her. And she wasn't leaving this room until she discovered what he wanted from Garrett.

∽

The duke settled into the chair across from the desk as if he owned it, lacing his fingers together and giving Garrett an unreadable look. His blond hair was perfectly coiffed, matching the gold embroidered thread through his coat. A pristine cravat circled his throat, and there was a sword sheathed at his side. He looked like a man who had the utmost confidence in using it too.

"I'll cut straight to the point," the duke announced, dropping the faintly amused smile. It slid off his face as if it had never been there. "I want to hire you to find someone for me."

Garrett leaned his elbows on the table and examined the duke. He had this itching sensation down the back of his neck. As though something here wasn't what it seemed. Perry's unusual reaction downstairs only pushed him closer to the edge.

"Of course, Your Grace," he replied smoothly. "I will be happy to review your case and set someone—"

"No. I want you to be in charge of the investigation. Not one of your little lackeys."

The arrogance of that statement made Garrett stiffen. But what the devil could he say? He still hadn't stood before the Council and pleaded his case. When he did, this man would hold Garrett's fate in his hands.

"Perhaps you could explain to me precisely who you want me to find." That wasn't a yes.

The duke stared at him through those arctic eyes. "I want you to find Octavia Morrow for me."

Garrett frowned. He had little acquaintance with the duke, but the name of Octavia Morrow seemed to access a memory somewhere. Then it struck him. "Octavia Morrow," he said bluntly. "Your supposedly deceased thrall."

"Octavia's not dead. She orchestrated the entire matter."

"Let me be blunt, Your Grace. Why the hell should I believe that? Blood was found all over your bedroom, half the manor was on fire, and there's been no sign of her since. Several of the servants claim to have overheard an argument between you earlier that day—" What else could he remember from the papers?

"Don't forget the bloodied shirt of mine that was found in the wash basket." The duke was clearly enjoying himself.

Garrett settled into silence. Either the duke was the best card player he'd ever seen, or he was telling the truth. "You're suggesting that she staged her own death and laid the blame on you. Why would she do that?"

For the first time, the duke's composure wavered. "I intend to find out," he said in the sort of voice that made Garrett's hackles rise.

The expression on the man's face was the one thing that convinced Garrett he was telling the truth. This man hadn't killed Octavia Morrow. No, he genuinely thought she'd staged her own death to implicate him, and he wanted revenge.

The case suddenly fascinated him. Garrett knew very little of it, as Lynch had dealt with it himself, but the case notes would be here somewhere. And if Lynch hadn't found anything, there hadn't been anything to find.

"There's no one else who held some sort of grudge against her?"

"Octavia was willful and made few friends, but nobody wished her any harm. No, I have full confidence that she ran."

"Why?"

The duke leveled a gaze on him, as if daring him to meet it. If Moncrieff thought Garrett could be intimidated, then he would soon learn he was wrong. Garrett had grown up in streets, where men didn't fight with words, but with any sharp—or blunt—instrument they could lay hands to. If you showed a hint of fear, of backing down, then they would cut you down just to prove that they could.

"We argued," the duke finally admitted. "Octavia disagreed with some research I was involved in."

Garrett frowned. "Do you have any idea where she might have gone?"

"I believe you might start with her father."

Taking up his spring pen, Garrett dashed off a few notes. "Was there anyone else who might have wished her harm? Or wanted to discredit you?"

"She ran—nobody harmed her."

"And I have only the word of a man accused of murdering her as proof of that," Garrett replied. "If you want me to investigate the matter, then I will. Thoroughly. I shall take your opinion into consideration, of course."

Surprisingly the duke smiled. "I see why Lynch likes you. Do as you will, then. I am quite open to being questioned, considering I have nothing to hide."

For the next ten minutes the duke answered his questions, leaving Garrett with a list of places to start. Miss Morrow had few friends among the Echelon—she'd been described as somewhat of a wallflower—but there were one or two debutantes she'd associated with. Nobody had seemed to hold any sort of grudge against her, but that was due more to her unassuming nature.

Garrett put down the spring pen. "I find myself exceedingly curious as to why you offered for her, considering her nature. You're a man of a certain standing. You could have had any debutante, but you chose an earl's daughter without any seeming accomplishments or grace in society. It baffles me."

"Society didn't suit her." The duke's eyes lost their focus for the slightest moment. "It didn't mean that she didn't have her own unique charm. Octavia had little interest in snaring my attention—a rarity, I assure you. I could have had anyone, but I chose the girl who didn't want me."

No doubt that appealed to someone of the duke's arrogance. Garrett stood. "I'll conduct some preliminary inquiries and meet with you again, once I have some of the groundwork in place. I assume you'll expect regular progress reports?"

The duke gave him a little smile. "You assume correctly. The sooner this matter is taken care of, the better."

"The Keller-Fortescue murders must be my priority, but I shall certainly give it my full attention once we have dealt with the murders."

"I would rather—"

"As *soon* as they are dealt with," Garrett interrupted, holding the door open for the duke.

Not a man given to being denied anything, the duke opened his mouth again.

"Actually," Garrett said, "you could help me with that—in the interest of solving the murders all the more swiftly…"

Moncrieff arched a brow, bowing to defeat with a certain sense of irritation. "Could I?"

"Last week you were with the party that guided the Russian Embassy group through the draining factory."

"Where the two girls were murdered," the duke drawled. "I've read about it in the papers. One can scarce imagine such a thing. But yes, I was with the party. I own an interest in the factory itself, as well as two others. Both the Dukes of Malloryn and Caine are also major stakeholders. Why?"

That was a surprise. He'd thought the factories were government owned. "Were you associated with either Miss Keller or Miss Fortescue?"

"I see. My dubious past rears its ugly head again. Of course I'm a suspect."

"I didn't say that, Your Grace," Garrett countered smoothly. "It's an unusual neighborhood for their bodies to turn up in. I'm trying to establish a link between the factory and both girls."

"You do realize I've been gone for nearly ten years. I've only been back in London perhaps two weeks. I have faint acquaintance of the Keller girl and her father. He and I do business together. Miss Fortescue, on the other hand, propositioned me the night I returned to society. Unsurprisingly. I *am* the only duke in London without a thrall and her proposition isn't the only one I've received. We danced once or twice, as I'm certain several sources will corroborate." He frowned. "I also believe we took a stroll in Hyde Park. Flavored ices. Yes, that's right. That was her. She didn't suit me."

How difficult it must be to remember one girl

among many. "And the Russians? Would either of them have come into contact with the two deceased?"

This time the glare was forceful. "Tread carefully, Master Reed. The Romanov court is a dangerous place. They're not like us, not at all. They don't understand our rules or ways of doing things." Moncrieff gave a brief laugh. "The humanists plaguing us should consider themselves fortunate that they only have the Echelon to deal with. As to whether the Russians knew either of the girls, I would consider such acquaintance fleeting at best. And the prince consort is most interested in furthering acquaintance with the Russians. If you ask too many questions in front of certain ears, you might find yourself…removed."

"I'm only trying to find a murderer."

"And I'm only warning you to be careful. Russia is an important potential ally. In the grand scheme of things, Misses Keller and Fortescue are of little consideration."

Unimportant, to be precise. For the first time Garrett had a flash of empathy for what Lynch had been forced to deal with all these years. It set his teeth on edge to be beneath notice like this—like his mother had been, like all the humans in the city, the mechs…even himself.

"Thank you, Your Grace. Perhaps Malloryn or the Duke of Caine shall be able to shed further light on the situation."

"Perhaps."

They crossed to the stairs, the duke surveying the room.

Movement shifted below as Perry peered out from behind the open doorway she was loitering—or almost hiding—in.

"I do trust that you'll keep my confidence," the duke threw over his shoulder as he started down the stairs. "From all involved."

"You have my word."

"Let me fetch your coat, Your Grace," Doyle said with deference he rarely showed.

Moncrieff ignored him, glancing around the room, his cold gaze taking in everything. It paused on Perry, a considering look.

"Have we met?" the duke asked her, a somewhat unsettling smile crossing his face. "You look like someone I used to know."

Perry remained frightfully still. She'd never liked dealing with the Echelon. It was the only time when her aplomb slipped and her shyness bled through. Garrett could understand that. A few influential men knew there was a female blue blood among the Nighthawks, and though it wasn't illegal, it was frowned upon. "Your Grace, may I introduce Miss Perry Lowell," Garrett said, making it clear she was under his protection. "She serves as one of the members of my Hand."

"Perry." Surprisingly, a smile ghosted over the duke's lips and he glanced at her. "The peregrine, no doubt?"

Again Garrett looked back and forth between them. A part of him didn't like the attention the duke was giving her. Or perhaps it was simply the thought of any other man paying attention to what was his.

Not *his*. Damn it, he could feel his thoughts warping, taking on a darker edge. It was getting worse. If he couldn't control this, then he never would.

Perry stared back defiantly. "Yes, I was named for the peregrine."

"Swift and deadly," the duke murmured.

"I try to be," she replied.

Garrett might as well not have been in the room. Perry met the duke's stare, her eyes slowly darkening. The sight of it stirred something dark and protective within Garrett.

Doyle came back into the room with the duke's overcoat and top hat. The duke's gaze dropped, as if nothing unusual had occurred, and he slipped his arms through the great cloak as Doyle held it out. That faint, mocking smile played over his lips again.

"Very well, then," Moncrieff said, accepting his hat. "I want this matter concluded as swiftly as possible."

The duke disappeared with Doyle. Silence fell, thick and heavy, as Garrett and Perry listened for his tread and waited until the front door had closed. Perry let out a breath, then turned to him. "What did he want?"

Garrett started loosening his cravat. He didn't know what was going on in her mind, but he was still irritated with her. "To hire me for a private matter."

"You're not going to tell me?"

"Are you going to tell me what's bothering you?"

That mulish look was back.

"I thought not," he replied, crossing to the decanter and pouring himself a snifter of blud-wein. He needed it badly. "Do you want one?"

Perry shook her head. "Don't get caught up in his games, Garrett. You know what the Echelon is like. He'll be moving you like a pawn, playing at some game himself."

"You don't think I know that?" He threw the glass

back. It eased something within him, but it wasn't enough. It would never be enough.

They stared at each other. At an impasse.

"You have your duties," Garrett said softly. "Perhaps you should go and bathe, then see to making a list of the Echelon's master smiths—or those mech artisans in the Enclaves that could possibly create such a thing as a mechanical organ."

She lingered. As if she wanted to ask him something. But he'd set the terms between them today. All or nothing. He was damned tired of reaching for her and having her throw it back in his teeth.

Still, Perry looked troubled. As though she was fighting some thought that was tearing her in half. He'd never seen her like this and it worried him. His irritation washed out of him and he lifted a hand toward her. "Perry—"

She stepped back, that smooth mask sliding into place again. "You're right. I need to get clean."

The moment was lost. Perry turned and Garrett was left staring at her back with the horrible feeling that something momentous had been decided.

❧

What the hell was she going to do? The duke had recognized her. That little mention of the peregrine—the symbol of her father's House—was a certain sign, but why had he simply walked out? What was he playing at?

Perry had always thought that seeing the duke would be the worst nightmare she could imagine, but it wasn't. Seeing the duke with Garrett, knowing that

he watched as Garrett stepped between them protec-
tively, was worse. It locked her chest up tight with
panic until her head grew faint.

This was why she'd fled in the first place and
never gone home. The first time she'd realized that
Hague was keeping girls in the dungeons and doing
something awful to them, the Moncrieff had promised
her that if she ever breathed a word of it, he'd kill
her father. The shock of that threat, murmured in an
almost gentle voice, had torn her from her safe world.

And so, when she'd finally escaped, she hadn't
gone home.

Knowing how much her father would grieve
hurt her, but at least he was still alive to grieve.
Her sisters were happily married, each with several
children of their own. Nothing could change that.
They were safe.

But was Garrett safe?

The truth was becoming clearer in her mind, solidi-
fying with each detail.

She couldn't stay.

Could she?

Perry groaned, raking her hands through her still-
wet hair. The silence of the room was deafening, and
Garrett's words kept echoing in her head. Demanding
more from her than she could give.

She didn't realize she was moving until she was
through the door. Damn it, what had the duke asked
of him? She needed to know.

Night had fallen with economical grace as she
made her way to his rooms. Too many random
thoughts swirled through her head, but what beat in

her chest was the steady, dooming beat of an executioner's drum.

Perry rapped at his door with her knuckles, bruising them in her haste.

"Come in," Garrett called.

A shiver of breathlessness ran through her. Her hands were shaking but somehow she managed to open the door.

And there he was.

Shirtless.

"Garrett." Perry stopped on the threshold as if she'd been hit, staring at the naked expanse of his back.

He'd been shaving. Lather still decorated one cheek and he held the blade poised against his skin, his eyes locking on her in the mirror in surprise. Water dripped down his bare chest in the reflection, gleaming on the muscles. He'd discarded his shirt haphazardly over a chair, and his leather pants fit him snugly enough for a part of her to ache.

She'd seen him in a state of undress before. But she'd not expected it now, and the shock stole all of the words she'd been thinking of. Perry could only stare.

It took a moment for him to recover too. He cursed under his breath as his hand slipped and a bright line of red sprang up against the lather. Holding his cheek taut, he scraped the blade down his cheek, his attention returning to his task. "What do you want?"

You.

Slowly she shut the door. "May I speak with you?"

"Only if you have something interesting to say." Another stroke of the blade. His cheek was bare now and he angled his chin to shave beneath his jaw, wielding the blade with a dexterity she couldn't take her eyes off of. Her gaze slid over the faint red line on his cheek. Healing now, but she could scent the blood in the air. Hunger burned in her throat.

"Something along the lines of what we spoke of today. Secrets, for example," he continued. Flicking the last bit of lather from his jaw, he put the blade down and dabbed his face with a small wet towel. His skin was slightly pink and smooth, gleaming in the gaslight. Again he caught her looking at him in the mirror. "Otherwise, I have work to do. I planned on seeing what I could find out about—That's right. That's between the Duke of Moncrieff and myself. I know how much you like secrets."

"Garrett—"

He tossed the towel aside and turned toward her. Gaslight cast alluring shadows over his body. She'd seen it before. Felt each hard line of it in that alley. But the reality of it left her unable to tear her gaze away, her breasts aching and her sex growing damp with need.

"Now that's not fair," Garrett murmured. "No touching. No kissing. No looking at me like *that*, Perry." Slowly he crossed his arms over his chest. The muscle in his biceps rippled and she knew he'd done it deliberately. "Otherwise we'd have to stop pretending these are games, wouldn't we? We'd have to deal with the fact that things *have* changed between us. No going back. No pretending otherwise."

"You were the one avoiding me," she blurted.

His eyes were hot flame. "So this is punishment?"

"No." She looked up at all that leashed fury and hunger, all of it just for her. If she didn't take this chance there'd never be another. "Kiss me." It was the only thing that made sense right now. The only thing she wanted to think about.

A moment of shock widened his blue eyes. Then they narrowed. "Make up your bloody mind."

I'm frightened and I need you… All of that got lost on her tongue as she stepped toward him. Then her hands were on his face and she was reaching for him—or maybe he was reaching for her. Perry didn't know. She was fracturing inside, splintering into a thousand little pieces, and then one of his hands slid up the nape of her neck, cradling her scalp, and the other locked around her waist. Holding her together. Their mouths met and it was everything she'd ever hoped for.

Real.

Not like one of the thousand dreams she'd had of this moment. This was *real*. Garrett was kissing her and she could feel how much he wanted her. How much she wanted him.

A kiss so long denied. A yearning so long held that she felt it quivering deep within her. His tongue met hers. Lashed over it. He was right; sometimes he wasn't a gentleman. He was angry. She could feel it vibrating through the tense line of his shoulders. Perry dug her short nails into his back and he grabbed her wrists, forcing her back, back…

Her back hit the wall, but there was nowhere to go. Only him. Each hard inch pressed against her, his mouth devouring hers as he held her wrists pinned to the fine wallpaper.

And it wasn't enough. It would never be enough. She bit him, teeth sinking into the flesh of his lower lip, hard enough to draw blood. The taste of it exploded on her tongue and then they were both tearing at each other, teeth and lips and tongues tangling in a sudden urge to drink the other in.

He slammed her back against the wall, one hand sliding under her arse. Perry locked her legs around his hips, feeling the hot grind of his erection right where she wanted it.

"Damn it," he whispered, stealing a breath. His lips met hers on a groan that vibrated through his chest. "This is not—I'm not doing this. Not until you give me something, damn it—"

This was all she could give. The moment she'd seen him, she'd known she couldn't stay. The Moncrieff had found her now and he wouldn't back down. Nor would Garrett if he knew who she was. It hurt. That this could be the last night they had together. Perry kissed him, long and slow and hard, her hands sliding up to cup his cheeks. A quiver ran through his body and she rolled her hips, nudging against him, riding over the heated flesh digging into her hip. *Yes. This. Now.* One final good-bye.

Garrett sucked in a sharp breath. Then her hand was sliding down between them, the hard muscle of his stomach flinching beneath her exploring touch. Perry reached the edge of his waistband before he moved, capturing her wrist and shaking his head.

"No," he gasped, his eyes glassy with desire—and something else. She saw shadows there, stealing through his irises, sweeping away the beautiful blue.

Fierce need. "Perry, I have to be in control." Another shudder went through him. "I *need* to be."

Perry slid down his body as he stepped back, her boots hitting the floor. What was he doing? Her eyes flared wide. He couldn't be saying no. Not to this. Not now.

But he caught her hips and then he was turning her, her hands hitting the wallpaper. Pressing her hard against it, until her forehead rested against the embossed green-and-gold print and her breath wet her lips.

"Fuck," he whispered, pinning her there. "You come to me like this? After today?"

"I could go," she threw back over her shoulder, her eyes meeting his for one strained moment.

"You would, wouldn't you?" Something in his eyes darkened. "Too late for that, love."

Garrett's hands slid over her hips and tugged her belt open even as he pressed her against the wall. She was pinned by his weight, by the strength in his hard body. A delicious shiver went through her.

Fingers slid into her hair, knotting around it until he drew her head back. His other hand deftly dealt with the buttons on her trousers. Perry gasped.

"You don't get to say no anymore." He bit her neck, then suckled at the skin. The shock of it echoed through her, reminding her of other hungers. This wasn't the first time a blue blood had taken her blood. And she'd liked it once, perhaps too much. The ache in her nipples intensified.

"You don't get to pretend this isn't happening." Fingers skating lower, over her hip. Down. Finding the slit in her drawers.

His fingers found her, hot and wet and wanting. They paused for a moment as if surprised at something, then whispered over her flesh with long, slow strokes that stole the breath from her lungs. Perry groaned, rotating her hips, wanting more.

"You don't know how much I want to be inside you," he whispered. One teasing fingertip delved into her, then out again, dancing over her sex. "Fucking my way into you. Nice and slow. Until you're begging me for more."

He was going slowly enough to kill her. Perry slid her hand over his with a gasp, pressed it harder. More. She wanted more.

One hand wrapped around her throat. Curling her back into his body, her head thrown back against his shoulder. Trapped there as he wrought delicious damage on her.

"Yes," he whispered against her ear. "Right there?"

Perry bit her lip, trapping a moan. Her body spasmed as his finger rubbed over that one special spot. Again. And again. Destroying her. Tightening every nerve in her body until she was quivering. If he hadn't been holding her up, she would have fallen.

Her short nails raked the embossed figures on the wallpaper. *Please. Don't stop.* But his fingers were slowing, slowing, tracing teasing little circles that left her grinding against him, desperate for more.

"Everything has changed," he whispered, his hot breath on her sensitive neck. Lips brushed against her skin, the graze of teeth. "Admit it, damn you. Everything changed. And you wanted it to. That's why you wore that bloody dress at the opera. You wanted *this*."

"*Yes.*" The plea burned over her lips. The only truth she could ever give him.

A muscled thigh slid between hers, spreading her legs. "You want me."

Perry shook her head, quivering on the edge of ecstasy.

"Say it," he hissed, one finger broaching the wet heat of her body. Then two. Filling her. Stretching her. He stopped moving, both fingers buried deep within her. Leaving her on the edge. Waiting.

"I want you," she whispered. "Please...please don't stop."

"I don't intend to." His thumb caressed the center of all that feeling, and the edge crumpled beneath her feet.

One touch to fling her into the heart of all that sensation. One touch to break her. Perry cried out, pressing her trembling forehead against the wallpaper and leaning on it. *Oh God...* A sob caught on her breath. She barely felt him tugging her around, pressing her back against the wall. Perry looked up, her vision glazing.

Another long, slow, drugging kiss. Her shaking hands slid up over his shoulders tentatively. Muscle tensed beneath her touch and he drew back just enough to look at her. His eyes were black as night, the muscle in his jaw locked tight. "But I won't let you lock me out. Not again. If you want this—want me—then you're going to have to damned well tell me a few things."

Her heart punched behind her ribs and he saw it on her face.

Garrett's expression darkened, one finger pressing against her lips. "Either you talk to me, or things don't go any further." He caught her other hand and slid it lower. Over the thick bulge straining behind his pants. "You want this?" His hips thrust against her touch, rubbing the entire length of his cock against her hand. The expression on his face lost its focus, just for a moment, then tightened again. "Then you have to let me in. I won't settle for less."

Garrett took her hand away. Wouldn't let her reach for him. "No."

Hands tugged at her pants. He was doing up her buttons. Sliding her belt back into place. One last tug to notch it tight. The ache between her thighs intensified. Unfulfilled.

Perry's lips stung. She licked them, trying to work out what was going on. "Garrett?"

"Tomorrow," he said firmly, drawing away from her. "I'll give you tonight to think, but tomorrow we're going to talk. I'm tired of all the secrets between us at the moment. Aren't you?"

Perry's heart curled into a small tight ball in her chest. There would be no tomorrow. Tonight was meant to be good-bye. She slid her hand over his jaw, stepping closer, but he turned away and her lips met the smooth skin of his cheek instead. A gentle rebuff. *Don't... Let me have this one night with you. Please.*

But he was turning away, holding the door open for her. Like a gentleman. The idea of that almost brought a pained smile to her lips. After everything he'd just done to her, she knew he was no gentleman. Not underneath the smooth, cultured cravats and coats he

wore. Like the clothes he wore, the cultured veneer
was just that…a veneer.

Perry darted inside his guard and pressed her lips
to his in a chaste, gentle kiss that lingered. She never
wanted it to end, but then his hand was stroking her
face, subtle signs of his body withdrawing from her.

"Remember that," Perry whispered as she backed
through his door.

She would.

                 ⊱⊰

The door closed and Garrett splayed his fingers wide
against the timber, letting out the breath he'd been
holding. The scent of her perfume lingered, a ghostly
fragrance that haunted him. Reminding him of what
they'd just done. Of how he'd forced himself to let
her go.

And if the scent of her was difficult to forget, the
throbbing of his cock was just another reminder. He
could have had her. Should have. He'd seen the look
in her eyes as she left. Perry was gathering her wits
together, and he preferred her off-balance. If he gave
her too much time to think, he was afraid she'd only
find some other excuse to shove between them.

But if he'd given in to her… He'd set the terms
today and he meant to stand by them. For the first
time in his life, sex wasn't enough. He wanted more.
Wanted to explore this attraction between them.

If he had time.

Garrett flexed his fist, looking up. He could hear
her walking away, her steps getting firmer with each
stride. A knot twisted in his guts. What was he doing?

Drawing her closer when he should be holding her at arm's length. Keeping her safe from him.

"Damn it." He turned and stared at his bedchambers. Was this what he had to look forward to? A slow decline until he could no longer hide the truth of his condition? Holding everyone at bay? Pretending that he didn't want her when the truth was so very different?

Slowly his back hit the door and he slid down it, his legs drawn up in front of him. Garrett raked his hands through his hair. Truth: his CV levels were only going to increase. He had months, at most, before he started showing signs of the Fade.

Months in which to lie in bed alone at night, listening to the tick of the clock.

Or months in which to live his last breath, make something of himself, let himself love.

A whisper of longing swept through him. If he didn't have this looming over his head, would he push her away?

No. He wanted her too much. All his life he'd wondered if he would ever feel this way about a woman. He'd searched for it, charming dozens of women into his bed. Some of them had almost been clever enough or funny enough that he'd lingered, hoping that something in him would shift, that this would be the woman he could fall for.

And it never happened.

Until now.

Slowly he dragged his cupped hands down over his face and breathed into them. Of all the women he'd met, Perry had snuck under his guard when he wasn't looking.

He knew her, inside and out. Perry was the one person he trusted more than anyone else in the world, the one person he knew he could go to when he didn't know what to do. After Lynch had passed the rank of Guild Master onto Garrett's shoulders and left to face his own execution, Perry had been at Garrett's side when he'd told Rosalind the truth and gone to rescue Lynch. Lynch might never forgive him for that, but at least, on some elemental level, Garrett knew Perry would always be there for him.

Love was something that he'd always regarded in an almost mythic way, something he'd wanted but couldn't quite understand. He'd seen men and women stricken by it, and wondered when, or even if, that lightning bolt would ever strike him. Instead it had crept up on cat-silent feet, sinking its claws into him when he wasn't looking. It wasn't mythic. It wasn't an equation that could be solved or even something he could classify. It was trust and respect and the solid, grounding feel of her hand in his when he faced his problems. It was the idea of his closest friend becoming his lover, of exploring this feeling between them.

And he was frightened that he wasn't going to have that chance.

Dr. Gibson would track him down one day, or Doyle would notice how swiftly his blood decanters were being depleted, and then they'd both be required by law to report him.

He had a choice. Leave things as they were and die, never knowing the one thing he'd always wanted. Or let himself love her, knowing that he could never have forever with her.

It wouldn't be fair for him not to tell her the truth about his condition. He had to have her approval before he pursued this further. But the weight on his chest lifted. He could have Perry—for a time. Love her fast and hard, and then at the end of it, when his CV levels hit seventy-five, he'd hand himself in.

Better to live the life he had left than to spend every last minute thinking about her and wishing he had taken this chance.

If she'd let him.

Fourteen

LIGHT SPILLED OVER HIS DESK. GARRETT BLINKED AND pinched the bridge of his nose. He'd been staring too long at the case file. Most of the night, in fact, for that was dawn's first light, if he wasn't mistaken.

Pushing to his feet, he stretched, shooting the case file a filthy glance. The name "Morrow, Octavia" was etched along its spine. There were numerous reports on the night she'd fled. Details on the forensic evidence gathered at the scene, but barely anything on Octavia Morrow herself or any of the events following the night she disappeared.

What the devil was going on? Lynch was meticulous, and Garrett knew his handwriting well enough to recognize the notations. Anyone else looking at the file might not notice anything amiss, but Garrett knew his former master. No stone unturned, no fact left unchecked... Yet to all appearances, Octavia Morrow hadn't even left a trace of herself in the paperwork.

Garrett raked a tired hand over his face. He needed blood and the decanter in here was empty.

Leaving his study, he followed the sounds of

quiet conversation to the dining hall, greeting each Nighthawk by name and then helping himself to the sideboard. Byrnes glanced up from one of several dining tables, flicking out the morning's news sheet. He paused when he saw Garrett, then offered a wary nod.

Curse it. Garrett poured himself a glass of blood and made his way to the table. Appearances were everything, and the men needed to see the pair of them working together. And perhaps Perry was right about the way he was dealing with this. Not that he liked admitting it.

"My powers of deduction tell me you haven't slept a wink," Byrnes drawled. He laid the paper flat and leaned back in his chair. "One would almost think that you had women troubles, but you never have those, do you?"

Garrett bared his teeth in a smile and took the seat across from Byrnes instead of planting him a facer, as he'd have preferred. There was little doubt what the other man referred to. "Women are the last thing on my mind at the moment. I have two murdered girls, a laboratory straight from a penny dreadful, and now a private commission that seems to be muddying up waters that were as clear as the Thames in the first place."

Byrnes poured himself some coffee. The scent of it made Garrett's stomach lurch, but Byrnes seemed to be able to stomach small amounts of it, at least. "Indeed? Muddied waters…that sounds intriguing."

Garrett lowered the glass. Why the hell not? Byrnes occasionally had his uses. "Have you ever come across a case file that seemed lacking?"

"Lacking? In what context?"

"As if certain notes were missing from it."

Byrnes frowned. "Lynch oversaw the final closure of all case files. He would have noticed something."

The same line of thought Garrett himself had had. "The only man with access to the files is the head clerk. I sent a note an hour ago. He claims nobody's tampered with any of the files in his care."

"Are you suggesting that the file was tampered with before it was given to Mr. Morell?"

The only man who could do that was Lynch himself. "I don't know what I'm suggesting."

"Hmm." Byrnes leaned closer. "Which file?"

"The disappearance of Octavia Morrow."

"That's almost ten years old."

"Never solved," Garrett replied. "Lynch hates letting go of a case unanswered. And now there's not a single note in the file about any attempts made to track her. Not even a photograph or portrait of the girl."

"Someone tampered with it. Lynch would never leave a case like that."

"Exactly."

For a moment they were in perfect accord.

"But who could steal into the clerical wing without being seen?" Byrnes asked. "And why the sudden interest in the Morrow girl?"

"She's the commission."

Byrnes was at his best when there was a puzzle to be solved or something to be found. "It seems like the past is certainly coming to light again. The Duke of Moncrieff's return and now this, the mystery of poor Octavia Morrow being dredged out of the depths."

Those bright eyes locked on Garrett. "Who requested the commission? I know the duke graced us with his presence yesterday."

No point denying it. Garrett gave a terse nod.

"How very curious," Byrnes said.

"I want to know more about the case," Garrett replied. "I remember a handful of facts, but only what was shouted about in the broadsheets."

"Perhaps you should ask Perry. She seemed quite taken with the story in the papers the other morning."

"Perry?"

"Tall, slim girl. Rather serious expression, quiet, seems to prefer breeches to gowns. Looks rather smashing in red silk, though, wouldn't you say?"

Garrett frowned. There was a sense of something lurking beneath the words. "I know bloody well who she is. It surprised me, is all. She's not said a word to me about the duke."

"I wasn't aware that you were speaking much at the moment. Either of you."

"What the hell does that mean?" Garrett growled.

"Miss Morrow isn't the only mystery around here. You're not sleeping, and the pair of you are frequently at odds these past few days. That in itself has never happened before. Then of course, Perry's tiptoeing around in the middle of the night—"

He was one moment away from dragging Byrnes across the table when that last sentence penetrated. "What do you mean, she's sneaking around at night?"

"Last night," Byrnes replied. "Ava said she saw Perry disappearing toward the steam baths."

"Perry can use the steam baths if she wants—"

"Pardon, sir. Did someone say my name?"

Miss McLaren appeared carrying a plate of kippers and fried sole. Her hair was neatly braided and she wore the same drab green gown they'd found for her the day before. She paused at the edge of the table when she saw their reactions. "My apologies. I didn't realize you were unaware of me."

Both of them pushed to their feet. Garrett held her chair out for her. "Simply business," he replied smoothly. "Byrnes was telling me how you were recovering."

"I've been better." Despite the haunted look in her eyes, she graced him with a smile as she sat. "But Master Byrnes has been very kind."

Not a word he'd ever associate with the man.

"A little blunt, but very solicitous," Miss McLaren corrected, sighting his expression. Stabbing a kipper with her fork, she popped it in her mouth. Then paled.

Byrnes swore under his breath. "Your body's not the same, and neither are your necessities. Food is no longer something you require."

As she pressed her fingers to her lips, Garrett hastily found her a napkin. Miss McLaren took it from him and used it to discreetly remove her mouthful. "Oh, that's ghastly." She looked down in dismay. "I adore kippers."

"Try blood," Byrnes replied. "You're a blue blood now."

A fierce little pinprick of hunger lit her eyes, but her skin paled further. "No, thank you. I believe it's an acquired taste. Much like others." This with a darting glance at Byrnes.

Garrett paused with his cup to his lips. Good God. Was that flirtation?

Byrnes gave her a smile. "Perhaps you'd prefer something a little fresher?" He flicked the button on his sleeve and drew back the fabric, revealing the inside of his wrist.

"Byrnes was telling me you saw Perry last night," Garrett broke in, with a warning glare toward the other man. The woman had been through an ordeal; this was the last thing she needed. Especially from Byrnes. The man was coldly calculating in all pursuits, including those that involved women.

Then he put his cup down. Byrnes knew how haunted some victims of crime could be. Garrett sat back and reexamined them. Byrnes had his arm slung along the back of her chair, seemingly relaxed—though tension rested in his shoulders— and Miss McLaren…she was leaning in toward him. Hands shaking a little around her cup, despite her weak smile.

Perhaps Miss McLaren saw Byrnes as some sort of protector? Safe enough to smile at, to try to make some attempts at what she perceived as normality.

Perhaps she needed this to heal? To forget the nightmare? And Byrnes was her version of safety?

"I did," Miss McLaren replied, her gaze dropping. For the longest moment she stared at the thumping pulse in the offered blue veins.

The devil knew, she needed someone to help her adjust to being a blue blood and she seemed to trust Byrnes. "Did Perry seem out of sorts?"

Miss McLaren jerked her gaze to the kippers. "I'm not quite sure, sir. I barely know her."

Garrett reached out and laid a hand over hers. "I'm

merely concerned about her. It cannot be easy being the lone woman in a building full of men."

"She—I promised I wouldn't say anything."

"I won't let her know."

Miss McLaren's eyes softened. "She looked surprised to see me there. As if she was hiding something. And she...she..."

"Please," Garrett asked, holding her gaze. Forcing her to look at him, to trust him. "She seems out of sorts of late and we argued yesterday. I only want to know if she's all right."

Again Miss McLaren seemed caught on the edge of a precipice. "She seemed upset. And, if I didn't know any better, I'd believe she left the building. Or at least, she had a small satchel with her. I was... My room felt so small that I spent most of the night pacing the hallways, and I never saw her return."

"Satchel?" Byrnes asked.

"Left the building?" Why the hell would she have needed to go out last night? A cold hand gripped the back of Garrett's neck as he shoved his chair back and stood.

"Yes," Miss McLaren whispered. "She asked me not to say anything to you."

Fifteen

THE TRAIN'S WHISTLE CUT THROUGH THE COMMOTION of the crowd, a huge billow of steam erupting from the smokestack. Garrett shoved his way through the milling passengers, his eyes raking the platform for her.

Don't let it be too late. He didn't know what the hell was going on, but desperation churned through him. Perry was leaving him. He'd known it the instant the words left Miss McLaren's lips. That had been two hours ago and he'd been practically running through the streets ever since, trying to track her.

Struggling through a knot of workmen, he staggered to a halt on the middle of the platform. The train bunched its iron muscles, throbbing with imminent tension. A young lad leaped aboard, the conductor grabbing his arm and steadying him. A pair of young ladies in dark bonnets stepped back, dabbing at their eyes with handkerchiefs as they waved him off.

Where was she? He could see dozens of young women, but none of them was Perry. Pushing past a workman, he strained to see along the platform. *Nothing.*

Pulling out the locating device, Garrett cursed

under his breath. Its faint metallic clicks meant she
was close. He could track her to her proximity—she
was here, somewhere—but the device was no more
specific than that.

If I lose her...

His vision grayed at the thought, violence playing
through him. Perry was the only thing holding him
together right now.

Movement flickered through his vision. Dark feathers bobbed over a stylish hat as a young woman glanced
through the window on the train, then back at her lap.
Garrett's breath caught. Perry. He'd been looking for
a young lady in men's clothes, but she wore the black
wig from the opera, her burgundy velvet coat buttoned
tightly beneath her chin. A young woman toying with
her gloves in her own compartment, nonchalantly
waiting for the train to depart.

It cut at him inside that she could look so uncaring.
Did she even give him a thought? She hadn't even bloody
said good-bye.

The whistle screamed and smoke poured from the
smokestack of the train. It let out a mighty hiss, then
the wheels started turning. In her compartment, Perry
looked up, her shoulders slumping in relief.

"Stand clear!" the conductor bellowed.

Garrett was moving before he thought about it.
The train lurched forward, the conductor swinging
the door shut. As the train started to move, Perry's
carriage came face-to-face with him.

Look at me, damn you.

Slowly her shoulders stiffened and she looked up.
There was no hint of recognition at first, only that

deadened gaze meeting his. Then her eyes widened, expression painting itself across the muted planes of her face and enlivening it. Garrett nodded at her and stopped walking, falling back into the curious crowd. Perry slammed herself against the window, palm splayed over the glass as she stared after him, her lips parting.

Carriages rocked past. Garrett started running, shoving people out of his way as the train sped up, carriages rattling past him. He glanced over his shoulder and saw the last carriage drawing up close to his shoulder. *One last chance...*

He took it, leaping out over the tracks, his hands catching the lip of the carriage roof. A gasp went up behind him, but he ignored it, swinging his leg up onto the top and crouching there for a moment to catch his breath.

Now you're mine.

❧

Perry's heart leaped into her throat as she threw herself against the window, straining to see where he'd vanished to. How had he found her? What was he doing? Was he letting her go?

Slowly she sank down into her seat, the skin of her cheek still imprinted with the coolness of the glass. The image of his face flashed through her mind, tight with a fierceness that almost made her tremble.

He'd never let her go. Not like this. She knew him too well. This was not good-bye.

Perry leaped to her feet, reaching up to tug her satchel from the overhead compartment. It caught and she tugged it free with a hard wrench. The satchel

spilled open, the few garments she'd managed to pack
tumbling into her face and then falling in a half circle
at her feet.

"Blast it," she swore, kneeling to stuff it all back
into her satchel. Her heart hammered in her chest,
tempting her to flee.

Perry buckled it shut and spun toward the door.
She had to move. She could almost feel him on the
train now, prowling toward her. Flicking open the
latch on the compartment door, Perry was reaching
for the handle when a man dressed entirely in black
stepped into view through the window.

Too late.

Their eyes met through the glass and Perry was too
slow to move. Garrett yanked the door open, a blast
of noise racketing through the private compartment,
and stepped inside.

His hard eyes raked over her, lingering on the suit-
case. Something dark shifted through his expression,
and then he turned and eased the door shut with a soft,
controlled click. Sound choked off.

"How did you find me?" Was that her voice? So
tight and dry?

"The more interesting question is where, precisely,
are you going?"

Light suddenly streamed through the windows as
the train left the station. The carriage rocked as it
began to move faster, forcing her to brace her feet.
Garrett moved with the sway of the carriage, yanking
the curtain down over the door so that no one could
see in. One glance at her face and she knew that he
realized she had no intention of saying anything.

"It wasn't difficult," he said curtly, responding to her question when she didn't answer his. She flinched at his tone. "If you were leaving the city, which was the only possibility, it was either by train or ship."

Which didn't explain how he'd tracked her. She'd spent hours backtracking across the city. There was no way he could have followed that trail and found her so quickly.

Unless he had help.

Fitz. That damned tracking beacon they'd been using in certain cases. She started patting herself down, trying to find where the small device must have been sewn into her clothes. "Where did you put it?"

Garrett said nothing. Simply stared at her. And Perry realized that he'd never have expected her to wear a dress. She yanked her skirts up, looking at the heeled boots she always wore. The only flaw to her disguise, but at least she could run and fight in them, and that had been far more important to her mind. "Damn you, is it in one of my boots?"

He wasn't watching her. He was staring at her boots… No, at her legs and the elegant silk stockings she wore. Perry sucked in a breath and stepped back, dropping her skirts. The intensity in his expression frightened her. It was something she'd longed for, for so many years. Something she'd dreamed about. Something she'd seen on his face that night at the opera and again last night.

Something that terrified her.

He looked up. "You didn't say good-bye." Soft, dangerous words.

"I…I tried."

Last night. She saw the knowledge dawning in his

eyes. His lip curled back, his teeth bared. The veneer of civility slid off him as if it had never been. He was feral. Furious. And so bloody gorgeous it hurt her heart to look at him.

"You tried?" He gave a breathless laugh, visibly reining himself in. "You tried to say good-bye? Do I believe that? Let's be honest, Perry." His voice hardened. "You were goin' to give yourself to me but you were never goin' to say anythin'." He took a step toward, his face flushed with anger and his words coming out hard and clipped, mangling the fine pronunciation. "You never let me in. You keep me here." Taking her hand he pressed it against his chest, her arm straight. "All the damned time. And I'm tired of it."

He wasn't wearing his body armor. There was no barrier between her hand and the racing thump of his heart, except for thin cloth. Perry jerked her hand back against her chest, but she could still feel the echo of his pulse against her skin.

"I was trying to… I didn't want—"

"What?" He took up most of the carriage, his anger filling the air.

"It's not the same for me as it is for you," she snapped. "I didn't want to be hurt—"

"What the hell d'you mean? When I what? Walked away? Is that what you think I planned to do?" The look on his face… She had the sudden choking feeling that she had made a grave error. Garrett's lips thinned and he swore under his breath as he realized how badly he was speaking. "Do you think"—he enunciated each word carefully—"for one moment that I would ever do that to *you*?"

And suddenly it all welled up inside her, spilling over her lips before she could control it. "You never *looked* at me! And I was to suddenly believe that things had changed? You like games, Garrett. You like the chase. I've seen it a dozen times before. Why would I be any different? Why would—"

"Because I care for you, damn it!"

Both of them fell silent, staring at each other with chests heaving. Half the train had probably heard them.

"Have you ever thought that perhaps you never *let* me see you?" His voice lowered. "You're right. You were my friend, but nothing else. You never gave me one hint that you were...that there was anything between us. And you were so frightened when you arrived at the guild that I didn't see you as a woman. I won't apologize for that. You didn't want me to."

She shook her head. But a little part of her couldn't deny it. It had been far easier to love him from a distance, knowing that nothing would ever come of it. But now that things were growing complicated...

Another step. He reached out slowly, both hands cupping her trembling jaw. "Where were you going?"

Perry tore away and paced toward the windows, her skirts swishing. Trying to still the racing beat of her heart. Easier to think of this, rather than all of the unspoken feelings she could never give voice to. It calmed her somewhat. "I can't tell you."

Nothing.

"Do you know how much that bloody hurts? Damn it, Perry. Where were you going? Were you leaving the city forever? Were you coming back? What are you running from?" His voice thickened. "Was it *me*?"

"I just… I needed to…" The words died in her throat. If Garrett knew what had happened to her, she had no doubt that he'd confront the duke about it. She'd seen it happen before, where Garrett had stepped between a whore and her pimp, or a wife and her husband.

In those moments, he wasn't the easygoing man she knew. There was a darkness in him, a fierce wrath against men who mistreated their womenfolk. He'd never been able to do anything for his mother, and she knew he saw Mrs. Reed's face every time a woman was harmed. Perry couldn't let him go up against the duke, a man who could crush him and wouldn't hesitate to do so.

"You're not going to tell me," he replied, reading the set of her jaw. "Damn it, Perry. You know you can trust me." His expression softened. "I'd never hurt you, you know that. I'd never let anyone hurt you."

Which was precisely the problem.

I'm protecting you.

"I was going to send you a letter," she stammered. "Once I reached the port." To tell him about her suspicions about Hague, at least, so no more women would have to fear that monster.

"Port? So you weren't even going to stay in the country? Would I ever have seen you again?"

"No," she whispered.

A thousand expressions danced across his face. She might as well have struck him. "So you won't tell me where you're going," he said. "You won't tell me why. How is a man not to let that eat away at him? How am I not to think that it's something that I've done?"

"If I could stay with you, I would."

"Has someone threatened you?"

This was why he was so dangerous. Anger would only blind him to the truth for so long. She couldn't let him start analyzing the situation. The thought of what she had to do burned within her. "No. No, it's not that. It's…" Her mouth wouldn't say the words, her heart twisting mercilessly in her chest. She would hurt him with this, and do it deliberately too. The thought made her feel nauseous, but somehow she lifted her chin and stared him in the eye. "I—I asked you not to pursue this between us. I never wished to hurt you, Garrett, but you kept *pushing* at me. I'm sorry, but I don't feel for you the way you feel for me. There's—there's someone else…for me."

Garrett stared at her. "You're lying," he said, but the words were a whisper. And for the first time in her life, she saw doubt in his eyes.

"No. I'm not." The hardest words she'd ever uttered.

"Who?" he demanded. "Who is it?" A strange, fanatical light came into his eyes. "It's Byrnes, isn't it?"

"*What?*"

Both of his hands gripped her upper arms, darkness swimming through his gaze. "This last month, when I forced you to work together. *Christ.*" He rubbed a hand over his mouth. "Fucking hell, this is my fault."

Perry couldn't say anything.

And then he blinked. "No. No, you wouldn't—" His eyes narrowed on her, dangerous now. "You lying, little… You made one mistake, my dear. You should never have come to me last night if you wanted me to believe this has anything to do with another man."

"It's not a lie," she said desperately.

"Really?" He cupped her chin and forced her to meet his gaze. The expression in his eyes sent a shiver down her spine. "So you expect me to believe that you came to my room last night and let me do what I did to you when you had another man in your heart?" Dangerous, dangerous eyes. "You're clever. And you know me well enough to know how to manipulate me, but I'm not stupid, Perry." His eyes darkened. "Not for long enough, anyway. This has nothing to do with me."

"It has everything to do with you!" she cried, shoving at his chest. Desperate for him to believe her.

"Prove it," he whispered, eyes glittering as his face lowered toward hers. His mouth whispered along her jaw, his body driving hard against hers, every inch molded to her softening body. "Prove that you don't feel any of this. Prove that I don't mean anything to you." Cupping the curve of her nape, he caught a fistful of her hair and turned her lips to his. "Prove that everything between us is a lie."

And then his mouth took hers.

She'd thought his advances rough the night before. She was wrong. He'd been deliciously gentle with her in comparison. This…now… His body vibrated with anger, with need, with the desperate urge to claim her.

And she couldn't deny it.

A strangled noise sounded in her throat as his tongue darted over hers. How could she fight him when she wanted him so much? Her own fist clenched in his hair, trying to hold herself up—hold herself together—under the onslaught of his embrace.

If I let myself, I'll drown in this...
And then he'd die.

Breaking away with a gasp, Perry shoved at him. If he got hold of her, she knew she wouldn't have the strength of will to push him away again. A firm hand circled her wrist and Perry couldn't stop herself from twisting free, swinging his elbow up behind his back—

He ducked beneath her move, twisting the other way and twirling her, almost like a dancer. Timber paneling met her back, Garrett forcing her hands above her head and pinning her there with his body. She'd barely seen him react.

In all of their sparring, he'd never moved like that before. All those times she'd thought she'd won... And he'd let her

"You bastard."

He pressed her back against the carriage wall, using his whole body to trap her, to nudge between her thighs and force them to part. Forearms on the wall on either side of her face, he dragged his mouth away, breathing hard. The black glimmer of his eyes burned through her. Good Lord, he was strong. She tried to move, to escape, but she was helpless.

His lashes lowered, lips parting in a soundless groan as he ground against her.

"Come now, my fierce little peregrine," he whispered, riding against her, the hard ridge of his cock grinding exactly where she wanted it. "I know you can get out of this...if you want to."

Perry tried every trick she knew. Wriggling and squirming, and nothing mattered because she could feel him, hands pinning her wrists against the timber, his hips rasping against her. Leaving her wet and slick, aching so desperately that she knew only one thing would assuage the emptiness inside...

She stopped fighting with a gasp. Their eyes clashed; he knew it, felt it in her treacherous body. "No," she moaned, turning her face to the side as he leaned closer.

"There's no one else for you," he demanded. Bit the soft skin of her throat. "Say it."

The sharpness of his teeth shot all the way through her, igniting something deep inside. Perry squirmed, but this time it wasn't to get away.

"Say it," he breathed, fingers curling through hers as her wrists lowered, locking their palms together.

Perry closed her eyes. Squeezed them hard against the emotion surging within. "There's no one else for me." There never would be. Never had been, from the moment she'd met him.

Thick silence settled between them, broken only by the harshness of their mingled breaths. Perry glanced at him. A fierce, furious exultation curled his mouth into a victorious smile.

It wasn't done. Not yet. "I can't stay. This doesn't mean anything."

Garrett's head jerked back and he searched her gaze. "No, it means *everything*." He let her slide down his body, wild and trembling, trying to still her own harsh desires.

"Let me say good-bye," she whispered.

"I won't let you go," he told her stubbornly. "I need you."

"You've never needed me—"

"I need you now."

The train began to slow, rocking from side to side. Perry glanced at the window. "We're coming into the next station. You should swap trains here."

Their bodies rocked together, a gentle, torturous sway. Garrett glared at her, still pressing her against the wall. The train's brakes squealed and an enormous hiss of steam erupted from the smokestack. The train shuddered to a halt at the station, people's voices ringing down the corridor. And still he pressed against her.

"Garrett—"

"I'm not leaving without you," he said stubbornly.

"You don't have a choice." She made her voice harden.

"Perry, damn it. I can't—" He looked away, jaw clenching. "I can't do this alone. I *can't*."

"Yes, you can—"

"My CV levels are at sixty-eight percent. And rising."

The words stole her breath. Of everything he could have said to her, she'd never have expected this.

"No." That was dangerously high. Almost double what they had been before Lord Falcone had tried to kill him. Worthy of reporting to the authorities. The heat washed out of her.

"Yes."

No. She didn't want to believe it. Shook her head.

"Fitz examined me after the attack. I should have died. Falcone had his hand around my bloody heart, I could feel it. Fitz thinks that my body wasn't strong enough to fight off both the craving virus and the damage that had been done to me, so it chose the greater threat. The craving virus healed me, but managed to colonize me at the same time." He looked at her bleakly. "Fitz knows, but I haven't alerted Gibson to how high my CV levels are. He'd have to report me to the authorities as a risk."

All of the defiance drained out of her. She knew exactly where that route would end. Twice she'd helped to bring back a blue blood lord who'd fled the authorities when he entered the Fade.

"You're the only one holding me together right now. I can't lose you. I honestly don't know what I'd do without you." He looked at her, and a part of her cringed at the bleakness in his eyes. "You don't know how hard it's been this last month." Garrett cupped her face between his hands. The pressure of the wall against her back rocked her slowly. She was trapped here, beneath that imploring gaze. "Damn you, please," he whispered, one thumb stroking her cheek; an almost desperate move. "Tell me what you're running from. I can help you. And I need you. I need you so much right now. You're the only one I trust—"

"The others wouldn't betray you."

"The only reason I haven't lost control is because you're there. At first I was afraid I'd hurt you, but in some irrational way, being with you makes it easier. Makes me feel as though I can breathe through it, keep control."

She understood only too well what panic felt like.

"You're my anchor, Perry. You're my breath when I feel like I can't catch my own. I don't think I can *be* strong enough to fight this alone." Blackness swept through his irises, stealing away the blue. Garrett clenched his eyes shut, sucking in a sharp breath. "I can't do this without you," he told her hoarsely. "I know I can't."

"That's not true."

But how could she leave him alone right now? This was the greatest fear a blue blood had. To face the start of the Fade, knowing that it would end in either execution or worse.

She'd have walked away to save his life. But how could she leave him behind when he was dying already?

"Don't," she murmured. "Don't you give up."

Garrett looked at her and she slid her arms around his neck and pressed his face against her shoulder as if to hide that hopelessness from both of them. The racing tick of his heart thundered through his chest, pressed so tightly against hers. Solid and *real*. Slowly his arms slid around her, as if he wasn't certain of her response. Or as if he didn't want to trap her, wanted to give her the choice in this.

Not that there was any choice. Not anymore. Perry slid her gloved hands through his hair, fingers fisting in the dark coppery strands a little too tightly, unable to stop herself from pressing her cheek against his temple to feel his skin against hers.

"Are you staying?" he whispered, the breath of his words stirring against her neck. "You're not leaving me, are you?"

One last hesitation. An image of the Moncrieff flashed through her mind, sending her heart thundering along like the train beneath them. "I'm not leaving."

His arms tightened, crushing her against his broad chest.

This is a mistake, something dark in her warned.

But Perry didn't care. All she could feel in that moment was Garrett's hard body pressed against hers. For once she could take guilty pleasure in letting herself melt against him.

❧

They swapped trains at the next station. This time the trip was silent, the compartment slowly rocking as she stared out the window and watched London growing larger, the train bringing her closer to home. To her fate.

A full yard separated them on the seat. She couldn't remember a time when Garrett had ever been this silent for so long. He was a man who liked the sound of his own voice, often stirring her out of the long silences she preferred. Teasing her. Tempting her into arguments that went nowhere just to amuse himself, arguments that left her hot and bothered and burning with life.

"Where were you going?" he finally asked.

"The colonies." It was the only place she could have safely vanished among the populace. Most of Europe was staunchly anti–blue blood except Russia, and that was far too close to Moncrieff for her liking. In the colonies, blue bloods mingled with humans, with little difference between the classes.

He stared at the empty seats opposite them, as if afraid to look at her. "Are you ever going to tell me why?"

This time it was her turn to look away, out through the window. But she could feel his eyes on her, both of them stealing little glances when they thought the other wasn't looking. Her gaze softened, focusing on his reflected image, rather than the dreary, gray city climes outside. Their eyes met in the reflection.

"I thought not. Devil take you." A soft sigh. "I suppose I must figure it out myself."

That made her head jerk up. Garrett could be astoundingly astute—while also incredibly blind—at times. If he started sniffing around her secrets, trying to unearth them…who knew how far he'd get?

"Don't! I want your word that you won't try such a thing, or I swear I shall get on the next train out of London, no matter what I promised you."

Those perceptive eyes searched hers with a thoroughness that felt as though he looked all the way through her. His brows drew together slowly. Thinking. Always when he was at his most dangerous. "I'd find you," he warned.

"How *did* you find me?"

"Not your boots," he replied, his voice sounding tight and dry as he looked out the window. "Do you remember that case with Lord Rommell several years ago?"

A shiver worked over her skin. It was the closest she'd come to dying since Moncrieff.

"I couldn't find you in the tunnels beneath the theater," he said, his voice still strangely quiet. "And it stank so bad that I couldn't track the scent of your clothes either." He swallowed. "Thought you were dead."

Almost… Beaten within an inch of her life, lying in the water of the sewers, thinking how easy it would be to just slip underneath them forever. To let the pain and the hurt wash out of her. Even a blue blood could drown.

"You found me," Perry replied, studying the tension

that was growing in his tall frame. Strong emotion wasn't a good thing for a man in his position to feel. He had to keep calm. Slowly she reached across the seat and slipped her hand into his. "I knew you'd find me."

"But I nearly didn't," he snapped. "I don't even know what led me down that tunnel. Maybe a noise... maybe some instinct. And there you were, all bloody and bruised. Facedown in that fucking water. Christ." He scraped a hand over the back of his neck, cheeks reddening. "I asked Fitz to make something so that I'd never lose you again. And then I attached it to the one thing you never go anywhere without."

Her knife. She felt the hilt of it dig into her breastbone, where it nestled neatly in the sheath built into her corset. Perry's fingers grazed the smooth velvet over her breasts and he nodded.

All these years he'd been watching over her. Knowing where she was at all times, what she was doing. It should have felt intrusive, but her heart gave a little twist in her chest. He'd cared. Even when she'd thought her own feelings unrequited.

Perry squeezed his fingers. "Take a deep breath."

It took long minutes before his breathing returned to normalcy. His fingers tightened on hers once or twice but Perry didn't draw attention to it. He needed her to be his anchor.

She just wondered whether she'd be strong enough to hold on to both of them when the storm finally hit.

The train rattled into London's Kings Cross station slowly, steam hissing like a kettle as the brakes squealed. Garrett looked down at the warm weight against his shoulder, reaching up to trace a dangling black curl off Perry's cheek.

She'd fallen asleep roughly an hour ago. The train's rocking motion had tipped her toward him, and Garrett had eased his arm around her, her head against his chest and the feathers from her bonnet tickling his nose.

He didn't want to wake her. It was…pleasant to sit here. Comforting even. For the first time in weeks, the hunger lay dormant within him. Garrett didn't particularly want to examine why. The hunger was part of him, his darker half, and it had driven him half-way to Bedlam when he'd realized that she was gone.

As if it knew something he didn't.

He wanted to taste her blood. The very thought sent need surging through his veins, but the idea of hurting her… It made the dark, furious side of the hunger snarl angrily inside him.

Even the darker side of his craving knew Perry was to be protected at all costs. There'd been blue bloods before—Lynch included—who had fixated on a partic-ular woman to a possessive degree. Last month, when Lynch had been driven into a blood-crazed fury by a chemical agent, he'd still been unable to hurt Rosalind.

The train rolled to a halt and Perry murmured something in her sleep as she turned her face into his chest and curled her fingers around one of the brass buttons on his leather coat.

"Perry," Garrett whispered, stroking the fine downy hairs at the back of her neck. Her own hair, not the glossy black curls of the wig she wore. It was fine, almost golden at the roots. He'd always thought she dyed her hair black to draw less attention to herself and make her look more like a lad than a woman, but now he wasn't so sure.

He wasn't certain of anything anymore, least of all her.

Perry's eyelashes fluttered against her pale cheeks. He wanted to wake up next to her, like this. Wake up with her in his arms.

She was fiercely beautiful in her own way, from those stubborn gray eyes to the slightly aquiline tilt of her nose and her thick dark brows. The more he looked at her face, the more he seemed to see it. As though he was still struggling awake from that first moment when he'd seen her in a dress, when the world upended itself around him as if someone had splashed ice water in his face.

"I see you," he whispered.

Perry's lashes quivered again, her eyes half opening. He watched the moment her gaze focused and she realized she was in his arms. Stillness slid through her, turning her to stone, then she pushed herself upright, the creases from his coat imprinting one smooth cheek.

"You should have woken me." She stretched, the dark red velvet tightening over her breasts.

Somehow she slid into a dress and it was as if she relaxed into the femininity she so disdained as a Nighthawk. As natural to her as the leathers she wore.

Which led him to a conclusion. Once upon a time, Perry had lived in dresses. It came too easily to her. Indeed, that night at the opera, she'd mingled with the Echelon as if she belonged.

"It didn't bother me," he replied. "And you were tired."

"I spent most of the night laying a false trail all over the city. I might have saved myself the time, if I'd known you had a tracking device on me, and come straight to the train station. You'd never have caught me."

Though she laughed gently, the words tore through him like a knife. He had to find out what had frightened her, or she could run again. And this time she'd make certain he didn't find her.

She'd warned him that if he started digging around in her secrets she'd leave. And from the relaxed way she peered out the window, it seemed she'd forgotten that he hadn't actually agreed not to do so.

Garrett had been very careful not to promise anything. Though he might have distracted Perry from the question, he hadn't forgotten it. Something had frightened her badly enough that she'd wanted to leave her entire life—and him—behind without even a good-bye.

If she thought he was just going to forget about it, then she didn't know him very well. But it seemed she was quite content to pretend nothing had happened, which was her usual modus operandi.

So be it. Until he could discover what she was hiding.

And he *would* find out.

Sixteen

GARRETT RUBBED HIS KNUCKLES AS THE HANSOM STEAM coach pulled up outside the guild. As soon as he'd made that quiet acceptance this morning—that there was nothing he could do about the craving virus—his mind had become very clear.

He wanted, more than anything, to drag Perry off to his rooms and finish what they'd started last night and on the train. But her shoulders were still hunched, her gaze distant. She'd agreed to return with him, but he couldn't push her or he had the horrible suspicion she'd flee again.

"Here," he said, helping her down from the coach. Nervousness lit through him, hesitancy he'd never known when speaking to her before. But then a part of him was terrified to say the wrong thing, in case she fled. "Are you up to working with me today, or do you wish to rest?"

"I thought I was on desk duty."

"You are." Where he could keep an eye on her. "Garrett…?"

"Yes?"

"I need to speak to you about something. It's... about the case."

Finally. He let out a relieved breath. "Of course. As soon as we've freshened up."

They parted ways in the foyer, with Byrnes strolling to the railing of the stairs and glancing down. He looked at Perry. Then looked again, his eyes widening slightly as she sailed past.

Just the man he needed. The thought irritated him, but Garrett couldn't put this off any longer. He'd let his own selfishness potentially affect the guild. "A word," he called.

Byrnes straightened. "You found her, then."

"Your deductive skills are legendary," Garrett drawled, climbing the stairs. "Don't ask her about it."

Byrnes arched a brow.

"Has Miss McLaren said anything yet?" Garrett asked, striding toward his rooms. Opening the door into the study felt a little like coming home. He'd never truly had a place of his own, only the small cell that most Nighthawks were allocated upon arrival.

"Enough." Byrnes's face closed as he slumped into a chair by the fireplace. "She's the daughter of an investment banker in Edinburgh. She can't recall very much, but she was returning home from a dinner when her carriage was stopped. Miss McLaren peered out the window to see what was happening, and someone hit her over the head and kidnapped her."

"Imagine being trapped in a bloody tank for months." Garrett paced in front of the fireplace, his hands clasped behind him. Someone—Doyle, no doubt—had stoked it.

"That's not all." Darkness swirled in Byrnes's eyes. "He performed regular experiments on her. She didn't go into detail, but I gather they were fairly horrific. But she was very specific on one thing—whoever the killer was, he didn't want her to die. One of the girls did once, when he had her on the examination table, and he tore the place apart in a fury. The next time he took Ava from the tank for her examination, he was more careful with her, and ever since."

Keeping his specimen alive. Garrett's lip curled. "Anything identifiable about him?"

"Tall, broad through the shoulders. He never spoke to her, but he would swear under his breath sometimes. Something foreign, she thought, though it wasn't German or French. Wore a pair of magnifying goggles and a mask over his lower face, like one of those breathing masks Rosalind gave us at the opera to filter the air so we wouldn't be stricken by the gas from the Doeppler Orbs."

Blast it. Could it be Sykes under the mask? There was no way of knowing for certain. "So maybe he didn't mean to kill Miss Fortescue or Keller? Maybe Miss Fortescue was a failed experiment and Mallory startled him in the midst of moving Miss Keller downstairs."

"So he kills her. There and then, and takes the heart with him." Even Byrnes paled. "That's incredibly twisted."

"Some men are. We're dealing with a man with both expert surgical and mechanical skills, a man who's intent on creating something no one else has managed. Someone who collects body organs—"

"A man with access to the craving virus," Byrnes added.

The man yesterday morning had been a blue blood. It had to be Sykes. Who else would follow them or fit the description? He'd thought one of the Echelon involved, but Sykes must be their blue blood. Still… "If it's Sykes, then someone in the Echelon is backing him." It wasn't unusual for scientists to be granted patronage from one of the Great Houses. Science was money and power these days. "That laboratory cost a good deal to set up."

"Someone with ties to the factory?"

"It makes too much sense." Garrett turned on his heel, snapping his fingers. "Now we have to trace whoever it is to the factory. Sykes is our killer, I'm sure of it, but someone else is involved—or knows about it."

They stared at each other, both in accord for once.

The door opened and Perry slipped through, stripped down to her leathers. She glanced between them. "What is it?"

Garrett explained his theory, watching as the color slipped from her cheeks. His heart beat a little harder. She wasn't entirely surprised at his words as she settled on the sofa.

He didn't like the questions that were mounting up. Perry knew more about this than she was saying.

"The Duke of Moncrieff admitted that he, Malloryn, and Caine own controlling shares in the factory," Garrett said. "Which means that any of them could be suspect."

"You're talking about questioning three of the dukes who rule the city, Garrett," Perry said in a small voice, her hands pressed between her knees where she sat.

"She's right," Byrnes admitted. "I might admire your brass, but don't expect me to call on you when you're imprisoned in the Ivory Tower."

"Unless…we don't do the questioning," Perry murmured. "I know you're not going to like this suggestion, but Lynch is a duke now. He could safely—"

"No." A hot flush of anger overtook him. There was no way in hell he would go before Lynch and beg him to help.

"Even if it means we catch this bastard?" She knew him too well. "Don't put your pride on the line."

Damn her. "I'm not asking." He didn't think he could stand to be dismissed again. It was ridiculous, of course. If it would help solve the murders, Lynch would help. "Will you do it?"

Perry nodded.

"I might speak to Barrons myself," he continued, dismissing Lynch from his mind. Or trying to. *Damn you, I could use some advice right about now…* "He and I have a friendship of sorts. He might be able to shed some light on whether his father, the Duke of Caine, has any involvement."

"And myself?" Byrnes asked.

Garrett gave him a considering look. He didn't like what he was about to do any more than Perry would if she understood it. But she was right. His pride wasn't worth the cost of the guild. And in facing certain truths, he had to acknowledge all of them. "I want you to coordinate a hunt for Sykes, the overseer. I'm almost certain he fled from us this morning, and that he's our man." All of the pieces of the puzzle were starting to come together. "I want you to handpick a group of the lads who are good at this sort of thing and direct them."

A slight thinning of the other man's mouth. "You're intent on saddling me with some fool as partner, aren't you? If there's nothing else, I shall take my leave."

"Considering I was one of those 'fools,' I wouldn't dally if I were you," Perry drawled.

Surprisingly, Byrnes stopped in front of her, slipping her hand from her knee and bringing it to his lips. "My lady, you were never a fool. Poor taste in men, perhaps, but I actually enjoyed working with you."

The sight of his lips pressing against her hand stirred something dark inside Garrett. That moment in the train came back to him, when she'd looked him in the eye and told him there was someone else. He knew the truth of that now, but a part of him wanted to tear Byrnes to pieces.

With a flourish—and a glance in Garrett's direction—Byrnes took his leave.

Perry read the harsh line of Garrett's jaw. Her lashes fluttered as she looked down. "I'm sorry," she said in a small voice, the mood of the room darkening. "I should never have said what I said."

"I know the truth. It still hurts." He met her eyes. "No lies between us from now on." He saw her open her mouth and held up a hand. "If you can't tell me something, then don't say anything at all. Just don't... don't lie to me."

"Thank you."

She wouldn't thank him if she had any idea of his plans. Garrett crossed the room and sat beside her. The moment he did, some of the tension drained out of him. He hadn't even realized how on edge he'd been, a bothering thought. If he was growing complacent with the grip of the hunger…

"You shouldn't be jealous of Byrnes," Perry murmured. "I cannot believe he was the first man who sprang to mind when I…when I said what I said."

The thought arrested him. He'd never *been* jealous before. "I daresay I'm not the only one who's suddenly noticed you're a beautiful young woman. Besides, you have been spending a great deal of time with him in the past month."

That earned him a pretty pink flush through her cheeks. She didn't take compliments well. Perhaps she'd never been used to them. "That was due to your machinations, not mine."

"Mmm. It doesn't help that I don't feel entirely rational when it comes to Byrnes." Slowly he reached out and brushed a strand of hair off her cheek. "It's getting long now."

"What are you up to?"

His fingertips trailed along her jaw and down. Her throat worked as she swallowed, but there was no other sign of movement. "Perhaps I'm trying to assuage my jealousy," he murmured.

She turned, sinking those small white teeth into his fingers. A sharp nip that drew his gaze to hers. "I meant, what are you up to with Byrnes? You had a certain expression on your face when you asked him to deal with the men."

He just wanted to keep touching her, but she wouldn't like this. "Byrnes wants to be guild master," he said, giving a little shrug as he withdrew his hand. "He needs to grow comfortable with giving the men direction."

The color drained out of her skin in dramatic fashion and she straightened. "You're grooming him?" A look of utter horror crossed her face. "No!" She shot to her feet. "You can't do this. You can't give up! You can't—"

"There is no cure for the craving virus," he admitted. "I'm not giving up, Perry, I'm accepting certain... necessities. Byrnes isn't a natural leader of men, but he's ruthless and cunning. He'd stare the prince consort in the eye and tell him no, if he had to. My own prejudices against him are selfish. I can't leave the guild without a master. Not in these times."

She was speechless.

"I've considered other options, but there are none." He tipped his chin toward her. "The Echelon would never allow a woman to lead, and Doyle's humanity works against him."

"I can't believe you're doing this!"

"I have a responsibility to the position." He caught her wrist and dragged her toward him. "Perry, I don't want to do this. Just let me...let me explain."

She looked utterly devastated.

"Despite what I think of him at times, Byrnes is smart. Dangerously so. He's also very good at—"

"That's enough," she declared. "I don't want to hear any more of this."

No point in pursuing this further. She'd never listen. He caught her fingertips as she tried to pull away. "Come. Sit and talk to me. You and I have some things to discuss."

Reluctantly Perry let him ease her onto the sofa beside him. "About what?"

"About us."

She didn't, as he'd expected, instantly deny there was anything between them. Instead she looked him in the eye. Wary but curious. "Then speak."

"Things have changed between us," he said bluntly. "And whether or not I never noticed you before, I'm noticing now. I want you to be my lover."

A thousand thoughts raced across her eyes and she drew her knees up to her chest. "I'm not certain that would be a good idea. What would the men think?"

Not a no. Not a yes, either.

"In other circumstances, I'd agree. I might have taken my time. Figured this whole mess out. But that's the one thing I am certain about, Perry. I don't have much time. My CV levels have increased nine percent in the last month." He took a shuddering breath. "I know this is hardly the romantic proposition young girls dream of, but it's the truth. I want you, Perry. You're the only thing I would regret if—"

Her fingertips against his lips stopped him. He turned into the touch, pressing a kiss to her fingers. Their eyes met.

"It's unfair to even ask you," he whispered against her touch. "I know that. But I also know that I've never wanted anything more in my life. And if this is all I have left of life…then I would want to spend it with you by my side. You don't have to give me your answer immediately. And if you feel that I'm asking too much of you, then you don't have to say yes—"

She kissed him, sliding into his lap, those elegant

FORGED BY DESIRE
257

fingers stroking his face, and something he hadn't expected to see smoldering in her eyes.

He'd never been so tempted in his life. "Perry—"

Lips touched his, gentle and soft. Beguiling. Garrett's fists curled up against her face. He needed to stop this. Talk to her about it. But she was making it hard to think. He captured her wrists. "You're not distracting me. Not this time."

"I bet I could." Her eyes *gleamed*.

There *she* was again. Garrett took a sharp breath. "I want to be your lover," he said again. "But I want you to be certain of this—"

She shook her head, and twisted in his grip, that stubborn look in her expression.

"Yes," he repeated, forcing her to meet his gaze. "I have months, at most, before someone notices... or before I hand myself in. I don't want to hurt you any more than necessary. I can't be selfish, not when it comes to you."

The look on her face tore at him inside. "Promise me you won't give up? People have been speaking for years of a cure for the craving. I'm going to find out what the scientists know. What they've discovered so far. I swear."

"If there was such a thing, I'd search for it myself. But you need to be aware that I'm not certain how long I can hold this off. Already I'm finding it hard to control my anger. When I heard about the factory, I wanted to rip Byrnes's head off."

"But you didn't," she pointed out.

"Perry, it's only going to get worse as my craving levels rise."

"What about me, then? Have you ever wanted to hurt me?"

"Of course not," he shot back. But he raked his mind over the last month, about how he'd felt when she was in the room with him. Wary, of course. Nervous to touch her at times. And he wouldn't deny that she roused his lusts—both of them. "I want your blood."

"I want yours," Perry whispered. "It doesn't mean I wish to hurt you, though I could."

"But your craving levels are much lower."

"Garrett, when you found me in the draining factory, my knuckles were bleeding. You didn't even notice," she argued. "Miss McLaren did, but you didn't. What were you feeling in that moment? It wasn't hunger. Your eyes were black, but you weren't thinking about my blood at all."

The words froze him. "I was…worried about you." He always worried about her in dangerous situations—but this had been more than that. Equal parts possession and fear. The last thing he'd been thinking about was the hunger.

"But you weren't thinking about my blood." Her warm touch against his cheek drew his attention back to her. Those smoky-gray eyes blazed with determination. "I won't believe that you can't beat this—that we can't beat this."

"Are you certain we're a 'we'?" he asked.

A dangerous question. For he wasn't sure. And he had the feeling he wouldn't be, until he knew what was going through her mind, why she'd left him.

"Yes," she whispered, leaning forward, her breath curling across his lips. "I was certain the moment I said

I'd return with you. And there you have my answer
to your question too. I don't need time to think of
the consequences. I'm tired of worrying and thinking
and deciding if everything I do is the right thing. I'm
tired of being afraid. Of wanting something that I can't
have…" And here her thumb brushed against his lip,
leaving him little doubt as to what she referred to. "I
don't want to think about it anymore."

Yes. She'd said yes. His hands dug into her thighs,
where they'd been resting, a dark exultation sweeping
through him. Garrett knew she wasn't truly his—not
until he knew her secrets—but this was a move he'd
been afraid she wouldn't take.

With quivering hands he took that final step across
the line drawn in the sand between them. His mouth
met hers, palms sliding up to cup her face.

Need boiled within him, but he kept the kiss
gentle. A tasting. Stealing her breath into his lungs.
The sweetest kiss he'd ever tasted; a moment he
wanted to savor for the rest of his life. For a moment,
just a moment, the hunger was a distant sensation.

And then it roared to life.

Baring his teeth, he turned his face into her shoulder. The hammer of her pulse was loud in his ear,
and he blinked and looked away, the room falling
to shadows.

Hands slid into his hair, lips pressing against his
forehead. "Don't be afraid," Perry whispered. Her hips
rolled against his, riding against the rough ridge of his
cock. Garrett sucked in a sharp breath, his need turning
from blood to something infinitely more pleasurable.

Somehow her hand found one of his and slid it up

against the soft linen of her shirt, settling his palm over
the heated curve of her breast. Her hips rolled again,
a slow, torturous temptation. Garrett turned his face,
nipping at her lip.

"You're definitely no innocent," he murmured, his
other hand sliding up her lean flank and over her ribs.
His cock ached hard enough to make him weep.

"Curious?" she whispered, throwing her head back
and arching against him.

Yes. It drew a hiss from between his teeth. "You've
never been with anyone. All these years." He would
have known.

"Haven't I?" Hot breath in his ear.

Jealousy surged again, burning far more fiercely
than even the hunger. He looked up, just in time to
see her lips curve.

"There is no other man for me," she whispered,
plucking open the first button on her shirt. "But I like
seeing this side of you."

"Jealousy, you mean?" He slid both hands up her
back, his lips finding her throat. She was still working
on those buttons. He took a shuddering breath, lips
trailing lower over naked skin that felt like cool silk
beneath his lips.

"Yes," she whispered. "I like to see you jealous."
Fists clenched in his hair, dragging his face up to hers.
"As I have been."

The shirt clung to her shoulders, barely hiding her.
But he couldn't have looked away from those black-
ening eyes if he'd wanted to. This was one of her little
secrets…something he'd never realized before. He'd
never been a monk and she knew it, all too well.

A blithe answer hovered on his tongue but he didn't give voice to it. There was something about her expression, about the way she held herself. This had hurt her and he'd never even known.

"You never said anything," he replied.

"What could I have said?"

A challenge if ever he'd heard one. Slowly his hands eased down her back, sliding over the curves of her arse. But he did nothing else. "Maybe if you had, I'd have realized what an idiot I was long ago. I won't apologize for what's in the past. But if you want the truth, there was always something missing. Something…" He shrugged helplessly. "You. You were what was missing."

Perry's head lowered, her fingertips tracing his collar and her expression opaque. Garrett brushed his mouth against hers. "And yes, I know it's completely unfair of me, but I'm insanely jealous that there's been another man in your life. And I'm also curious"—he slowly rolled her onto her back on the sofa, pressing his weight over her—"very curious about just how innocent you are." He kissed her throat, her chin, her jaw. Then paused. "I wouldn't want to hurt you, if you were not very experienced."

Her voice was smoke. "You won't hurt me, Garrett."

"No?" He brushed her collar aside, exposing a breast band. Meeting her eyes, he tugged it down, revealing the faintest tip of her nipple. The sight of it locked up every muscle in his gut. Every instinct in him wanted to bury himself inside her. Take her. Make love to her in every way he knew.

Jealousy reared again. And possession. And emotions

he didn't think he could even name. All of them alien to him. "You're mine, my fierce lady peregrine," he whispered, leaning down and tasting the smooth curve of her breast. The ache inside deepened, tightening his balls. The body beneath him was so familiar—lean and lightly muscled, the strength in her apparent as her fingers curled around his biceps. But she wasn't fighting him now, and as he pressed down between her thighs, the sensation was completely new between them.

Tugging apart her shirt, he brushed his lips against her bared breasts, tongue darting over one nipple. A gasp stole from her and he looked up, meeting her startled gaze. No sign of gray in them now. Only darkness; only hunger, need, the fierceness of the craving. But it wasn't blood she was hungry for. Not now.

He used teeth and hands, learning her, delighting in each little hissed intake of breath he earned. He rocked forward until her hips cradled his and it was torture and pleasure for both of them. Garrett pressed his face against her breast, breathing hard. *Need her. Now.* But he'd never had the urge to prolong the experience so much before. He wanted to remember every moment, every sweet caress between them as he took her for the first time. To make love to her, truly.

How different it was to be doing this with a woman he cared for. With Perry. Every time she gasped or squirmed beneath him, he loved it. Slowly he worked his way down, leaving her nipples pink and glistening. Nipping at the smooth skin of her hip. Tongue darting into her navel…

Perry bit back a moan, sinking her hands into his hair. "Oh… Garrett."

"Are you wet for me?" he whispered, the rasp of his stubble leaving marks on her porcelain skin. She was so fucking beautiful. All long legs and smooth skin. Lithe and sleek, like a cat.

Color burned in her cheeks. A hint of shyness. He liked it when she was flirtatious and sensual, but this too was Perry. "Garrett—" she choked out.

He smiled against her hips, his lips brushing against the buttons on her breeches. He tugged one between his teeth, then looked up at her. "Yes? Or no?"

She was biting her lower lip so hard that she would leave a mark. "Yes," she whispered.

His heart thundered in his chest. Surrender. He felt it as she relaxed back onto the sofa. Felt it as he reached for the buttons on her pants.

A sharp rap sounded at the door. "Sir?" Doyle called.

Garrett looked up, breathing hard. "You've got to be bloody kidding me."

Perry jerked the two halves of her shirt together and rolled onto her side, her cheeks turning a furious pink. "Damnation!"

"Stay there," he growled, planting another kiss on her startled mouth, far too tempted to linger. He looked at her—then at the door. "What the hell is wrong?"

The guild had better be on bloody fire.

"You've a caller, sir," Doyle replied. "The Duke of Moncrieff."

"Again?" What rotten timing. "Tell him I'll be a moment." He needed to straighten his shirt and stifle the raging cock-stand in his pants. He shot Perry a frustrated look, but the expression on her face froze him. "Perry?"

She seemed to shake off the fugue that had overtaken her. Gave him a weak smile.

"Duty calls," he said dryly. "Time to see what His Grace wants this time."

"Garrett"—she caught his arm—"wait."

"Later." He bent and kissed her, capturing the protest on her lips. Perry's fist curled in his shirt, holding him there. "There is definitely going to be a later. I won't have this rushed—"

"Wait," she blurted. "I need to talk to you. About the case. About the...the duke."

"Can it wait?"

"No." She shook her head. "Please sit." Definitely nervous. "I meant to talk to you. I think...I think I know who the killer is."

Seventeen

THERE WAS NO OTHER WAY TO TELL HIM.

"I said once that this case was personal," Perry blurted out, dragging her knees up in front of herself and locking her arms around them. Her whole body felt shivery, tingling with the echo of his touch. But the thought of what she was going to tell him cut straight through the lust. "I told you it was because it reminded me of what had happened to me. I lied."

His gaze shot to hers. Intense. "I'm listening."

"I thought that I'd killed the man who infected me with the craving," she said carefully. "But I'm beginning to wonder... I don't think he died. I think he's still alive, and I think he's the same man who kidnapped Ava and Alice, and killed those girls."

"Why would you say that?"

Good. Let them stick to facts. That was something she could manage to deal with. "The laboratory under the draining factory. It's virtually the same as the one he trapped me in years ago. The same smell, the same instruments... He was exploring the effects of the craving virus on healing—exploring just how much

damage it could heal. And then, of course, there are
these rumors about that monster prowling the mists of
the East End—of Steel Jaw. Garrett, I cut half his face
off. It was…hanging." She swallowed hard, pushing
away the memories. "His name was Hague, and he
was a scientist who performed illegal experiments on
women. I think Hague is Steel Jaw. And I think he's
also masquerading as Sykes."

"Why didn't you tell me this? How could you
think to leave without letting me know such a thing?"

"I was going to send a letter." She saw his expression. "Garrett, he broke me," she whispered. "I'm
frightened and I'm trying not to be, but I…I can't.
You don't know what…" An icy shiver ran down
her spine, her gut locking tight. "It makes me feel ill
when I think of what he did to me. I can't breathe at
times. I have these…these moments of hysteria—you
saw what I was like at the factory.

"It hasn't been so bad of late, because I thought
he was dead. But now, now that he might not be…
Others will be hurt. I just wanted to get away from
here." She buried her face in her hands. "Even now,
he's stripping me of my self. He makes me less, every
time I think of him. I want to be brave. I want to hunt
him down and get justice for what he did—what he's
still doing. But I don't know if I have it in me."

And that was the horrible, shaming truth. Everything
that she'd fought for in the last nine years was a sham.
Every time she'd forced herself to enter the dark
tunnels of Undertown or to track down some killer,
she'd thought that she faced some inner demon. But
it was a lie. The moment Moncrieff reentered her

life—bringing that monster back into it—she became nothing more than a victim.

Warm hands covered hers and then Garrett slid his arms around her, tucking her in tight against his body. Perry couldn't move. Her whole body locked up tight as her shoulders shook.

"I'm frightened," she whispered. "I'm so frightened and I don't know what to do anymore."

"There are many different types of courage, Perry. Sometimes simply surviving is the bravest thing a person can do," he murmured, hand splaying over her back and rubbing. "To reforge a life after such trauma. You're not a coward for being frightened. Indeed, you'd be a fool if you weren't, for you know firsthand the horror of the situation." His voice dropped an octave. "And you came back, knowing what he did to you. Knowing you might have to face him again. If anything, I admire the hell out of you."

The words stole through her, warming something deep within.

"My mother survived," he continued, "when my father forsook her, and did what was necessary to feed both herself and me. That too is bravery, in its own way. She taught me that the man with the biggest fists or the best skills in a knife fight isn't always the strongest or the bravest. It's those who survive the worst life can throw at them and keep on fighting."

"But what if I face Hague and freeze?" Her head lifted from his shoulder. "What if I can't breathe again? What if—"

"Then we deal with such when we face it," he replied, cupping her cheek in his hand. "But I don't think you're going to panic when you come face-to-face with him, Perry. And if you do, then I will be there to help you breathe. I promise. Now what did you want to tell me about the duke?"

A part of her was still hoping that she could protect him from this. "Perhaps... I just have a suspicion he's involved."

"Because of what happened to his thrall? Octavia?"

Strange to hear those words from his lips. "Yes. Because of what he did to Octavia."

Garrett stared at the window, his chiseled profile stained by the afternoon light. It bleached the tips of his chestnut lashes, highlighting the blue of his eyes. "I think he's up to something too. He's tasked me with finding Octavia. He doesn't think she's dead."

Perry could barely hear for the sudden roar of her heartbeat in her ears. "He wants you to find Octavia?"

"Thinks she ran away from him. I'm not certain if I believe him or not. I only know that something strange happened with that case. There's virtually nothing in the case file."

But the duke had looked at her. Looked *right* at her, then away. Only that one jest he'd made, about her taking the name of the peregrine, her family's House sigil, gave any hint that he'd recognized her.

Then Garrett's words penetrated. Nothing in the case file. The *only* person who had the authority to do that was Lynch.

He'd known all along who she was.

Perry slid off his lap. "What are you going to do?"

Garrett straightened, tidying his coat and breeches with a rueful glance at her. "I'm going to see what he wants this time. No doubt a progress report. He was adamant I devote my time and attention to this, rather than the Keller-Fortescue case."

"And your intentions?"

"The duke can kiss me arse," he replied with a devilish gleam in his eyes and that roughened Bethnal accent reemerging for a second. She liked the way the words sounded. His tone was warmer in its natural state. Not as crisp and precise, as if he had to say each word carefully to ensure its accuracy.

Garrett leaned one knee on the sofa and bent down to press a gentle kiss to her lips. "If only because of his appalling sense of timing."

The taste of his lips warmed against her, his tongue sliding over hers in a teasing thrust. Slowly the back of his hand brushed against her shirt, rasping over her taut nipple. The knot in her abdomen tightened with an ache that desperately wanted her to reach up and drag his weight down upon her. To feel every hard inch of his body on hers, pressing her into the soft cushions of the sofa. She slid her hands into his hair, dragging him down, his tongue spearing into her mouth as she tumbled against the back of the sofa.

She needed this so much right now. Something to take away the panic, the fear. To remind her that she wasn't alone.

And he gave it to her, his own movements just a little desperate.

Hot. Hard. Drugging. She'd never been so aware of her body, every nerve ending tingling beneath her skin as his elegant fingers curled over her breast, palming the aching flesh. *More.* The angle of their position denied her, no matter how much she arched against him. She needed to ride her hips against his, to feel the heavy surge of his erection between her thighs.

Garrett dragged his mouth aside with a groan, breathing hard against her neck. Cool breath shivered over her skin and then he wrenched away from her, mouth parted, gasping, the fierceness of his hunger staring back at her with predator eyes.

"Stop looking at me like that." Something flickered through his gaze. Heat and need, a shiver of the darkness within. His lashes lowered, palm splaying over her breast, cupping it through the thin lawn of her shirt. "I'm trying to be dutiful."

Let the duke wait. For the first time in years, she felt nothing more than a flash of heated irritation at the thought of him. Damn him. Her fist curled in Garrett's shirt and she reached for him—

"Later, my love," he breathed harshly, drawing away from her. "Bloody hell. I'd almost managed to forget what we were up to before we were rudely interrupted. Almost. Now you've given me a cock-stand again."

"I could take care of that," she replied in a smoky voice that stiffened every muscle in his body.

Garrett stood in front of her, staring down at her with the kind of look that heated her through. He swallowed. "How?"

Leather glided beneath her palms as she slid her hands up his thighs, shifting her hips to the edge of the sofa. In that moment, fear was a distant memory. She liked herself like this, liked being bold and reck-less. The way he looked at her made her feel distinctly

feminine in a way she'd never particularly wanted to
be before. But this… For the first time she understood
what it was like to feel comfortable in her own skin.
For a man to want her with no expectations, no
demands that she change and be more like the standard
vision of femininity.

Perry pressed her lips against the leather straining
over his muscled thighs. Higher. Looking up at him
and letting him see exactly what she intended.

Garrett sucked in a breath and caught her wrists.
"*Fuck.*"

Someone hammered at the door again. "Sir?"
Doyle called. "Are you coming?"

Garrett threw a glance over his shoulder. She could
sense him weakening, trying to decide which need to
satisfy. "I'm bloody trying to," he muttered, letting
go of her wrists and stepping back out of reach. "If
someone would stop interrupting us."

Perry laughed under her breath.

Closing his eyes, he tilted his head back. Thinking.
"I shall see the duke. Then I have something important I must attend to in the city. Shall we meet here
at five?"

Perry also had matters to attend to. She nodded,
tipping her chin up and staring into those hot blue eyes.
The smile melted off her lips, the languid warmth washing out of her as the danger of the situation struck her.
As much as she wanted Garrett, she had the feeling she'd
never be entirely free of the Moncrieff. Unless…perhaps
she should confront him? Find out what he wanted?

The thought stilled her. She'd been running for so
long now that the idea of confronting the duke had

never occurred to her. But if she didn't, these stolen nights with Garrett would always be overshadowed by him. And she was tired of hiding, of running, of being afraid.

"You'll be careful?"

"Always." Garrett shot her a wicked smile as he backed toward the door. "You have a promise to fulfill, and I intend to make you keep it."

❧

Garrett paced Lynch's parlor, watching the clock tick steadily through the half hour. He'd expected to wait—or to be turned away at the door—but the time still dragged at him. Moncrieff had lectured him for almost an hour on the lack of progress with the Morrow case until Garrett had abruptly escorted him to the door. Now this. Another waste of time perhaps, but he couldn't be certain. Fingers flexing, he cursed under his breath.

Footsteps suddenly echoed on the stairs in the foyer. Lynch. Garrett recognized that brisk step immediately, a hard lump forming in his throat.

The double doors swung open, the man himself outlined in the haze of light from the foyer. Lynch wore stark black from head to toe, except for the white cravat at his throat. No doubt he was on his way to some Echelon function.

"The butler said you had a case you wished to discuss?" Lynch asked without so much as a welcome.

Garrett hated to even say this—it smacked too much of begging—but his own pride wasn't worth risking Perry's safety. "No, it's a personal matter."

The echoing silence was answer enough.

"I wouldn't be here if this wasn't important. Or if I had anyone else to ask. After Falcone attacked me, my CV levels increased. I'm not used to dealing with the…side effects." He looked Lynch dead in the eye. "I need to know if I'm a danger to Perry."

A hint of consideration in those glacial eyes. "Why Perry in particular?"

At least Lynch intended to hear him out. "Matters have evolved between us." Especially that afternoon.

"Do you *think* you might harm her?"

"I don't know. I don't feel as if I wish to, even when the craving hits me, but…can I risk it?" Garrett wet his lips. "When you were in the grip of the blood frenzy, the only person you responded to was Rosalind. You didn't hurt her, even when you wanted to kill everyone else. I have hope—"

"Rosalind is my one exception. Even when roused, the darker half of me sees her as something to be protected. Someone to kill for—to die for." Lynch frowned as he thought about it. "We blue bloods often speak as though the craving is a separate part of ourselves, but I do not think it is. I often wonder if the gentlemen of the Echelon use that excuse to deny the sheer primal need of their own nature. We are supposed to be men, in control of ourselves and not driven by our lusts, but that is what the craving is.

"Most of the time I am one with my rational self, and I love Rosalind more than anything. Therefore, when the primal part of my nature rises, I am incapable of harming her—for that primal part is still me.

The craving virus is a constant dichotomy of character. Lust versus the intellectual nature of man. Both parts of me, primal and rational, need her. Even when I was drugged into a blood frenzy, my desire to protect her was still stronger than my blood-lust."

"One might argue that falling in love comes from the primal side of one's nature, rather than the rational," Garrett countered gruffly. "At least, I find little that makes sense in any of this."

The silence stretched out. A month ago, Lynch might have even jested with him about it. "In answer to your question, do I think you will hurt her? No. I do not. Your feelings for Perry while in control of your nature would only be emphasized when the primal side rises. Or at least, so I believe."

"I have nightmares," Garrett admitted softly. "Of what I could do to her."

"Nightmares are often formed of what we fear most," Lynch replied. "Perhaps they are simply that? Nightmares."

For a moment Garrett was back in the past, talking through a case or a personal matter with Lynch, the way they used to. The way Lynch dissected the problem made sense somehow, in a way that Garrett couldn't have worked through on his own.

"Was that everything you wished to ask?"

That sense of camaraderie evaporated as if it had never been.

No. "Yes." Garrett squared his shoulders. "Thank you for seeing me."

It was more than he'd expected. And more than he deserved, perhaps. With a clipped nod, he strode toward the door, but the moment his hand gripped the handle, he couldn't seem to move any further.

Resentment was a hot flush within him, no matter whether he'd earned this dismissal or not. He couldn't stop the words from boiling up, spilling over his lips as he turned around. "I never had a father. Only my mother, and she was lost to me far too young. There was no one to teach me the right of things…only you. You showed me what honor is. What a man could build in his life if he had the will for it.

"And then you asked me to stand by while you went to die. So yes, I told Rosalind what you intended when you set out toward the Ivory Tower. I couldn't stand by and watch as you sacrificed yourself for her… I know that I failed you. I know that you'll never forgive me for it, but I'm not sorry. I couldn't just let you die. And telling Rosalind what you were planning—with the risk that she would sacrifice herself in your stead— was the only answer I had at the time. And if you want the full truth, I knew what choice she would make. I knew—I hoped—that she loved you enough to sacrifice herself for you."

Another long silence. Lynch's fingers tapped on the back of a chair, his face expressionless. "Rosa is something that I never thought I would ever have. She is my happiness. If I had died in place of her, then it would have been worth it."

Garrett laughed humorlessly. "This might appeal to your sense of irony, but I understand that now. I understand what it's like to almost lose something so infinitely precious that you can barely breathe for the near loss of it. I know"—he looked down—"why you hate me. I know you'll never forgive me. I just wanted you to know... You asked too much of me."

The words fell into the silence, seeming to echo in the small parlor, until Garrett couldn't stand it anymore. He gave another clipped nod and darted through the door, feeling that overwhelming sense of censure following him.

～

"Well, that was interesting."

Lynch's hand jerked away from the curtains, and he let them fall as Rosalind entered the parlor behind him.

"Listening at the door, my love?" he asked.

"Of course. You only tell me the boring bits." She crossed to his side, twitching aside the curtains to watch as Garrett disappeared into the traffic. "So Perry has finally made her move."

"So it seems," Lynch replied, glancing down at Rosa's pretty, upturned features. "You did predict it, after all."

"At least he has someone by his side," Rosa murmured.

"That's enough," Lynch warned, sliding a hand over her elbow. Devil knew that she'd taken every opportunity in the last month to point out how stubborn he was being. He was weary of it.

"Far be it from me to point out that if Garrett hadn't done what he did, you wouldn't be alive right now to enjoy our marriage. I, at least, have him to thank for it."

"That we're both alive is a miracle," he replied tightly. "We could both have died."

"And I could have shot you when we first met and none of this would have happened, either."

"That's not a valid argument."

"Then neither is yours," Rosa pointed out.

He ground his teeth together.

"I think you're feeling guilty," Rosa murmured, reaching up to straighten the lapels on his coat. "He's right, you know. Asking him to let you die was cruel. I remember the conversation he and I had when he told me the truth. You deliberately told him that if he tried to use the Nighthawks to rescue you, they'd be slaughtered. And you used Perry's name in particular, because you knew he'd never risk her. Now you're angry with him because you backed him into a corner and he took the only way out he had left. He came to me."

Lynch rubbed his knuckles along her jaw. She was right, damn it. And he'd known it for far longer than he'd admitted. He sighed. "How the hell do I deal with this mess?"

Eighteen

PERRY STALKED INSIDE THE BIRMINGHAM GENTLEMEN'S club, her cap pulled low over her face. The servant at the door tried to stop her, until she showed him the harsh leather body armor of a Nighthawk beneath her coat. A flash of five pounds told her exactly where the Moncrieff was.

The library was located upstairs, a room crammed with floor-to-ceiling shelves full of ancient books, and plush leather chairs that gleamed with polish. The thick scent of cheroot smoke and cognac assaulted her nostrils, as well as an overabundance of cologne. It was the kind of place where rich blue bloods gathered to survey the papers and discuss the major political events of the realm in hushed tones.

A pair of blue bloods lingered in chairs near the door, murmuring over snifters of blood-laced cognac. Behind them, an armchair faced away from the door, the gaslight gleaming on the fine golden threads of the Moncrieff's hair.

The usual gut-twisting reaction gripped her. *I'm not afraid of him. I'm not.* She didn't know who she was trying to fool. Best to get angry. She jerked her head at the pair of blue bloods and gestured toward the door. One of them paled, the other opening his mouth to protest. Perry slid her coat open and eased a hand over the hilt of her knife.

They vanished, the door clicking shut behind them.

Be brave.

"What a pleasant surprise," the Moncrieff murmured, turning the page of his paper. "I didn't expect to see you here…Miss Lowell, was it?"

Her reflection gleamed in the window in front of him.

Perry strode across the room. "Enough games. I refuse to play them anymore."

"Unfortunately, you don't get a choice."

She had the knife drawn, the blade pressed against her forearm to hide it, and the hilt warm in her hand as she circled him. "Do you think this is amusing? What are you playing at?"

He looked up then. "I'm reading the paper. You're the one accosting me."

"Don't pretend this isn't what you wanted."

His lashes lowered as he examined her, his eyes turning soft and molten. Dangerous. "Put the knife away, my dear."

"Or?"

"I'll take it off you."

Maybe he could, but maybe he couldn't. And though ten years stretched between them, she could remember just how easily he'd snapped a blue blood's neck back then. Moncrieff rarely displayed how dangerous he was, which made him all the more unpredictable. She wasn't quite certain if she could best him.

Perry put the knife away.

"So you have finally come to see me," he said, lowering the paper and looking satisfied.

"How did you find me?"

"One of my old acquaintances thought he saw you at the opera last month with a group of Nighthawks. Imagine my surprise when I opened *that* telegram."

"So you came all the way to London for me," she demanded.

"Don't be arrogant. I already intended to reinstate myself here. I had no intention of staying in that wretched hellhole in Scotland. Your reappearance is simply a ser-endipitous moment I intend to take full advantage of."

Then why all the subterfuge? Why? Unless... "That's why you haven't come for me yet, isn't it? You wanted me to crawl here to you. You think you hold all the power."

"I *do* hold all of the power. Do you know that this is the only gentlemen's club in the city that will accept me?" He smiled, a chilling sight indeed. "Everybody believes I killed my thrall." His gaze raked over her. "I don't like what you've done with your hair."

"What do you want?"

Moncrieff shook out the paper again and opened it. A grainy photograph of the queen stared out at her from the front page, endorsing the upcoming exhibi-tion. "I want the truth to emerge."

"The truth?" she challenged, snatching a fistful of the paper and forcing it down. "Or your version of it?"

He looked up. Slowly.

Perry let go and he shook the wrinkles out of the paper in a careful manner.

"You will return to my house and resume your duties as my thrall, as you agreed to do ten years ago. You will fulfill the terms of our contract, and I will see to your every comfort and continued good health for the rest of your life, as I promised to do in your thrall contract. You will attend balls on my arm, and we will let it be known that you are very much alive and well. As for everyone who accused me of dirtying my hands with your blood, I will rub their faces in the truth until *it blinds them*."

She swallowed. "You think I believe you mean me no harm?"

"I don't particularly care if you do or not," he replied.

"And Hague?"

"Is unimportant."

Her temper flared. "I know he's damned well alive, Moncrieff. He's responsible for the deaths of those two girls, isn't he? Girls you brought into his sphere. He saw you with them, didn't he? Saw them somehow and wanted them for his collection, the way he wanted me. You think I can look him in the eye and not want to cut his throat?"

"You didn't do such a good job of it last time."

That roused her ire. "How can you look the other way and ignore what he's doing? All those girls… How many have there been? How much blood is on your hands?"

The duke's eyes narrowed. He flipped a page of the paper. "I only need him for a little longer. He is a means to an end. Then the good doctor will have outlived his usefulness."

"And until then? What of the girls he'll take between then and now?"

"There won't be any," he said firmly. "I'm in London now, and I fully intend to hold his leash. I'll choke him with it, if need be."

"I'm sure that shall stop him," she snapped. "You told him to keep his hands off me, did you not?"

The duke looked sleepy eyed. Dangerous. "Hague learned how much he cost me over that unfortunate incident." His eyes met hers. "I hold both of you responsible for my exile. If you'd stayed, Octavia, you would have seen how I dealt with the matter…"

Despite her feelings for the monster, she almost shivered. "And the girls here? You wouldn't have wanted him to draw attention to whatever you're planning. How long has he been here? Why the hell did you let him off your so-called leash?"

She'd scored a point; she saw it in his expression. "Unfortunately, his current experiments require a great deal of blood. My investment in the draining factories last year provided too good an opportunity. Nobody would miss the blood here, and I could provide access to the factory for him."

"And—"

"Enough." He held up a hand.

Perry's nostrils flared. "No." It was the hardest word she'd ever said. But it was easier the second time. "No. I won't come back."

"Won't you?" A silky threat. "Don't make me kill him, Octavia."

A chill ran through her, like ice in her veins. "Kill whom?"

"Your lover."

The world seemed to freeze. All she could see was the Moncrieff's gaze slowly scanning the article he was reading. As if she meant nothing to him, as if Garrett meant nothing to him. Her throat thickened. "Garrett's not my lover."

The paper lowered. "Did I say his name?"

She stared at him, realizing that she'd only confirmed his suspicions. The Moncrieff wasn't just clever, he was cunning too. "He's my friend," she whispered.

"But you love him."

"No, I don't—"

"Then why did you come back?"

She lost the ability to breathe. "What?"

"On the train. You were going, weren't you? Fleeing me. But something he said convinced you to come back."

The heat drained from her face.

"I have every road, rail, and ship watched, Octavia. Even yourself. So if you think you can escape me this time, I pray, think again." A slither of darkness blackened those eyes, and she realized that his calmness was just a veneer, as it had always been.

Trapped. She could almost feel the iron bars closing in around her and it hurt, because she realized that for a moment, she'd almost thought there might be a chance. Garrett had given her that, made her believe that she wasn't alone in fighting this, and the Moncrieff was ripping it away.

"I won't kill him at first." The Moncrieff must have taken her silence as doubt. "I'll take everything away from him to begin with. I'll destroy any chance he has

of becoming Master of the Nighthawks. I'll take his
friends, his reputation, his health. I will cripple him;
you know I can. I know precisely what a blue blood
can survive, just how much damage the body can—or
can't—heal. I will make him regret ever meeting you,
until your name is just a curse in his ears, or what is left
of them. Then, and only then, I will kill him."

"Not even you have the right to murder a man,"
she whispered.

"Can't I? Perhaps I don't have to." He smiled. "All
I have to do is tell him what I'll do to you—what I've
done. I've met the man. I made a point of that. It's
always wise to know your adversary. He's intent on
protecting you, my dear, which means he won't have
a choice but to challenge me."

And she could see it, just as clearly as the picture he
painted for her. The Moncrieff had the power to do
exactly what he'd just threatened. The only thing she
could do was sacrifice herself to protect Garrett. As the
Moncrieff no doubt planned.

"He's a better man than you'll ever be," she whispered, knowing that the words were capitulation.

"I don't want to *be* the better man," he replied,
folding the paper and putting it aside. "I'm the Duke of
Moncrieff. However, I'm not entirely cruel. I shall give
you a day to say your good-byes and gather your things.
You will come to my house tomorrow at four in the
afternoon, when you will put aside that hideous thing
you're wearing and dress appropriately. Coincidentally,
I'm hosting a ball, something of a welcome back to
civilized life. You're to be my special guest."

He'd never once doubted that she would appear. He

must have been planning this for weeks, manipulating her into a position where she would have no choice but to face him. Giving her a day to say good-bye was just a sign of how much power he held over her, nothing more.

"I hate you."

"That's irrelevant," he replied. "I might have given a damn once, Octavia, but nine years of humiliation tends to wear away at a man's pride. There are a number of ways I could punish you for this, but I simply wish to put this behind me and move on. I have a reputation to regain and you have a reneged contract to fulfill."

"And what shall we tell the world about my absence?" she asked bitterly. "Since you seem to have thought of everything else?"

"You tripped and hit your head," he replied, "which led to a temporary loss of memory, and in your disorientation, you fled my manor. You have been living in the city serving as a governess for a merchant banker, until I found you and helped you regain your memory."

"I'm terrible with children."

"Use your imagination, my dear. I'm certain you'll be fine. You seem to have lied your way into the Nighthawks quite adequately. Unless Lynch was aware of your identity the entire time?"

The way his gaze focused on her chilled her. A warning that any answer of hers might only implicate Lynch. "I didn't find my way to the Nighthawks until three months after Octavia had disappeared. Lynch doesn't ask questions. He's not interested in our pasts, only what we can make of ourselves."

The Moncrieff stared at her for a second longer, then nodded shortly, accepting the story.

"And my father?" she demanded. The words almost stuck in her throat. She would rather face the Moncrieff before she could look her father in the eye again. "I don't want to see him."

"Hardly the thing, Octavia."

"Perry," she corrected absently.

"Octavia," he repeated. "I'm afraid that everything you've known for the last nine years is about to be buried."

The words were a chilling reminder of the threat facing Garrett. "I don't want to see my father," she repeated. "I won't. I can't look him in the eye and lie. Not about this."

"He'll want to see you," the duke replied.

"Then tell him I don't want to see *him*." It was the only way she could protect him.

They stared at each other. The duke gave a short, clipped nod. He could afford to be magnanimous, and if her father didn't believe her lies, then Moncrieff was the one who would have to deal with the Earl of Langford.

He would do it too.

"Is there anything else?" Perry asked hollowly.

"Not at this stage."

"Then I have my own conditions."

Interest flared in his eyes. The man had always been charismatic enough to charm, but few charmed him. He'd always enjoyed the challenge she'd presented. "Intrigue me."

"I'll fulfill my contract as your thrall, which means

you have every right to my blood. But I won't give you my flesh rights." She had once, before she'd known the true depth of the monster before her.

"Challenge accepted," he purred.

Suddenly her temper snapped. Perry had the blade to his throat before she even knew what she was doing. The Moncrieff didn't even flinch. "You will never bed me again," she ground out harshly. Blood welled as the tip of the knife dug into his pale flesh. "If you touch me, I will kill you."

Her gaze dropped, drawn despite her hatred for him to the sudden droplet of blood that ran down his throat. Something stroked over the back of her hand. His thumb.

"I like *this* change in you," he whispered. "Why don't you taste it?"

Their eyes met, his thumb digging into the back of her hand, forcing the edge of the knife across his throat. Blood welled.

Perry staggered back, dropping the knife. All she could see was the line of blood across his throat, the scent of it flavoring the air. She could almost *taste* it in her mouth.

"I won't force you, Octavia. I won't have to. You think you can control your hungers? Your passion? I know just how deep it runs. How much it aches to hold it back." He smeared the blood across his hand, drawing her hypnotized gaze again as he sucked it from his fingers. A hint of darkness crept through his irises and Perry took a half step toward him.

She realized what she was doing and froze.

"When you are beneath my roof, you will take your blood from me, or not at all," he stated, tugging a snowy white kerchief from his pocket. He dabbed at his throat. "In return, I shall not demand your flesh rights or touch you in any manner other than is necessary for the blood-letting."

"I'd rather starve."

"Then you will," he replied, lowering the handkerchief. There was no sign of the wound. His CV levels must have been astoundingly high.

"Keep Hague away from me. If I see him, I'll kill him." How confident she sounded. Inside, she trembled, but the duke nodded as if accepting her terms. "You will also cause no harm to Garrett or any of the Nighthawks, either by your own hand or anyone else's, or by any political maneuvering."

"I won't need to. Unless they move against me."

Which would be her task to manage. Perry gave a brief, abrupt nod. "You'll give me your word?"

"You have it." A look of dark satisfaction shadowed his expression.

Perry suddenly felt tired. This was the moment she'd been running from for years. It was almost a relief to have it over and done with.

"Then I will see you on the morrow." The strength was starting to wash out of her, leaving her knees quivering beneath her. A certain sense of hopelessness settled over her. She needed to get out of here. She needed to walk, to clear her head, to be alone to think.

"Octavia?"

She paused on the threshold and glanced over her shoulder at him.

"I shouldn't care to be pushed on this. You've been given my terms. If you don't appear tomorrow at four, then you will regret it."

The finality with which he said the words made her shiver.

෴

Perry couldn't return to the guild. Not just yet. Instead she walked out into the heavy rain, barely feeling the icy sting of it on her face and head. People hurried past with parasols and umbrellas, and one poor girl selling oranges shivered on the corner, holding a bedraggled newspaper over her head.

She walked for hours, not knowing where she was going or why. The rain came down like a curtain, obscuring the world and sinking through her clothes until the wet leather clung to her clammy skin and her teeth chattered with the cold. She staggered to a halt and looked up, staring at a white Georgian manor in Kensington. Suddenly she knew where she'd been going.

Perry shivered in misery as she waited for someone to answer her knock. At this time of night, most blue bloods would be out doing the social rounds and she would be lucky if the servants let her in.

Footsteps sounded, then an imperious-looking butler cracked open the door. Butter-yellow light flooded out, and for a moment she felt like she'd found her balance again.

"Yes?" the butler intoned.

"I need to speak to Lynch."

An imperious eye raked over her. "His Grace is not at home."

Perry pushed past, dripping water all over the white marble floor. She couldn't stand to be out in the rain a moment longer.

"What's the problem, Haversley?" A voice rang out.

Lynch strode to the edge of the gilt balcony above the entry, his gaze raking over her. His knuckles tightened on the rail at her appearance and he turned to the butler. "I want drying cloths and a flask of blud-wein sent up to my study, and a bath drawn in the guest chambers. Have something of Rosalind's laid out for her."

"Your Grace—"

Lynch took the stairs two at a time. "If I wished for your opinion, I would have asked for it."

He caught her by the arm as she swayed, his nostrils flaring. "Bloody hell, you're freezing. What have you been doing?"

"I need to talk to you," Perry said hoarsely. "I need your help."

He gave the butler a glance to warn her and nodded. "Upstairs. The fire's lit in my study. We can speak there."

Somehow he got her up the stairs. Perry was so cold, she was shivering almost violently by the time he helped her through the door. He pressed her into an armchair, despite her protestations about being wet.

The butler reappeared with several maids, and Lynch conferred with them quietly before returning with some towels. He dragged her coat and boots off her and dried her as best he could.

Finally he knelt in front of her, his dark head bent as he took a deep breath. "What's wrong?

"You had to know," she whispered. "You're not stupid. You had to know who I was. And the investigation closed shortly after I found the Nighthawks. You've never given up on a case before, not like that."

Lynch stared at her for such a long time that she

thought perhaps she'd been mistaken. Then he jerked his head. "Do you need me?"

The power of the Duke of Bleight against the Duke of Moncrieff. It was a tempting offer. And it might have worked.

But it would also draw Lynch and Rosalind into Moncrieff's schemes. And who knew what the Moncrieff would do? If he was having her watched, then they were good at what they did, for she hadn't seen them. Which meant that one of his men could potentially get close to Garrett. Or perhaps they were already close enough to hurt him.

"No," she whispered miserably. She had run from the duke years ago. It was time to pay her dues. "But I do need you to do something for me."

Lynch's expression softened. "Anything."

"I have to go back. I have to—" She swallowed hard. "I need you to look after Garrett for me. I know you're angry with him for what he did, but I need you to promise me that you'll forgive him, that you'll make sure he doesn't do something foolish."

"Perry, I—"

"Your word!" she replied, feeling her own anger rise. "After everything he has damned well done for you over the years! He needs you now."

Lynch turned on his heel and paced to the decanter in the corner, pouring them both a shot of blood. "We'll discuss this in a minute."

"He needs you," she repeated stubbornly.

Lynch handed her a glass of blood and then threw his own back. "As you're all intent on reminding me at the moment."

"Please. His virus levels have doubled. From the Falcone attack. They're at sixty-eight percent."

Lynch froze.

"He's always thought of you as a father. You know that. And he *needs* you to forgive him."

"Bloody hell." Lynch let out a harsh breath. "And you? Will he forgive you?"

"No." This was the second time she wouldn't say good-bye. "No, he won't."

A bleak look crossed Lynch's face, and then he sighed and knelt beside her. "Perry, are you certain?" A hand reached out to stroke her cheek, one of the few times he'd ever touched her like that.

"Please. *Don't*—" Perry couldn't stand his gentleness. She felt as though one kind word or touch would shatter her right now, like a rock pitched through a stained-glass window. It would smash her into a thousand tiny pieces that would never quite fit back together again. "Just promise me."

"I'll forgive him." Lynch's hand lowered. "I'll find…some way to help him through this."

"There is no cure," she said bleakly, the first time she'd ever voiced it. The first time she could contemplate what that meant for Garrett.

"There have been rumors of late—I'll look into them, I promise. And perhaps I wasn't speaking of his craving levels."

Their eyes met. He knew how she felt. She saw it.

"How?" she whispered.

"Rosalind," he replied. Then more gently, "Does Garrett know how you feel?"

"He—I—"

Again he understood. "He won't let you go so easily."

"I know."

Another favor she was asking from him. Another debt that she would never be able to repay. And more. "Can I stay here tonight?"

He disapproved, she saw, but he nodded. "Are you going to say good-bye to him?"

"I *can't*."

And suddenly Perry realized that this was the end. She could never see Garrett again, never touch him, never tell him how much she loved him, how she'd always loved him...

Lynch saw it in her face. Hard arms wrapped around her, dragging her tight against his chest. Perry couldn't hold it in anymore. She broke, sucking in huge raking gasps of air, her hands fisting in his coat to hold herself up. A sob tore loose. Then another.

"Shhh," he murmured, stroking her damp hair. "I've got you, Perry. I won't let anything happen to him, I swear. We'll work this out. We'll do something..."

A thousand meaningless words that she couldn't hear anymore, but they soothed her when nothing else could. This was Lynch. The man she'd once believed could do anything, save anyone. Not herself perhaps, for there was no saving her, but he would look after Garrett.

She heard someone come into the room. Rosalind, from the fresh scent of lemon verbena perfume. A murmured question, then Lynch was lifting her in his arms as if she weighed nothing.

"Come," he murmured. "I'll put you to bed."

Like her own father had done, once upon a time.

Perry clung to him, feeling as though she could sleep for a hundred years.

"Thank you," she whispered.

Nineteen

GARRETT RUBBED AT THE BRIDGE OF HIS NOSE AND pushed the case file away from him. Where the hell was Perry? She was supposed to meet him back here at five, and that was hours ago. To take his mind off matters, he'd been poring over the nonexistent case file for Octavia Morrow in the hope that something would give him a lead. He'd even sent Doyle to look through the boxes of books he'd packed for Lynch. Somewhere in there was a *Guide to the Great Houses of the Echelon*. If he had nothing on Octavia, perhaps he could look into the entire Morrow family. See if anyone there might have had a motive to kill her—or to hide her.

Footsteps echoed in the hallway and his head jerked. Too heavy for Perry. The moment a rap at the door sounded, he knew who it was.

"Come in," he called.

Byrnes strode into his study as if he owned it. He was covered in mud and God-knows-what, and the smell of him hit Garrett in the face like a punch.

"Christ," he muttered. "I thought you were hunting Sykes. Not rats in the sewer."

Byrnes's own lips twisted. "Much the same thing, it appears. Caught sight of a man matching your description, but he ran into the tunnels beneath the draining factories."

Another scent lifted the hairs on the back of Garrett's neck. "Is that blood?"

"Sykes was prepared for a hunt. The whole place is rigged with traps. We lost him, and then I had to bring two of the lads back to Gibson. Thought I'd let you know, then I'll head back out. The bastard's not getting away from me this time." A strange glint gleamed in the other man's eyes.

"How bad?" A blue blood could heal from almost anything, and Dr. Gibson's help was rarely required.

"Mind if I have a drink?" Byrnes asked, tipping his head toward the decanter.

Garrett nodded and poured them both a snifter of blood. "How bad?" he repeated.

"Might lose Kennewick. Took a wooden shaft straight through the chest. Jansen's leg's hanging by a tendon or two, but that should heal if Gibson can stitch it all back together."

"Bloody hell." His first month as master, and already one Nighthawk was at death's door. "How many men would you need to hunt him down safely?"

Byrnes considered it. "Give me a squad of twenty-five. The best you've got."

Garrett nodded. "Brief them on what to expect. Then see if you can pick up Sykes's trail."

"It's hard to track—he doesn't have a personal

scent, but I can smell the faintest hint of chemical on him." Byrnes looked nervous for a moment. "It'd be easier with Perry. She can smell things even I can't."

Their gazes locked. The hair on the back of Garrett's neck rose, darkness flickering up over his vision.

He fought to think through it. It was only his protective instincts, forcing him to act irrationally. Byrnes was right; Perry was the best they had. And if she knew he'd kept her out of the action to protect her, she'd have his head.

Or worse, she'd think that he didn't trust her abilities.

He nodded. Could barely speak for the wash of fierceness sweeping through him. "She's not here at the moment. She might have told Doyle where she was headed. Just don't let her get hurt."

"Not a scratch," Byrnes promised.

A moment later Doyle poked his head in, squinting at Byrnes. "Not interruptin'?"

Garrett waved him in. "You found the book?"

"Aye." Doyle placed it on the desk and glanced at Byrnes. "You run afoul of the Thames?"

Byrnes bared his teeth, then swiftly explained. Doyle sank into the chair on the other side of Garrett's desk and scratched at his beard. "Case keeps gettin' muckier and muckier," he growled, and Garrett knew he was thinking of Kennewick, who he'd trained as a novice.

Garrett flicked the book open, swiftly searching until he found the House of Langford's section. "Do you know where Perry went?"

"Never said. 'Ad that look in 'er eye, though… That determined one."

Garrett frowned. Then his gaze jerked back to the sigil engraved next to the House name. "Bloody hell." His jaw dropped.

A peregrine, stretched out in a hunting strike.

He'd seen that before. On the coin that he'd stolen from Perry's pocket the other afternoon. Why the hell would she have a coin with the Langford crest engraved on it?

"What's wrong?" Byrnes asked.

"Have you ever seen a coin with this sigil on it before?" he asked, pointing to the page.

Byrnes shook his head but Doyle squinted. "Nope, and I ain't likely to. Not like some scion from Langford 'Ouse is goin' to come marchin' through them doors, and they certainly ain't for sale."

"What do you mean?"

"They were in fashion 'bout twenty, thirty year ago. All the Great 'Ouses were 'avin' 'em made—one for every member of the family. Birthin' gifts, most often. And if you ain't a Langford, you ain't gettin' one."

It hurt to breathe.

No.

But so many things fell into place. Roughly nine years ago Perry came to the guild, not long after Octavia Morrow disappeared. Her dyed hair. The way she'd reacted with the Duke of Moncrieff, the way she'd fooled half the Echelon into believing she belonged at the opera, the way she'd fooled him.

Perry.

Who was frightened of something, frightened enough that she'd tried to run.

Moncrieff. His vision went white with rage. What

the hell was the duke playing at, coming here and asking him to look for Octavia when he had to have guessed who Perry was?

And where the devil was she? Little fingers of cold licked up his spine. *Think, damn it, think.* His immediate instinct was to hunt her down himself, but something—years of discipline under Lynch—stayed his hand.

If the Moncrieff was intent on revenge, then Garrett was considerably out of his depth. He needed allies and he needed absolute confirmation that what his gut was telling him was true. It made too much sense not to be, but before he went up against the duke, he had to be certain that Perry was Octavia Morrow.

And he had to be certain that he could control himself. The force of the craving was no ally in this; it could cost him his wits and, therefore, everything.

"Rouse the guild," he said, urgency making his voice harsh. "I want you all out on the streets searching for her."

"Who? Perry?" Doyle frowned.

"The whole guild?" Byrnes asked incredulously.

"The whole guild," Garrett repeated, snapping the case file on Octavia closed and tucking it under his arm. "And quietly. I don't want anyone to notice." He tugged the location device from his pocket and tossed it to Byrnes. "This should help. I've set a tracking chip on her."

"What about Sykes?" Byrnes asked, holding it in his hand.

"I think I know exactly where Sykes has been hiding." If Sykes was the man who'd hurt her, then the bloody duke had a hand in it. Moncrieff had to be the link between the factories and Sykes. "Just find Perry and bring her back here. Keep her under guard until I return."

"Where are you goin'?" Doyle called.

"To see the Earl of Langford. And if the Duke of Moncrieff returns, *don't*, under *any* circumstances, let him near her."

Time to find out the truth behind this entire maze of deceit and trickery. And to work out exactly what type of game the Moncrieff was playing with him.

∽

Langford Hall loomed out of the mist like some enormous gargoyle, carved of heavy gray stone with Gothic columns. The elegance of youthful beauty clung to its lines, but the stone was slightly water-stained, the curtains not quite right, like some middle-aged matron who'd once been a diamond of the first water.

Garrett swung down out of the steam carriage and stared up at the manor. An odd feeling of foreboding traveled down his spine, the tiny hairs along his arms rising. He could guess at some of the facts of the case, but he needed more. He needed to know why she'd fled from the duke.

"Want me to ring the bell, sir?" Jamie Cummings asked, pushing the driving goggles up on top of his head. The young novice had driven him out here, and rings of coal smoke circled his eyes from the city's pall.

Garrett shook his head. "You might as well pull the travel rug out and sit in the carriage. I doubt I shall finish here very swiftly."

The lad gave him a grateful look and Garrett slowly strode toward the door. It was barely two hours' drive from London, but it might as well have been another country, for the quiet that lay like a thick blanket.

Garrett had rarely been out of the city environment. The lack of noise made his ears ring slightly. There was always noise in London, even at night.

It seemed an eternity before he heard the shuffling footsteps of someone coming to answer the door, and when it opened, an elderly butler peered out at him. "Sir."

"My name is Garrett Reed, Acting Guild Master of the Nighthawks. I wish to speak to the Earl of Langford."

"It's late, sir. He may not be receiving."

"If you would emphasize the importance of my visit, I would appreciate it."

The butler shuffled away, leaving Garrett standing in the entry, examining the manor and tapping his foot impatiently. Glassy eyes stared at him from a stag's head, and ancient banners hung from the stone walls, most of them bearing that damning House sigil.

It seemed to take minutes, but the butler finally returned, his rheumy eyes full of disapproval. "His lordship shall see you now."

Garrett let out the breath he'd been holding. It was more than he'd been expecting. Langford had been in seclusion since Octavia's death.

The butler led him to a sitting room on the north side of the house. Heavy drapes were pulled across all of the windows and a fire flickered in the grate. A man sat before it, staring into the flames from his seat in a heavy, studded leather armchair. The flames reflected back off his blue eyes, and he seemed not to notice Garrett's arrival until Garrett cleared his throat.

The earl looked up, his vision coming into focus. There was a blankness to his face, as if he'd simply stopped feeling, as if he'd stepped back from the world and events that went on around him. "You're not Lynch."

It seems like the world is intent on reminding me of that. Garrett accepted it as his opening and stepped into the room. "My lord, my name is Garrett Reed. I serve as Acting Guild Master for the Nighthawks following Lynch's abdication."

"He retired?" the earl actually seemed surprised.

"He is now Duke of Bleight."

"Ah."

The fire crackled in the grate. Garrett gestured to an armchair beside the earl's. "Do you mind if I sit?"

"Do as you will. Though I have no doubt I shall be of little use to whatever avenue you pursue."

"I'm interested in your daughter's disappearance," Garrett said carefully.

The earl's face darkened. "She didn't disappear. That bastard killed her."

"The duke?"

All of the vitality that had been lacking in the man seemed suddenly to have found a spark: hatred.

"Moncrieff," he spat. "He killed my daughter. He took her away from me—" The earl's voice broke and he shut his mouth abruptly, nostrils flaring as he looked away. "He didn't even have the decency to accept my challenge afterward."

Despite what he knew of the duke, Garrett thought

that might have been a single act of mercy in the morass of what had happened.

"What was Octavia like?" Garrett couldn't hide the interest in his voice.

"Octavia was my youngest daughter. She was stubborn, spoiled. I adored her." The softening of the earl's features told the truth. "Her older sisters, Daisy and Amelia, were beautiful, kind girls…but Octavia… she was mine." His voice roughened. "I failed her. She wrote me several times, begging me to break the thrall contract. I thought it simply nerves, or her inability to conform to a traditional role.

"We never had a son, and I fear I allowed Octavia far too much freedom. I encouraged her to learn the sword, to ride, to take up masculine pursuits, and it wasn't until too late that I realized how much she would struggle to become what was expected of her. When she begged me to get her out of there…" The earl shook his head. "I *wanted* her to conform. My daughter is dead, because I ignored her."

"What reason did Octavia give for asking you to break the thrall contract?" Perry had been hurt by someone—had it been the duke who gave her the craving? The duke who put that fear in her voice and hurt her? No, no, she'd said it was Sykes—or Hague. Garrett squeezed his fists together, forcing the memory of her haunted expression away.

Control yourself.

"Why are you here?" the earl asked bluntly. "This was investigated years ago by Lynch."

"I've been asked to reinvestigate the case."

The earl was no fool. His head lifted, those blue

eyes locking on Garrett with a clarity that reminded him of someone. "Who hired you?"

"The Duke of Moncrieff."

Blackness slithered through the earl's eyes, his nostrils flaring. "Get out."

"The duke claims that he is innocent," Garrett said, finding his feet. "He believes that Octavia wanted to escape her thrall contract and staged her death."

The earl staggered upright, vibrating with rage. "That filthy snake lied through his teeth."

Garrett stared him in the eye. "I believe him."

"Get out! Bentley! Bentley!" The earl started for the door, calling for the butler.

"Wait!" Garrett went after him.

"You despicable—"

"Wait!" He shoved a hand into his pocket, withdrawing the one thing that might still the earl's wrath. "Do you recognize this?"

He held the coin up.

The earl froze, breathing harshly. "Where did you get that?"

"It belongs to a young woman I know. A Nighthawk. She calls herself Perry, and she's been with us for almost nine years. I need to know if this belonged to your daughter. I need to know if the woman I know as Perry is Octavia."

All of the color drained out of the earl's face. He simply stared, unable to speak or to move, his breath coming in short, harsh gasps.

"Do you have a portrait of her?" Garrett asked instead.

"In the hallway," the butler replied, peering through the door.

Garrett shot him a glance, then gestured to the earl. "Do you have some fortified blood? Something for him?"

The butler nodded and Garrett strode out into the hallway. Portraits lined it, but he'd not noticed them before. He paced past dozens of them, then stopped, his breath catching. There it was.

Three young girls stared out from the painting, sprawled in a rural scene with an enormous hound at their side. The elder two girls were beautiful, with bright smiles and plump, heart-shaped faces. One wore bright yellow and the other wore pink as she sniffed a handful of meadow flowers, peering mischievously over the top of them.

It was the third girl who stole his breath. She was young, perhaps only fifteen or so, looking solemn and serious as she petted the wolfhound. Silky blond curls tumbled over her shoulder, and her eyes were as gray as a stormy sky, staring out at the viewer as if she could see straight through them. She wore a green gown, as though to blend in with the grass around them, her head tucked shyly against the hound's shoulder.

"Is it this one? Is this Octavia?" Garrett stabbed a finger toward the girl in green, although he knew. Oh God, he knew. How many times had he seen that exact expression over the years?

The butler followed his gaze toward the portrait. "That is Miss Octavia with her sisters. Directly before she signed her thrall contract with the duke."

"It's her, isn't it?" the earl whispered, taking unsteady steps toward him. "She's alive, isn't she?"

Garrett gave a short, harsh nod.

The man shut his eyes, pressing a quivering hand to his mouth. "She's alive," he whispered. "But she never came home. She never let me know."

"Maybe she couldn't," Garrett suggested. The coldness was building in him again, a thunderstorm flickering within. "If she fled from the duke, then maybe she had cause. And maybe that threat, that fear, included the reason she couldn't come home."

"What are you going to do?" The earl's voice was becoming stronger.

Garrett eyed him. The man he'd first found would be no help to him, but there was a hint of something in the earl's voice that promised a growing strength. Maybe he needed this too.

"I'm going to find her—" And not wring her bloody neck as he wanted to. "Then I'm going to discover why she's frightened of the duke…"

"And then?"

"I'm going to make certain he can't hurt her anymore." The words were soft, but deadly menace echoed in them.

"Why do this for her?" the earl asked, his eyes keen. "You have to know that the duke will move to crush you."

There were a thousand things he could have said. A thousand reasons. Instead, he chose the one that burned the strongest within him: "Because I love her."

"Enough to die for her?" the earl challenged, clearly trying to test how far Garrett's loyalty would stretch.

"No." Garrett let out a small, harsh laugh. "I have no intention of dying. Not yet. But enough to destroy the duke. Or anyone who stands in my way." He stared the earl down. "I will not falter, my lord. I won't betray her and I won't turn back at the first hint of danger. Perry is my light in the darkness. I would burn the world to ashes to keep her safe, if it comes to that."

The earl stared at him for a long moment. "Then you have my blessing—and any help that I may offer you."

"Excellent. First I need to know my enemy. I need everything you know about Moncrieff. His strengths and his weaknesses."

"You have it, on one condition."

Garrett arched a brow.

"The duke is mine," the earl said grimly. "I failed her once. I won't fail her again."

"We might have to flip a coin for that honor."

Twenty

GARRETT STRODE INTO HIS STUDY, SLIDING THE COAT off his shoulders as he raked a hand through his wet hair. His fingers were shaking. Looking at them, he turned and crossed to the decanter of blud-wein, downing two glasses before he could even begin to sort through the mess in his head.

"Bloody hell." He turned and kicked a chair out of the way violently. The encounter with the Earl of Langford had only increased his tension. The Moncrieff was well nigh invincible. Reportedly the best swordsman in a generation, with the power of the Council of Dukes behind him and as rich as bloody Croesus. In comparison, Garrett had no true power—the duke would crush him if he moved openly—and barely any allies of consequence now that Lynch wanted nothing to do with him. He couldn't challenge the duke to a duel, he couldn't set the Nighthawks against him, and he couldn't buy him off.

The only weakness the man had was arrogance. Garrett was a Nighthawk, so far beneath him that the duke would barely see a challenge. It was the one thing he could exploit, if only he could think how to do it.

A sharp rap sounded at the door. Byrnes leaned against the door frame, his gaze riding over the bloodied glass on the desk and the forlorn chair on the floor. He said nothing, but it grated on Garrett's nerves, notching the tension within him even tighter.

"Have you found her?"

Byrnes's left eyebrow inched toward his hairline. "No."

"What do you mean?" Garrett froze.

"No sign of her. No trail, not even a hint of one." Byrnes held up a knife, the one with the tracking beacon inside it. "Found this near Covent Garden, tossed in an alleyway. No sign of a scuffle. Why? What's going on? Has she run again?"

"Nothing is going on," Garrett murmured, accepting the knife. One he'd designed himself, just for her. A muscle ticked in his jaw. "You've got four hundred Nighthawks out on the streets and you can't find her?"

"My, my, aren't we in a fine mood?"

"Now is *not* a good time."

Byrnes stepped inside, shutting the door behind him, blatantly ignoring the warning. "It would help the search if I had all the pieces of the puzzle. Something's bloody going on. You looked white as a ghost the instant Doyle handed you that book." His hand slipped into a pocket inside his coat and came up with a small piece of parchment. "Perhaps this has something to do with it."

"What is it?"

"Lynch arrived an hour ago. He's still here somewhere, but he grew tired of waiting. You know what he's like. Went to see the lads. He left this for you."

"Give it to me," Garrett demanded, his gaze narrowing on the piece of parchment. What could Lynch want? He'd made it quite clear their friendship was over. Something fisted tight in Garrett's gut. Longing. Christ, he wanted so badly to be able to ask what the answers were, to talk this through with the one man he'd admired above all others, but that was over now.

Every action had a consequence. At the time, he'd thought the price was one he was willing to pay, but now he wasn't so certain.

"No," Byrnes replied, circling the room with the piece of parchment still between his fingers. "I want to know what's going on."

"That's not your place."

"Then what the hell is my place?" Byrnes snapped. "I kept an eye on Lynch, helped him when he needed it, did what I was supposed to do as one of his lieutenants. I can't do that with you because you don't trust me. I might as well be just a damned tracker."

"You might have thought of that before you made my bloody life difficult when I accepted this role," Garrett snapped. "If I don't trust you, it's because you earned it. Give me the note."

Byrnes held it out to him, his lips firming. Garrett snatched it, recognizing the elegant writing immediately.

I'm sorry. I know I promised I would help you, but I have decided to resign from the Night-hawks. I can't come back. Lynch will explain what he can.

A strange ringing filling his ears. This was good-bye. Again. And she hadn't stayed to say it to him; she'd sent him a fucking note. His fingers curled into a fist, crumpling the letter in his hand. He could barely see for the sudden fierce wash of blackness that swept through his vision.

"Why is she leaving?" Byrnes asked, his voice coming from a great distance. "What the devil is going on between you two?"

Garrett was moving toward the door, but suddenly something shoved him back. Byrnes. His gaze focused again, and he couldn't hold it back any longer.

Garrett caught the other man by the lapels, dragging him close and snarling in his face. "Get. Out. Of. My. Way."

Byrnes's fingers wrapped around his wrists. "Not when you're like this."

Suddenly the other man was flying through the air, hitting the desk and rolling across the top of it, papers scattering everywhere. The inkwell rolled, black ink dripping like viscous blood from the edge of the desk. Garrett's gaze focused on it. Blood. He wanted blood. And he knew where to get it.

The world faded. The next thing he knew, he had Byrnes by the throat, forcing his chin up. The other man kicked out, legs wrapping around Garrett's hips, twisting, flinging him off balance. Then they were rolling across the timber floor, smashing into a chair and sending pieces of it flying.

"What the hell—?" Doyle's voice reverberated through the roaring in Garrett's head.

He turned, tracking the man. If he wanted human blood, it was right there in front of him.

"Get Lynch!" Byrnes hit him hard, his shoulder driving into Garrett's midriff. They went over the desk, Byrnes snarling down at him as Doyle fled. "I'm doing you a bloody favor!"

Garrett drew his arm back and punched him. Blood spattered across the wall and Byrnes shook his head, his fists tightening on Garrett's shirt.

"Is that the best...you can do?" Byrnes spat blood, laughing down at him.

He wanted to kill. Wanted to tear someone apart and Byrnes was there. Byrnes, who'd been the thorn in his side for the past month. Byrnes, who'd taunted him for years in the ring because Garrett refused to push himself to the edge, refused to hurt his comrades in what he considered sport. Perry flashed through his mind. Gone. He had to get to her, take her back. Lock her in the fucking cells if he needed to, so that she could never escape him again.

But first...

He smashed Byrnes across the face again. And again. Blood painted his knuckles, some of it his, some of it Byrnes's. It felt so damned good, he kept going, until Byrnes's hands weakened on his shirt and suddenly Garrett was on top, his fingers digging into the other man's throat—

Something hit him with the force of a train, driving him straight into the wall, his arm yanked up behind his shoulder and his face ground against the embossed wallpaper. The ringing in his ears got louder, his entire vision washing with darkness. He was going to kill whoever thought they could stop him from getting to Perry—

"Breathe." The voice was shockingly familiar. "Breathe through it, damn you."

Lynch.

Garrett's body jerked, heat and shame flushing furiously through his face. He bucked hard, but Lynch pinned him ruthlessly, forcing his arm higher until the screaming pain in his shoulder cut through even the black haze that blinded him.

"You're not alone," Lynch whispered in his ear. "I'm here. And I know how you feel. You need to breathe through it. Nice and slow. Let it in. And out again."

A hiss of breath escaped Garrett. He shoved against the wall but Lynch held him firm. No escape. Not from this, or from the black haze in his mind.

"That time that the humanists drugged me into a blood frenzy and you had to chain me to the bed, I remember you sat beside me the whole time," the voice said in his ear. "You wouldn't let Doyle or Byrnes kill me, because you knew that I could come back, that you could hold me there until I did." Lynch's grip shifted on Garrett's arm. "I've got you, lad. I've got *you* now. I won't let you lose control." He squeezed again. "She needs you to hold on. Perry needs you."

Not alone. Garrett collapsed against the wall, Lynch's body pressed against his. He sucked in a huge breath, feeling it expand against the tightness there until he felt like he could breathe again. Heat flushed behind his eyes, bringing with it a surge of shame.

"Don't fight it. Just breathe."

He could hear Byrnes getting slowly to his feet, could smell the blood in the air. His body tightened and Lynch felt it.

"Get out of here," Lynch ordered, "and clean yourself up. I want you back here in ten minutes."

Garrett tracked Byrnes through the room by sound, relaxing only when he was gone. He slumped again and opened his eyes, blinking through the shades of gray.

Lynch's harsh face came into view, examining him for a moment. Then the pressure was gone and Garrett collapsed to his knees, pressing his forehead against the wall. There was blood on his hands, his knuckles split. He had to get rid of it. Had to stop breathing in the scent of it. Garrett wiped his hands on the carpets, again and again, until his hands were crusted with dried blood. They shook.

A hand came out of nowhere, an offer of help.

"Why are you doing this?" Garrett asked hoarsely.

A considering look flashed through those gray eyes. Something he thought he'd never see in his master's eyes. "Because I abandoned you when you needed me," Lynch replied quietly, "and someone we both know reminded me of that fact."

Perry. Garrett stole another slow, steady breath, trying to fight the urge to descend back into the pit. They were words he'd hungered for, knowing that he didn't deserve them. That didn't stop the sound of them from aching like a knife to the chest. Lynch had turned his back on him, and he was right. Garrett *had* needed him. He was the only man Garrett had ever trusted—someone Garrett thought of as the father he'd never had—and he hadn't been there.

"You doctored her case file," he said, instead of everything he wanted to say. "You knew who she was when you declared the case unsolvable. You removed the photograph of Octavia Morrow so that no one would ever realize who she was."

"Ah." Lynch caught Garrett's hand, knowing he wouldn't take it. He hauled Garrett to his feet. "I wondered how much you knew."

"Not enough." Christ, the room was a mess. The desk was cracked right down the middle, the splintered remains of a chair scattered across the floor. He couldn't recall doing any of it. Garrett raked a shaky hand over his face. "I don't know why she fled from him or why she was so frightened." His voice cracked. "I don't know where she is."

"She's gone back."

Back. There was a hand on his arm and Garrett looked down, blinking through the sudden rage. Lynch's grip was a reminder. He needed to control himself right now.

"She's gone back to Moncrieff," he echoed. "Why would she do that?"

"That's what we need to discover," Lynch replied. "I never asked her about what happened all those years ago. I never let her know that I'd realized who she was. I should have."

"Perry wouldn't have answered anyway."

"No. Probably not. And she would have never completely trusted me again." Lynch frowned. "But how do we find out?"

Garrett stared at the destruction in the room. "We go to the source." His voice hardened. "Perry owes me a damned good-bye."

Twenty-one

THE ONE THING THE DUKE OF MONCRIEFF COULDN'T control was the weather.

Lightning lashed the stormy skies over the city, and rain dripped down the window, obscuring Perry's view. She stared at it, watching each drop coagulate and streak toward the bottom of the pane, not allowing herself to think of anything else.

Behind her, an abigail silently arranged the blond curls of her wig over her shoulder. Every so often she'd catch a glimpse of herself in the mirror of the vanity, and the sight always made her gaze jerk back to stare at the young woman in red.

The Moncrieff had arranged for everything. The red silk dress had been laid across the bed for her when she arrived, with a note from the duke. He thought the color would suit her, a sign of what she'd become.

All it did was remind her of Garrett—of that night at the opera when she'd worn red silk and this whole mess had begun.

"There we are, miss. You look beautiful," the abigail murmured shyly.

Perry didn't even have the heart to ask her name. She simply stared at her own reflection, at the clear, crystalline gray of her eyes and the blondness of her wig. A stranger. One who looked slightly uncomfortable in her borrowed finery, as though she'd almost forgotten what it was like to wear silk gowns and diamond chokers.

Or perhaps she'd changed so much that it was no longer her. In a way, she'd buried Octavia so completely that the foolish young girl no longer seemed to exist, even within herself.

"Thank you. That will be all."

The abigail bobbed a curtsy. "As you wish, miss."

Perry waited until the door shut. A sudden sense of restlessness washed through her. She couldn't stand to be trapped in this room any longer, with its wash of pale-pink Chinese wallpaper and lacy cushions piled on the canopy bed.

Your room, my dear.

She despised pink. She always had.

Perry crossed to the door and eased the handle around. It turned, but the door wouldn't open.

The abigail must have been under orders to lock her in. For a moment she was furious, and then an unwilling smile crossed her lips. If the Moncrieff thought that a simple lock could trap her, then he truly did not understand who he was dealing with anymore.

She tried the windows and found them latched too. A jest, really. Perry slid one of the pins from her hair and swiftly picked the lock. The window slid up, rain spattering across her skin as she breathed in the London air. Not enough to assuage the feeling of restlessness. She glanced out. The rain was beginning to soften, large fat drops instead of a steady downpour. Perry looked down at the silk dress and realized she truly didn't care about it.

Grabbing a fistful of her skirts, she eased out of the window and crouched on the narrow ledge. The heeled slippers impeded her enough for her to remove them and throw them back into her pink jail. Then, with wind whipping through her hair and skirts, she swiftly leaped from window ledge to window ledge, until she reached the upper terrace.

Say what she would about the Moncrieff, he had impeccable taste in housing. The view from the terrace stretched out over Hyde Park, a hint of greenery among the denseness of London. On a better day, she might almost be able to see the prince consort's Exhibition Building from here.

Potted oranges were pruned into exact shape, and chairs rested neatly around a wrought iron table. The glass doors to the orangery ran along the entire terrace, a veritable jungle beckoning from within. Perry's skirts began to cling wetly to her legs. In the distance, thunder rumbled.

It was exactly what she needed. Some chaos amid all of this ruthless order. A reminder that not everything in life could be controlled. A reminder that she still lived. That in itself was victory.

The shower of rain came down heavier, wetting her through in seconds. She ought to go back in. Her dress and hair were ruined. The duke would be furious if he saw her, and his guests would begin to arrive on the hour.

Still…as Perry twisted the glass door to the orangery, a part of her resisted the thought. She didn't *want* to go back.

Lightning flickered, its reflection dancing through the glass doors. Perry bowed her head and pressed her forehead against the door, rain spattering across her bare shoulders and her fingers splaying wide on the glass.

Something splashed in the puddle behind her. Perry froze, her eyes slowly opening and water dripping off her lashes. A nervous twist in her stomach reminded her that she hadn't caught sight of Hague yet. But a quick glance in the glass showed a reflection too tall to be that vile monster. Not Hague. Her heartbeat sped up. For a moment she almost wished it were.

"You forgot to say good-bye." *Garrett.* She pushed herself away from the door in surprise, her mouth dropping open.

He didn't look happy to see her. He looked furious. Raw. Rain dripped from his lashes and his chestnut hair turned dark as it clung to his scalp. Droplets of water slid down the molded leather carapace covering his chest.

It was everything she'd spent the last twelve hours hoping for.

And her worst nightmare come to life.

"Garrett," she whispered, pressing back against the glass door. "What are you doing here?"

❧

What are you doing here?

She had the nerve to ask him that? Garrett scraped

a hand across his mouth, feeling the roughness of his stubble. He'd forgotten to shave that morning. A brief glance in the mirror earlier had shown that he looked just as savage as he felt.

Perry stared at him with wide eyes, the silk of her dress clinging wetly to her body. He couldn't take his eyes off her. Here she was. Again. Running from him. Pushing him away when he could damn well help her. *His*. His heart wrenched at the thought. The idea of losing her was more than he could bear. Shadows flickered through his vision.

"Perry," he murmured. "Or should I call you Octavia?"

Her head jerked a little and she took a half step back. "You know then?"

Know? Hell, he almost laughed. He knew barely more about her than he had before he learned the truth. Only that she had once been born to the Echelon, to a man who still grieved for her loss; that she'd let the world believe she'd died; and that she'd been running from the Duke of Moncrieff all this time, only to return to him.

"I don't have a bloody clue," Garrett snapped. "All I know is that you couldn't trust me with the truth."

"I didn't want anyone to know—"

"I'm not anyone, damn you." How dare she? "I've told you everything about my life and I knew that you didn't want to speak about your past, but I respected that. I thought there was little to tell."

"There isn't anything to tell."

"To me?" Garrett questioned, taking a threatening step toward her. "You told Lynch." He searched her eyes, desperate to see some sign that she gave a damn.

"Only what he needed to know."

"Incredible. I thought we were partners, Perry. Friends. I always knew that you had my back, but you never thought the same, did you? Of any of us."

"That's not true," she cried, showing the first sign of agitation.

"You used us for what we could give you, but you never gave anything back. You kept everything locked up inside so that no one could get close. So that no one could ever guess your secrets. And now that you've gotten what you wanted, you're discarding us, like some fucking soiled robe—"

She slapped him.

The vibration shivered through his jaw, turning his head aside. Garrett touched the hot sting slowly, the blackness receding from his vision.

Rain fell, splashing in the puddles at his feet. She was breathing hard. So was he.

"You need to leave," Perry said, her fists clenched at her sides and her body quivering. She turned on her heel, all that glorious, wet red silk clinging to her lean body. "I'm never coming home, Garrett. It's over. Don't come back."

His gaze followed her hungrily. Then he was in front of her, slamming one hand against the wet glass wall of the orangery. Perry flinched back but he trapped her, reaching out with the other hand to lock her in. Rain slid down his wrist, inside the sleeve of his coat. It didn't matter. He was wet through. Wet and furious and aching so badly for her to give him just one hint that she'd ever given a damn about him.

Perry pressed herself back against the glass, her head turned slightly to the side. And he realized that she was waiting for something…a blow perhaps, or harsh words… Garrett froze. What had happened—the slap—that wasn't Perry. If she'd wanted to hit him, she'd have balled her fist and planted him one straight in the face. The slap was a reaction, something she might have done years ago, before she learned how to hit. Instinct. To push him away. Make him stop. Make the words stop.

He reached up, brushing his knuckles against her cheek. Perry shivered, closing her eyes as if she couldn't meet his gaze. Nothing made sense. He ran his fingertips down over her wet skin, tracing her lips.

"I shouldn't have hit you," she whispered, finally looking up. "I'm sorry."

Something he'd said had struck a nerve. Garrett searched her gaze, trying to push through the anger and the hurt. When she was frightened or scared, she attacked. And he had pushed her somehow.

Ten years ago she'd run from the duke. Why? Something had happened, something awful and frightening enough that she'd never returned home.

And now she was back in the very place she'd run from.

That didn't make sense.

"Why return to him?" Pieces started tumbling into place like clockwork. The duke coming into the guild and asking Garrett to look for her. Perry's reaction at the time hadn't spoken of a woman desperate to return to a man who'd once been her lover. No, that was fear, leaving her frozen and trembling on the stairs as she tried to make herself unnoticeable. He saw it now. "What did he threaten to do to you?"

"Nothing," Perry snapped, bringing her arms up inside his and knocking them aside. A dark, desperate glint echoed in her eyes. "I've simply agreed to fulfill my thrall contract."

"You're lying."

She stepped closer, glaring into his eyes. "The duke didn't threaten me. I choose this of my own free will. I was born to this life. Perhaps I want to go back."

Garrett glared back, searching for anything to tell him the truth. Now she was fighting. Which meant he had her cornered. "You always try to pick a fight when you're upset."

"I'm not fighting you," she shot back. "I'm telling you what is going to happen."

"You're lying."

"Damn you, Garrett." She pushed at his chest, without much success. One fist hit him above the lungs, then another, pounding at him, pushing, even when he caught her wrists and held them trapped there, the wet silk of her gloves gripping his fingers.

Slowly the aggression eased from her. Her shoulders fell, a quiver running through her lower lip. She looked so lost in that moment, as if she barely had the strength to fight. "How many times do I have to tell you what I've decided?"

He wanted to be her strength in that moment. To hold her up when she was so clearly struggling. Garrett smoothed his thumb across her cheek, tilting her face to his. He was so certain now. "You could tell me a hundred times. A thousand. It doesn't matter, Perry. I'm not leaving you behind. I'm not letting you slip through my fingers, not this time." His hand slid around the back of her neck, cradling her scalp and drawing her closer to him. "All this time, you were there. And I never saw you. I never knew. But now I do."

Perry froze, looking up at him hopelessly. "I can't do this." The words were a whisper. "We can't."

"I will give you everything."

And still it wasn't enough. He saw the longing in her eyes. For a moment, a droplet of water slid down her cheek, almost as if she'd shed a tear herself. Then she shook her head.

"I *can't*."

"I would sacrifice everything to be with you," he told her. "*Everything*."

"But *I* won't."

Garrett searched her gaze. A horrible suspicion fell into place. The only reason she could be doing this. His entire body froze, stillness leaching through him. *No.* "He didn't threaten *you*, did he? He threatened me."

Perry shook her head vehemently, but the diamond glitter of her eyes was its own truth. "Garrett—"

The darkness swirled within him, a vortex of sudden fury. "I'll kill him."

"No!" This time she was adamant. Fear flickered in her eyes as she tried to catch his wrist. "Promise me you won't do anything foolish!"

"I'm right, aren't I?" He held his fist up, out of reach, and she tried again. Caught it.

"Garrett—"

"You say you won't sacrifice everything. That makes me wonder where you'd draw the line, and I know you, Perry. I know the one thing you'd never sacrifice. Me. That's it, isn't it? That's what he threatened you with."

She swallowed. And reached for him with her other hand. "He'll destroy you—"

The confirmation shook him. No. Not this. He looked past her, into the depths of the orangery. That fucking bastard. Trapping her like this, using *Garrett* himself to force her back into a situation she'd fled from. He'd rip the duke's goddamned heart from his chest

Perry shoved at him. "No!" she whispered harshly. "No!" Hitting him with her fists, forcing him to step back, out of the orangery, which he hadn't realized he'd entered.

Garrett caught her wrists and she twisted, fighting him, her own desperation bleeding across her face. "Don't undo this. You can't beat him. No one can. He's a duke."

"I don't care if he's the king!" he snapped.

"He's the greatest bladesman in England. You barely know one end of a sword from the other!"

"I'm not going to bloody duel him," Garrett snarled. "And I can work out which end's the pointy one. I'm going to shove it up his ducal—"

Perry's hands fisted in his collar, a determined expression crossing her face. She was surprisingly strong. "I *won't* let you do this."

Garrett cupped her face, stroked her cheeks, her

lips, wetness gliding beneath his thumbs. "You made your choice. I'm making mine."

"Let me go, Garrett. Please."

Rain dripped down the windows, splashing across both their faces. A single drop gathered on the top of her lip. He wanted to lick it off, to taste it.

"Never," he said, sliding his hand around to cup the back of her head.

His mouth met hers, claiming it. A fierce, undeniable urge to protect swept through him, focusing solely on the woman in his arms. She'd done this for him. Because she loved him. Even if she'd never said the words, she didn't need to. Even if he hated the cause, he couldn't stop himself from crushing her against his chest and squeezing her tightly.

His hands cradled her face as he pressed her back against the rough brick wall of the house. Perry's fingers clenched in his coat, a breathy little mewl sounding in her throat. Her mouth was hot sin. She kept nothing back, kissing him as if her life depended on it, kissing him as if the world was going to end and they only had minutes left, seconds...

Everything that stood between them washed away in the pouring rain. All of the doubts he'd had. Whether this would ruin their friendship, whether he could stop the inevitable spiral of the craving... It didn't matter. Nothing mattered except this. Right here. Her mouth on his, tongue darting against his own, her hips undulating against him as he sank a hand into the flesh of her arse and hauled her tight against him. Kissing her, drowning in her...

It wasn't enough. Somehow he had a hand clenched

in the wet silk of her skirts, dragging them up her thighs. Perry threw her head back as Garrett ran his lips down her throat. Her pulse kicked against his lips and he didn't dare linger, need lighting him on fire as he kissed his way down her wet skin, licking the water from her breasts.

The silk clung. He couldn't get it off. Didn't need to. Her nipples were hard and tight behind the silk and he bit her there, teeth scraping gently over her stays, his mouth following as he suckled. Perry gasped, hands fisting in his hair.

He sucked the moisture from the silk, heating it with his mouth. Yanking her skirts higher and higher, until he had them bunched at her waist. Behind his leather breeches, his cock raged for release.

"Hold your skirts," he commanded.

She did, leaning back against the wall and biting her lip as she watched him go to his knees before her.

The flesh of her thighs was ice cold against his lips as he found her drawers and tugged them down. Even they were wet and cold, but he knew there was heat here somewhere. And as his palms slid up the back of her legs, parting them, he knew he'd found it.

Garrett's breath refracted back at him, hot on her clammy skin. One of her hands slid into his hair as she trembled and he kissed his way up her thigh, pressing his face against the small tangle of blond hair at the junction of her hips. She smelled clean and wet, and he wanted her, needed her… So much so that the ache almost knotted him in two.

"Garrett!" Perry sucked in a harsh gasp as he licked at her, nuzzling into her sensitive flesh.

The taste was exquisite. Garrett let go of control, losing himself in his need for her. So many months spent denying himself, denying her. And now, right when he was on the verge of losing her, he had this one last chance…

Each gasp he wrung from Perry's lips felt like victory. Each time her fist clenched in his hair and she cried out wordlessly, her body folding over him. He coaxed her thighs wider, shifting one knee up and over his shoulder. And then she was his and he kissed her deep and hard, feeling the tension in her begin to tighten.

"God. Oh, God," she cried, hips thrusting against his mouth.

He felt her shudder. *That's it. Just a little more.* And then she cried out, jerking hard against his mouth as both hands curled around his shoulders.

"Garrett. *Please.*"

Another rippling spasm. Garrett tongued her deep, suckling on her clitoris. Perry had a hand to her mouth, biting her knuckles to hold back a scream. With her other hand, she pushed him away, her whole body collapsing back against the wall.

"No," she whispered. "No more. Enough."

Garrett drew back, pressing a kiss to her thigh. "Never enough," he warned.

Her leg slid off his shoulder, and he caught it at his elbow, their eyes meeting. Then he surged to his feet, locking her leg around his hip as he kissed her.

Perry was shuddery, weak. But he felt her starting to throw off her lassitude, her hands darting down between them. The urgency in her actions bit at him. This wasn't done between them. And it wasn't enough by half. He wanted to brand himself on her skin—deep within her—so she'd never be able to walk away again.

"You belong to me," he whispered, feeling those greedy little hands tearing at the buttons on his pants. "I won't give you up, Perry. Not now. Not ever."

His cock sprang free into her eager grip. Garrett shifted her in his arms, hooking her other leg up around his hips and shoving the acres of wet red silk out from between them. Then he thrust hard, sinking into her wet heat and moaning.

Bliss. It felt so right that he almost came, right there. Perry's body was a tight, silken fist around his cock, her teeth sinking into his lip on a moan as he thrust again. Garrett shoved his hand out, holding them both up against the wall, his other arm locked around her, grinding her close against him.

There was nothing of gentleness in this. A claiming, pure and simple. She belonged to him, and he wanted to etch that fact on her memory so that she'd never think of another man again. Their greedy hands tore at each other, Perry's half-drugged gaze meeting his, and then she was moaning again as he pumped his cock inside her. Little desperate pleas in his ear that drove him wild, crazy with need. Her teeth sinking into the tender flesh where his neck met his shoulder.

He knew what she wanted.

"Take it," he gasped, dragging the knife from his belt and pressing it into her hands.

Perry let out a low moan. "I *can't*."

Garrett wrapped his fingers around hers and brought

the knife up. The edge was a sharp sting against his throat as blood welled. Perry's eyes narrowed in on his throat as blood mingled with the rain, a look of such intense need that he almost came.

"Do it," he whispered, offering her his throat. "You want it. I want it. *Do it.*"

The first brush of her mouth sent a shudder through him. Perry gasped at the taste. Then her mouth suckled at his skin, drinking his blood, the sensation shooting all the way through him until his balls tightened. Garrett slammed her back against the wall as her tentativeness gave way to hunger, burying himself inside her. It felt so damned good. She owned him in this moment, could have asked him for anything. The sweet pull of her mouth against his throat was drugging. Suddenly he was fucking her, feeling the pull of her mouth in other places, desperate to sink into her flesh, as if the two could become one.

Perry drew back with a gasp, her eyes flooded with blackness. Lips consuming hers, he tugged at the pins holding her wig in place. He shoved the bloody thing aside, and then his hands were sliding through the short silken strands of her own hair.

She looked like herself again. But more. Wet and sensual and so bloody beautiful that it made his heart clench in his chest. *You. It was always you.*

The thought pushed him to the heights of pleasure, his gut clenching as heat flashed through his balls. Garrett groaned, pressing his face against her throat. He didn't want this to end, because he knew that she still wasn't with him fully. The second he let her go, her clever little mind would start coming up with every rational excuse she could find to fight this.

"Perry." He slid his hand between them, thumb rasping over the seat of her pleasure.

Perry sucked in a sharp breath, her wide gray eyes locking on his. Her body tightened around him and then she shattered, her mouth forming a little "Oh" of surprise as she threw her head back, clenching around him, shudders racking through her.

The world disappeared, became nothing more than heat and wet and sex. Each thrust became a little rougher, more urgent. Rain spattered across his face as he ground her against the wall, coming with a harsh gasp.

His thrusts slowed as he shuddered within her. Suddenly he could feel the harsh brick rasping against the backs of his hands as he held her in place. The sting of the rain was so cold it seemed to shock him back to life. A flash of lightning lit up the sky. Garrett lifted his face from her shoulder, breathing hard.

Perry's quivering fingers slid roughly over his mouth, her gray eyes locking on his as if she still couldn't quite figure out what had happened. Solemn, serious eyes. He wanted to kiss the frown from her brow, make her forget all of the doubts that were suddenly creeping back in.

Garrett took her hand and kissed the backs of her fingers. "No regrets, my love," he said hoarsely. "You belong to me now."

Twenty-two

LONG MINUTES DRIFTED PAST AS GARRETT HELD HER pressed against the wall, slowly breathing as he came back down from the heights of ecstasy, his body still tangled with hers.

"This doesn't change anything," Perry whispered against the skin of his throat.

His heart clenched in his chest. Garrett's hands tightened on her. "Tell me you don't love me," he said and withdrew from the warmth of her body, tucking himself back into his breeches.

Perry's eyes widened, rain dripping down her cheeks and turning her eyes almost blue. He watched the emotion evaporate from her face as she smoothly put up her walls, shaking her skirts back into place.

"I don't love you," she lied.

"Tell me you never did."

"I never did… I never will."

So blank, that mask. As if nothing could ever penetrate it. And he needed to get under her skin, to force her to fight for this too.

"We promised no more lies." Garrett stroked his

thumb over her kiss-ravaged mouth. "So I will give you my truth. I love *you*," he told her. "And I won't let you go, I won't make any promises to go away and leave you to fight this alone." His thumb traced away some of the wetness on her cheek. "The way you think your father did."

Perry's entire body stiffened. He could almost see her working through his words, deciding what she could and couldn't deal with. It was little surprise when she focused on the statement he thought she'd choose. "Why would you say that about my father?"

"I met him, last night."

Another flinch. The mask was starting to slip, her eyes searching over his shoulder, as if to find something that would help her escape this, escape him. "Love has conditions attached, Garrett." Her lower lip quivered. "I'm not a fool. I learned the hard way. My father loved me—he doted on me—but he wanted me to change. He wanted me to accept..." Her breath caught. "I couldn't be what he wanted me to be. What the world wanted me to be."

"Have I ever asked you to be anything you're not?"

Nothing in her expression changed. But she hesitated. "No."

"And I don't think you're giving your father enough credit. You sent him letters asking him to break the contract between you and the duke. Did you ever tell him what was happening? What you were frightened of? I've seen your father, Perry. He's a broken man. He feels that he failed his daughter, and he's had to live with that for the past nine years."

Perry slammed her hands up, her palms hitting him

hard in the chest, both guilt and rage flooding her eyes with black. "Don't," she warned as he staggered back a step. "Don't you dare mention him. Don't—" She turned around, wiping the wetness from her face as if just noticing the state of her dress and hair. "Oh, God," she whispered. "I have to go. I have to get ready for the ball."

Garrett grabbed her upper arm. "Perry—"

"I'm wet. The dress—" She shook herself free, panic painted across her face.

He'd pressed her too hard. Too fast. She was facing demons that he could only begin to guess at. And the first thing she did was try to put some order back into her life.

"I have to go."

"I'm not letting you—"

"You don't have a choice," Perry snapped, grabbing fistfuls of her skirts.

He held his hands up. "I could throw you over my shoulder."

"I could kick you in the ballocks," she shot back. "This is not your choice to make. It's mine, Garrett. I know you don't like the price, but I can't see any way around it, for now. He's *dangerous*."

"So am I."

Perry paused by the door to the orangery, her hand on the handle. "I know you are. But the duke—he has resources, power… You're just a Nighthawk in this world, Garrett. And I won't risk you."

"Because you love me too," he pushed.

Perry's nostrils flared. "Because you're not a killer, Garrett. Not at heart. And he is."

"I do what I have to."

"Precisely. You hesitate every single time it comes to taking a life. The Moncrieff kills because he likes it." She shook her head and opened the door. "I've made my decision." Her voice broke. "I'd rather have your hate than see you hurt."

They stared at each other. Garrett realized she wouldn't back down, not from this, not now. "You always were a stubborn chit."

"Good-bye, Garrett," Perry said softly.

The door opened and she slipped inside, becoming little more than a red-and-white wraith moving behind the wet glass.

"Good-bye," he said as the door clicked shut. "For now."

～⁓

Perry strode along the hallway in her bare feet, her skirts clinging damply to her legs. She was so upset she could hardly speak, let alone think. *"He feels that he failed his daughter…"* The words tore through her, igniting a maelstrom of emotion. She wanted to scream. *He did. He did fail me. He wasn't there when I needed him so badly…*

And worse. The words that hurt the most. *I love you.*

She'd loved Garrett for years, both the man she'd thought he was and the more complex part of him that she'd just come to realize was there. But a part of her had never expected to hear those words from his lips. It was easy to love him, for he never looked at her, never noticed her. Her feelings for him were safe, because she would never have to examine them further, never have to face his disappointment in her when she couldn't be what he wanted. It frightened her and the first thing she'd thought when he'd said it was, *No*.

Every man in her life who'd told her those words had placed conditions on them. *I love you but…I want you to change.*

Her father had spent years teaching her to fence, to ride, to manage the enormous estate they called home. And then when she'd turned sixteen, suddenly it wasn't enough. His focus had turned to her debut, and the sudden realization that his daughter didn't fit the same mold as every other dashing young debutante. When she'd captured the duke's eye, he'd been not thrilled but relieved, as if in his secret heart, he'd doubted her ability to ever land a thrall contract.

The duke had said those words, luring her into quiet corners during their courtship. *"I love you, Octavia, but when the contract is signed, I will expect certain behavior of you. I shall engage a finishing tutor, just for you. Consider it a gift, dearest."* And she'd been so desperate to prove herself to her father—and the duke—that she'd agreed and called it love.

I love you, Garrett had said. The words still hammered at her, fighting to sink through her determination to hold them at bay. *Have I ever asked you to be anything you're not?*

She couldn't think about that right now or else she'd lose control. A part of her wanted so badly to throw herself into Garrett's arms. To believe him. To beg him to take her away from here. To run. Together. She couldn't escape the feel of him, as if he'd imprinted himself onto her skin—and beneath it. The inevitable had finally happened, and she knew that a part of herself would never feel the same.

I love you.

A door in front of her opened and the Moncrieff himself came out, toying with his cuff links. He looked flawless in his evening attire, his black coat gleaming in the gaslight.

They both stopped. His hard gaze raked over her, a challenging eyebrow tilting up.

"I wished for some air," Perry told him, a dark edge coming over her thoughts. Ever since those first few months as a blue blood, she'd never come close to losing control of her darker nature, but it was there tonight, bubbling within her like the storm outside. Pushed to the limits by a man who claimed to love her.

One hand lashed out, caught her chin, and tilted her face toward the nearest gaslight. "I told you that you were to take no other man's blood."

"I believe the precise words were, 'When you are beneath my roof, you will take your blood from me, or not at all.' I was on the terrace, Your Grace." She jerked out of his grasp and held up a handful of her damp skirts. Color was draining out of the world, her senses growing even sharper, until she could see fine grains of hair along his jaw where he'd recently shaved. "I was very clearly not beneath your roof."

Quietly: "Get yourself cleaned up." A muscle in his jaw tightened. "You look like some filthy Covent Garden slattern."

She bared her teeth at him in a silent snarl.

I love you. I love you. I love you. It hammered at her from within, slowly breaking down the walls she kept in place to protect herself. She couldn't fight it, couldn't stop hearing the words. They were drowning her, slowly getting louder, beating in time to the rush of her heart.

And this man in front of her was the one thing stopping her from everything she had ever wanted.

The fear washed out of her, leaving her pulsing with her own dark power. Perry stared at the Moncrieff. He'd always terrified her. She had known, beyond a shadow of a doubt, that he could and would destroy her if he had the desire. That she was completely alone in the world, for not even her father would help her. The one man she'd always run to, the one man she could trust to always be there for her.

He hadn't been, and the realization had crushed her. Yet she'd forgotten that she was no longer that frightened young woman. She was a blue blood now. And there was a man out there who loved her. A stubborn, stupid, reckless man who refused to take no for an answer. No matter what she told him, Garrett would try to rescue her. She was no longer alone.

Never alone again.

I love you.

It gave her the strength she needed so badly. Perry shoved the Moncrieff against the wall, his eyes widening in surprise. She stepped closer, her fingers curling into claws in his coat. "You will never speak to me like that again."

Blackness bled through his own eyes. "I will speak to you however I damned well please—"

Perry plucked a pin from the wig in her hand and jammed it into his abdomen. The duke snarled, throwing her back, but his legs gave way almost immediately, the hemlock racing through his system and paralyzing him. All of her pins had been dipped in the small vial of poison she'd brought with her for protection.

He crumpled to his knees, shock turning his face white. Perry picked up her skirts and circled him as he slumped onto the floor, still trying to fight the poison.

"I will play your games. I will let you parade me on your arm tonight and show the world that Octavia Morrow didn't die. But I won't let you treat me like some insipid little toy you think you can kick around if it misbehaves. Make whatever threats against Garrett you can, but I promise you this… If you hurt him, I will kill you. I will cut your heart out of your chest while you lie helplessly like this on the ground, and I will *burn* it."

Grabbing a handful of her skirts, Perry spun on her heel, her bare feet sinking into the plush Turkish red carpets.

"Octav-ia."

The word was strangled but clearer than it ought to be, considering the paralysis.

She turned.

The duke struggled to roll onto his side, fury painted across his face. His CV levels must have been staggeringly high for him to be moving already, a fact she wouldn't forget.

"My name is Perry." She'd never been Octavia; she'd never truly understood her.

"If you ever…do this to me again… I shall give you to Hague."

Perry stared at him, seeing the bodies again. Those poor young girls in the cellar of the duke's mansion, bound by iron collars to the walls. Missing…things. But still alive.

"It's amazing what the body can survive, Miss Octavia…" Hague's voice whispered in her memory as he injected something into her arm. *"This won't hurt at all."*

A little shiver worked its way down her spine, the blackness draining out of her vision as she stared down at the Moncrieff. All of her newfound confidence evaporated at the thought of the monster, her breath coming sharply.

"You knew," she whispered. "You knew all along what kind of monster he was."

The duke struggled to his hands and knees, listing dangerously. "The price is worth the gain."

Again that cellar flashed through her mind. Helpless. Unable to move, while Hague jerked the bright light closer to her face and then started cutting. Forcing the craving virus he'd injected her with to heal her, until her skin was unblemished and the table was covered in blood.

It helped the virus to "bloom," he'd told her. In normal circumstances, it could take weeks or even months for the full infection to set in. However, if her body was healing the damage, then it couldn't fight off the virus.

And once she was infected…the virus would heal

any wound Hague inflicted on her. He could experiment with creating functioning mechanical organs to his heart's delight.

Perry jerked out of the memory. Some things were never meant to be relived. "You bastard." There was a familiar hollow feeling in her chest. She fought to breathe through it, feeling the hot rush of one of her bouts of hysteria latch onto her lungs.

Moncrieff bared his teeth, straining to push himself upright. "You wouldn't understand. Knowledge is power. And Hague can do things no one else can."

"But the price—"

"Sacrifice for the greater good," he taunted her. "Those improved iron lungs they're outfitting coal miners with who do you think came up with the design? He's a genius."

"He's a monster."

The blackness was bleeding back into her. She let it, fighting to breathe. Darkness stirring within. Perry took a step toward him. She was shaking so violently she could hardly walk, but if she killed him, right here, right now, then no other girl would have to suffer for his cause. She'd be able to breathe again. She could find Hague. She could…she could…kill him…somehow…

"You deserve to die," she said, sliding the knife from the inner lining of her corset.

The Moncrieff barked a laugh. "Probably." He met her eyes. "Hague knows how to reverse the effects of the craving."

Everything in her went still. *Everything.* The world froze to almost crystalline precision. "That's impossible."

"I assure you it's not. He's created a device for

me—why the hell do you think I keep him alive?" His
eyes narrowed. "High CV levels, my dear?"

Suddenly her lungs opened up and Perry fought to
stay upright, not to curl up into a ball, shaking. A cure.
A way to reverse the effects of the virus. A blaze of
hope swirled through her that made her dizzy.

If he knew what she wanted the information for,
he'd only have one more thing to hold over her head.

"It's something every blue blood fears," she managed to say. She could save Garrett. All she needed
was the technology. He'd never have to be afraid to
touch her again. Wouldn't sit there with that icily
calm expression on his face as he outlined what would
happen when he was...gone. He'd live. For years.

Which meant she couldn't kill Hague. Or the
duke. Yet.

No more girls, though. It had to be soon. She'd
have to find out what Hague knew and then she could
destroy him.

"Precisely. And I control it."

The realization triggered another in her mind.
"That's why your exile ended early, isn't it? You gave
the technology to the prince consort in return for a
seat on the Council."

The Moncrieff dragged himself to his feet. "I can
own the empire with what I know."

He could own *her*.

Just how far would she go to save Garrett? She
knew the answer only too well. There was nothing
she wouldn't sacrifice to save the man she loved. "I
want that information."

The Moncrieff's gaze narrowed on her. "It's

him, isn't it? Not you." A smile crept over his lips.
"That's why you came back. What will you give me
for the information?"

The world seemed to narrow in around her. "What
do you want?"

"Complete and utter surrender."

A moment to reconsider. To walk away. Then
Perry whispered, "I want your word that no more girls
shall be harmed."

A brief nod. Her head lowered in defeat. "You
have my surrender."

⋘∾⋙

The guests began arriving shortly after dusk fell, a line
of steam carriages stretching back for miles. Everyone
who was anyone seemed to be attending, despite the
inclement weather. No doubt they were all afire about
the Moncrieff's return and the promise of a night he'd
avowed would be like nothing they'd ever seen.

Perry watched through the window. The abigail
had returned to repair her attire, and she now wore
midnight blue silk with elegant silver embroidery
stitched across sections of her bustle. The poor abigail
trembled as she replaced Perry's hairpiece with a fresh
one, fumbling with the gloves until Perry had taken
pity on her and put them on herself.

Now she was alone, silently tracing patterns on the
glass with her silk gloves. The Moncrieff would send
for her when the ball was in full swing. He intended
everyone to be there to witness her resurrection from
the dead.

After tonight, there would be no going back. She

had given her word to the duke. All she had to do was get through tonight and tomorrow morning, and he would give her what she wanted at the opening of the exhibition tomorrow. He'd promised. Garrett would never have to fear the Fade again.

A thousand things she'd wanted to say over the years to Garrett. A thousand times she'd bitten her tongue, forced herself not to admit the depth of her feelings to him. All that time she'd wasted.

A rap at the door broke her thoughts, jerking her away from the window. "Yes?"

The door opened and the duke stood there, imposing in black. There was no sign of their earlier struggle in the hallway. His cheeks were flush with color, his eyes glittering with satisfaction. Here was the moment he'd waited nine years for.

"It's time," he said, extending his arm.

Perry smoothed her skirts, a delaying tactic she'd once used when she'd been a debutante to ease the tangle of her tongue and her shyness. "Of course."

She took his arm and swept out into the hallway.

Music echoed through the halls, an elegant, restrained waltz that mingled with the soft hush of laughter and conversation.

"Tonight will be a success." Excitement burned through the duke. "And after tomorrow's showing of the device at the exhibition, the entire Echelon will be bowing at my feet."

It was as if he were alone, speaking solely for his own benefit.

The music grew louder. It itched along her skin, marching her inevitably to the next chapter of her life.

The gilded doors opened at the end of the hallway, the laughter and conversation swelling.

The ballroom stretched out below them, the floors so polished that it seemed as if twice as many dancers circled the room as were actually there. Mirrors lined every available surface, and the riot of color was almost painful to the eyes.

Moncrieff led her to the top of the stairs. It took a moment for people to begin to notice them, curious eyes turning their way and whispers starting. A smile stretched over the duke's mouth, his predatory eyes surveying the room.

Once he had captured everyone's attention, he glanced at her. "Shall we?"

They began the descent, conversation slowly dying as people began to realize who she was. Faces paled, gasps echoing in the room. The entire waltz ground to a halt as debutantes strained to see what all the fuss was about.

Perry hated every moment of it. This was a world she'd never truly understood.

"Who is she?"

"What is going on, Gerald?"

"Hush. By gods, that's Octavia Morrow!"

Not a single person moved. Fans fluttered to a halt and the orchestra finally gave up. Silence reigned, except for the underlying whispers that choked the room.

Then a man near the foot of the stairs stepped forward, clad in strictly tailored black. The silk of his lapels gleamed under the candelabra, and a ruby stickpin winked in the snowy white cravat at his throat.

Barrons, the Duke of Caine's heir.

He bowed slightly, his dark eyes showing no surprise at all. "Octavia. You are well?"

That sent the room into another flurry of whispers, for the use of her name presumed that he knew her and well. The question he was asking, however, had nothing to do with anyone else. She had at least one ally here tonight.

Suddenly she didn't feel so alone. "It's good to see you, my lord."

"A friend sent me," he replied quietly.

Garrett.

At her side, the duke stiffened. "As you can see, she's perfectly well. And alive," he added, in a slightly louder voice before he swept her past Barrons and into the crowd.

The following hour was a nightmare. Perry could barely function as the duke introduced her to lords and ladies she only half remembered, and some she'd never met. The excuse for her absence—her amnesia—seemed to satisfy some of them, but their ravenous curiosity was insatiable as they hounded her with question after question, which the duke smoothly negotiated. She could feel the itch start deep within, the darker side of her nature threatening to emerge.

"I need something to drink," Perry whispered to the duke.

"In a moment—"

"Now." She dug her nails into his arm and he shot her a sharp glance, taking in the bleeding blackness of her eyes.

"As you wish," he demurred, looking entirely too pleased with himself.

A passing debutante gasped as she saw Perry's eyes, and suddenly everyone was looking at her again. Seeing the signs of the craving virus upon her. She didn't care. She needed blood, needed to get out of this crush for a moment.

Several servant drones circled through the crowd, champagne glasses littering the trays they carried on their heads. The small machines were easy to track, for an exhale of steam followed them throughout the crowd. Perry snatched a glass of blud-wein but the duke intercepted it before it touched her lips.

She turned to snarl at him, but he smiled and sipped it himself. "Only from me, Octavia."

The thought curdled her stomach, but the hunger was burning in her throat. She *needed* blood. She'd never been so close to lashing out before, never understood just how hard it had been for Garrett in the last month.

"I could have been lenient," he continued. "If you hadn't disobeyed me this afternoon. Consider this your punishment. Come."

Eyes tracked them as they swept through the ball-room. The scent of warm flesh and perfume filled the air, along with the underlying hint of blood. Several thralls wore diamond collars to hide the healing slash marks on their throats, but Perry could still smell the blood, and it drove her further into the grip of the hunger.

The crowd parted, a dark form materializing in the midst of a dozen white-gowned debutantes. The duke stiffened at her side and Perry's heart leaped as Lynch forced them to stop.

"Your Grace," Lynch said, inclining his head toward the duke at her side.

Rosalind was with him, wearing an exquisite gown of crushed violet silk with mink fur at the collar. Piles of coppery hair were melded into an elegant chignon, and her gloves concealed her mechanical hand. The eyes that examined the Moncrieff were cold and hard as she sipped at her champagne. Eyeing him as one would an adversary.

"Your Grace." Moncrieff sounded surprised. "How...interesting to see you here."

Which meant Lynch hadn't been invited. The Moncrieff had wanted to separate Perry from all of her friends.

"An interesting night all round," Lynch replied, with the faintest of smiles. He was tall enough to rival the duke in height and he stared into Moncrieff's eyes, letting him know that he wasn't at all intimidated. Lynch had been the original Nighthawk, used to dealing with murderers, madmen, and the Council of Dukes. His gaze flickered to her.

"Breathe," he told her and the iron band around her lungs suddenly vanished.

Lynch would never let her face this alone. Heat flushed behind her eyes, and the crushing grip of the hunger eased until color flooded back into her vision.

"This must be your lovely wife." The Duke of Moncrieff stepped forward, reaching for the duchess's hand.

Rosalind smoothly offered him her left hand,

and he pressed his lips to the back of it, hesitating minutely. No doubt he'd realized it wasn't flesh he held but metal.

"How intriguing," he said. "I wasn't aware that you'd married a mech."

The word was a complete insult. Rosalind held a hand out, suppressing Lynch's sudden, furious intake of breath.

"If you hurt her, I will kill you," Rosalind whispered, triggering something within the mechanics of her hand. A blade hissed through the silk of her glove, narrowly avoiding the duke's lips. She smiled as he let her go abruptly.

"It's never a successful evening without at least one threat," Moncrieff replied haughtily. To his credit, he extended his hand toward Rosalind again. "May I have this waltz with your wife, Lynch?"

It was a threat, but the pair of them exchanged glances, then Rosalind stepped forward, accepting the duke's gloved hand. The blade slowly vanished back within her glove. "Go," she told her husband. "Dance with Perry. The duke and I shall discuss the mechanics of my latest bill."

"It sounds fascinating," Moncrieff replied dryly, shooting Perry a warning glance as he swept the duchess into the waltz. He hadn't expected her to accept.

For the first time since she'd arrived, Perry's shoulders relaxed. Lynch took her gloved hand and rested it on his forearm, holding it in place. "Are you all right?"

"No," she whispered, then attempted to smile. "But I have been in worse places and survived."

"Dance with me."

Perry nodded and then Lynch was leading her toward the dance floor and smoothly sweeping her into the waltz.

To dance with Lynch was strangely comforting and she realized that they moved perfectly together. For years they'd waltzed with blades, knowing how the other moved, knowing each fluid line of the other's body. This was simply a different style.

"You're not alone," he told her. "Don't give up."

"Thank you, sir."

Lynch gave her an amused smile. "How long do you think Moncrieff will last with Rosa before she drives him insane with her latest proposition for Parliament?"

"Perhaps I should join her cause. I can bore him to death."

Lynch's grip tightened, just a fraction. "Do you want me to challenge him?"

"No," Perry replied. "I need him alive." She looked up. "I need you alive."

There was a long moment of companionable silence between them as Lynch swept her in circles around the room. They'd never needed an abundance of conversation between them to be comfortable.

"*Need* him alive?"

Perry glanced up at him from beneath her lashes. "He has a device that can reverse the effects of the craving. Or control it."

A slight intake of breath. That was the only sign that he'd heard her, but for Lynch, he might as well have set off a fireworks display. "And the price?"

"Me."

He nodded sharply, looking across the ballroom.

His gaze locked on something, his eyes narrowing just a fraction as he stared at the duke. "That device could be dangerous."

It reminded her that Lynch was no longer simply the Nighthawk, but one of the Dukes who ruled the city.

"He doesn't intend to share how it works," she replied. "But if tonight goes well, he'll allow the Echelon a preview at the exhibition tomorrow. He'll control the device, of course, but he'll allow blue bloods to use it for a small price. And he'll give me access to it."

"I see."

It unnerved her, for she feared he knew exactly what she meant. "What is Garrett doing tonight?"

The waltz slowed, Lynch rocking her to a halt. "He's here, of course. For you."

His gaze lifted over her shoulder and Perry felt a prickling awareness run down the back of her neck. She glanced over her shoulder just as the crowd parted and Garrett stepped through, immaculately clad in black, with the white of his bow tie gleaming. Just that easily he slipped into the coat and looked as though he belonged here in a way she'd never mastered.

"No." She panicked, jerking at Lynch's hold.

Lynch leaned close enough to whisper in her ear. "If I ask him, I know what the answer will be. The price is too much, Perry. It's time you learned to let someone else help you for a change."

"I can heal him," she whispered. "I can save him."

Another long, slow look. "Speaking as a man who has recently had his wife try to sacrifice herself for him, the gesture won't be appreciated. If a cure exists, then there's still hope. That's enough."

"Might I cut in?"

The voice shivered over her skin, under it. She held on to Lynch until the last second, a wash of heat sweeping through her. Then Lynch gently disentangled her and passed her into Garrett's arms.

"She's all yours," Lynch replied, and the words sounded vaguely prophetic.

Music started up, a hint of a Middle Eastern hum rasping over the strings. Perry's gaze jerked to Garrett. The *assah*. A dance designed to tempt, to display a thrall or debutante's best assets to a blue blood.

"You look beautiful," he said, sweeping her into the dance. Of course he knew the steps, though she didn't ask how. There'd been affairs in his past with ladies of the Echelon, and Garrett had always been able to master any skill with minimal effort, damn him.

He turned her in a slow circle, holding on to her wrists from behind. "Though I prefer you in red." Another turn, drawing her back against his chest, his voice whispering over the skin of her neck. "And wet."

One hand curled around her waist, drawing her in tight against him. Perry slid her gloved hand over his, holding it in place, her breath trembling through her chest. "You shouldn't be here. You're going to ruin everything."

"Precisely."

The dance swept them apart again, Garrett twirling her in elegant circles. Then she was back in his arms as if she belonged there. Oh, how she wanted to stay. This dance was forbidden, but the feel of Garrett's arms made it seem as if the world had vanished around them, as if they could create their own world. Somewhere safe, just for them.

"I told you to go!" she whispered harshly. "I made my decision."

"If I recall, I don't believe I actually agreed with it." Garrett twirled her in a pirouette, their eyes meeting for a brief smoldering moment before she was back in his arms.

"You're a stubborn bastard." Despite her anger, a tiny part of her warmed.

"We're well matched." His breath tickled her hair. "I'm going to give you stubborn children, my love."

Perry flinched. She couldn't focus on that. Not now. And he knew it. "He has a cure for the craving," she murmured, trying to force him off balance as much as she was.

Stillness leeched through the hard body holding her. They paused in the middle of the dance floor. "If you tell me this is why you're doing this, I'll wring your bloody neck."

"Then I won't tell you."

Perry twirled, giving him a sharp look to keep going.

Garrett glared at her, moving sullenly into the next step. "I'm not leaving without you tonight. I did it once. Not again. And you can argue all you damn well like."

Perry glanced over his shoulder. The Moncrieff prowled the edges of the dance floor, watching her with a dark, possessive look on his face. She jerked her gaze back to Garrett. "He'll kill you."

"Not here, he won't," Garrett replied with considerable aplomb.

"This isn't a jest!"

At that his eyes darkened and he leaned close to her. "I'm not laughing, Perry." His grip tightened on her until their hips were almost pressed against each other, his lips trailing against her cheek. She trembled at the rasp of his stubble.

"Damn you for a stubborn fool."

"People in glass houses, my dear."

Perry drew back enough to be able to see his face. "What are you planning?"

Another swirling circle, where she caught a glimpse of the duke, strolling slowly through the crowd. Their eyes met, then she was swept into Garrett's arms, her back cradled against his chest.

"Best if you don't know."

"Garrett," she whispered over her shoulder.

His gaze locked across the room. The duke stared back, a tight expression on his face. Perry couldn't stop herself from grabbing Garrett's hand reflexively.

"He's not alone," she whispered. "Whatever you're planning, you need to know that he'll protect himself first." She hesitated. "Don't forget about Hague."

Garrett's attention snapped to her.

"You know what he did to those girls." Her chest seized, but she kept going. "It's not the first time I've seen such a thing. It's not the first time…" She couldn't go on, shook her head. "I escaped, Garrett. I'm the only one who ever has." The words were coming faster now. "The duke told me the cellars were out-of-bounds, and I should have listened to him. But I was curious. And there were…strange noises sometimes. Crying. At night. That was why

I begged my father to get me out of there. I should never have gone searching. I should never have opened the cellar door, but I did."

A thumb stroked her hand, drawing her back out of the nightmare. Perry looked up bleakly as he swirled her gently in his arms. Garrett said nothing, letting her say what she needed to say. His presence was an anchor against the fear and horror.

"When they found me, I was trying to free one of the girls. The duke told me that if I ever breathed a word of it, he'd kill my father, and Hague…he wasn't supposed to touch me. I had to live there, knowing what was going on. One night the duke went out, to his club"—she was babbling—"I tried to free them again and Hague took me. He h-hurt me. He just wouldn't stop cutting me, no matter how much I screamed." She wet her lips, seeing it all over again. Garrett's hand caught her chin, forcing her eyes to his. Forcing her to see him, rather than the blood on the blade.

"You escaped," he said quietly.

Running down that long hallway in the duke's mansion. Slipping in her own blood. And there, over the fireplace, a pair of crossed broadswords. She'd been so desperate by then. "When Hague came after me…I thought I'd killed him," Perry whispered. "The blade went through his face, his jaw. I don't know how anyone could have survived."

"And then you ran."

"Hague had injected me with the craving virus. So that I'd survive his experiments. By the time I fled, I wasn't in my right mind. I could barely fight off the hunger, let alone actually think about what I should do. And my father—I couldn't go home. It was the first place the Moncrieff would look. And he'd threatened—"

"It's all right," Garrett whispered, his hands stroking her hips as he rocked her. "You don't have to be frightened anymore."

So easy to surrender to that gentle touch. She wanted to. "You don't understand. The duke knew what Hague was doing. They have no conscience, no…no empathy. You can't arrest them. You can't duel them; only a blue blood of the Echelon can. With this ability to reverse the craving, the duke *owns* the prince consort. Any court case would simply vanish, and the witnesses too."

Garrett's hold tightened. "So you'll stay with him. Knowing what he did."

"I will do what I need to."

"And so will I," he said quietly.

"Don't."

"If I asked you not to stay with the duke, would you obey?"

Perry's jaw tightened.

"I thought not," he replied. "So don't ask me to watch the woman I love go with another man to save my life. I won't have it, Perry."

"Stop saying that."

"I'll keep saying it until you believe me." His arms locked around her, drawing her close, his breath a harsh exhalation against her cheek. "I love you, Perry. I'll always love you. And I'll tell you every day for the rest of our lives if you need me to."

She couldn't keep fighting him anymore. And the dance was drawing to a close, people's eyes turning their way. He was holding her far too closely for even the *assah*.

Her eyes met the Moncrieff's. The duke was waiting for her on the edge of the dance floor, a blank expression on his face. Too blank.

"Trust me," Garrett whispered.

It broke something inside her. "I'm frightened," she admitted. "All of this... Everything I've done... I can kill a man with one blow, but as soon as I see the duke, I'm just a frightened young girl again. I hate it."

"The problem is that you still think you're alone."

She looked up.

"And you're not," Garrett said fiercely. "You have me—you'll always have me. And Lynch and Rosalind, Byrnes...even Barrons is here... Do you think we're frightened of the duke?"

Hope stirred, that fickle bitch. "What are you going to do?"

"Promise me you haven't given up." He used her own words against her.

Another darting glance at the Moncrieff. Perry wet her lips. "Garrett..." She wanted to believe him. In her entire life, she'd never met anyone who gave her as much hope as he did.

"Swear it," he demanded in a fierce whisper.

Their heads were curled together. He was barely rocking her now, both of them cocooned in their own little world. Perry tasted his breath on her lips. Her heart gave a wild thump. To take this step frightened her almost as much as Hague did. She'd been trying to protect Garrett, to protect her father, but if she didn't do something, she'd be trapped forever.

There would always be someone the Moncrieff could use against her. *And I don't want to do this anymore.* Her heart twisted again. *I want to be with Garrett.* "I swear it."

The hard line of his shoulders softened. "Good. My first impulse was to come in here with that recurring pistol Fitz has been dabbling with and kidnap you like a pirate, but Lynch and Barrons—and common sense—have convinced me to wait until we have a workable plan. We're putting things into place for tomorrow at the exhibition. I still need to contact several people, but I needed you to know you weren't alone." Gloved fingers brushed against her hair. "I'm not going to duel him, Perry. Though I damned well want to. But this is another world and I'm going to play by their rules."

"And me?"

"Be prepared," he whispered. "For anything. Lynch will give you the details at the exhibition—I daresay I won't be allowed close to you." For a moment his eyes darkened. "Moncrieff won't hurt you? Tonight?"

"I can handle him," she stressed, her voice a little stronger now. "He can't afford to hurt me. Not now. In a way, returning to the Echelon was the safest thing I could have done. He can't do anything to me without destroying his standing in society."

"What about Hague?"

"There's been no sign of him, and I doubt I will see one. The duke knows how I feel about that. And Hague is disciplined, despite everything. He will be working on the device."

The muscle in his jaw ticked and he shut his eyes,

his chest expanding as he took a slow breath. "If he lays one hand on you…"

"If he touches me, I'll break his fingers," Perry whispered, squeezing his hand. That warmth was spreading through her now. Belief. She had the ridiculous, light-headed feeling that they were going to do this. "You know I will."

For a long moment she didn't think she'd convinced him. Garrett opened his eyes and stared at her, releasing the breath he'd been holding. "Tomorrow," he said. Then, foolishly, "I don't want to let go of you."

"I don't want to let you go, either."

His eyes searched hers. "You mean it."

"I always meant it," Perry whispered. "Even if I never dared say it."

The light in his eyes almost made her smile. But neither of them dared, at this moment. Garrett squeezed her hands where they were laced through his. "Don't tempt me to take you out of here," he growled. "Tomorrow, when this is done, I'm going to lock you in my bedchambers and make you tell me that until you're hoarse."

"Tomorrow, then," she whispered.

"I'll hold you to that." Garrett glanced over her shoulder as if meeting someone else's eyes. Perry didn't dare look; she could feel the Moncrieff's gaze drilling between her shoulder blades.

Slowly she rubbed her thumb over the back of his hand, bringing his attention back to hers. "Trust me."

"Tomorrow." He said the word as if it was a promise, then he gave a taunting nod to someone behind her and, turning, strode away through the crowd.

A hand locked around her elbow. "What the hell is he doing here?" the Moncrieff hissed.

"Saying good-bye," Perry whispered, watching as the crowd swallowed up the man she loved.

Twenty-three

PERRY HAD BARELY GOTTEN A WINK OF SLEEP FOR THE
nervousness that racked her and the fear that something was going to go wrong, that Garrett would be
harmed. That was truly her worst nightmare. To come
so close to being in his arms—his heart—and have it
all torn away from her. To lose him forever.

"You look rather unimpressed," the Moncrieff
murmured at her side, tearing her thoughts from the
man who held her heart.

Perry blinked. She'd barely noticed any of the
exhibitions they'd passed, or the chorus of amazed
exhalations from the attendees. Everyone was curious
about her, of course, and though she'd exchanged
small pleasantries, they'd been distracted ones at best.

"The exhibitions are truly first-class," she said,
meaning none of it. "The prince consort shall be
overjoyed with their reception."

Feathers bobbed as ladies fluttered fans and the echo
of conversation hummed through the air, floating up
toward the glass ceiling high above. The enormous
building was formed of glass, and light streamed

through the panes, highlighting every curtained par-
tition and the brass gleam of the latest standard
of automaton, or enormous threshing machines an
American company had shipped all the way from
Manhattan City. Businessmen and nobles from all over
the world had come to see these marvels of modern
engineering. Ahead of them, light sparkled off what
appeared to be a line of mirrors—a mirrored maze in
the heart of the aisle.

The duke offered his arm, tucking her gloved hand
into the crook of his elbow and holding it there. A
possessive gesture. "The best is yet to come. This way,
my dear. Let me show you the device."

Anticipation sat heavily in her chest. He'd spent
most of the night locked away with the device, after
offering her his blood. Perry had taken it, despite a
moment's hesitation. Though the thought disgusted
her, she had wanted to be at her best today. "The
device you use to neutralize the craving?"

He checked his pocket watch, then tucked it within
his embroidered champagne-colored waistcoat. "All
will be revealed within minutes."

Drat it. Perry tried not to let her disappointment
show, but he saw it, a tiny smile playing over his lips.
"Do try to pretend you're interested in me, rather than
my machine."

"Why lie?"

His laughter rang through the room as he led her
toward a large, curtained-off exhibit directly opposite
the grand staircase. A walkway lined the upper floor,
providing excellent vantage points.

Dark midnight-blue skirts swished around her

ankles as he directed her to a spot beside the bloodred curtains. Another dress cut to fit her perfectly. Black lace edged the neckline and dripped down her bustle, and her gloves were gleaming black satin. The amount of thought the Moncrieff had put into her wardrobe was unnerving. Planned. No doubt everything that had happened up until this point was part of his game.

Not everything. She caught a glimpse of Barrons across the crowd, sipping at his blud-wein, with that outrageous ruby dangling from a hoop in his ear. At his side stood the young Duke of Malloryn. In the light, Malloryn's hair gleamed like polished copper, and she almost thought it was Garrett until he raked the crowd with a cold, dismissive gaze. Young but deadly, as he'd have to be to keep his seat on the Council.

She didn't dare look for Garrett. He'd told her he'd get word to her somehow, but she couldn't give him away. Instead Perry watched as the Moncrieff strode to the center of the curtain, waiting for all eyes to notice him.

A hush fell and skirts rustled as people began to edge closer. Someone brushed against her and Perry found Mrs. Carver at her side, her burnished bronze eyes gleaming in the light as she fanned herself. There was no sign of her brutish verwulfen husband, but at her side stood another young woman in delicate condition, wearing a sternly cut charcoal day dress that hinted at the soft swell of her curves. From the similarity in their features, they had to be related to each other.

"This is my sister, Honoria." Mrs. Carver introduced them. "She wanted to see the device they're about to reveal. She's the sister I spoke of at the autopsy, the one with the interest in science."

"How do you do?" Perry murmured.

"Quite well, thank you," Honoria replied.

"Don't look now," Mrs. Carver said through lips that barely moved, "but your man is behind you. On the gallery above us."

Perry glanced up, but Mrs. Carver caught her hand and tilted the large black ostrich feathers in front of their faces as if she were sharing a humorous *on-dit*. "Don't give the game away," she whispered. "It's very important that the Moncrieff doesn't know Master Reed is here yet."

Here. Watching her. Instantly Perry's shoulders relaxed. She glanced at Honoria, wondering how much she knew, but the woman was watching the stage intently. "And your husband? I didn't think he'd allow you here without his presence." It wouldn't be easy, being verwulfen in a world that thought such creatures little more than recently released slaves.

"He didn't," Mrs. Carver replied dryly. "He's at the back of the crowd, with my sister's husband." She leaned closer, her voice dropping. "I was the only one they didn't think the Moncrieff would suspect and...I owe Barrons a favor or two. He asked me to let you know that things are proceeding as planned. However, they need to get the Moncrieff alone."

"Alone?" She could certainly lure him away...

"Not you," Mrs. Carver replied. "Master Reed wants you to stay here, in the crowd, where it's safe. He and the Duke of Bleight have matters in hand."

"Of course they do." Keeping her nice and safe

while they planned to ambush the Moncrieff. The thought made her unaccountably nervous. "Thank you for helping then, Mrs. Carver. I shall owe you a favor myself."

"Lena, please. I feel so terribly ancient when someone calls me Mrs. Carver." The vibrant young woman flashed her a smile. Then it faded. "Tell me, did you find the man who killed Miss Keller and Miss Fortescue?"

"I believe we're both about to meet him." Perry felt ill at the thought, a ring of coldness circling her temples.

"Don't be frightened." Lena squeezed her hand. "I can smell it," she admitted when Perry shot her a sharp look.

"I'm not frightened." She had friends. And a man who loved her. The thought warmed her from within, burning through that trembling, breathless feeling in her chest. Perhaps she'd always have such a feeling whenever she thought of Hague, but at least she was learning to manage it. She'd survived once. She would do it again. She just needed to keep believing such a thing.

"Ladies and gentleman," the Moncrieff called.

Instantly the room hushed and people gathered closer.

"As announced last night, the prince consort and I have a demonstration of particular interest and magnitude." He gestured to the side and the prince consort stepped forward with a smug smile.

Light gleamed off the gold breastplate the man wore beneath his pale blue frock coat, as per his usual custom. He hadn't aged in the ten years since she'd last glimpsed him, though his skin was paler and even his hair had lightened. Those almost colorless eyes surveyed the crowd, settling on something for a moment. Following the prince consort's gaze, Perry saw that it was Lynch and Barrons, standing at the back of the crowd with expressionless faces.

Danger stirred the fine hairs on the back of her neck.

"My queen." The Moncrieff nodded to the small woman behind the prince consort. "Would you do me the honor of stepping forward? Duchess?"

Queen Alexandra's skin flushed a healthy pink, and she looked around warily as the crowd surveyed her. "As you wish."

Another young woman took her arm, leading her forward with an iron grip on the queen's gloves. Together they were the sun and the moon—the human queen with her dark, glossy hair and warm complexion, and the tall, icily regal duchess with hair the color of flame, ruthlessly gathered into a chignon. Perry had barely known the Duchess of Casavian, but she recognized her immediately.

Lady Aramina Duvall was the only acknowledged female blue blood in London, and one that held a substantial amount of power. Not only did she sit on the ruling Council of Dukes, but she had thwarted numerous assassination attempts and even fought her own duels. Cold as an arctic breeze, the Echelon whispered, but Perry rather thought that the woman had to be, in order to survive in such a world.

The Moncrieff slipped his superfine coat off and handed it to Perry. He began working on the buttons of his sleeves. "Last night, you both attended me at the conclusion of my ball. I took a measure of my blood and tested it with a brass spectrometer that the duchess provided herself. Lady Aramina, could you inform the crowd of what my craving virus levels were?"

The duchess arched a defined brow, smoothing her cream-colored skirts. "Your CV levels were sixty-two percent."

"Your Majesty, will you confirm this?" Moncrieff asked.

"I confirm it," the queen replied, glancing at her husband as if to seek his approval.

"Could Mr. Thomas Wexler step forward, please?" the Moncrieff called.

The crowd parted around a tall man in a gray suit, who looked rather surprised at being named. "Yes, sir?" he asked with a distinct American twang.

"Mr. Wexler owns Wexler and Sons, a fine American company that produces the Spectrum 300, the latest—and supposedly greatest—example of brass spectrometers in the world. Some of you might have noticed his exhibit next door," the Moncrieff said. "Mr. Wexler, would you mind if I borrowed your device for a simple experiment?"

The man offered a rakish smile. "As long as we can discuss the commission afterward."

Laughter echoed. The duke returned his smile. "Consider this an endorsement."

The brass spectrometer was brought forward and the crowd craned their necks. Even Perry was growing curious now. She glanced up, just once, but she couldn't see any sign of Garrett.

She could sense him, though, the gentle caress of his gaze on her back, like the faint tracing of fingers.

"Duchess, would you do me the favor of checking my CV count?" the Moncrieff asked.

"I should be delighted," Lady Aramina replied, in a voice completely devoid of such stated expression.

Stepping forward, she withdrew a small case from her reticule and removed what appeared to be an elegant fléchette. Taking the duke's hand, their gazes meeting, she slashed the blade across his finger, then turned and dripped the welling blood into the mouth of the spectrometer.

The small device gave a whirring sound, swiftly overwhelmed by the creak and rustle of clothing as everybody leaned forward.

A little slip of paper shot out and the duchess held it up. "Your CV count is—" The words stopped suddenly, her eyebrows arching in surprise. For a moment her face looked softer, younger. A woman of warmth and emotion, rather than the ice princess who'd stood there but a moment ago.

The Moncrieff tied a small linen around his finger until the cut healed. "My CV count is…?"

"Forty-six percent," the duchess said. "That's impossible. I saw it with my own eyes last night. The levels of virus in your blood can't have dropped almost twenty percent within hours. That's simply—"

"Miraculous," the duke finished for her, with the most satisfactory smile Perry had ever seen on his face. Success. He studied the crowd, dwelling in the moment, knowing that every eye in the place was upon him. "And I assure you, quite possible." Taking a step back, he grabbed a fistful of the curtain. Waited.

"For years, we blue bloods have ruled the world,

victim only to the violence of the disease and its inevitable consequences. Living in fear of that moment when our CV levels finally reveal to us the end: the Fade." His fist tensed in the curtain. "No more."

With a flourish he yanked it down, revealing an enormous brass device. The crowd gasped. A chair sat between two glass cylinders, with several wires and tubes running between them. Blood filled one of the cylinders, and rearing above them were a pair of conductors, the type that spat charged lightning between them.

Honoria sucked in a sharp breath. "That's how he does it," she whispered. "He drains as much blood as he can and then replaces it with human blood to dilute the CV levels." Her straight brows drew together. "A rather temporary notion, I'd suspect."

The two sisters glanced at each other, momentarily forgetting Perry. "So it's not a cure?" Lena whispered.

"I don't believe such a thing truly exists... Used regularly enough, it should control the craving levels, however." Honoria slid a hand over Perry's wrist and leaned closer. "If I were to propose a theory, it's entirely possible that this would be the perfect time to rid oneself of the duke. He'll be recovering from the blood loss, and the lower limits of craving virus in his blood will slow his healing and reaction times. For the moment, he's made himself rather more human than he anticipated—or indeed, has probably thought of."

"How do you—"

"She knows what we're about," Lena murmured.

The perfect opportunity. "Could you relay this information to Lynch?"

Lena nodded and faded into the crowd. Perry's heart started to beat a little faster, her gaze locking on the duke.

"The process takes several hours," the duke admitted, "which is why I spent most of the night hooked up to the device in order to provide proof of its authenticity. Some of you may doubt my word, but do you dare dispute what the queen and the duchess—no friend of mine—saw with their own eyes?"

The Moncrieff sat in the chair, resting back like a king on his throne. "This technology is the first of its kind in the world. The only known management for the craving virus! It's not a cure—and truly, who would not wish to be a blue blood? But with this, who knows, perhaps we could live forever." He reached inside his shirt and withdrew a long key on a chain. "And to prove my loyalty to the Crown, after the demonstration I will give the key to the prince consort, who my own doctor has been personally treating for the last month." Tucking it in his pocket, he stood and bowed to the prince consort.

"'Tis true," the prince consort called. "An incredible device. My CV levels have dropped remarkably since I began treatment and continue to improve with regular infusions."

"How does it work?" one of the Russians called in a heavy accent.

"Is it dangerous?" another gentleman asked.

Murmurs sprang to life.

"For this, I call upon an old friend of mine to explain and demonstrate. A genius, able to comprehend the very workings of the virus itself." The

Moncrieff gestured into the shadows at the sides of the curtain walls. "Dr. Hague, of Delft."

Cold eyes met hers as a shadow detached itself from the edge of the stall. Wearing the thick, false beard he'd worn in the alley, the man she'd given chase to— the man she knew as Sykes—stepped forward. His hair was lighter than it had been once, but she suddenly realized that might be the effect of the craving virus upon him. Most blue bloods took longer than ten years to reach the Fade, but who knew what experiments he'd performed on himself, if any?

A tremble started down her spine and Perry's fingers curled into fists. She wasn't alone anymore and she wasn't weak. This time she was going to finish the job she'd started so many years ago—to stop this monster from continuing his evil.

No more girls would ever have to suffer.

❧

Hague. Everything in Garrett went still as the bastard stepped out of the shadows. Perry stiffened, and Mrs. Carver's sister, Honoria, settled a gentling hand in the small of her back. It wasn't enough. He could see the fine trembling begin in her body, her shoulders jerking as if her lungs had arrested.

He liked to cut…

Perry's words echoed in his ears. Instantly the world dissolved into shadows and Garrett found himself pushing his way through the crowd, cutting a silent, deadly path between silk-clad debutantes and thralls and their blue blood masters.

He couldn't take his eyes off Hague. The man was

demonstrating how the device worked, rolling up the duke's shirtsleeve to insert a fine needle into the vein on the inside of his elbow.

"Using human blood to flush through a blue blood's veins until the desired cleansing has been achieved…" the duke called. "It lasts several months, until the virus gains hold again, but the effects are instantaneous and significantly decrease the CV percentage. Regular infusions lower the percentage further each time, though the lowest we've been able to manage is twenty-one percent."

Reaching out, Garrett slid his palm across the smooth taffeta covering Perry's back. Through it, he could feel the boning of her stays. "I'm here."

Honoria Rachinger gave him a grateful look and stepped aside. Perry's shoulders sank and she half glanced over her shoulder. "Should you be?"

"I want to get Moncrieff alone," he replied, rubbing circles in the small of her back. "Which means I need his attention on me. This will do it. We're going to deal with him first, then arrest Hague. Are you armed?"

"I couldn't—in case the duke noticed."

Garrett slipped her thin stiletto dagger from inside his coat and pressed it, sheath and all, into her hand. Perry's fingers curled around it and she flashed him a grateful smile.

"I'm being brave," Perry whispered. "It's not as bad as I expected. Not with you here."

He bit his tongue against the admonition that he'd never doubted her bravery. That was her doubt to overcome, not his. "Just don't be reckless."

"This coming from you?"

"There's too much at stake," he admitted, sliding his hand over her hip and stepping closer. Tucked in the shadows near the edge of the curtains, they were out of the way enough that he could take certain liberties. "How was last night?"

"I had to take his blood," Perry replied, watching Hague like a hawk. He felt the tension tighten each muscle along her spine and her voice grew unusually quiet. "There was no way to avoid it."

The last thing he wanted to think about was Perry in another man's arms. But that was his primal side speaking, furious at the thought of another man taking what was his right. "You did what you had to," Garrett said gruffly. Then hesitated. "He didn't touch you?"

"No. He had to receive his transfusion. It kept him away all night."

Relief loosened the tight knotting in his gut. Garrett kissed the smooth skin at her nape, earning a small gasp from her. "Good. I hate to even think of his hands on you."

Tension curled down her spine, but this time it wasn't fear. Sweet, delicious tension. Garrett's fingers stroked her hips, curving under her bustle to cup her bottom.

A swift intake of air crossed her lips. But her attention had dropped from Hague, which was what he wanted.

"Garrett, the duke is looking at us."

"Good," he murmured, pressing another kiss to her bare shoulder and looking up at the duke.

Moncrieff glared pure hate back at him, unable to enjoy his and Hague's triumph. His weren't the only eyes watching, either.

This was a direct challenge to the duke's stated ownership of her, and those watching knew it. Another layer to add to the mystery and drama of Octavia Morrow. He'd have to marry her now. For her reputation, of course.

"Here he comes," Garrett murmured. "Stay here."

"Be safe."

"Always." He moved to intercept the duke.

"A word?" Moncrieff's smile was sharp edged enough to cut.

"Perhaps several?" Garrett murmured.

"This way." The duke gestured through the crowd, toward the end of the exhibits, where they'd have some semblance of privacy.

Twenty-four

"I MUST HAVE MISSED YOUR NAME ON THE GUEST LIST," the Duke of Moncrieff murmured, slipping two glasses of cognac off the tray on a passing servant drone's head. "I believe only those of noble birth were invited to attend the first day."

Garrett smiled and held out his arms, displaying the elegant coat he wore. "One only has to look the part. Besides, what is nobility, if not the sense of impunity to do as one wills?" He'd learned that, if nothing else, from the streets. Watching as the prince consort slowly ground the human classes beneath his heel.

"You have stones, at least. I could almost admire your courage." The duke's smile slipped. "Or perhaps 'stupidity' is the better word." He set one of the glasses on a small stand at the end of the row. "Would you prefer it neat? Or bloodied?"

Garrett's gaze narrowed on the flask in the duke's hand. Darkness stirred within him, his vision changing. He forced it down. Blood would only affect his focus. He already wanted to kill this bastard. The rational side of his mind fought his primal side; the only way to beat the duke was to outthink him. "Neat."

"I hope you don't mind if I choose to have mine bloodied. It's the way I prefer it."

"Not at all."

The duke offered him the crystal-cut glass. Garrett took it, staring into the amber liquid. Everything depended on the next few minutes.

"I assure you it's not poisoned," the duke remarked, swirling blood through his own cognac. He took a sip, watching Garrett over the edge of the glass with dangerous eyes. "I prefer more direct methods of removing a man."

It was excellent, as predicted. Garrett stared up at the enormous exhibit in the center of the aisle. One of the Scandinavian kraken submersibles, if he wasn't mistaken. It hung from iron wires, the long strands of its propellers streaming like a windswept flag behind it. "Your direct methods confuse me, I admit. This whole game of asking me to look for Octavia Morrow, when you knew who she was all along. I'm afraid I don't quite understand why you bothered to waste my time."

"Have you ever been hunting?"

Garrett shook his head. *Only thieves and murderers.*

"In Scotland we shoot pheasant. First we send the beaters out, to frighten them out of the heather. They're cunning birds. It's only when they take flight that one gets a chance at them. Otherwise they lie in hiding, nothing moving but the frightened beat of their hearts."

"So you were using me to force Perry's hand."

"I knew where she was. I just needed to flush her out."

She'd been so out of sorts this week. Garrett could only imagine how afraid she'd been to come back to the duke. The thought stirred his protective instincts, which was dangerous. Only one thing could undo this. He downed the rest of the cognac to calm himself and put the glass down on the drone's tray. "You've thought of everything."

"Always."

"Do you gamble?"

The duke arched a brow. "Of course."

With a smile, Garrett reached out and upended both his and the duke's empty glasses. "Have you ever seen the three-cup trick? They play it out on the streets, to gull passing flats out of their chink. I used to turn my hands to such tricks when I was a lad."

"You seem to have risen beyond your means." The duke was unimpressed.

Garrett held up a penny and then turned one more glass over until they were arranged in a row. "It's simple, really. First you give the flat a chance. Let him win a game or two." Slipping the penny under a glass he began to move them, slowly at first. A little faster. "Once he's getting confident, you start playing a little faster..."

"Is there a point to this?"

"Watch closely, Your Grace. I'm trying to explain the rules of the game." Garrett stilled his hands. "The coin is here, of course." They could both see it through the glass. "It's called misdirection. I want you to watch the cups. Not my hands. Now where is the coin?"

It was gone. The duke looked down. Each glass was empty. Garrett held his hands up with a smile.

"The penny is worthless." Garrett shrugged. "I do, however, have your key. The one you used for the device. I slipped it from your pocket as we moved through the crowd. One of my associates has it now."

The duke sneered. "A thief as Master of the Nighthawks? No matter. Keep your key. Hague has a copy of it."

Only two of them. "Yes, but now that you've given the device to the prince consort, who is going to control Hague's key? Yourself? Or the prince consort?"

This time the duke's eyes met his. He wasn't sneering anymore. "You little bastard, you think you can blackmail me into giving up Octavia? I *own* the prince consort. If he wants my technology, he'll crawl at my feet if I will it. I have the prince consort in my damned pocket, you fool. If I want him to jump, then he'll damned well jump. I own him. I own them all—they just don't know it yet."

"That makes you a powerful man," Garrett murmured, a knot of nervousness twisting in his gut. This was the moment he began to move his hands a little faster, metaphorically speaking. "I never realized you were so ambitious."

"Ten years ago, that bastard exiled me," the duke replied. "*Me*. After all of our years of friendship—everything that I had done for him—he turned his back on me to retain the favor of the masses."

Time to steer the duke away from this topic, make sure he didn't realize the game. "You sound like a man who shouldn't be crossed."

"Just so you know what you're dealing with." Moncrieff flicked lint off his coat. "I'll warn you this once: Octavia is mine. I shall make her suffer for all the trouble she caused me. You don't think I know her best? I'll lock her up, trapping her in her bedroom, all alone, until I wish to parade her in front of my peers. She'll perform her duties as my thrall, giving me both flesh and blood rights, and I'll remind her of your name every time I come to her bed. Sometimes, I might even walk her past the guild, just to let her know how close to freedom she is—how only a wall separates the pair of you…"

"And here I thought you wanted me dead."

"Death is closure, Reed. No, I want her to have hope. And when she gets close to breaking, I shall take her out and remind her that you're still out there. Alive. Free. I will make her hate you."

"You're truly an evil man," Garrett replied, seeing for the first time the true monster beneath the duke's polished veneer. Hague was his own brand of evil, but Garrett wasn't certain who was worse. "I almost feel sorry for the prince consort. For those on the Council. For they're next, aren't they? For the slight they gave."

"Let's just say, I have plans for the Council." The Moncrieff straightened. "I'd advise you to leave immediately and return to the guild. I promised Octavia that I wouldn't harm you if you kept your nose out of this business, but I'm not generous enough to give second chances. You have five minutes to remove yourself."

"And if I don't?"

"Then I shall see you removed."

"I see." Garrett straightened. "You're a dangerous enemy, Your Grace. Too powerful for a simple Nighthawk to take on and expect to win. I can't duel you, I can't kill you, and I have little doubt that if I went to the prince consort with the information that you sought to manipulate him, I wouldn't survive to meet him."

"Precisely. Your word against mine." The duke glanced around. "And I like holding meetings such as this so publicly. Nobody can get close enough to overhear." His smile gleamed. "Now get out of my sight before my mood becomes less generous. I'm done with you."

Now the reveal. Where's the penny, Your Grace? Garrett smiled, reaching inside his coat. "I'm not quite finished with you yet. Do you see this?" He held up the small brass disk with its clockwork cogs. "This is called an ECHO recording device." Garrett wound it back to the start and inserted the small gramophone into the slot at the top. A tinny rasp sounded.

The next words were the duke's. "*...own the prince consort. If he wants my technology, he'll crawl at my feet if I will it...*" Garrett stopped the recording. "I believe I know several people who might be very interested to hear your words."

The duke's jaw whitened with tension, the blue of his eyes vanishing. His nostrils flared. "You think you can defeat me with such childish tricks?"

One flick of the duke's cane sword sent the ECHO tumbling to the floor. The duke stepped on it and ground it beneath his heel, then shoved the tip of the cane into Garrett's chest, forcing him back a step. Moncrieff bared his teeth in a smile.

"You pathetic little shit." He shoved and Garrett took a step back, shooting a glance at the crumpled device. The Moncrieff slowly lowered the cane sword. "I would kill you now. But it isn't quite the done thing at an exhibition one is hosting. See yourself out," he snarled. "I have guests to attend to."

Giving Garrett his back, he stalked toward the milling crowd. Garrett followed, not quite finished with the duke.

A dozen heads turned their way. He saw Lynch in the crowd, moving the Duke of Malloryn and the Duchess of Casavian into place at the stairs. On the other side, by an Egyptian exhibit, Barrons tipped a glass of blud-wein back and saw him over the rim. Instantly he smiled at something his companion said and excused himself, gesturing to an elderly gentleman who stood beside Byrnes.

In front of him, Moncrieff strode through the crowd. Garrett struggled to keep up, his shoulders striking first one rich lordling, then another. Despite their protestations, he paid them no mind. The prey was in front of him, climbing the stairs toward where the prince consort resided with his nervous queen, holding court along the gallery.

At the top of the stairs, Perry stood between Mrs. Carver and her sister. Their eyes met and Garrett gave her a smile. The world didn't exist for him in that moment. Just her. *Nearly done.*

Lynch paused halfway down the stairs, stopping Moncrieff in his tracks. "Did you get what we needed?"

Garrett nodded and slipped a hand inside his waist-coat pocket. The Moncrieff glanced behind him, his brow furrowing when he saw who stood there. "What the devil is going on?"

"I was trying to explain," Garrett announced, climbing the steps with slow deliberation. The duchess looked interested now, turning to see what had caught Lynch's attention. The Duke of Malloryn echoed her movement. "How easy it is to gull a flat. You see, I kept telling you to keep an eye on the glass with the penny. But all the time, my hands were moving behind the scenes." He tugged out a second ECHO and swiftly rewound the clockwork.

The instant he stopped, it clicked into motion and the duke's tinny voice echoed out. "...*have the prince consort in my damned pocket, you fool. If I want him to jump, then he'll damned well jump. I own him, I own them all—they just don't know it yet...*"

The Moncrieff's face drained of color.

Check. Mate. Garrett met the duke's gaze with vicious satisfaction.

The Duchess of Casavian took several steps down the stairs, her embellished cream skirts swishing around her feet as she reached for the device. She looked up, a devious little smile curling over her red-painted mouth. "Oh, Moncrieff. Bested by a pup. And a rogue, at that." She laughed.

The duke's hand slid over the hilt of his sword. Garrett stepped past him, shooting him another deadly look. "I did try to warn you about the rules of the game. You weren't paying enough attention, Your Grace."

Perry's eyes were wide as she stared down at him.

For Garrett, none of the others existed. He climbed toward her, reaching out to cup her face. "You're free. I have him over a barrel."

Perry's lips quivered, then her gaze slid past him toward the duke. "Don't turn your back on him yet, Garrett."

The duke looked furious. His black eyes raked over the group, seeing no sign of any potential allies.

"I believe the prince consort will be most interested in this," the duchess said, tapping the ECHO against her cheek. She tipped her chin to Byrnes and the pair of Nighthawks that had materialized at the Moncrieff's side. "Arrest him. For collusion against the Crown."

They took one step toward him, the duke bristling with fury. "You lay one hand on me and I'll remove it," he snarled, then turned his attention to the duchess. "You'll regret this."

"I doubt it," Lady Aramina said, holding up the key that Garrett had slipped to Byrnes.

"Whoever owns the cure, owns the Echelon." Garrett lifted his voice. "Isn't that correct, Your Grace?"

All of the Council members shifted uncomfortably.

Those black eyes turned on him. "You insolent little prick." The sword slid free of its sheath with a steely rasp, but Barrons stepped forward.

"Are you offering challenge, Moncrieff?" Barrons asked. "To the Master of the Nighthawks?"

Garrett's eyes locked on the duke. *Do it.* He'd been holding himself back, but the sudden urge to spill the duke's blood was almost overwhelming.

Perry squeezed his arm in warning. "Don't you dare," she whispered.

"Master Reed's not of the Echelon," Lady Aramina stated. "The duke cannot offer challenge."

Moncrieff's eyes glittered as he surveyed them. Finally his gaze locked on something—or someone—just past Garrett's shoulder.

Footsteps echoed on the marble as all eyes turned to the aging Earl of Langford. Perry's grip tightened on Garrett's arm, her face draining entirely of color.

"*I* offer challenge," the earl said, one hand sliding to the hilt at his side. He never looked away from the duke. "You gave your word that you would care for my daughter." His nostrils flared. "I failed her once. I won't ever let you touch her again."

Perry let out a small gasp. Garrett slid his fingers through hers and squeezed, but he never took his eyes off the duke.

"Father," Perry whispered. "I won't let you do this."

Her father glanced at her, his blue eyes sad. "I'm sorry, Octavia. So sorry I didn't believe you." His hand closed around the hilt of his sword. "I must make things right."

Perry lurched forward, slamming the sword back into its sheath and holding his hand there. "No! Dying won't make anything right!"

"I don't intend to die," he replied.

"Come, old man," Moncrieff called. "No one else can challenge me. Let my steel taste blood today."

Perry looked up into her father's face, silently pleading with him to say no. The earl gently removed her hand from the sword hilt. "Let me do this," he said. "Let me make amends."

Only Garrett saw the stubborn change come over

her face and recognized it for what it was. There was a moment where he could have stopped her. The "no" even formed on his lips, but something held his tongue. Perry needed to do this. She needed to prove to herself that she could, and only he, with his own nightmares, understood precisely why.

Perry threw her father's hand off and grabbed the hilt. Steel screamed as she withdrew it, spinning on her heel to face the Moncrieff.

"So be it," Perry whispered, staring at the duke. "I challenge you to the death."

Twenty-five

"OCTAVIA!" HER FATHER, OF ALL PEOPLE, REACHING for her shoulder.

She threw him off, stepping out of his way with a subtle grace. All of her attention was locked on the duke. Somewhere deep inside, she'd always known it would come to this point. She needed it. To bury the past, once and for all. That was why she'd taken her father's lessons and used Lynch to hone her skills.

The duke's gaze flickered between her and her father. He didn't want this, she realized. No, he wanted to kill someone else, someone that she loved. If it couldn't be Garrett, then her father would be enough to twist the blade deep inside her.

"I was born of the Echelon and I am a blue blood," she called out. The entire Echelon knew it after last night. The girl who'd seen her eyes at the ball had spread the rumors, no doubt. "Thus I have the right to challenge you."

"She states the law," the Duchess of Casavian added.

"She's a woman. I'm not dueling a bloody woman," the duke snapped.

"Are you afraid?" the duchess asked mockingly, and Perry glanced her way.

Perhaps not an ally, but the duchess seemed to have some sort of disagreement with the duke. And perhaps she understood what it was like to be a female blue blood in this world.

"Coward," Perry said softly. She reached down and fisted a handful of her skirts, slashing them off just below the knee. "The Duke of Moncrieff is a coward and a fool."

Oh, those black eyes narrowed on her. He drew his blade with a hiss. "Nobody calls me a coward. Not even you, Octavia."

"I just did," Perry replied, giving him a tight little smile as she kicked off her heeled slippers. Her stockinged feet slid on the timber parquetry beneath her, flexing a little as she found her balance. It all seemed so easy now, like slipping into an old routine.

A muscle ticked in Moncrieff's jaw.

"You will never take power," Perry taunted. "The prince consort will likely strip you of your title and execute you for your plans." She let a small smile show. "And you were defeated by a *Nighthawk*."

"I accept." The duke yanked at his coat and tossed it aside, his broad chest straining against the gleaming white silk of his waistcoat.

"Perry," Garrett warned.

She didn't look at him. She couldn't, at this moment. Still, he deserved something. "Trust me."

"I do," he replied. "It's him I don't trust."

"A wise assessment," the duke muttered.

Whispers had started in the hall below. People were

straining to get a better look, lured by the sight of bared steel.

"Perry," Lynch called.

She let her attention shift to him.

He nodded at her soberly. "Remember that you are a Nighthawk."

Fight like one. She nodded back, saluted him with the sword, and then turned to face the duke, feeling whole for the first time in years. "*Allez,*" she called, and the duel began.

᭰᭰

"Tell me, Master Reed... Do you enjoy soiled goods?" the Moncrieff mocked.

Garrett surged forward, but a hand came out of nowhere and locked around his upper arm.

A gasp went up as the duke's sword slashed across Perry's cheek, cutting her from ear to eyebrow.

He swam through the darkness, finally focusing on Lynch's face. Lynch shook his head sharply. "You're distracting her."

Garrett let out the breath he'd been holding and glanced away. It was true. The duke had scored three slashes in the last minute alone, while her attention was divided. But Garrett's hands quivered, the hunger aching inside him. This was his woman, and it was harder than he'd thought to watch her fight her battles.

Lynch stepped into his field of vision, forcing him to step back. Steel rang on steel, and the crowd gasped.

"Control yourself," Lynch murmured. "Let her do what she needs to do."

"She's losing—"

"Yes." Those gray eyes bored through him. "Because she's thinking about his words. About the effect it's having on you."

"It's not just me," he snarled, following the path of Perry's frequent glances. Hague leaned against the Egyptian exhibit, his beard so thick it almost seemed to engulf his face.

As if sensing his gaze, Hague turned, a steel monocle enlarging his pupil grotesquely. Light reflected back off the fellow's jaw, gleaming on a plate of steel beneath the beard.

Garrett shot Perry an anguished glance as another chorus of *oohs* and *aahs* echoed in the hall. Steel screamed against steel and Perry was forced back against the rail overlooking the great hall below. She ground her teeth together as the duke's blade forced her own close to her face.

Come on. Garrett's fingernails left little half-moons in the palms of his hands. Their eyes met, and he silently prayed for her to disengage.

"*Hit him*," he mouthed. Then tapped his forehead.

Her eyes widened momentarily, then she realized what he meant. Her arms gave way, bringing the blades dangerously close to her throat, and the Duke pushed forward. Perry dealt him a stunning crack to the head with her forehead, shoving with the sword at the same time.

Blood splattered on the white marble floors as the Moncrieff staggered to the side, a slash welling on his smooth cheek. He looked shocked. Only for a moment, though. Then the tip of his steel lashed out at her.

Perry dove out of the way and the blade sheared through the railing, sending shards of gilt flying. She spun, lashing out with her foot and hitting the Moncrieff high in the chest. He staggered again, but Perry was already running, pushing through the crowd to get more space at the top of the stairs.

"Go," Lynch ordered Garrett, giving him a shove as the duke gave chase. "Take care of Hague. I'll watch. I promise you, I won't let her fall."

Garrett shot her another anguished look. She was dancing like a lithe shadow, the swagged gathering of her bustle curving over her bottom and the long, elegant muscles in her legs flexing as she lunged, her stockinged feet slipping on the parquetry floors.

He tore his gaze away. Hague stalked slowly through the crowd, his hands clasped behind his back as he watched Perry with an intensity that was unnerving. He was moving to place himself within her vision again.

"Take Byrnes," Lynch said. "To watch your back."

Both Byrnes and Garrett stared at each other. Garrett gave a short nod. "I'll need someone. Wouldn't be the first trap the duke's planned." It was as much of an apology as he could give.

Tension drained out of Byrnes's shoulders. "Finally. Some action."

"I want him alive," Garrett snarled.

❧

Garrett was gone. So too was Hague.

Perry ducked beneath a swipe meant to cut her face. She'd started to notice something in the last minute. The duke's chest rose and fell with startling alacrity. He hadn't expected her to last this long, and from the way his blows were becoming wider and more aggressive, he was hoping to finish this quickly. She was outmatched in strength and reach, but she was faster than he was and her endurance was better.

"I'll hazard a guess," she panted, "that Scotland is notoriously free of fencing masters. Or any opposition of reasonable skill."

The duke's lip curled and he lashed out. Their swords squealed as Perry riposted, locking the hilts together.

"Where's your man now?" he spat.

"Taking care of old business," she shot back, disengaging and meeting his next strike with a clever *prise de fer.*

"Hague." The Moncrieff actually smiled. "I hope that ends well for him."

Perry danced clear. Something about his tone sent a shiver through her. "What have you planned?"

"Why, nothing, my dear." His tone was almost solicitous as he cut through her sleeve. The tip of the sword bit into her bicep, and Perry cried out as he wrenched it free with a nasty little smile. "You do realize how very predictable this is? Him showing up here to ruin my exhibition? I couldn't have extended him a better invite."

The crowd gasped and Perry staggered into a debutante in acres of pastel pink skirts. Her foot slipped on the silk and the Moncrieff lunged forward. Perry threw herself onto the ground in a roll, coming up on her feet as the girl screamed behind her.

The Moncrieff yanked his blade from the girl's

shoulder and shoved her out of the way. "Clear the bloody floor!" he snapped as a matron screamed and caught the fainting girl.

Perry tried to thrust but her arm felt so heavy. Thick, viscous blood dripped down her sleeve, the lace of her cuffs clinging wetly to her skin. The bleeding would stop soon, but the injury deep within the muscle paralyzed her movements. The duke's next thrust tore the hilt from her hand. The rapier slid across the parquetry and landed by the top of the stairs.

No time to look for it. The Moncrieff thrust toward her heart.

It was all she could do to drop beneath the blade. Perry hit the polished timber, her hands slapping the ground as the rapier whistled overhead. She had only a bare second to react, for she was vulnerable in this position.

Hooking her foot behind his, she kicked it out from under him and rolled. The duke hit the ground with a curse, but Perry was already up and sprinting, sliding to her knees to snatch up her rapier with her left hand.

Boots echoed behind her. She came up and swung just in time to counter another attack.

"I see," Perry gasped, "that your thrusts with a blade are almost as ineffective as your attempts at seduction."

Fury filled the duke's eyes and he beat her back with furious lunges she could barely deflect.

"Tell me," the duke demanded. "Would you like your lover's heart on a plate once Hague is through with him? Or in a box?"

Hitting her *corps-à-corps* in the shoulder staggered her back, and Perry's eyes widened as the heel of her foot found no purchase.

She was at the edge of the staircase.

❧

"Bloody mirrors," Byrnes muttered, staring at the mirror maze exhibit. "Of course he had to go in there."

Garrett glanced behind him, listening for a second to the sound of steel clashing on steel. If he could still hear it, then she was still alive.

Byrnes muttered something under his breath, glaring at the distorted view of himself with an enormous forehead. A plaque at the front read: *There is only one way out of the maze, but to find it is to find your way within.*

"If there's only one exit, we'll have to separate. I'll enter through it and meet you in the middle," Byrnes said.

"We'll trap him there," Garrett replied and stepped through into the maze.

Twenty-six

AHEAD OF HIM HE COULD HEAR FOOTSTEPS AND HARSH breathing. Garrett darted through the mirrored passage, a thousand distorted images of himself reflecting back at him. What a damned foolish exhibit. Designed by some German philosopher to examine the perception of self. He looked at the bug-eyed image staring back at him and wondered how that would ever make him understand himself better.

His quarry thundered ahead of him, darting through the maze. Not even an attempt at stealth, but then perhaps the bastard didn't realize what was hunting him.

He liked to cut...

Perry's whisper haunted him. Years of nightmares and fear, forever carved into her soul by this man. The darkness in Garrett curled through his veins in delicious anticipation. He needed Hague—needed the information about how to work the device—but the less rational side of him, the side that hungered for revenge, was dangerously ascendant.

He couldn't stop seeing Ava and Alice and the other girls trapped in those hideous aquariums. That could have been Perry. Or worse. She could have suffered the same fate as Miss Keller or Miss Fortescue. His hands quivered. Easy to end this. Easy to make sure Hague never hurt another woman again…

Ahead of him a corner loomed. He could see a dark shape distorted in the image and pressed his back against the mirror wall. One hand dropped to the pistol at his side. Then away again. For this he wanted knives. Something bloody.

"Just you and me now, *meneer*." Hague's voice was deeper than he'd expected. Almost guttural with the accent. "You good with knives? As good as me? I like knives. You should know this. *She* did. She knew how good I was with knives."

Garrett's teeth gleamed in his reflection, bared in fury. Blackness washed over him. The urge to tear this bastard apart with his bare hands. "I think you know more about them than I do," he shot back. "Like how a blade feels when it carves through half your face. Did you like that? Did you know there's not even a single mark of what you did to her on her flesh, but you… You can't ever forget what she did to you, can you? You'll wear it always. *Monster*. Steel Jaw. A sign of exactly what you are so that no one ever forgets."

There was a snarl of rage, then a fist smashed through the glass next to his ear. Garrett caught it, using the man's momentum to slice his own forearm to shreds as he hauled him through the gaping hole. Thousands of glass slivers splintered over him, cutting at his face and hands. Then Hague yanked back and his arm disappeared.

All Garrett could smell was blood. It fired his
nerves, left his heart pounding in his ears. He darted
around the corner, but Hague was already running
down the passage. Away from him.

Coward. He pounded after him, images dancing
away from them. Dozens of images of Hague, but
only one of them was bleeding. Droplets of it painted
a clear path on the floor. Garrett leaped forward and
tackled the man, driving him into the reflective wall.
Cracks screamed out through the glass and Garrett
spun the bastard, grabbing his coat lapels and smashing
him back against the mirror.

The thick beard had half torn away, revealing the
cold gray gleam of the man's iron jaw. His teeth were
metal too, half of his mouth revealed behind the mess
of his lips. Or what was left of them. A nightmare in
itself. For a moment Garrett just gaped.

Then Hague's hand came up, a pistol gleaming
in the light. Garrett shoved Hague back as the pistol
discharged next to his ear. Glass cascaded from several
mirrors as the bullet struck behind him—and exploded.

Not the first time he'd come across firebolt bullets.
Rosalind and her humanist contingent had been
responsible for unleashing them into the human population. When the bullet struck anything, the chemicals
inside it would mix, resulting in an explosive reaction
that could even kill a blue blood.

Garrett grabbed the pistol, wrestling with Hague
for control. He smashed their hands into the sharp,
ragged edges of a broken mirror and Hague screamed,
dropping the bloody thing. Garrett kicked it out of the
way, going for his knife.

Movement stirred at the corner of Garrett's vision, distracting him for just a moment, then something hot and sharp stabbed into his back. Twisted. Garrett went down on one knee with a grunt, his vision blazing out in a haze of white. Heat and ice quivered over his flesh. He could smell blood, feel the sting of it as the knife was withdrawn.

Byrnes skidded to a halt with his preferred weapon of choice, a pair of *sai*, in his hands.

"What took you so long?" Garrett snapped, twisting free.

"One way in, one way out—they're both the same," Byrnes snarled. "Had to double back around and follow you in."

Not quick enough to dodge the next blow. Blood splashed the glass behind him, the sting igniting his upper arm. *Careless.* "Work with me," he snapped at Byrnes.

They fell in together, both of them circling Hague. Every movement sent a shudder of pain up Garrett's healing back. Catching a glimpse of Byrnes's cold blue eyes, he feinted forward and Byrnes mirrored him. Hague darted to keep them both in sight, but it was clear he was uneasy. The knife spun but Garrett blocked it, punching hard beneath the man's arm. Once, twice...three times.

A hiss of breath hit him in the face and he sliced open Hague's ribs. Letting the blood hunger rise was so easy here. To feel it swamping him, drowning him in the vicious need. He lost track of movement, became nothing more than reaction. This man had hurt Perry. A snarl curled his lip. His forearm came up to block another blow, the knife an extension of his arm as Byrnes darted in on the other side.

Blood welled. *Kill him.* Garrett swept his knife across the back of Hague's knee, and the bastard screamed as he went down. Another blow had the knife sinking up to the hilt in the man's chest, leaving his heels kicking as he gasped and choked on the floor. *Finish it.* Garrett twisted the blade in Hague's chest and stopped that awful gurgle.

Slowly he looked up, silence ringing in his ears. Byrnes stared at him, mouth slightly agape. "Could have let me know you had that in you."

"I don't like to kill," Garrett said, his voice strangely metallic. "Doesn't mean I can't."

The coldness leached out of him, the hunger receding like a purring, contented cat, its furious need glutted on blood and death. The next step he took, his leg went out from underneath him. Garrett staggered forward into Byrnes's arms, looking down in surprise. Blood gushed from a stab wound in his thigh. He hadn't even felt it, lost in the fury of his primal self.

Strong hands held him upright, pushing him back against the wall. "Easy, easy. Here, drink the blood." A flask pressed against his lips. "You'll heal."

He already was. He could feel it burning through him as the craving virus healed the knife wounds in his back and thigh. And just that easily, the hunger washed out of him, leaving him cold and shivering, his vision a riot of color. Of red. A thousand shades, painted across the glass. Across his hands. He looked down at the faint tremble in them. *I did that. Or the part of me that could be a monster did.*

Byrnes arched an incredulous brow toward the dead man at his feet. "You moved like—"

"It's because my CV levels are higher than normal." Made him stronger, faster than he had been.

"So I'd noticed." Their eyes met. Byrnes shrugged. "It's easy to reprint the percentages on your spectrometer if one knows what to do. Fitz wanted me to keep an eye on you."

All along he'd known the truth. And he'd kept Garrett's secret?

"Why?" he asked, draining Byrnes's flask.

Byrnes gave a soundless laugh. "You were always Lynch's favorite. I shouldn't…" He lowered his head. "I wasn't angry with you when I was overlooked."

"You gave me hell."

"Likewise." Byrnes returned his stare with an equally cold one. Then sighed. "He made the right decision."

"Did he? I've made a right muck of this." Garrett sighed. "Perry told me I had too much pride."

"Maybe in that, we're truly brothers." Byrnes held out a hand and helped Garrett to his feet. It was as much an apology as either of them could give. "You should go. They're still fighting."

"And the body?"

"I'll deal with it."

"Try and find his key—we'll need it to use the device." Garrett paused. "I'll need it."

"Good luck," Byrnes muttered, riffling through Hague's clothes.

The newly knit muscle in Garrett's thigh tore apart as he half ran, half hobbled toward the stairs and the gallery. Dozens of blue bloods had flocked from all corners of the exhibition, drawn like vultures as the clash of steel on steel rang.

He could barely see her. Just a darting form dancing out of the way as the heavier-set duke advanced on her. It felt like years since he'd gone after Hague, but the face of the central clock showed only ten minutes had elapsed. And Perry was still fighting.

A gasp went up from the crowd. Garrett shoved through the gathering, his gaze locked on her, so fierce and defiant. Fighting for her self, as well as her life. She had nowhere to go, her back foot feeling for purchase on the lip of the stairs and a swift glance over her shoulder showing that she knew it. Coldness gripped him with harsh claws. He barely felt the muscle tear in his thigh as he started running.

The duke stepped back a little to give himself space for the final blow. "Good-bye, my sweet Octavia."

Garrett's hand dipped into his coat, locking around his pistol. He wasn't close enough. The bloody thing only had an accurate range of forty feet, but he had to do something.

The duke's arm drew back.

Garrett shoved through the crowd, forcing his way past foreign dignitaries and princesses alike, cocking the hammer back on the pistol as he ran.

The blade began to fall.

"No!" He lifted the pistol.

And Perry lunged into the thrust, her own blade sinking home. Her body jerked as the duke's blow struck, the razor tip of his rapier sliding through her back as if through a bag of sand.

"No!" Garrett screamed.

He ran up countless stairs, his thighs burning, his leg threatening to give out beneath him. She was falling, the point of the duke's blade piercing through the back of her blue dress. A dark shadow bloomed against the silk in a spreading blot and Perry began to topple backward...

Garrett caught her, hands snatching at her tenderly as he tried to lower her to the floor. Blood stained his hands, the front of her dress, everywhere he looked... He could hardly see for the overwhelming rise of the hunger, but her shocked eyes locked on his and became the center of his world. Beside him the Earl of Langford reached for her, both of them helping to lower her onto Garrett's lap.

"I've got you," he blurted, patting her cheek. His fingers left blood there and he wrenched his hand away, wiping it on his coat.

"Hague?" she whispered.

Garrett swallowed hard as blood broke on her lips. "Dead." He couldn't stand to see the rapier sticking out of her chest. "Dammit, Perry. Don't you dare leave me." His voice broke.

She gave a weak smile. "Not this time."

"Promise."

"Promise." The word was a whisper. Then her head lolled to the side as she tried to see what was going on.

The duke was on his knees, the hilt of Perry's rapier sitting dead center in his chest. He looked shocked, his fingers touching the hilt as if to wonder how it had gotten there. Slowly he crumpled forward, his forehead bouncing on the timber floor as his body slumped. Blood pooled around him.

"Got him," Perry whispered. "I knew I could do it."

Lynch knelt down beside them grimly, his fingers wrapping around the blade in her chest. "Give her blood," he said. "We have to get this out. It's close to the heart."

"What if it cuts her inside again?" her father demanded, stilling Lynch's hand.

"If it begins to heal around the steel, she'll only lose more blood later," Lynch replied grimly. "And if she moves, we don't know what it will do to her heart."

The earl looked devastated. "Oh, Octavia... What were you thinking?" He swallowed hard and reached for her hand. "You should have let me do it."

"I killed him," she whispered, triumph gleaming in her eyes. "I finally ended this."

But at what cost? Both Garrett and Lynch exchanged a sharp glance, then Lynch nodded. Time to do this.

Garrett slashed his wrist against the rapier and pressed it to her lips. Perry's eyes flickered, the focus draining out of them, but some hint of the hunger swirled to the surface, her pupils becoming little black pinpricks at the scent of his blood.

"Drink," he urged her brokenly. Thank God his craving levels were so high. The virus would help to heal her, if he could get enough blood into her...if the blade came out cleanly...if it hadn't hit an artery or the heart...

"One, two..." Lynch yanked the blade clear on "three," pressing his palm down on her chest to put pressure on her wound.

Perry's teeth sank into Garrett's wrist and she screamed. The pain of it barely touched him. Garrett felt as though he existed outside of his body at the moment, watching as she panted. Words tumbled from his lips, urging her to drink, telling her he wouldn't let her go. Ever.

Slowly her hands clutched at his arm and her lips locked around the healing slash. The wet rasp of her tongue set it to bleeding again and then she was suckling at his skin.

Her eyes locked on his, her mouth greedy. Garrett could feel the pull. A month and a half ago, their positions had been reversed. He suddenly wondered whether she had felt like this, begging him to drink as he choked on his own blood. Wondered if her own chest had felt tight as a drum, hoping to a God he didn't believe in that it would be enough. Her lips left his skin in one final kiss, and she sucked in air as if she'd been drowning. But she was alive. And her eyes were black with the force of her own hunger.

"I love you," he whispered. "I don't know if I've told you that today. But you need to heal, so that I can tell you again tomorrow. And the day after that. I made you a promise—"

Her eyes fluttered closed in dreamy surrender, her body slumping into his arms. Unconscious.

Slowly the world began to come back into focus. Lynch was standing, bellowing at the curious crowd to stand clear. The Earl of Langford's eyes were locked on Garrett, seeing everything that he couldn't be bothered to hide.

"Jolly good show," one of the American blue

bloods said, clapping an earl on the back. "It shall be the talk of the exhibition."

The crowd began to clap.

Garrett curled his lip back off his teeth. Getting her out of this vulture's nest couldn't come too soon.

Twenty-seven

A SPARK CRACKLED IN THE GRATE.

Her eyelids weighed down by heaviness, Perry sighed and rolled onto her side. Warmth cocooned her. Blinking against the thick darkness of the room, she pushed some of the blankets off herself and then stilled, her senses finally beginning to make some sense of the situation.

The Moncrieff. His sword sliding through her chest as if through paper. And Garrett begging her to stay with him as he lowered her to the floor and tried to stop her from bleeding.

An ache throbbed in her chest and Perry sat up, glancing down at the frilly spill of lace around her throat. Someone had dressed her in a lawn nightgown, the kind of thing that debutantes wore. Perry rubbed between her breasts. There was no twinge from a wound, but she could feel it deep inside still, where the craving virus sought to heal her.

"You're awake," a hoarse voice whispered.

A large form dissolved out of the shadows, Garrett pushing away from the fire he'd been staring into. Its warm, golden light licked the tired planes of his face as he turned, highlighting the blue of his eyes and the dark circles that shadowed them.

"You look awful," she rasped.

His mouth tightened, but he said nothing. Merely stared at her with a hungry, yearning look in his eyes.

Perry's chest tightened again, but not from her wound. She lifted her arm and gestured for him to come to her. As if the action had unlocked some door, he spilled into motion, crossing her bedroom in firm strides and drawing her into his arms.

"Oh, sweet Lord, Perry," he whispered, crushing her against his chest and burying his face in her hair as he knelt on the bed. "You're not to do that again."

"I shall definitely duck next time," she agreed, sliding her arms up under his shoulders and closing her eyes. For the first time, she could simply enjoy the sensation of being in his arms without guilt or fear forcing her away.

There was a harsh quiver in his body. She froze, one hand caressing the dark hair at his nape. "Garrett?"

He shook his head and clung to her, unable to breathe even a hint of how he felt inside.

"We survived," Perry whispered. The truth hit her. Both the duke and Hague were gone forever. She would never have to fear them again, never have to keep looking over her shoulder. For the first time in ten years, the future stretched out before her, bright and beckoning and...

And then she realized.

"Garrett?" She pushed him back, trying to capture his face in her hands. "You killed Hague. You weren't meant to kill him. He knows how to work the device, how to—"

Thick dark lashes flickered up over bright blue eyes. "It's all right. Byrnes found the key on Hague, and Lynch took the device into custody in all the confusion. Honoria Rachinger helped me use it. Not long enough to drop my levels beyond sixty percent, but it will put off the inevitable for a while longer. The prince consort has the device now."

"He won't allow you access to it."

"I know," Garrett shrugged. "But we have time. Lynch has heard several rumors of a cure—out of the East End, actually. He's been discussing it with Barrons, who seems to have more information."

"How long do you think you have?" she asked, sitting up.

"Hopefully long enough." He wouldn't meet her eyes. "Perry, must we discuss this now? I've just gotten you back. Let's simply enjoy the here and now."

"But I want forever," she told him hotly.

"And I will do what I can to be here for you."

"Promise me."

He drew back onto his knees on the bed, the stubborn line of his jaw tightening. "Perry, I knew that we could evade the duke. This is different... This is...inevitable."

"I spent nine years hoping you'd notice me. Nine years! And now that you have, I'm not going to let you go. Not now. Not ever." She slammed her open palm against his chest. "You made me promises."

"Stop it! You'll hurt yourself. Your chest—"

"You said that you would tell me you loved me

every day for the rest of my life. You made me believe
that! It was the only thing that kept me going"—and
here her voice broke—"at a very bad time for me.
You can't break your word." Another useless wrench
against his grip. "You can't."

"Perry." He dragged her into his arms as if she
weighed nothing, her hips straddling his thighs. "Stop
it. I don't want you to hurt yourself."

"You seem to have no such compunctions."

Suddenly she was flat on her back on the bed,
with Garrett leaning over her, pinning her wrists to
the sheets. His eyes blazed black with fury. "That's
enough," he snapped. "I'm not going anywhere. Not
yet. You need to calm down."

"Promise me," she whispered. "Promise me you
won't leave me."

His body sagged, pressing her against the mattress.
"Damn it, Perry, I promise." He sighed and rested his
forehead against hers.

"I want you to say the words," she pressed. "Say, 'I
promise I won't ever leave you.'"

Garrett reared back just enough to stare at her.
Shadows limned his face, caressing his high cheekbones.

"Don't think I haven't noticed how often you *seem*
to agree to do what I say," she shot back with a glare.

"I was rather hoping you wouldn't realize."

"Garrett?"

He shifted to the side, resting on one elbow and
letting her wrists go. The expression on his face was
impenetrable. "I promise I won't ever leave you."
One hand stroked her jaw. "I don't *want* to leave you.
I love you."

All of the fight went out of her. She'd dreamed of this. Feared it with equal measure. But it was time to leave fear behind her. Time to be brave. Perry cupped his hand against her face. "I…I love you too. I always have."

Garrett shut his eyes, a shudder running through his broad frame. "That's the first time you've said it, you know."

"I couldn't before. Because then it would make it real and I didn't want to lose it."

He knew. His eyes blazed with fierce desire.

"Where did you find this?" Perry cleared her throat, fingering the nightgown. Time to speak of other things.

"Your father insisted on sending for it. For a great deal of your things, actually." Garrett's head tilted toward the corner, where a weather-beaten old trunk rested. She recognized the crest on it. "He's kept them all these years."

"Is he here?" she whispered, rubbing at her chest again. The ache had intensified.

"Yes. He's asleep in one of the cells. Do you want to see him?"

"Not just yet. Give me time. I still feel a little lost and…guilty, I suppose. I was angry at him at the time, and frightened the duke would hurt him and—" Her voice dropped. "I don't want to have to face anyone just yet. I want to stay here. With you."

"Just you, then. And me," he whispered, his fingers tracing the fine lace of her neckline, trailing over the lawn. His gaze had dropped, smoky blue now with heat. "It's pretty."

A month ago, she would have thrown those words in his face. She'd spent so many years pretending not to be a woman, pretending she didn't have a woman's needs or desires. For so long she'd been a different person. Now a part of her felt cut loose, as though she wasn't quite certain what to make of herself.

A Nighthawk didn't wear lace-trimmed night-gowns. But something in her liked the way he was looking at her. For the first time in her life, she felt like a woman—not a coltish girl, uncertain of herself, or even a woman forced to wear men's attire. There were no expectations of who she should be. Garrett simply liked what she was.

Garrett's fingers tugged on the strings holding the nightgown together and Perry's breath caught, her nipples hardening behind the fine lawn. He noticed, of course, his gaze flickering to hers for one long, melting moment before a smile graced his lips.

Thick, delicious tension curled through her lower abdomen, and she couldn't stop her hand from lifting and brushing against the soft linen of his shirt. Her nightgown fell open beneath his touch and then he kissed her throat, the coolness of his breath drifting across her skin.

Perry shivered. That afternoon in the rain had been imprinted on her skin and burned into her very bones, but she liked this too, this gentle seduction. The cool trace of his lips as he caressed her throat and chin, then cupped her face and turned her mouth to his.

He stole her breath, tongue dancing with her own. A kiss that consumed her, let her know just how much he knew about this, about sex and hot, wet kisses and the desperate ache between them that felt like it could never be assuaged. Her teeth sank into his lip and she arched up beneath him, his palm curving over the slight swell of her breast.

Yes. There.

"Kiss me," she whispered, tugging at his shirt.

A swift glance at her, then he licked his way down her throat, his tongue dancing over the throbbing beat of her vein. He knew what she wanted without being told, one hard thumb rubbing delicate circles around her nipple, ruching the fabric. Then his mouth was there, suckling her through the fine lawn. Perry yielded with a gasp, her hands dragging his shirt over his head, his lips parting from her skin just long enough to get it off. Then her hands were sinking into the thickness of his hair, dragging his mouth back where she wanted it.

In all of her many dreams of this, she'd never quite realized the meticulous care he'd take. He loved her body as if there could be no greater pleasure than this, as if each whispered cry and moan he wrung from her lips was more precious than gold. A man sure in his skill and his reading of her.

One hand slid along her inner thighs. "Part for me," he whispered and coaxed her thighs to fall open.

She couldn't deny him. The feel of his palm against her skin was a devastating tease. Just resting there. Making her arch her hips as if to beg for more of his touch.

"Please." She needed that touch. Needed something to slake the vicious hunger.

Fingers danced up her inner thigh, finding the wet

curls there. Garrett drew back just enough for her to see his eyes consumed by the same hunger that afflicted her. His lips curved. "You're wet for me."

"Always."

Slow, silky touches. Torture. Perry entwined her arms around his neck and moaned, her nipples aching for the return of his mouth. He knew it too, his eyes dancing with amusement as he bowed his head and took one aching bud between his teeth just as his fingers drove into her. The sensation speared through her, igniting the feel of his fingers thrusting slowly into her body.

"Faster," she whispered, but he took no heed. Each light caress only slowed further, until she was begging, grinding against his hand, her own fingers clutching at his wrist in desperation.

Then his hands were gone and he came over her, hips pressing against hers, right where she needed it. Perry sucked in a shuddering breath, his hands pinning hers to the bed. His erection strained against the leather of his trousers, grinding hotly against her until she came with a harsh exhalation, the world vanishing around her until only he remained.

She collapsed back on the sheets, panting.

"There she is," Garrett whispered, his lips caressing her jaw. "My fierce little peregrine. Sweet and sensual and so damned beautiful. I've dreamed of you like this. Dreamed of fucking you." His hand circled her throat and stroked down to her chest. "Of taking blood from you. Hearing you cry out." He bared his teeth, the hunger in him all-consuming. "Stop me," he begged.

"Never."

And then he was as lost as she was. Kissing her, his tongue mating with her own, his body riding her back to the edge of something so strong she almost feared it.

Sweet Lord, he was strong. Perry's fingers flexed in the hard muscle of his biceps, gliding over the heated satin of his skin. She dug her nails into the flex of his shoulders, gasping a little as his hips ground down upon hers. Garrett captured the gasp with a surging kiss, his touch growing a little stronger, a little more desperate now...

With a soft moan, she slid her legs around his hips, the lawn pressing damply against her. Reaching between them, she found the buttons on his leather trousers and fumbled with them in the warm dark.

Garrett bit her chin, pressing soft kisses there. "Here, love." He reached down and tugged the buttons open, letting the heated weight of his cock spill into her hands.

Dark lashes closed over smoky blue eyes as he moaned. His cock clenched beneath her tightening fingers, and when he looked up at her through passion-glazed eyes, she loved it.

The next kiss took her by surprise, hard and demanding, his lips possessing hers with slow, languid skill. Hips rocking against her, her hands sliding over that smooth, polished length, wringing other soft noises from deep within his throat...

Then he cursed under his breath and rolled to the side, tugging the tight leather down his muscled thighs. Perry rolled onto her elbow, her fingertips dancing down the hard ripple of his abdomen. She

liked the sudden sense of urgency she felt in him, as
though he couldn't control himself with her.

Firelight gleamed on his pale skin, caressing each
long muscle. He truly was a work of art, built to fight,
to kill, to hunt... As her palms skated over the planes
of his abdomen she couldn't help wishing she owned
some kind of artistic talent, some way of capturing this
moment forever.

Muscle flexed in his arm as he threw his pants
aside, then he turned back to her with a predatory
gaze and reached for her. Perry pushed at his shoulder
instead, coming onto her knees over him as he fell
flat. Hot, wicked eyes met hers as he understood her
intentions. Then he was dragging her onto his lap, her
thighs parting around his as the nightgown bunched
around her hips and dangled off one shoulder, revealing her breast.

Fine hairs rasped against her inner thighs as he
shifted her into place. Then his hands skated along her
thighs, lifting the hem of the nightgown. The lazy,
heated look he gave her burned through her.

"Off," he demanded, sliding his hands up beneath it.

Perry plucked at the hem and dragged it up over
her head, before tossing it aside. His gaze dropped in
appreciation, a small growl echoing in his throat. That
look of his... It stole any sense of self-consciousness
from her. She was beautiful, here, now, in his eyes...
And she'd carry that with her forever.

"It seems that you have been hiding something," he
murmured with wicked delight as his fingers brushed
against her breasts. His smile warmed her. "How did
I not notice these?"

Then his smile dipped as he traced the healing scar beneath her breasts with the pads of his fingers.

She didn't want that memory coming into this. Perry caught his hands and cupped them around her breasts, her hips surging as his roughened hands slid over such sensitive skin. The glide of his erection beneath her made her quiver. A vivid picture of that last time flashed through her mind, of him burying himself to the hilt inside her, pressing her into the brickwork... Wetness slicked between her thighs, an empty ache, just begging to be filled.

Garrett sucked in a hissed breath as she threw her head back and moaned. Each slow glide tortured both of them, sensation fracturing through her. Garrett rocked up onto his elbows, his palms sliding up her back as his hot mouth locked around her nipples. It forced her knees deeper into the mattress, her body riding the exquisite length of his cock.

"Damn it, Perry. I wanted to take my time."

She could feel the head of his erection dipping into the wet heat of her body. Perry rocked her hips, gaining another inch. "I've waited long enough. I feel like I've waited forever." Cupping his face in her hands, she claimed his mouth as she sank down the length of his shaft. It stretched her, filling that aching emptiness until she knew she'd never be alone again.

"Christ," he whispered, kissing her, biting at her mouth as his hands raked her back and buttocks. "I'll never get enough of you."

It thrilled her to the core. Nails skittering down his naked skin as she plundered his mouth. "Garrett." Her soft little cries broke the silence...

Mercy… So good… She moaned and kissed him as deeply as she could.

Darkness filled her—and she glorified in it. The warm golden light vanished from the room as her hunger rose. Perry bared her teeth and gasped, clutching him, riding him. Trying to consume him. The fierceness of her desire rocked her. That she could feel like this, naked and exposed and so entangled that she could barely tell the degree of separation.

"Garrett," she whispered, sinking her teeth into the hard muscle of his shoulder. She wanted to draw blood, to lick his skin, taste the very essence of him…

A strangled sound spilled from his lips. Garrett tumbled her onto her back, his narrow hips pumping into her and his hands hot and hungry on her body. Hovering above her, his arms straining with the effort as he rode her with increasing frequency, he slowed, each thrust deep and torturous.

She'd thought once that she'd known what desire was. But this was…necessity. As vital as breath and as furious as the blood hunger. It tore her apart and left her aching for completion. Yearning. *So close…*

Then he captured her knee and drove it higher, forcing her body to tilt until his cock ground within her, finding something so exquisitely delicious that she almost exploded.

Perry's eyes shot wide, her nails scoring his back. Her gaze locked on his, and as she shattered, the last thing she saw was the blazing need for her darkening his own eyes.

Sensation rolled through her like a summer storm, hot, vivid, and electrifying. Destroying her. Leaving her gasping and wrung out beneath him as he drove her into the mattress. She could almost feel the moment his thrusts began to slow, his teeth sinking into that lush bottom lip.

"Yes," Perry whispered, wrapping her arms around him and using her whole body to clench around him. It wracked her anew, throwing her back into the eye of the storm until she tossed her head back and cried out in pleasure.

The muscles in his throat strained, a vein standing out in his temple. Garrett gasped and then he spilled his seed within her, strain quivering through his body. Perry held on to him with desperate hands. She had to, for fear that she'd fall and never stop falling.

With another shattered gasp he collapsed against her, his breath coming hard against her bare throat and her breasts crushed between them. "Perry." He stroked fingertips down her throat and over her collarbone. Then his weight came back down and his hand splayed flat over her ribs. "You are so beautiful, do you know that?" A quivering kiss against her jaw. "So wild, so brave…"

She clung to him, her feet rasping over the smooth muscle of his buttocks. Garrett lifted off her after long minutes, shuddering as his cock spilled from her. Rolling onto his side, he drew her into his arms and collapsed onto his back, one arm thrown over his eyes.

Warmth from the fireplace caressed her naked skin and Perry lay still for long minutes, listening to the beat of his heart beneath her ear. She'd never dreamed how much peace she would find in this moment, with his fingers lazily tracing circles on her shoulder.

"Nine years?" Garrett whispered, breaking the silence. "You've loved me for that long?"

Only he would dwell on such a thing at a moment like this. Perry curled her arms around him and rested her head against his chest. "For someone who thinks they know women, you never had a bloody clue."

Twenty-eight

NINE YEARS OF LIVING AMONG MEN HAD IMMURED Perry to the worst, or so she thought, but she'd never truly realized what a pack of old gossips the Nighthawks were. Doyle was the worst. The moment he'd discovered she was sharing Garrett's chambers, he'd dug his heels in like a chaperone protecting her nonexistent virtue.

It didn't help her temper that she'd met with her father that morning. It hurt to see him so tentative and uncertain of his welcome. He'd wanted her to return to the hall with him but Perry had shaken her head. She fully intended to stay with the Nighthawks. This was her home now, not the Echelon or society. Though she wanted, more than anything, to have him visit her each week. She'd missed him.

Stalking toward Garrett's study, her ears caught a hint of conversation within. Several voices she recognized, and some she couldn't quite place.

"Come in," Garrett called when she knocked.

The room was crowded with people and chairs: Barrons, Lynch, Rosalind, Garrett, Lena Carver, her husband and sister, and a stranger who stood behind Honoria's chair with his palm resting on her shoulder.

Perry shut the door, instantly feeling uncomfortable in the focus of everyone's gaze.

"Miss Morrow." Barrons stood, gesturing her to take his chair. "You look better than last we met."

"Thank you," she muttered, easing into the seat.

Garrett stole a glance at her, arching a questioning brow. She flashed him a slight smile, letting him know that the meeting with her father had gone well.

"Perry, you know Mrs. Carver and her husband, Will," Garrett said. She nodded and he gestured to her right, where Honoria sat. "This is Lady Honoria Rachinger and her husband, Sir Henry."

What were they doing here? Why had this meeting been called?

"Yes, I met Lady Rachinger. How do you do," Perry replied to the woman's husband.

She couldn't quite take her eyes off Sir Henry's crushed velvet waistcoat. The crimson color was shockingly vibrant in the room, highlighting the stark leather of his coat, and were there…razors at his belt? The kind a barber used? The man's green eyes watched her examining him, then he gave a crooked smile—a dangerously wicked smile—and held out his hand to her. "Blade," he said in a thick Cockney accent.

Perry's eyes widened. "The Devil of Whitechapel?" she blurted. Three years ago the queen had knighted him, but she'd never realized his name was Sir Henry.

"One and the same," he replied, shaking her hand. "But I prefer Blade."

Barrons offered her a glass of blud-wein. "You'll forgive me, but I asked Honoria and Blade to come. There's been much discussion between myself and Lynch since the exhibition, and…I feel Honoria might be able to shed some light on this situation with the cure the prince consort now owns. She has some interest in this field and has been following all of the latest innovations in the search for a cure."

Perry exchanged a flushed glance with Garrett, swiftly sipping her blud-wein. It was rather like having a living legend in the room.

"As several of you know, I was able to use the device to lower my CV levels before the prince consort took control of it," Garrett said, nodding toward Honoria. "I'm happy to relate my experience with it if you desire."

"You got 'igh CV levels?" Blade asked.

"Relatively," Garrett replied. "They're lower now, but I expect them to increase with time."

Blade circled the room like a creature on the prowl, his hands clasped behind his back. Even Lynch tensed slightly as he passed by. "Let's cut straight to the point. This ain't got naught to do with the cure, you're all fox-in-the-'en's-'ouse 'bout the prince consort controllin' it."

Barrons and Lynch exchanged a glance.

"Some of us are interested in the cure itself," Perry corrected, meeting and holding Blade's gaze.

He shot Garrett a look, then nodded. "Fine. Some of us wants a cure. Some of us are concerned about that pasty-faced vulture ownin' it."

"I still hold Hague's key to the device," Lynch

replied. "But the prince consort has his own, as gifted to him by Lady Aramina."

"He's getting dangerous," Barrons said.

"He's always been dangerous," Will Carver snorted, crossing his arms over his enormous chest.

"You're not on the Council," Barrons retorted. "You don't see his moods or the swift change in them. In the last three years, the Council has gained several new members. The prince consort no longer controls the way they vote. The device is his way of controlling the situation again."

Garrett circled behind Perry, his hands sliding over her shoulders. "Everyone will want to use it. If he figures out how it works, then the prince consort's power is absolute. He'll own the Echelon."

She knew what he was thinking. He'd made his thoughts on the prince consort quite clear, every time they saw a child living on the streets or men and women crushed and bloodied after a riot by the brutal hooves of the prince consort's metal Trojan cavalry. The Nighthawks were the ones who cleaned up the bodies. The ones who knocked on houses and had to break the news to a loved one inside. Perry slid a hand over his and squeezed. The Council of Dukes might be guilty of some matters, but they were the only ones who had the power to stand against the prince consort if they willed it.

Until now.

"Bloody hell." Lynch rubbed his jaw. "We'd never overthrow him."

"Unless the cure is widely available to everyone," Barrons agreed.

"Is that what we're doing?" Perry asked, looking around the room. "Seeking to overthrow him?"

All of them stared back at her. Rosalind looked grim, her gaze dropping to her lap. Lynch's fierce gray eyes were intensely focused on Barrons, and Barrons… He looked uncertain. Of the others, the most interesting thing she saw was the look Blade gave Honoria.

"The prince consort has grown increasingly erratic over the last few years," Barrons finally said. "Offering the Moncrieff a Council seat was clearly a sign that he was trying to control the Council vote again. Moncrieff—and his cure—was the prince consort's means of shifting power back, and now that the duke is dead…"

"The prince consort is going to start growing desperate again," Lynch concluded.

"That wasn't a yes," Perry pointed out, looking back and forth between the pair of them.

The moment stretched out, dust motes swirling through the haze of weak sunlight. Then Barrons laughed under his breath. "So it comes. The point where we have to put voice to the thoughts that have been troubling all of us." He smiled at her. "Yes, my lady. It is becoming conclusively clear that the prince consort needs to be overthrown."

"Yes," Lynch murmured.

Rosalind wet her lips and squeezed his arm. "Yes."

"So we steal the device?" The idea was impossible. It would be heavily guarded, under lock and key in the Ivory Tower, swimming in Coldrush Guards…

"What if there was no need to gain the device?"

Honoria asked suddenly. "You all say the device gives him ultimate power, but what if there was another way to control the craving?"

"How?" Lynch murmured, all of the movement in his body vanishing as his knuckles whitened on the armchair's sides.

Barrons turned away from the window, the light behind him obliterating the distinctive lines of his face and casting him in a halo of sorts. He looked like no angel, however. "Honoria, are you certain?"

"There is another…cure," Honoria replied. "I discovered it almost four years ago, and both Blade and Barrons have been using it since. That's why Dr. Hague's machine interested me so much."

The words hit Perry like a fist to the chest. "A cure?"

"And you didn't think to mention this?" Rosalind demanded. "Everyone fears the Fade." Surreptitiously her gloved hand slid over Lynch's, though she didn't look at him. "It would shift the entire power of the Echelon."

Perry let out a breath, feeling a little dizzy. She didn't dare glance at Garrett. This couldn't be true… She could barely allow herself to hope.

"Whoever controls the cure controls the Echelon," Barrons said grimly. "And whoever discovered that cure is worth more than their weight in gold. The prince consort would lock them away and never let them see the light of day again—or he'd assassinate her so only he knew its secrets. We were protecting her."

"Perhaps that was wrong of us," Honoria said. "I didn't realize so many other people would be affected by withholding such information." This with an apologetic look at Garrett. "It's a vaccination my father discovered. It doesn't affect a blue blood, but if he drinks his blood from a human who has been vaccinated, it slowly decreases his CV levels until he reaches a plateau."

"If we hold this information, we can regain power on the Council," Lynch murmured.

"No," Honoria replied. "I won't see this information used for the Echelon's games."

"If we give it," Blade said, "then we give it to all. If the information's free, then can't nobody use it for their own terms. The prince consort loses all that power." His smile held a dangerous edge to it, and he winked at Will Carver. "That's somethin' I'll drink to."

Honoria took a deep breath. "I shall publish all of the information in the scientific journals and the newspapers."

"That's still dangerous for you," her sister Lena murmured.

"If you can live as a verwulfen, then I can reveal my hand."

"Publish it anonymously," Perry replied.

"An excellent idea," Honoria replied with a warm smile. "Or perhaps I shall publish it under my father's name. Sir Artemus Todd. He discovered it, truly."

"And then?" Garrett demanded. "You said you mean to overthrow the prince consort, not just counteract him. Are you all insane? He owns the Coldrush Guards and the legions of metaljackets—who outnumber the Nighthawks, might I point out!"

"We're not without our own allies," Barrons murmured.

"A handful of Nighthawks, a couple of dukes, and the Humans First Party, I presume?" Garrett asked, glancing toward Rosalind.

"The verwulfen ambassador," Will Carver added, "and all the verwulfen under me command."

"Count me in," Blade muttered. "And me men."

"There are humanists scattered throughout the city from when I ruled the revolution." Rosalind's voice was stronger now. "And…preparations were laid to go to war, if the humanists ever grew strong enough to topple the Echelon. Those preparations are still in place."

"All we would need," Barrons said, "are the Nighthawks."

The world seemed to slow down. Perry felt very small all of a sudden and glanced at Garrett for comfort. The word "war" seemed to hover in the air. She knew what it meant. People would die. Friends and enemies alike. But hope also shimmered in the air between them. *No more bloodied bodies and riots.*

"Is that your cost?" Garrett asked. "For your cure?"

Surprisingly Blade shook his head. "You'll 'ave the cure. You've me word on it, regardless o' what you decide."

Garrett glanced at Lynch.

"It's your decision," Lynch replied. "They're your men now."

"Aye, and if I don't agree, I'll be the one forced to send them after you once the prince consort gets wind of this," Garrett snapped. A red flush crept up his throat and he turned away, clasping both hands behind his head as he stared at the study wall.

Rosalind shot her a look but Perry ignored it. This

was his decision to make, and she refused to see him coerced into it by his friends.

Crossing toward him, she reached out and stroked the hard leather carapace of the back of his body armor to let him know that he wasn't alone in this.

"What do you think?" Garrett asked.

Perry considered the question. She didn't particularly like the answer that was forming in her mind, but she couldn't very well turn her back on the truth. "If it doesn't happen now, then it will happen eventually. I think it's inevitable. You only have to look back on the last few years and increasing tensions between humans and the Echelon.

"The prince consort has crushed too many riots, forced martial law down upon the city more than once, and increased blood taxes to a dangerous level. Once he rebuilds the draining factories, he'll have to put the blood taxes up again to fill them. The working class will rise by themselves, sooner or later, and he will crush them." *Or we'll be forced to*.

"And you?" he murmured. "If I make this decision, then I'm throwing you straight into the heart of this war."

Perry knew immediately what held him back. She'd nearly died, and he had watched it happen.

"Now or then, Garrett. It will come eventually."

He stroked her face, gentle fingers brushing against her cheek. "I'm afraid. For you."

"I know," she replied, cupping his hand and turning her lips into the palm of it. "Then we fight back to back. The way we've always done."

The doubt slowly faded from his eyes. "I want this," he admitted, and she knew he was thinking of Mary

Reed, forced into prostitution by rising taxes and the Echelon's greed. Of all those women and children he *hadn't* been able to save over the years.

Perry's lips curled up in a rusty smile. "We survived against the Moncrieff and Hague... We can survive anything, Garrett. With you by my side, I know there's nothing to fear."

"Your father is going to have my head. I promised him I'd keep you safe."

That surprised her. "When did you—?"

"We had a certain type of discussion this morning, while you were sleeping," he replied.

"Why didn't you tell me?"

A knowing light came into his eyes. "It's the type of discussion a father has with the man who's bedding his daughter. Consider it between him and me." The humor in his eyes faded and he turned back to the room in general. "I don't entirely like this. I think we need to consider the effects of what we speak of before we commit to such a course." Garrett met all of their eyes in turn. "But for what it's worth, it's done. You have the Nighthawks."

Both Lynch and Barrons let out a breath of relief.

Garrett, however, wasn't finished. "But first, there is something else to plan. Perry is going to do me the honor of becoming my consort."

"I am?" she asked, arching a brow at him.

"You wouldn't want me to break two promises to your father, would you?" he asked, that devilish little smile she loved so much tickling at his lips.

Acknowledgments

To my agent, Jessica Faust, for always being there on the other end of the email and supporting me whole-heartedly, no matter what.

My heartfelt thanks to Leah Hultenschmidt for acquiring the series and setting my feet on this path; and to my wonderful new editor, Mary Altman, for putting her time and energy into this book. My project editor, Megan, for catching all of the glitches and making me think. Thank you also to the entire team at Sourcebooks who do all of the behind-the-scenes work and helped whip this book into shape!

Special thanks to my amazing support crew, the ELE girls: Nicky Strickland, Dakota Harrison, Kylie Griffin, and Jennie Brumley! Wonderful writers all, who are always there to share the journey and helped me with the beta read. For all of my readers, Facebook fans, and Twitter followers: you make this all truly worth it. I love getting to "ooh" over covers and share book recommendations with you all—it keeps me sane!

To my family and friends, who understand my

hermit-like ways and are always pushing me to chase my dreams. To Beryl Raselli, Sarah Holland, Evelyn and the local library ladies, and Chris Day-Plush for helping to spread word of the books in town.

And last, but certainly not least, to my boyfriend, Byron, for getting excited over the little things with me, understanding why I have to work so many hours, being the first to tell me to quit my job so I can write full time, and generally for being my best friend, always. This book is a special one, written just for you.

In case you missed it, here's an excerpt
from the groundbreaking first novel in
Bec McMaster's London Steampunk series

Kiss of Steel

IF ONLY SHE'D BEEN BORN A MAN...A MAN IN WHITECHAPEL
had choices. He could take up a trade, or theft, or
even join some of the rookery gangs. A woman had
opportunities too, but they were far more limited and
nothing that a gently bred young lady would ever
aspire to.

A mere six months ago Honoria Todd had owned
other options. They hadn't included the grim ten-
ement that she lived in, hovering on the edges of
Whitechapel. Or the nearly overwhelming burden of
seeing her brother and sister fed. Six months ago she'd
been a respectable young woman with a promising job
as her father's research assistant, hovering on the edge
of the biggest breakthrough since Darwin's hypothe-
ses. It had taken less than a week for everything she
had to be torn away from her. Sometimes she thought
the most painful loss had been her naïveté.

Scurrying along Church Street, Honoria tugged the
edge of her cloak up to shield herself from the inter-
mittent drizzle, but it did no good. Water gathered on
the brim of her black top hat, and each step sent an

icy droplet down the back of her neck. Gritting her
teeth, she hurried on. She was late. Mr. Macy had
kept her back an hour at work to discuss the progress
of her latest pupil, Miss Austin. Scion of a merchant
dynasty, Miss Austin was intended to be launched
upon the Echelon, where she just might be fortunate
enough to be taken in as a thrall. The girl was certainly
pretty enough to catch the eye of one of the seven
dukes who ruled the council, or perhaps one of the
numerous lesser Houses. Her family would be gifted
with exclusive trade agreements and possibly spon-
sorship, and Miss Austin would live out the terms of
her contract in the extravagant style the Echelon was
acclimatized to. The type of style Honoria had once
lived on the edges of. Before her father was murdered.

Church Street opened into Butcher Square. On a
kinder day the square would be packed with vendors
and thronging with people. Today only the grim
metal lions that guarded the entrance to the Museum
of Bio-Mechanic History kept watch. The city wall
loomed ahead, with the gaping maw of Ratcatcher
Gate offering a glimpse of Whitechapel beyond. Fifty
years ago the residents of Whitechapel had built the
wall with whatever they could lay their hands on.
It stood nearly twenty feet high, but its symbolism
towered over the cold, misty square. Whitechapel had
its own rules, its own rulers. The aristocratic Echelon
could own London city, but they'd best steer clear of
the rookeries.

If Mr. Macy found out Honoria's address, he'd
fire her on the spot. Her only source of a respectable
livelihood would vanish, and she'd be facing those

damned *options* again. She'd wasted a shilling tonight on a steam cab, just to keep the illusion of her circumstances intact. Mr. Macy had walked her out before locking up the studio where he taught young ladies to improve themselves. Usually he stayed behind and she could slip into the masses of foot traffic in Clerkenwell, turn a corner, and then double back for the long walk home. Tonight his chivalry had cost her a loaf of bread.

She'd disembarked two streets away, prompting the cab driver to shake his head and mutter something beneath his breath. She felt like shaking her head too. A shilling for the sleight-of-hand that kept her employed. It didn't matter that that shilling would keep her with a roof over her head and food on the table for months to come. She still felt its loss keenly. Her stockings needed darning again and they hadn't the thread for it; her younger sister, Lena, had put her fingers through her gloves; and fourteen-year-old Charlie...Her breath caught. Charlie needed more than the pair of them combined.

"'Ey!" a voice called. "'Ey, you!"

Honoria's hand strayed to the pistol in her pocket and she glanced over her shoulder. A few months ago she might have jumped skittishly at the cry, but she'd spotted the ragged urchin out of the corner of her eye as soon as she started toward Ratcatcher Gate. The pistol was a heavy, welcoming weight in her grip. Her father's pistol was one of the few things she had left of him and probably the most precious for its sheer practicality. She'd long ago given up on sentimentality.

"Yes?" she asked. The square was abandoned, but

she knew there'd be eyes watching them from the heavily boarded windows that lined it.

The urchin peered at her from flat, muddy-brown eyes. It could have been any age or sex with the amount of dirt it wore. She decided the square jaw was strong enough to name it a boy. Not even the constant rain could wash away the dirt on his face, as though it were as deeply ingrained in the child's pores as it was in the cobblestones beneath their feet.

"Spare a shillin', m'um?" he asked, glancing around as though prepared to flee.

Honoria's eyes narrowed and she gave the urchin another steady look. If she wasn't mistaken, that was a rather fine herringbone stitch riddled with grime at the edge of the child's coat. The clothing fit altogether too well for it to have been stolen, and it was draped in such a manner that it made the child look rather more malnourished than she suspected he was.

She took her time drawing her slim change purse out and opening it. A handful of grimy shillings bounced pitifully in the bottom of it. Plucking one out with reluctance, she offered it to the little street rogue.

The urchin reached for the coin and Honoria grabbed his hand. A quick twist revealed the inside of the child's wrist—and the crossed daggers tattooed there.

His wary mud-brown eyes widened and he tried to yank his hand away. "Leggo!"

Honoria snatched her shilling back and released him. The boy staggered, landing with a splash in a puddle. He swore under his breath and rolled to his feet.

"I've more need of it than you," she told him, then swept her cloak to the side to reveal the butt of the pistol in her skirt pocket. "Run back to your master and tell *him* to give you a coin."

The boy's lip curled and he glanced over his shoulder. "Worf a try. Already bin paid for this." He flipped a shilling out of nowhere and then pocketed it just as swiftly. A stealthy smile flashed over his face, gone just as quickly as the coin. "'Imself wants a word with you."

"Himself?" For a moment she was blank. Then her gaze shot to the child's wrist and that damning tattoo of ownership. She tucked her change purse away and tugged her cloak about her chin. "I'm afraid I'm not at liberty this evening." Somehow she forced the words out, cool and clipped. Her fingers started to shake. She thrust them into fists. "My brother is not well. And I'm late. I must see to him."

She took a step, then shied away as a hand caught at her cloak. "Don't. Touch. Me."

The boy shrugged. "I'm jus' the messenger, luv. And trust me, you ain't wantin' 'im to send one o' the others."

Her mouth went dry. In the ensuing silence, she felt as though her heartbeat had suddenly erupted into a tribal rhythm. Six months scratching a living on the edges of the rookery, trying to stay beneath the notice of the master. All for nothing. He'd been aware of her, probably all along.

She had to see what he wanted. She'd caught a glimpse of the *others* who were part of his gang. Everybody in the streets gave them a large berth, like rats fleeing from a pack of prowling toms. Either she could go of her own volition, or she could be dragged there.

"Let me tell my sister where I'm going," she finally said. "She'll be worried."

"Your neck," the urchin said with a shrug. "Not mine."

Honoria stared at him for a moment, then turned toward Ratcatcher Gate. Its heavy stone arch cast a shadow of cold over her that seemed to run down her spine. Himself. Blade. The man who ruled the rookeries. *Or creature*, she thought with a nervous shiver. There was nothing human about him.

Of Silk and Steam
by Bec McMaster

— ✑ —

Enemies. Allies. Lovers. How far will they go to protect their hearts?

When her father was assassinated, Lady Aramina swore revenge against the Duke of Caine. Leo Barrons, the duke's heir, has long been her nemesis, and when she discovers he's illegitimate, she finally has leverage against the one man who troubles her heart and tempts her body.

Sentenced to death for his duplicity, Leo escapes by holding Lady Aramina captive. A woman of mystery, she's long driven him crazy with glimpses of a fiery passion that lurks beneath her icy veneer. He knows she's hiding something; he doesn't know it's the key to saving his life.

— ✑ —

Praise for Bec McMaster:

"McMaster continues to demonstrate a flair for wildly imaginative, richly textured world-building." —*Booklist*

"Bec McMaster brilliantly weaves a world that engulfs your senses and takes you on a fantastical journey." —*Tome Tender*

For more Bec McMaster, visit:

www.sourcebooks.com

My Lady Quicksilver
by Bec McMaster

— ❧ —

I will come for you...

He will find her no matter what. As a blueblooded captain of the Nighthawk Guard, his senses are keener than most. Some think he's indestructible. But once he finds the elusive Mercury, what will he do with her?

It's his duty to turn her in—she's a notorious spy and traitor. But after one stolen moment, he can't forget the feel of her in his arms, the taste of her, or the sharp sting of betrayal as she slipped off into the night. Little does Mercury know, no one hunts better than the Nighthawk. And his greatest revenge will be to leave her begging for his touch...

— ❧ —

"Set in an alternate version of London ruled by vampires...the perfect choice for readers who like their historical romances sexy, action-packed, and just a tad different."—*Booklist*

"One of my top books of 2013... just amazing."—*Royal Reviews*

For more Bec McMaster, visit:

www.sourcebooks.com

Heart of Iron
by Bec McMaster

---- ✈ ----

No one to Trust

Dangerous. Unpredictable. That's how people know the hulking Will Carver. And those who don't like pretty words just call him The Beast. No matter how hard Will works to suppress his werewulfen side, certain things drive him beyond all control. And saucy Miss Lena Todd tops the list.

Lena makes the perfect spy against the ruling Echelon blue bloods. No one suspects that under the appearance of a flirtatious debutante lies a heart of iron. Not even the ruthless Will Carver, the one man she can't wrap around her finger and the one man whose kiss she can never forget. He's supposed to be protecting her, but he might just be her biggest threat yet...

---- ✈ ----

"Edgy, dark, and shot through with a grim, gritty intensity, McMaster's latest title adds to her mesmerizing steampunk series with another gripping, inventive stunner."—*Library Journal* Starred Review

"McMaster's second London steampunk book dazzles and seduces...will leave readers breathless."—*RT Book Reviews* Top Pick of the Month, 4.5 Stars

For more Bec McMaster visit:

www.sourcebooks.com

The Highland Dragon's Lady
by Isabel Cooper

❧

He's out of the Highlands and on the prowl...

Regina Talbot-Jones has always known her rambling family home was haunted. She also knows her brother has invited one of his friends to attend an ill-conceived séance. She didn't count on that friend being so handsome...and she certainly didn't expect him to be a dragon.

Scottish Highlander Colin MacAlasdair has hidden his true nature for his entire life, but the moment he sets eyes on Regina, he knows he has to have her. In his hundreds of years, he's never met a woman who could understand him so thoroughly...or touch him so deeply. Bound by their mutual loneliness, Colin and Regina must work together to defeat a vengeful spirit—and discover whether their growing love is powerful enough to defy convention.

❧

Praise for Isabel Cooper:

"Cooper's world-building is solid and believable." —*RT Book Reviews*

"Isabel Cooper is an author to watch!" —*All About Romance*

For more Isabel Cooper, visit:

www.sourcebooks.com

To Love a King

The Court of Annwyn Series

by Shona Husk

---- ❧ ----

He's trying to reclaim the past

To keep the balance between good and evil at the court of Annwyn, Prince Felan ap Gwyn has two weeks to marry and take the crown. But he wants more than just power—he wants love; a love he once had but was too stubborn to hold on to.

She's struggling to face the future

It took years for Jacqueline Ara to put her life back together after Felan abandoned her. She's moved on, even if her heart still burns for him. But with war in Annwyn looming and death bleeding into the mortal world, Felan and Jacqui will need to heal old wounds and rekindle the passion that once welled between them…or face losing everything.

---- ❧ ----

"Shona Husk's engaging voice and vivid, creative world-building make every one of her books a must-read!"
—Larissa Ione, *New York Times* bestselling author

For more Shona Husk, visit:

www.sourcebooks.com

About the Author

Bec McMaster lives in a small town in Victoria, Australia, and grew up with her nose in a book. Following a lifelong love affair with fantasy, she discovered romance and hasn't looked back. A member of RWA, she writes sexy, dark paranormals and adventurous steampunk romances. When not writing, reading, or poring over travel brochures, she loves spending time with her very own hero or daydreaming about new worlds. Visit her website at www.becmcmaster.com or follow her on Twitter @BecMcMaster.